Also By Stuart Yates

The Sandman Cometh
Splintered Ice
Roadkill

BYZANTINE HISTORY SERIES
Varangian
King of the Norse (Coming soon)

PAUL CHAISE SERIES
Burnt Offerings
Whipped Up

As Glen Stuart

Cold Hell In Darley Dene
The Pawnbroker
Interlopers From Hell

THE TRILOGY OF TERROR
The Well Of Constant Despair
Accursed Dawn
Death's Dark Design

TALES FROM ISLAND ANIMAL RESCUE
Dark Times At Animal Rescue
Dark Wings Over Animal Rescue
Farewell To Animal Rescue

VARANGIAN
King of the Norse

*Being the second installment of
The Byzantine histories, featuring
Harald Hardrada*

STUART G. YATES

Rebel ePublishers
Detroit New York London Johannesburg

Rebel epublishers
Detroit, Michigan 48223

All names, characters, places, and incidents in this publication are fictitious or are used fictitiously. Any resemblance to real persons, living or dead, events or locales is entirely coincidental.

Vatangian – To Be The King of the Norse
© 2014 by Stuart G. Yates

All rights reserved. No part of this publication may be reproduced, distributed, or transmitted in any form or by any means, including photocopying, recording, or other electronic or mechanical methods, without the prior written permission of the publisher, except in the case of brief quotations embodied in critical reviews and certain other noncommercial uses permitted by copyright law.

For information regarding permission, email the publisher at rebele@rebelepublishers.com, subject line: Permission.

ISBN-13: 978-0692339688
ISBN-10: 069233968X

Book design by *Caryatid Design*
Cover design by *Littera Design*

ACKNOWLEDGEMENTS

As with any work such as this, huge thanks must be given to all those who encouraged and helped me in my efforts to bring Hardrada's story to the page. Without the tireless devotion of Jayne, my knowledgeable and witty editor, this novel would not be as polished or accomplished as it is. I am forever grateful to everyone who has helped in giving me the opportunity to place Hardrada in his rightful place as the last, and greatest of all Vikings.

This book is not history, but many of the incidents within the pages did happen. For those who wish to investigate further the life of Harald Sigurdson, I can recommend the work of John Marsden, and his biography of Hardrada, *The Warrior's Way*, an accessible and immensely readable account. It makes clear the sometimes rambling and confusing sagas, upon which I based story, and guides the reader to a broader appreciation of just how great Hardrada really was.

For my true friends and the home I miss.

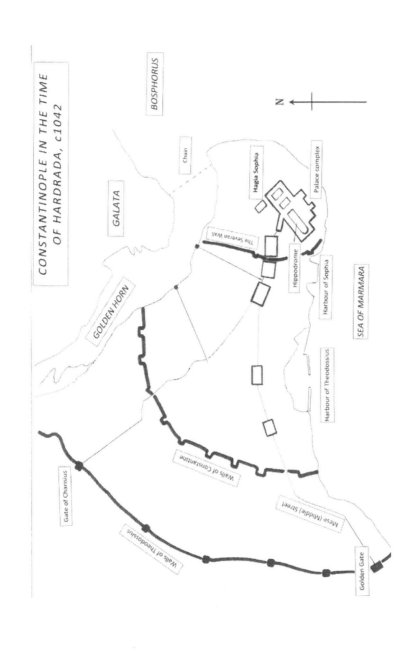

Landing

England, early September, 1066

The wind cut like hounds' teeth, biting deep into the exposed flesh of Edgar's face and neck, and he screwed up his eyes in a gargoyle mask of misery. He stood on the headland; feet planted wide against a gale so strong it almost bowled him over, and stared out to sea.

Amongst the boiling fury of the sea, the waves cutting up in a rage of spray and noise, he thought he saw a ship. A tiny dot, barely visible through the sheets of rain that lashed down, it couldn't possibly stay afloat much longer. He strained forward for a better view and witnessed his fears become reality. It *was* a ship, battling through the mad maelstrom, tossed and thrown as if it were a mere toy, fragile and flimsy. As he looked, the vessel reared up, seized by the waves to spin in wild, haphazard violence, control all ripped away.

The vessel came clean out of the water and slammed down again, with a crash louder than the roar of the boiling sea. Wooden sides shattered amongst the foam, and the ship yawned and pitched, and at last capsized, disappearing under the screaming water, to sink into the seething, swirling depths. Gone, consumed by the raging ocean.

Edgar dragged a hand across his face, bunched his shoulders, and turned away. If he believed there were people on board the stricken ship, he showed no sign of caring. Besides, how could anyone survive in that? Any cries of desperate men lost amongst the howling wind, hope lost. He put his head down and tramped through the sodden grass, putting all such thoughts from his mind. Life, for him and everyone he knew was hard, brutal and quick. No time to spend thinking about the deaths of others.

He was fifteen summer's old. As with everything, this was more guesswork than accurate calculation. He may have been sixteen summers old for all he knew, perhaps even seventeen. As his mother had died two summers ago, he had no real way of checking. Father, who rarely came home, seemed infinitely old. A great bull of a man, massive shoulders, arms like tree trunks, a gnarled face framed by a wild beard that gave him a ferocious look. Eorl Hereward the people called him, if they spoke to him at all; most quaked in his presence. On the few occasions Edgar saw him, any words he may have wished to utter, he kept inside. Hereward seemed like a man troubled, his face grim with concern, the lines cut deep around eyes lost in thought. So the villagers stayed away, and Edgar kept himself far in the background.

The small, bustling village lay in the bowl of a fertile valley, the various houses and outbuildings placed haphazardly in a crude circle, in the centre of which stood a large meeting hall. Edgar came over the far rise, the rain streaking down from a leaden sky, and shouldered through fellow villagers, all busy with the constant daily battle to survive. He drew the neck of his cloak tighter around his throat and scowled upwards. How long had it been since the sun last shone? Edgar couldn't remember. He knew the crops were in danger of being ruined, the ground so clogged with mud. Peas and beans might still grow, but the wheat. The wheat was something else.

He put his head down and moved on, stumbling almost at once into Roderic, the village elder, who swore at him, and threw out a backhanded blow, which Edgar nimbly dodged.

"Look where you're going!"

The old man turned away, bent forward against the lashing rain. Edgar moved on without a word. He had been about to tell Roderic of the ship, but the old man, always so quick to temper annoyed him, so he left it. Why was it the old became so cantankerous? Was that how it was with age, he wondered. Other elderly folk appeared indifferent to life's grinding turn, but they seldom smiled, and Roderic least of all. Perhaps the responsibility of his position made him so tetchy? Edgar didn't care. Let him find out about the wrecked ship for himself, when the bloated bodies washed up on the beach.

He reached the house he shared with the sons of Stowell the baker, and ducked in through the doorway. He pulled off his sodden cloak and fell down in front of the fire to dry himself. Great clouds of steam rose from his clothes, and he drew up his knees and held them close to his body with arms that dripped moisture. It was supposed to be summer, or so the birds told him. So where had the sun gone? What did it mean?

A shadow fell over him and Edgar turned to see Gyrrth, a thegn of immense stature, filling the doorway. Almost as large as Edgar's father, Hereward, he grunted when he saw Edgar, and stepped inside. He kicked Edgar's discarded cloak. "We must go," he said simply.

Edgar watched him move over to the far corner, where he rooted around amongst various objects stacked up there. Edgar coughed. "Go? Go where?"

"King Harold has called a general muster of all the fyrrd. News has come of an invasion, in the far north." He swung round, hefting in his great hands a large, round shield together with two sturdy spears. "We are to assemble over at Sparrow Hawk Hill, then march across to London."

Without warning, Gyrrth threw a spear sideways towards Edgar, who shot out his hand and caught it around the thick shaft. Gyrrth grunted, impressed. "You'll do," he said, his voice flat, without emotion.

Edgar turned the weapon and studied the metal point. "My father always said that when I first saw battle, he would give me a sword."

"Well, your father's not here. He went north at least two moons ago, when the reports came about the Norse bringing their black ships back to our land. Your father left with a group of housecarles to meet up with Lord Morcar to face those pagan scum. We've heard nothing since."

"I know." Edgar did not want his voice to betray any of the emotions that rumbled away inside. His father's departure had been sudden, unexpected, and he'd left no word of where he was going, or why. Edgar suspected that something of enormous importance had occurred somewhere, but this was only a guess. He had no evidence to back it up, until now. Gyrrth's announcement suggested events were moving fast. "Are we going to the north too, to find my father?"

Gyrrth hawked and spat into the hard-packed earthen floor. "Your father ... no one knows what has happened, whether battle has been joined, lost or won. All we know is that the Norse are here. On our land."

"When must we leave?"

"Now." Gyrrth scooped up Edgar's cloak and tossed it to him. Edgar caught it and held it out before the fire. "Unless this cursed rain stops, our march will be longer still. I will try to acquire a horse, but I doubt if there will be any. Stowell had a pony, but he will use that for himself."

"Stowell is also going?"

Gyrrth gave the boy a measured look. "I told you, this is a *general* muster. Every man must be ready."

Edgar nodded, gathered the cloak over his still soaking shirt and shivered. "How far do we have to go?"

"That is as much a mystery to me as to where all this rain comes from! All I know is that today we go to Sparrow Hawk Hill and there we will receive our instructions. Rumour has it that the king and his brothers will be there, together with many lords and earls of England, and their housecarles."

"It's serious then."

"Boy," Gyrrth couldn't keep the impatience from his voice. "It is more than serious – it is *Vikings*. The enemies of our blood."

Edgar watched the great man disappear outside and turned to stare at the fire. So, the King himself, Harold Godwinson, lord of all he surveyed, was come to call the people to arms. The Vikings, the Norse had returned. Why now? What force, what ambition had spurred them on, he wondered. It was common knowledge that for longer than Edgar had been alive, the Norsemen were no longer the power they once had been. He knew the stories, had listened to the elders talking around the campfires at night, tales of raids, terror and death. How an ancient King, Alfred, had tamed them and how a Viking had once sat on the throne of England: Cnut. The stories described him as a great man. But a confessor had restored the land to Saxon blood, and Godwinson gave it strength. And now, they were back, back to reclaim what they believed was theirs.

This land.

He dragged a hand over his face; a face still wet from the rain, and realized he was desperately tired. The call made, battle lines drawn across the dirt, he had no choice but to comply. Edgar stared into the flames and wondered what manner of man could bring the Norse back to greatness? A man who had to be great himself.

A man unlike any other.

One

The Magnificent City of Constantinople, 1042.

"We need more men," said Ulf, letting out his breath in a blast as he lowered the large box onto the stone floor of the quayside. Immediately, Haldor sat down on the box and leaned forward, putting his face into his hands. Ulf slapped him on the shoulder and said, "Feeling like death, old friend?"

Haldor barely looked up. "Only when you are here."

Ulf chuckled. "Nice to see you're still in a good mood. Well," he glanced towards his other companion who stood like a great tree, solid, inscrutable, "what say you?"

The port lay still and quiet, the only sound water gently lapping against the harbour walls, the occasional clink of coiled chains waiting for the return of ships. The endless blue stretched out towards the horizon, sea merging into sky. Empty. The eye of the world made blind.

Distant voices travelled across the quayside from far away. The city licked its wounds from the recent battle, soldiers and citizens alike mourning the fallen and the occasional wail reminding them all of how terrible the fight had been. But to Ulf's question, no answer came.

Harald Hardrada shifted his broad shoulders, turned and studied his older companion for a moment. Hardrada nevertheless looked every inch the veteran warrior, aged before his years. A young man in his mid-twenties, many believed him older, a lifetime of adventures having hardened his body to the consistency of seasoned oak. Enormous in stature, the muscles in his arms bulged like pieces of thick, coarse rope. He wore a simple hauberk of chainmail over a white, red-trimmed tunic and rough leggings lashed around the calves with leather thongs. He held a large double-headed axe in his fist, and a sheathed sword dangled from the broad leather waist belt. Tangled hair hung loose, draping his face, caught by the breeze, ignored by Hardrada, deep in thought. When he at last spoke, his voice sounded heavy and tired. "This is not good. I had hoped that at least one ship might be here, but for there to be nothing …" He turned again to survey the empty quayside. The port of Constantinople, one of the greatest cities on earth, usually teemed with life, with ships coming and going from every corner of the world, dockworkers scurrying backwards and forwards, off-loading the merchandise from a hundred different lands. Grain and spices, silks and linen. Olive oil, fruit and vegetables. Gemstones, ore and flax, all of it maintaining the most magnificent Empire known to Man. Constantine the Great's city, New Rome, capital of the world silenced by the excesses of a mad Emperor, overthrown and blinded before being banished."Where by Odin's beard have they all gone?"

"Probably got wind of the trouble. You know what these effete seamen are like," Ulf chuckled again, walked over, and stood beside his friend. "Harald. We are not going to leave this day. Perhaps not for many days."

"Damn your eyes, Ulf, if we don't ..." His voice trailed away, leaving thoughts unspoken.

Ulf, ever the prophet of doom, said, "What, the Lady Zoe will have your balls?"

"Aye, she will at that. Yours too, perhaps." He sighed again. "We'll all feel her wrath, in some way."

"Leave me out of this," shouted Haldor from his seat on the box, "I never coupled with her."

"Not for want of trying," grinned Ulf. His features soon changed, becoming serious. "We need men, Harald. A lot of men, if we are to break through the chains which protect the harbour and sail north. That is what you're thinking, yes?" Hardrada grunted. "Perhaps we could send out word, hire mercenaries?"

Hardrada shook his head. "I need loyal, willing warriors to follow me, not craven purse-robbers. My cause is just and I want them by my side because they accept me as King, not because I fill their pockets with Byzantine gold." He shook his head. "No, they will come when I call – they are Varangian Norse." He slapped his thigh. "I haven't travelled this far to be denied because of the fear and cowardice of others. Damn these Greeks, always looking out for themselves, thinking of ways to make more money. News of Michael's fall will have travelled to every corner of this creaking Empire and men will be looking farther afield to swear their allegiance now they think Byzantium is weak and leaderless."

"Which it is."

"Not for long, I'll wager. Maniakes no doubt has it all worked out." He pressed his fingers into his eyes for a few seconds before turning to Ulf. "We'll go back to the city. I'll talk to Maniakes, come up with a deal. He needs me, needs all of us. With the Scythians gone, the city is left undefended."

"He has the Varangians, Harald. The City Guard too. Maniakes is a viper, you know that more than anyone. He will do whatever he can to keep himself in power, and he sees you as a threat, an obstacle to his ambition."

"No," Hardrada shook his head again, "he needs us, Ulf. He knows I command the respect of the Norse and will want me to lead the Varangians, return them to their former glory. Not as mercenaries, but as loyal soldiers to the Senate and Emperor, whoever that might be. Once we have established order, we will leave. Not as bandits, but as noble men."

Haldor gave a cough before raising his voice. "In that case we will need to convince the General that your counsel is wise, and your honour absolute. Simple." He laughed, a harsh snap that resounded loudly across the empty port. "That shouldn't be too difficult for a man like him, a twisting, loathsome liar."

Haldor hobbled across the stones to join them, hand clutching his side. He still suffered from his clash with the giant Scythian, Crethus. Harald, studied the grimace set on his old friend's face, the drawn, yellow flesh, and did not like what he saw. "What ails you, friend?"

Ulf sighed, "He caught a blow in the guts is all! For pity's sake, man, get yourself some wine, have a lie-down."

Haldor ignored the barbed sarcasm and made a face at Hardrada. "Maniakes will not be easy to convince. You'll need Alexius on your side. He trusts you, and what's more he *owes* you."

Hardrada knew this to be true. Certainly, to have such a strong ally, the Holy Patriarch of the city, to vouch for his sincerity would prove priceless. "Aye, you're right. I'll find a way to gain audience with him. He'll understand, will want Zoe back on the throne, but at the same time require security. Something I can provide." He reached out a hand and clutched Haldor's arm. "More pressing is your need for rest, my friend. Where did he strike you?"

Haldor shook his head, "I'll be fine. I just

need a few moments, no more. Like Ulf says, perhaps some wine."

"*Where did he strike you?*" repeated Hardrada, not wanting to keep the edge out of his voice. Haldor appeared weak, close to the edge of collapse, like a wet rag in Hardrada's hand. The huge Viking did not believe he had ever seen his old friendlook so frail before. It worried him more than he dared admit.

Haldor looked from one Viking to the other and shrugged. He gingerly pulled up his thin, woollen jerkin to reveal a large, angry sword cut that ran across his right side, just under the ribs. The skin hung down in an ugly flap and the swollen, mottled blue and green bruising around the wound pulsed horribly. Blood and pus seeped from the large, oozing slice in slow, thick trails.

Ulf sucked in his breath whilst Hardrada spoke in a voice not much above a whisper. "You need that tended to. The wound is deep, and your ribs ... they could be broken. If a bone has pierced your vitals ..."

Haldor gritted his teeth and readjusted his jerkin. "I've had worse, I promise you. Like I said, just some rest is all I need."

"You were always a stubborn oaf," said Ulf, unable to keep the concern from his voice.

Haldor smiled at his old friend, but it froze on his face, as his eyes grew dark. "For the moment, I think we have other more pressing things to worry about."

The others turned to look in the direction of Haldor's gaze, towards the far end of the port.

Striding across the quay, a large group of

fully armed Byzantine Royal Bodyguard marched in unison, their hobnailed boots crunching over the dressed stone, banners held aloft, bronze helmets glinting in the sun. At their head marched a young, resolute and determined-looking officer.

"Andreas," Hardrada hissed as they drew closer and he gripped the shaft of his axe as the ice ran through him and settled in the pit of his stomach.

Two

Nikolias, officer in the Imperial Guard, pulled off his helmet and wiped away the sweat from his brow. He watched the Lady Zoe move towards the Forum of Constantine. He had done his best to dissuade her, making it perfectly clear what awaited her; the terrible scenes of death and destruction, the masses of dispossessed, traumatised citizens, fearful, confused and desperate. She listened, steely-eyed, the determination obvious. Nothing he'd said made her change her mind.

The battle which had raged through the forum and around the steps of the Royal Palace, furious and terrible, leaving dead scattered everywhere, mangled flesh, headless corpses, limbs hacked and tossed into every corner only served to convince her of the need to address her people. The stench of decay clung to the very stones of the once-fabled and magnificent city, but it seemed to Nikolias the Empress Zoe cared not a fig for such horrors. Her people needed her now more than ever, and her sense of duty overcame any feelings of revulsion or despair.

She glided serenely away, even refusing his offer to escort her, and her strength of character buoyed him up, made him realise this was a woman of great fortitude, grace and determination.

Zoe, Empress of Byzantium, wife to two dead Emperors, adoptive mother of a third knew her own mind and, despite every setback, she remained stalwart and confident in her abilities. Surrendering, Nikolias let his shoulders relax and turned to the men who helped fetch Zoe from the monastery where the previous Emperor Michael V had banished her. "You are dismissed, lads. Go back to the barracks, await further orders."

The men exchanged uncertain looks before shuffling away. Nikolias watched them for a moment before he too made his way back to the complex of the Royal Palace.

It was as quiet as the grave, the buildings shrouded with gloom. A stark contrast to how it used to be, with courtiers scurrying back and forth, soldiers snapping to attention, heralds announcing the arrival and departures of a dozen emissaries. The ancient walls of the divine palace once rang with the sound of a thousand voices, proclaiming this as the centre of the world, the pulsing heart of the sacred Empire of Byzantium. Now, not even echoes remained, with nobody except the occasional corpse to grace those hallowed corridors.

From beyond the walls surrounding the

complex came the sound of citizens returning to the Forum, no doubt anxious to know what would happen next. They had risen up against Michael, and many had paid the ultimate price. Nikolias, charged with bringing the Empress Zoe out of her enforced banishment to the monastery on the island of *Prinkipo*, missed the bulk of the fighting. News of the Varangian victory over the Scythians soon reached him, and the evidence lay all around in the bloody contorted lumps of mangled flesh amongst the marbled pillars of the palace. Citizens and soldiers, woman and children, the vicious struggle making no exception to rank or privilege. Members of the extended royal family, wives of dignitaries, sons and daughters of government officials, mixed with those of ordinary folk, broken bodies twisted in the unspeakable horror of their last few moments. Throats cut, abdomens ripped open, heads and limbs strewn wherever he looked.

He closed his eyes, fighting back the tears. Nikolias knew much about death, having fought many times before, but the realization that so many of the dead were children brought anguish and revulsion to the very pit of his being. He slumped down on the steps, glaring at the corpses of three or four Scythian soldiers. Never ones to baulk at the slaughter of the defenceless, the sight of them brought him a curious sense of joy. But the hideous signs of their handiwork, the murder of innocents so intimate, so close, proved his undoing. He put his face in his hands and wept.

It was some time before he found the courage to stand up and slip through the main doors.

What lured him to the palace, he could not say. Curiosity, or something more. A constant, niggling concern played around inside his guts, refusing to leave; something, or someone guiding him here, urging him to continue. Although he attended mass, listened with hushed reverence to the Patriarchs and the priests as they chanted out their prayers, he believed religion was little more than a duty. If God did exist, Nikolias always wondered why He allowed so much suffering to continue. The priests told him, when he gathered the courage to ask them his question, it was Mankind's fault. Apparently, God had given Man the freedom of choice. What he did, he did of his own volition, and justice would have to wait.

Mankind, mused Nikolias, had to answer for much. The hearts of men, blackened by corruption, jealousy, covetousness. These things led to the recent spate of killing, the vile excesses of Michael V, his brief but cruel reign seeming to mock every righteous corner of the glorious capital of Constantinople. New Rome, plunged into the mire of vice and sexual perversion. Was God's hand in any of it? The Emperor was God's chancellor on earth; what he did, he did through the power and guidance of God. Was God now undoing the corruption, returning Zoe to power, bringing Nikolias here?

The vast corridors rang out with the sound of his hobnailed boots crunching across the marble floor, causing him to slacken his pace and move with caution. If any Scythians lurked amongst the shadows, he would be an easy target for a well-aimed arrow. He bunched his shoulders, his eyes roaming, peering into the shadowy depths. Pillars rose like a forest to the vast, ornate ceiling, the work of decades, a testament to the eternity of the glorious city. Nikolias remembered his history; over seven hundred years before, the greatest of all Emperors, Constantine, made the city his own. Whilst in the West the old Empire crumbled, Constantine secured his power base and removed external threats with extreme prejudice. Men like Nikolias helped quell internal revolts, bolstered up the reign of Emperors, and created the supreme power on earth. However, not all Emperors were the same. Nikolias knew Michael, more than any army ever could, undermined it all and almost brought disaster to everyone. Now, within a breath of the centre of power, Nikolias tightened the grip on his sheathed sword, ready to strike out at any sudden attack; stragglers of that corrupt and debauched ruler may still lurk in the gloom.

He turned a corner and stopped. Two Royal Guards lay dead against the towering double doors of one of the many royal apartments. One door yawned open, weak light flickering from within, and he moved closer, heart pounding in his ears, body tense. Nikolias drew his sword and used the point to ease open the door a little more. He gasped when he saw her.

Leoni.

She sat on the edge of the bed, head down, faced covered by her hands. Nikolias held his breath and gave the room a quick once-over before crossing to her.

A body, slumped in the corner, came into view, head smashed and unrecognizable. Next to it, a heavy, gold candelabrum, covered in congealed black blood, gave testament to what had occurred. With great care, Nikolias sheathed his sword and stepped up next to the girl.

He reached out to pull away her hands. Startled by the unexpected touch, Leoni's face snapped up, wide-eyed with terror. She squawked, hand flying to her mouth, and scurried backwards across the bed, lashing out with her feet, whimpering like a wounded animal.

Nikolias raised his hands, "No, wait!" He tried to keep his voice calm and reassuring, but he failed as Leoni slammed herself against the far wall, wrapping her arms around her knees and began to wail. "I'm not here to hurt you," he said.

Breathing raggedly, uncontrolled, her eyes red-rimmed with tears flashed as she gasped, "You keep away from me, God damn you!"

Nikolias stepped back, lowering his hands. "I promise you, I mean you no harm."

He studied her. She wore a long, cream silk shift, tiny threads of gold sewn through the material. The garment, virtually transparent, revealed every line of her young, slim body. Numerous tears speckled the bodice, merging to form larger damp smudges. Without thinking, he allowed his eyes to settled on them, for perhaps a moment too long. She drew her knees closer to her body. "I am a servant of the Empress, so take care," she hissed.

He blinked, aware of how his gaze might be misconstrued. He threw out his arms, "No! No, I didn't mean ..."

Her body shook, terrified, her brave show seeping away. Nikolias tried a smile, and she answered it with a scowl. "I know you," she said. "You're that guard the General sent. Sent to keep me locked away, to seduce that vile man, the one they wanted to become Emperor?" She shook her head wildly, growing braver as her features hardened. "Well, he's gone – and I didn't seduce him, so there. I'm not Maniakes's little puppet any more, do you hear me?" She clutched at the hem of her shift, bunching up the material in her fists. "He's used me once too often, and I won't do it again, I tell you. What he forced me to do with Michael ... never again, you understand? So, you go and tell that to your precious General, if he's still alive."

"I don't know who is alive or dead, I truly don't. Whilst the battle raged, my mission lay elsewhere. The only thing I do know is that Zoe is about to present herself to the people."

"*Zoe?*"Leoni's voice cracked, incredulous. "But, but they sent her away. Michael, he banished her."

"Like I said, I had my mission. To bring her back." Nikolias shrugged, took a tentative step forward. She stiffened again, and he stopped. "I don't know anything more. For all I know Michael too is dead. The city is quiet now, the fighting stopped. And the Scythians have gone, probably also dead, the whole scurrilous lot of them. So ..." He forced a smile. "I am a sworn officer of the Imperial Guard, obligated to ensure the safety of her gracious Highness, the Empress, and all of her servants." He smiled again, and this time he saw no responding look of disdain. "So, you're safe."

"*Safe?*" She rubbed away at her face, drying away the traces of any remaining tears. "No, anything but safe. If the General still lives, he'll want to know what happened with Constantine." She swung her legs off the bed and stood up, smoothing down the dress. She took in a shuddering breath, pausing to compose herself. "He didn't send you?"

"No. I just ..." He shrugged again, acutely conscious of her body beneath the silk, and glanced down at his feet. "I ... I needed to know."

"Know? Know what?"

"Whether ..." He gestured around the room. "So where is he? This Constantine?"

"I've no idea. He ran off, with Christina."

Nikolias frowned. Ran off? Where would he run to? He nodded towards the corpse. "Who was he?"

Leoni shivered, holding herself, averting her eyes. "I don't want to talk about it."

He grunted, looked around the room and

saw what he wanted. He crossed over to where a shawl lay forgotten on the floor, picked it up and went to her. She tensed as he drew close, but relaxed a little as he brought the heavy material around her shoulders. "You're cold," he said. "And you will need this if we are to go."

"Go? Where am I supposed to go? The General ..." She shook her head. "My orders were very precise, and I have failed. I have served my usefulness now, and he will want to discard me as soon as he can. But I don't care. I'm not his slave any longer. What he would have me do ..." She shuddered and drew the shawl closer around her. "I thought he cared for me, but it was all a lie, his only thought to have Michael under his control. So, my talent for seduction came into play and the Emperor, he ..." Her voice trailed off and more tears tumbled from her eyes. She turned away, pressing the shawl into her face.

"You cared for him, didn't you?"

"Cared?" Her face, when she let the shawl fall, appeared red, angry. "He used me, and now ..."

"I meant the Emperor. Michael."

She went silent, her mouth opening slightly. "I ..." She returned to the bed and slumped down. "At first he was vile. But the more we ...well, I'm sure I don't need to give you the details."

"No. I think I have a fair enough idea."

"Do you? I wonder. To you I'm nothing more than a whore, isn't that right, using my body to further my ambitions, or the ambitions of others? Well, you may well be right, but not anymore. The General, he played me for a fool, fucking me like a wild thing, leaving me gasping, desperate for more ... but there was never any *passion.* You understand? Never any *love.* With Michael, it became different. He wanted so much to please me, to give me everything he could."

"He was a monster, Leoni!"

"Was he? Why, because he wanted to rule alone, have all the power of the Empire for himself? Is that so monstrous?"

Nikolias looked to the open door. "You should keep your voice down. If anyone should hear they'd—"

"I'm past caring. Michael's gone, I know that. Replaced. If I ever had any feelings for him, they've gone too." She shook her head. "The General is the real monster, twisting, conniving and if he's alive, he'll find me and have me flayed."

"In that case," said Nikolias, smiling broadly, "I think I know precisely where you will be safe."

Three

The great Byzantine General, George Maniakes, stood beside his horse, stroking the beast's neck whilst he smiled to himself. So far so good, the past few days had proved stressful beyond belief, but now he could allow himself a few moments to unwind. The main threat, Michael V, former Emperor of New Rome, had gone, ferried away to a distant and somewhat bleak monastery to live out the rest of his pathetic existence in isolation. Forgotten, and blinded. Fitting punishment for his excesses – his attempts to become a new Caligula or Commodus.

There were those in the senate who demanded the Emperor's death, to set his head upon a pike, and parade it through the streets to spit upon and jeer at like some obscene manikin from the very worst of street theatres. Maniakes resisted, knowing full well how history would judge such acts. This wasn't *Rome* after all! With Michael's fall, the Scythian guard destroyed, there remained only a few minor obstacles to the General's ambitions, mere irritations soon resolved. He was pleased with his decision to send Andreas, together with a body of men to the port to arrest Hardrada. As soon as he told Zoe what the Viking's intentions were, her eyes clouded over and the orders made. Andreas, as Maniakes knew he would, set off without a pause, a murderous look on his face, no doubt hoping Hardrada would resist.

A wave of elation coursed through the general, plans falling into place, the future looking bright. True, some of Michael's more outrageous schemes wrong-footed him at the start, but soon Maniakes recovered and outmanoeuvred the young, corrupted Emperor. His remaining opponent for power, John Orphano, chief eunuch of the Imperial court and head of the vast Byzantium bureaucracy, fell almost as rapidly as Michael, undermined and disgraced. God alone knew where he ran off to, but Maniakes no longer cared. The fat slug's departure ensured the power of New Rome lay within the General's grasp. His plans to place Constantine, his latest creature, on the throne meant all would be well.

A movement to the right made him turn. The Empress Zoe glided towards him, resplendent in her courtly robes. A smile played at his lips, but he mastered the desire to break into a broad grin, and bowed deeply. "You look ravishing, Your Highness."

Within arm's reach, her perfume invaded his nostrils and, not for the first time, he contemplated taking her to his bed to conquer her body, make her his own. Her penchant for lovers was well known, and she preferred them domineering and well endowed, both attributes he possessed in abundance. But when he raised his eyes to hers, he knew such a course was beyond even his machinations. Zoe may well be beautiful and eager, but she had her own mind and the bedroom, not the throne, was the place for domination. A pity, as her body was lithe and supple, her skin smooth and taut, but such an opportunity would never develop into anything more than mere fantasy.

"You have gathered the Imperial Bodyguard, prepared the way for my procession to the forum?"

Maniakes gave a pained look. "Highness, the city streets are still filled with dead. I beg you to reconsider."

"Your servant, the boy Nikolias, told much the same thing. I caught sight of the carnage before coming here. I have seen worse."

Maniakes doubted it, but he remained impassive. "Highness. The horrors visited upon the city mean there can be no procession, not in the way you envisage."

"I envisage only the rejoicing of my people when I ascend the throne, General. But they will expect a certain sense of ... *pomp*, would you not agree?"

Zoe, always a great believer in spending as much money as possible in making the royal family resplendent, loved the splendour of being Empress. Unfortunately, her excesses had drained the state treasury and now, with the capital still in the grip of fear and uncertainty, what the citizens needed was reassurance, not great shows of majesty and wealth.

"I take it from your silence that you do not agree, General." She pressed her lips together, rustled her heavy gown, and flicked away an imaginary piece of dust from the shimmering material. Interlaced with gold and silver panels, the coronation robe seemed to glow of its own volition, an excess Maniakes did not approve of, fearing the reception she might receive, appearing so fine after such suffering.

"Many hundreds have been killed, Highness," he continued, his voice low. "The people love you, that much is certain, but they need to know all will be well from now on, that the killing has ceased and they are safe."

"Of course they do, and that is precisely what I will tell them."

"Telling them may not be enough, Highness."

"Do not presume you can teach me how to rule, General. I have had more than one lifetime of experience, married to two great and resourceful Emperors. I know what I'm doing."

Maniakes felt his cheeks redden and he bowed, partly to mask his indignation, partly to give himself time to think. "Highness, it was never my intention to—"

"Enough of this," she waved him away, "I am indebted to your service, General, but you are a soldier, *not* a politician, least of all a diplomat. Your answer to everything is a cut of the sword, whereas mine is a more subtle and considered response. I know the people's suffering, as they do mine. And believe me,

General, I *have* suffered." She pulled in a tremulous breath. "Michael's time on the throne may have been brief, but it was full of woe. Why I ever assented to adopting him I will never know. I must have been mad, or drugged, or both. Whatever the reason, I do not believe I have ever made such a calamitous error of judgment. To welcome that boy into the royal family was folly beyond belief."

Maniakes, his head still bowed, mumbled, "You were not to know what he would become, Highness. None of us did."

"That is as may be, and you are right – at first he seemed so sweet, so ... *subservient* and willing to learn. Something took hold of him, some evil, and it corrupted him, turned him into a monster."

"He was given false council, Highness. Not all of it was of his making."

"You think not? Well, you could be right. You knew him better than most, did you not?"

Maniakes almost yelped, his heart palpating alarmingly. "Highness, I knew nothing of—"

"Spare me your indignation, General. I know full well you had my handmaid, Leoni, service his every desire in the hope of ensnaring him into one of your many plots."

"Highness, I promise you—"

"Don't take me for a fool, General, because I am not. I have survived two dead husbands, one lunatic adopted son, and the people *love me*. That is something you never understood, or perhaps believed. They know me for what I am, of royal blood, destined to be Empress of the divine Empire of Byzantium. With God's good grace, I will nurse this earthly wonder back to its rightful place as the capital of the Christian world. And it begins today, General, with my addressing the people and assuring them the darkness is overcome and a new dawn awaits."

With a great theatrical flurry, she swung away and glided off towards the forum.

Maniakes trembled as he straightened his back, a trickle of sweat rolling down his spine, cold and unwanted, like that royal bitch's oratory. He snapped his head towards a pair of guards who stood some way off. "Escort her royal majesty," he barked and watched them spring into action. Only when they were safely out of sight did he allow himself to drag his hand across his brow and try to settle his pounding heart.

***

With Maniakes standing next to her, the Empress Zoe looked out across the sea of faces gathering in the Forum of Constantine, a huge open space bordered with acacia and lime trees. Its once pristine facade, however, had lost much of its former beauty, besmirched with the blood of the dead. Even now, soldiers carried bodies away, piling them into two great heaps, one for citizens and Varangians, the other for the despised Scythians. These same bodies, tossed in burial pits and forgotten not long afterwards. Zoe sniffed, raised her chin and drew in a deep breath.

Maniakes gazed upon her, standing so majestic, so in control. When he'd caught up with her a few moments before and told her of the duel with the mighty Scythian captain, she'd stopped, face like alabaster, cold and without emotion. She'd turned to him, aware of the triumphant glint in his eye. He'd taken great joy in giving her the details of her lover's death, of Hardrada's ecstasy at decapitating him. She'd allowed no outward sign, but Maniakes knew inside her heart broke, all hope gone. Until she'd spoken, when his doubts resurfaced. "Crethus was a gentle and attentive lover, General. In another life, I might have wished for so many things, to have him beside me, his strong arms protecting me as I ruled in the day and he loved me in the night. But such things could never be. I am Empress and he is dead."

Maniakes marvelled at her resolve and accepted her triumph in silence.

***

Zoe regarded the General with slight amusement. He knew nothing of what went on in her heart, although he believed he did. Crethus would soon be nothing more than a distant memory, placed to the back of her mind and forgotten, like the many other dead.

Not so Hardrada.

In the days before Michael Calaphates – thanks to her support – ascended the throne, she feasted upon Hardrada's flesh, before discarding him when news of his betrayal reached her ears. As Emperor, Michael Calaphates, corrupted by power, led the Empire into disarray, ordering the slaughter of Hardrada's Varangian Guard in order to secure his tyranny. By making an enemy of the

Viking, Michael paid with a heavy price – blinding. Meanwhile, Zoe conducted herself with far more subtlety, biding her time, waiting, like a mantis, for the opportunity to strike. Up until now, because the Empire required his talents, Hardrada had managed to survive. Zoe smiled. The Viking would meet his end soon enough, without ever suspecting where the order originated.

Zoe turned away, knowing her lack of remorse for the dead Crethus irked the General, dulling his triumph. Belittling him, however, might prove dangerous so curbing the General's avarice required careful planning, the loyalty of his men legendary. The hero of Sicily, the victor of so many battles, his latest triumph against Michael's Scythians further ensured his esteem amongst the citizens. With a little luck and a great deal of subterfuge, she might find a way to remove both him and Hardrada at the same time. Now there was a delicious thought!

She smiled at him before ascending the steps. "Thank you, General. Your continued support fills me with great joy. Let us now present ourselves to the people and bask in their love. For both of us." She took a deep breath and walked out into the sunshine.

The people raised up their voices in one, prolonged tumultuous cheer.

***

He ran through the maze of streets, lined with squashed, squalid tenements, ignoring the curious look of the occasional citizens hanging out of an upper-storey window. Constantine had never been in this area before, so unlike the splendid surroundings of the Palace complex. Here the stench of filth filled his nostrils, brought bile to his throat but more than this, the sense of threat bore down on him, made him wary and uneasy. He plunged on, like someone possessed, eyes moving but not focusing, his only thought to escape.

Next to him, the girl, held in his grip, whimpered. Dismissive of her protests, he cared nothing for her, keeping her close with the hope of using her as a means to bargain for his survival.

When they'd left the Palace, Constantine had crouched behind a nearby tree and watched the young Byzantine officer disappear inside the magnificent, vaulted entrance to the royal apartments. He'd held the girl's face between forefinger and thumb, glaring at her. "Don't make a sound!"

They'd sprinted off, tripping over dead bodies, snaking a path from the complex towards the port.

The distance proved longer than he expected and soon Constantine slowed, gulping in air, gripping his side in agony. The girl tried to wrestle free, but he maintained his grip, gritted his teeth and snarled, "You wouldn't be wanting to leave me would you, my pet?" His face twisted into a leer. "I haven't done with you yet," and he yanked her behind him.

Soldiers roamed wherever he turned, soldiers the like of which he had never seen before. Huge men, longhaired, muscular, the looks on their hard faces enough to chill hearts, turn bowels to water. He knew if such men spotted him, death would be the outcome. So he kept close to buildings, crouching in doorways, slinking inside shadows, managing to steer well clear of danger. Now, in the tenements, the silence proved deafening. He suspected most people had either fled or gone to some designated meeting place to await news. Of Michael's victory perhaps, or his defeat?

He wondered about Michael, and Maniakes, the organiser of Constantine's return to the capital through a series of secret messages. Since his arrival, however, Constantine had received no word, nothing, left alone in the vast, empty palace, pacing the room, partaking of the girl Christina with increasing passion but growing ever more impatient.The other girl, Leoni, despite resisting his charms, had shown her mettle by dashing out the brains of the Scythian dog who'd burst into the apartment. She acted quickly, without thought, her actions saving all of their lives. With no other course open but to flee, Leoni refused to leave. If Constantine harboured thoughts of bringing her with him, the arrival of the Byzantine officer put paid to them all. With no time to argue, he ran, taking Christina. When he became the true power in Rome, as promised by Maniakes, there would be any number of girls to choose from, to sate his most demanding palette. For now, a royal handmaiden might prove a good insurance policy against those who might wish him harm.

An old crone appeared from a doorway and cackled. "Which way to the port?" he snapped. His plan was simple – to hire a boat or bribe a fisherman and get back to the safety of his island home from where he could dictate more advantageous terms with Maniakes. Not even his brother, John Orphano, the royal eunuch, could eclipse Constantine's diplomatic and administrative skills. The Empire needed him now more than ever, and that made him valuable. But not safe.

The woman pointed a gnarled finger over to her right, "Around the next few bends, then follow your nose. You can't miss the stink of fish."

Constantine dragged the girl with him, the crone's fading cackling setting his teeth on edge, until at last they stepped out into the wide expanse of the port. Here all the business of the Empire took place, ships from every corner of the known world bringing in their wares and goods. The Byzantine Empire flourished through the complex system of trade routes developed since before the great Roman Empire split, its riches beyond measure, eclipsing even the ancient city of Rome itself.

Constantine stopped and gaped, his stomach turning over, his legs pieces of thin string.

The place lay deserted, silent, dead. A lone gull soared through the azure sky, its mocking cry echoing across the open expanse, the gentle lapping of the sea against the quayside walls the only other sound. No ships docked here; no men worked. Nothing.

Christina took her chance and tore herself free from his grip. She rubbed her wrists as tears trailed down her cheeks. "You hurt me," she hissed. "Bloody bastard that you are."

"Stop your moaning," Constantine said, gazing towards the empty horizon.

"What will you do now, eh?" She laughed. "You're finished, you know that? When they find you, they'll kill you."

"*They*?" He turned and studied her as if for the first time. Slight, no substance to her at all. What was she, seventeen? Young, a waif of a girl, who nevertheless proved receptive to his advances, never complaining, who opened herself to his every whim. He enjoyed himself at first, relishing her lithe body, the way her arse stuck out, so big and round against the slimness of her waist, the way she begged him to take her 'just one more time'. But now, the conquest complete, he wasn't sure if he needed her anymore. The plan was to take her with him, but with no available ships, things would have to change. Besides, her constant moaning frayed his nerves. He rubbed his chin. She was more of a burden than a prize.

"Why are you looking at me like that?"

She took a step backwards, still rubbing her wrists, and her mouth trembled. A mere slip of a girl. Seventeen.

Without a word, he went into a crouch, bringing out the knife from the folds of his robes. Her eyes became like saucers, locked on the blade. "What are you going to do?"

"It'll be all right," he said, inching forwards.

"It won't hurt, I promise."

He made a sudden lunge, but the girl was faster, dancing away from the slash of the knife and he lost balance. He made a wild, backward cut, stumbled and fell to his knees. Cursing, he spat and stood, slashing again and again as she dodged out of range, the knife striking nothing but air. She turned and ran, bare feet slapping on the dressed stonework. Constantine roared, gnashing his teeth in frustration, knowing he could never catch her. He rolled his fists into tight balls and cursed God and Maniakes and his brother for ever having brought him to this detestable place.

A noise someway behind him caused him to whirl around. His heart jumped.

A group of well-armed soldiers approached, spears held aloft, bronze lamellar armour glinting in the sun, marching in perfect unison, shields emblazoned with the sigil of the Imperial Guards. Their officer, a young man, chin hard, face set, strode ahead and beside him three others, one of whom was a giant, the biggest man Constantine had ever seen. The officer, however, took all his attention, the man's livid, burning glare boring into him. Constantine deftly slipped the knife into his robe and pulled in a breath as the group came to within a few steps and stopped.

"I am Constantine, soon to be Grand Domestic in the service of the Empress Zoe. That girl," he wagged his finger at the diminishing figure of the fleeing Christina, "tried to assassinate me – no doubt on the orders of some ingrate traitor. I demand you escort me to a place of safety."

The huge warrior beside the officer guffawed and for a moment, everyone stood in silence.

The officer took a step forward, one hand falling to the hilt of his sword. "I saw your knife," he said, eyes flashing red and dangerous.

Constantine's throat went dry and he threw up his hands. Later no one could attest to what truly happened next, such was the speed of the officer as he slipped inside the big man's guard and threw him to the ground with a jarring smash.

Yelping, Constantine writhed on the hard stone, clutching at his back, his face twisted in agony as the officer relieved him of the knife. A strange sounding voice said, "By Christ, you move fast, boy."

And then the reply, "You had best remember that, Viking. For one day, my knife will sink into your flesh."

Strong hands hauled Constantine to his feet. A fist slammed into his gut and the vomit spewed from his mouth. The ground loomed up towards his face as his knees cracked against the hard ground. He screamed then something very hard and very solid struck his jaw and the lights went out.

Four

"It is an advantageous outcome," the Patriarch said, "and gives us all time to reconsider our options."

"Advantageous!" Maniakes brought his fist down on his desk with a tremendous smash and rose to his feet, his face twisted with rage. The guards at the entrance stiffened. The atmosphere grew tense. "How in the name of God can it be termed 'advantageous'?"

Alexius, the Patriarch of Byzantium winced. "Please, General. Don't blaspheme."

"Pah!" Maniakes struggled to keep himself under control, pressed his fists down onto his desk and leaned forward. "Constantine was our one trump card, Your Holiness! Now, he has been disgraced, thrown into a dockside pigsty with a bunch of cut-throat pirates. And all because of that snivelling little shit's notion of honour," he jabbed a finger towards Andreas, who stood ramrod still, gazing ahead. "Thanks to him, everything could go arse over tit!"

The Patriarch pressed a hand to his face. "*Please,* General."

Maniakes steamed, blew out a loud breath, and strode around the desk to face Andreas. "What the hell were you thinking of?"

"I had no idea who he was, sir. I saw him attacking the girl ... we all saw it, sir. A young girl who just happened—"

"I couldn't give a monkey's toss who the bloody girl was! I want to know why the hell you put that poor bastard in the brig."

Andreas blinked. The General's face was so close he could count the pores on his nose. "Begging your pardon, sir, I thought it preferable to killing him."

"Did you, by God?"

"Yes, sir. Indeed I did, sir."

"Well, *sir,* thanks to your high-handed efforts, we may have lost the services of the ablest man in the whole fucking Empire! The man who was going to help us out of the mess we are in. Guards!" The two soldiers came to attention. "Take him outside and hang him naked on the Lion Gate, after you've castrated him."

The men stepped forward as Andreas paled, his legs buckling, and he pitched forward.

"General!" Alexius stepped forward, intercepting the soldiers, and catching Andreas before he fell to the ground. "General, for the love of God! This boy has served the Empire well. You cannot punish him so severely for one, thoughtless mistake."

Maniakes shook his head. "*One thoughtless* ... you may be forgetting, Holiness, but

Constantine was the only sure way we had of re-organizing the administration, of putting this Empire back on its feet. If he decides to give it all up, return to his island, then what will we do? The Empire is teetering on the brink and we need a capable man to guide us clear of the shit Michael has left us. God help us if the Normans get wind and attack, for we will have no means to defend ourselves."

Alexius helped Andreas onto a chair and shook his head. "There could be other avenues to explore."

"Oh, and what might you have in mind – or *who*?That dog Orphano? I'll not have that viper back in a seat of power."

"No," said Alexius with a grin. "No, I have another plan. One that I believe could be the best possible outcome for everyone – the Empire, you, the Church and, of course, the Empress."

The General chewed at his lip. "This had better be good, Holiness."

"I believe it is." He clamped his hand on Andreas' shoulder and smiled at him. "All will be well, Andreas. Just next time, think before you act."

Andreas, recovered from the shock of the General's cruel judgement, bowed his head. "I will not fail you again, Holiness." He turned to looked at Maniakes. "Nor you, sir."

Maniakes grunted, played his tongue across his teeth, and sighed. Finally, he went back to his desk and sat in his chair. "Very well. Give me the details of this plan, Holiness. Then I'll consider what to do. But, in the meantime, you keep that idiot out of my sight for the next few days, whilst I try to calm down."

Alexius inclined his head in assent and gave Andreas over to the guards who each took an arm and guided the young officer out of the office. When the door closed, Alexius turned to the General.

"I believe we can still win over Constantine. What happened is nothing more than a slight step backwards. Once he has recovered, I will put my influence behind what I propose. I think you will agree that my plan is quite frankly ... *brilliant.*"

***

Looking up from the bubbling pot, Nikolias's mother smiled over at Leoni sitting at the crudely worked dining table. "You seem tired, my dear. Hungry too."

Leoni barely lifted her head, offering only a slight quivering of her mouth in response.

The old woman motioned her son to come closer, and took him away into the corner of the room, out of earshot.

"Who is she, Niko? She looks terribly frightened."

"She is, Mother. I had to rescue her from the Palace and almost certain death."

"The Palace?" His mother looked over his shoulder and studied the girl once more. "But who *is* she?"

Nikolias, with no time to think anything through, had taken Leoni to his home; the one place where he could guarantee her safety. Now, he wasn't so sure of the soundness of his decision. His mother, a widow of many years, found life increasingly difficult. Not just the onset of old age, the aching joints, the loneliness, but with her husband long dead, killed in battle, making ends meet was nigh impossible. All the servants had gone, soon followed by the grand house they once shared before the money ran out and debts mounted. Nikolias's pay didn't amount to much and, after much soul-searching, they had moved into this cramped, damp little place. His mother did her utmost to make it comfortable, homely. Whenever he managed to get away from his duties, Nikolias often found her quiet, reflective. And now this, burdening her with Leoni, whose life could be snuffed out in an instant. By aiding her, his life – and his mother's – were in danger. With reality striking home, regrets multiplied.

"She is the concubine of the General," he said in a quiet voice, not truly understanding the enormity of the situation until now. Uttering the words brought everything into perspective, He squeezed his eyes shut, "Holy God, I should never have brought her here."

"Well, you have." She gently patted his cheek. She smiled. "These things happen, Niko. You always were a thoughtful boy, too kind for your own good to be honest. But if, as you say, her life is in danger, we have no choice." He went to speak but she pressed her finger against his lips. "We have to help her. She can stay here for as long as needed whilst you try to sort something out."

He nodded, knowing there was no

alternative and not wishing his mother to suspect, even vaguely, at what stirred within him. Maniakes would want to find her, and his men would scour every corner of the city, working diligently until they succeeded. After that where would Nikolias be? An officer in the Imperial Guard he may be, but never beyond the clutches of the General. He knew he was treading a very fine line between life and death, a death terrible to contemplate: public castration, flayed alive. He shuddered.

"Are you sick?" His mother brushed her hand across his cheek again.

"No." He took her hand and squeezed it. "I have to go, report back to duty. I will return later and we will talk about what we can do. Thank you."

"What else is a mother supposed to do?"

Nikolias went to Leoni and sat down next to her. She didn't flinch, lost in some dark recess of her memory, reliving the horror. "I have to go," he said. "Mother will look after you, feed you, and give you fresh clothes if needed. I shall come back this evening." From somewhere, he found the courage to reach over and take hold of her hand. There was no response. "Leoni, I swear to you, I will do whatever is in my power to keep you safe."

At that, she at last raised her head and he almost gasped in shock. Her eyes, red-raw from crying and lifeless, her cheeks puffy, lips quivering, hair limp and lank. "You're risking your life for me, and I am so thankful, but ..." She shook her head, despair leaking from every pore. "You cannot save me, Nikolias. I am lost, lost forever. The General will never stop, and you know it. He will find me eventually, and when he does ... I'm a danger to him, a threat. The things I could say, the people I could tell. It would be the end of him, so he must destroy me. And when he discovers you have helped me, he will destroy you also. You must take me back to him, tell him you found me in the palace after Constantine fled, leaving me for dead. You *must,*it is the only way."

"No. I have another way, Leoni. I have a half-brother who lives in Hadrianopolis. I can take you there." He ignored his mother's piercing glare. "He will help, Leoni, and you will be far enough away to be out of the General's reach."

"Hadrianoplis? But that is a journey of *weeks,* Nikolias. We will never make it!"

He squeezed her hand. "We will. I have friends, debts I can call in. I will take leave, Leoni, and—"

"You can't!" Her eyes grew large, bulging. "Not now, not when the city needs you most. Nikolias, I thank you for everything you have done for me so far, but you have to face facts. We cannot leave the city."

Nikolias's mother placed a bowl of steaming broth in front of the girl, together with a spoon and some hunks of bread.

"You go, Nikolias," she said. "She will be fine."

"Yes, you're right." He stood up, repositioned his belt and went to pick up his helmet from the far side of the table.

"Nikolias?"

He stopped and turned to Leoni, whose eyes glazed over with a distant look. She gave the tiniest of smiles. "Thank you."

It was all he needed. His heart swelled and he left.

Five

Marched under sword point to a secure area in the far part of the city, well away from Varangian eyes, the three Scandinavians, unceremoniously pushed into a squat watchtower, heard the door bolted from the outside. As the sound of hobnailed boots receded into the background, Hardrada groaned and paced the small, square room whilst Ulf sat in the corner, chewing his nails in silence; Haldor closed his eyes as if in sleep.

"This is just how it was before," Hardrada spat, causing Ulf to start. "Another bloody prison cell my reward for helping them. The journey to the north, returning with the Varangians and overthrowing Michael. And what do I get?" He pounded the slimy, damp drenched walls with both fists. "To be locked up, like a criminal. Damn their eyes."

"It's not the same," said Ulf, his voice sounding thick with tiredness. "This isn't a prison cell, Harald. They won't keep us here long."

Hardrada swung around. "You have more optimism than me, old friend! This is the General's doing, I can sense it. The bastard will do anything to keep me out of the way. And what about my treasure, eh?"

"We just have to be patient. There is no point thinking the worst. If Maniakes wanted us dead, it would already have happened."

"You're treasure is safe," said Haldor, without so much as a flicker of his closed eyes. "Maniakes is cooking something up, you'll see, and once he sets us free, we will go and retrieve it. Until then," he turned over onto his side and gave a groan, "try to sleep away the hours."

Ulf sniggered, "He has a point, the old bastard. No point in fretting, Harald."

Hardrada pressed his back against the wall. "I wish I knew what was happening. Who do you think that fat bastard was down at the quayside?"

"His name is Monomachus," muttered Haldor. "Constantine Monomachus. He's related to John Orphano as far as I can remember, brother or half-brother I think." His eyes fluttered open and he winced as he shifted position. "He's the ablest administrator in the Empire and a notorious glutton and sexual deviant to boot."

Ulf laughed. "Not much different from his brother, then."

Hardrada frowned at his old friend, "How do you know all this, Hal?"

Haldor shrugged. "I hear more than I tell,

Harald. But I know this, if, as I suspect, the general's plan is for this worm to become Emperor, we will all have to tread carefully."

"You said he wouldn't kill us."

"I hope I'm right," continued Haldor. "Maniakes cannot seize the throne for himself. He knows the people would never accept him as he is not of royal blood, despite his exploits on the field of battle."

"But neither is this Monomachus."

"No, but Zoe is."

Hardrada frowned. "You think Maniakes will try to bring the two of them together? In marriage?"

"Why not? It would make a good plan – no? – having an Emperor under your control. Maniakes has ambitions far beyond being the greatest general Byzantium has ever known. He wants total power."

"There are many who say that without you, Harald, Constantinople would already have fallen. People revere you even more than the illustrious general."

Hardrada looked at Ulf and forced a smile. "It's true we had some *interesting* debates about strategy, the good General and I." He shook his head. "So he's another Michael, this Monomachus?"

Haldor shook his head. "I don't think the Empress would suffer another monster. No, he's not like Michael. He is subtle and clever. More dangerous by far."

"In that case, don't you think we should escape before he gets wind of who we are," said Ulf. "We have no choice."

Harald closed his eyes and slid down the wall to sit on the rough ground. "Like I say, we're right back where we started."

***

Not so very far away, in the Royal apartments, a small flock of handmaidens was busy fitting the Empress Zoe with a new ceremonial robe. She stood in the middle of the private room where soldiers had seized her and marched her down to the quayside. They'd manhandled her onto a waiting ship to take her to a monastery and a life of obscurity. It seemed so long ago now, as if a terrible dream. So much had changed in the passing of a handful of days. Michael, overthrown, Maniakes triumphant. Crethus, dead at Hardrada's hand.

One of the girl attendants tugged at her waistline a little too vigorously. Young, flighty little things, with a tendency to break into giggles at the slightest jape. Zoe longed for her old, trusted servants, especially Leoni. The Empress sucked in her breath. "Careful, girl, this dress is worth more than you will ever see in your lifetime!"

The girl's face blanched and she fell to her knees, babbling, all light-heartedness gone in an instant. "Highness, forgive me, I did not mean to—"

"Enough!" Zoe pulled herself away, not caring to listen any longer to their inane cackling, incompetent every single one. "Get out the lot of you." The girls hesitated, wringing their hands, unable to decide what to do. "I want Leoni. Send me that officer, the one who brought me back from the monastery. Nikolias. I wish to speak to him."

"But mistress, the General has said that we must prepare you for an audience with the Senate."

Zoe slowly turned, the last straw broken at last. Her eyes narrowed. "Find Nikolias. *Now!*"

***

The General poured himself a generous goblet of wine and downed it in one. He smacked his lips with relish and peered over the rim towards Alexius, who sat across the table, arms folded, doing his best not to look uncomfortable.

"What's the matter, Holiness? Not used to a soldier's way of doing business?"

"Nothing of the sort, General. I am merely waiting until you feel able to speak."

"Mmm …" Maniakes reached for the wine jug and poured himself another full measure. This time, he savoured the alcohol, rolling the wine around his mouth before swallowing it with an exaggerated gulp. "We are the greatest Empire on earth," he said, holding up the goblet. "From all over the known world people bring us olive oil, fruit, spices, silks … and a hundred other things. Including this majestic wine. Are you sure you won't try some?" He arched an eyebrow and grinned at the Patriarch's stony silence. "We bask in our glory, granting trading rights to every adventurer who wishes to strike out and find new markets. And yet …" he tilted his head before draining the goblet. "And yet, we still do not have the power to *crush* those who threaten us."

"Times have changed, General. New Rome is not the power it once was. We need to use different methods now, ones that don't expose us to the wrath of the barbarians."

"Barbarians?" The General tipped up the jug and let the last few drops dribble into the goblet. "They are no longer barbarians, Holiness. They are sophisticated, ruthless, and intelligent. Resourceful too. Russians, Bulgars, Pechenegs. All of them covet our lands. The Normans especially."

"You have encountered them before, General. You prevailed and, in Sicily, taught those Normans a lesson they are never likely to forget. Faith in God and the justness of our cause will mean you will prevail again." He unfolded his arms and leaned forward, his tone less severe. "I know it will be so whenever you are called to defend our Empire."

"Hardrada aided me in Sicily, don't forget that."

"And still you put him behind bars. There is no love lost between you, that is certain."

"The man has ambitions. He has grown tired of Byzantium and needs to find his own way, have songs sung about *him*, not us. He cannot be trusted."

"Yet he did vanquish the Scythians. Without his influence, the Varangians would never have come and crushed those heathen dogs, and Michael would still rule."

Maniakes studied the dregs of his wine, declining to answer or lend support to the holy man's words.

Alexius breathed a long sigh. "However, as I have said, we are overstretched. We no longer possess the resources to defend all of our borders. Therefore, we must use diplomacy as the main tool for our continuance, not force."

The General nodded once. "You're taking this somewhere, Holiness. I can see it in your eyes. You have your plan and now I think it only fair you reveal it in more detail. Boy!"

Instantly, a youth came into the room, head bowed low. Maniakes thrust the jug towards him, "Fetch more wine. Some bread and olives too."

The youth took the proffered jug and went out again. The General stretched out his legs. "I want you to tell me everything, Holiness. We have to work together to ensure Byzantium flourishes. My plans have waned a little, now that Constantine Monomachus is somewhat indisposed. The poor sap is a jabbering idiot after what Andreas did to him."

"He will recover, and when he does we can move forward."

"But Zoe has already paraded herself before the people, and you have indicated you will crown her with all the usual pomp and ceremony afforded an Empress of New Rome. So what's to be done? We need Monomachus's skills, his ability to make money!"

Alexius, about to reply, stopped when the servant returned. Both men waited in silence whilst the youth placed bread, oil, olives and wine on the table. When finished, the boy bowed and left. The Patriarch absently ripped off a piece of unleavened bread, drizzled oil over it and crammed it into his mouth. Maniakes watched him, pouring himself more wine.

"On Lesbos," said the Patriarch, licking the oil from the tips of his fingers, "Constantine Monomachus was exiled by the esteemed John Orphano ..." Alexius paused, gave a wry smile, "... one of the eunuch's more, how shall I put it, *questionable* decisions ... but Monomachus now holds his brother in contempt."

"Contempt? I'd call it hatred. Brothers or not, Orphano is an eel, always has been. Perhaps Monomachus is the same?"

"I believe him to be intelligent, affable, *pliable*. With the correct guidance, he could be placed at the head of our Empire and lead us in a new direction. A new belief."

Maniakes sat back in his chair and popped an olive into his mouth. "I thought the original plan was to put him in charge of the administration, now that Orphano has disappeared?"

"That was *your* plan, General. To outflank Orphano, and in some way implicate him with Michael's schemes."

"You've been doing a lot of digging, haven't you, Holiness? Tell me, where do you come by all of this information?"

"Your constant attempts to outmanoeuvre Orphano are common knowledge, General. With Orphano out of the equation, perhaps your plans are becoming more ... how should I put it, more *ambitious?*" It was the Patriarch's turn to eat an olive.

Maniakes leaned to his right and spat out a stone. "I'm sick of Constantines and Michaels and every other bloody fucking Emperor." He waved away Alexius's look of horror. "I'm a soldier and I speak bluntly. My only ambition is to see Byzantium *safe*. I have no desires for the throne, if that's what you're getting at."

"Then you agree? We groom Monomachus and prepare him for an audience with the Empress?"

Maniakes guffawed. "She'll take one look at that fat bastard and throw up." He shook his head. "She'll never be persuaded to saddle herself with him."

"I have often deliberated over that myself, General." His eyes twinkled. "I believe I have a way out of this particular predicament. If you will humour me ..." He swivelled in his seat and called, "Guard!"

A soldier entered, and Alexius snapped his fingers. After a brief pause, a taut, lean individual stepped inside, bare-chested, bristling muscles, with a fine chiselled face. He brought himself to attention and saluted. "*Ave!*"

"A Roman?" spluttered Maniakes.

"This is Marcellus Flavius, General. He trains boxers for the seasonal games in Hadrianoplis."

Maniakes allowed his eyes to run over the man's body and grunted, impressed. "He looks a solid enough fellow. But I don't think Monomachus would make a particularly good fighter, Holiness."

Alexius suppressed a chuckle. "General, Marcellus will train Monomachus, but not for fighting. He will trim his fat, harden his muscles, and transform him into something that the dear Empress will find irresistible."

Maniakes considered the proposition, sipped at his wine and finally sat back to consider the superb specimen of manhood standing before him. "You think you can do this, Marcellus? Have you seen him? Years of eating rich food and guzzling gallons of wine have made him soft."

Marcellus looked to Alexius, received a curt nod, then smiled. "I will get him ready, General. His lifestyle requires re-education – his stomach will soon follow."

Maniakes laughed. "My God, Holiness, you've excelled yourself with this one! If you can make Monomachus turn his back on dates and oil and afternoons spent sleeping on his couch, Marcellus, then you'll have served the Empire well."

Marcellus inclined his head. "This I can do, General."

Maniakes smirked, dismissed the Roman with a wave of his hand and chose another olive. When the man had gone, Maniakes continued, "I bow to your thinking, Holiness. If it works, and we can use this Monomachus to aid Zoe, the Empire will be well on the way to restoring itself."

"It will take more than Monomachus alone to do that, General, despite his unquestioned skills at administration. Years of neglect have left us weak, institutionally and militarily.

Like the man himself, we have grown soft. Michael was the result of years of ineptitude and incompetence. We should have acted sooner."

"But Michael acted first. He outmanoeuvred us, Holiness. *All* of us."

"And thank God we had Hardrada to save us."

The General pulled a face and munched down another olive. He spat the pip across the room. "And what of the lovely Zoe herself? What happens when her sister arrives? Whatever happened to your more fanciful plan of placing them both on the throne, to have them ruling as joint Empresses? You change your mind too frequently and play too complicated a game, Holiness."

"I am guided, General. Through my prayers." Alexius spread out his hands, "The people love the sisters, but they will not be assuaged until a man is at the head of our Empire."

The General fixed Alexius with a penetrating stare. He well knew the holy man's penchant for intrigue, dressed up as it was as religious fervour. The man was dangerous and would need careful watching. True, he had saved Constantinople from the excesses of Michael V by convincing Hardrada to bring the Varangians back to the great city and destroy the detested Scythian guards, but how much wider were his ambitions? Were they similar to his own, might they reach as far as the throne itself? "I will think on this, Holiness. Give me a few days. Monomachus is in a state of shock, but if Marcellus can work a miracle ..."

Alexius nodded his head. "As you wish, but I think Monomachus will not prove troublesome. Isolated on that island of his for seven years, he is bound to take some time to adjust." He stood up. "In the meantime I shall speak to Theodora, prepare her for her reunion with her sister."

"You're still going to pursue that line, despite your words?"

"She has a right to share in our decisions, General. She is a member of the royal dynasty. There have been too many intrigues and lies. We need open, shared government if the people are ever to support our future decisions."

Swallowing down the urge to smirk, Maniakes ruminated over the Patriarch's words, the hypocrisy ladled thick over every utterance. Alexius may well declare his desire for 'open and shared government', but that did not prevent him from sending his acolytes to spy on friends and allies. He was the same breed of rat as they all were; the only difference being he wrapped himself up the ornate robes of his office, believing they set him apart, gave him authenticity. They didn't and Maniakes knew it.

"I will inform the Senate. The more of them we have on our side, the better." Alexius gave the slightest of bows and went out.

Maniakes steepled his fingers and brought them to his lips. His own, personal ambitions would have to remain secret, despite the

Patriarch's obvious suspicions. For now, Alexius was a powerful ally, someone to keep close. The idea of bringing Monomachus to court, to school him in the finer arts of leadership, hone his body and mould him into someone controllable, a mere figurehead, was something Maniakes had long contemplated himself. If Zoe, who preferred the comforts and trappings of *being* Empress rather than the responsibility, were to couple with a man under the General's command then overall power would at last be in his grasp. If he still wanted it. Perhaps the arrival of Zoe's sister might change things, open up alternatives.

He finished his wine, stood up, collected his helmet and went outside.

The guards snapped to attention and Maniakes paused to adjust his headgear, pulling the leather strap tight under his chin. He was a big man, but the huge Imperial Guards flanking the entrance to his office dwarfed him. He sighed, nodding to one. "I want you to find Andreas and send him to the stables. I will be leaving within in the hour, so do not tarry."

The guard saluted and marched off. The General closed his eyes and turned his face skywards. The early afternoon sun beat down and Maniakes allowed himself a moment before striding off, with the second guard in tow, through the Royal enclave.

Almost a city within a city, here stood all the apartments and offices of state, the beating heart of the Empire. The massive bureaucracy that maintained the lifeblood of

Byzantium, pressed in around the many boulevards and avenues, countless offices and rooms staffed by competent, highly literate men who strived endlessly to ensure money continued to flow. Here they ratified trade agreements, resolved land disputes, recorded requests and bequests, checked and filed. The Empire was vast, dominating central Europe and the Near East, but external pressures from jealous enemies grew and Byzantine's armies stretched thin. Nowadays a different army, armed with pens, not swords, kept the peace. The Patriarch's words came to him, the idea of peaceful diplomacy being the way forward. As enemies became more numerous and bolder, Maniakes knew his troops would be hard pressed to keep them at bay. Centuries ago the same problems overwhelmed Rome, leading to its fall, the once great eternal city a shadow of its former self; great monuments, buildings, streets, houses, all left to rot. To consider that such a fate awaited Constantinople was too horrible to contemplate.

He had grown tired. Not only physically; war and intrigue, his two constant bedfellows, had lost their allure. He longed for peace and solitude, a chance to live out his life without forever worrying about what might happen. Once safely ensconced on the throne, Monomachus would retire with a fat pension, as reward for years of service. Perhaps the two royal sisters would erect a monument in his honour, a fitting conclusion and a place in history.

As he moved through the tree-lined boulevards, his thoughts turned to home. A few days to relax, to settle his mind, reach conclusions. That was what he needed, not the heat and stress of the past few weeks. Michael's brief reign had been one of lunacy and callous indifference, but now the former Emperor festered in some godforsaken hellhole in the arse end of the world, broken and useless. After dragging him away, the guards had returned to report that Michael, now blinded, ranted and raved, damning the entire world, venting his fury at anyone who would listen. Hardrada, he screamed, had carried out the deed. At every turn, the spectre of Hardrada loomed and not for the first time Maniakes considered killing the giant Norseman. Maniakes wondered if he still had the energy to see through such an endeavour.

By the time his leisurely stroll brought him to the stables, Maniakes's horse was waiting, saddled and tended by the young groom. Looking resplendent in his full guard's uniform, Andreas stood close by and came to attention as Maniakes stepped up to the horse and nuzzled into its face. The animal responded, blowing hot air from its nostrils, flicking its mane, returning the affection. Maniakes spoke to it in a whisper as he breathed in the thick aroma of sweat that clung heavily in the narrow stall.

"I love the smell of hay," Maniakes said with a grin, nodding towards the young officer. "Well done for getting here briskly, Andreas."

"At your command, General."

Maniakes smiled. "Yes." He reached over to caress his horse's neck with long strokes of his hand. "Listen, I am returning to my villa for a few days to take in the sweeter air the country provides and catch the last of the summer sun. I want you to prepare everything for Theodora's return. The heralds have already approached her and she will be here within a few days. The Patriarch will send for you, so make sure that everything is made ready, and you will inform His Holiness of my intention to meet with the Senate on my return in two days. Theodora needs cosseting, Andreas. She has been living a life of seclusion for almost twenty years ... returning to the clamour of the court may prove stressful for her. So watch, protect and, above all else, support her. When I get back, I shall speak to her." He nodded to the groom, who held the horse's reins whilst Maniakes pulled himself into the saddle. He reached forward and stroked the horse's neck again, calming it. "Constantine Monomachus is recovering after what has happened. I want you to attend to him also, to persuade him of the need for a slightly more considered and respectful way of conducting himself at court. The days of gluttony and sexual gratification are at an end. We want no more Michaels, understand me?" Andreas lowered his head and brought his heels together in attention. "Monomachus will be attended by a gymnast of some repute, a man who will train him, bring some muscle to his flesh." He noted the frown crossing

Andreas's face. "The Empress needs a man, Andreas. We *all* need a man on the throne. And talking of men, Hardrada is spending some time in quiet contemplation. The Empire has need of his services, Andreas. You would do best to make sure no harm comes to him."

Andreas's mood changed, his eyes darkened and his mouth became a tight, thin line. "I would rather you didn't give me such a charge, sir. Not for that man."

Maniakes studied the young officer, well aware of the hatred he bore for the Viking. It was something that could be used to his advantage, the General mused, and he smiled. "Andreas, your loyalty to the Empire is beyond question. So much so that on my return, I will be making recommendations to the Senate regarding your status, recommendations that will see you well rewarded, with titles and estates of your own." He ignored Andreas's dropped jaw. "So, do as I say, despite the obvious hatred you harbour for the man. He is useful, and we will need him in the weeks and months to come. And remember, you swore a holy oath, before God, that you would cause the Viking no harm. Remember?" Andreas nodded. "So, until such time as the Patriarch releases you from that oath, if you value your eternal soul, you will not break the promises made." He gathered up the reins and led his horse out of the stable. "I shall be back in two days, Andreas. I expect everything to be as it should be. I hold you responsible, is that clear?"

"More than clear, sir."

"Very well, see to it then." He spurred his horse and moved away, knowing Andreas bristled with indignation, softened by a tiny tremor of curiosity, wondering what the General's recommendations to the Senate might be.

SIX

Through the many holes and gaps, the wind cut like a knife into the flesh of the men huddled together in the high-vaulted hall. A sound like a demented banshee whistled through the wooden walls whilst without, the cold heralded another harsh, unforgiving winter.

Strewn over the long tables the detritus of the previous night's feast mingled with pools of vomit from those who had partaken too much of rich wine, their slumbering bodies hyphenating the scene. Threading his way through these inert clumps, Yaroslav, king of the Rus, went to the head of the room, lifted up a goblet of wine and drained it. Swathed in a sheepskin-lined robe, the cold still bit hard, and he rubbed himself with trembling hands, crammed some goat's cheese into his mouth and washed it down with more wine.

He looked about the gloomy interior, early morning sunlight sending thin shafts through the cracks in the wooden slats of the walls.

Partially completed, another year would pass before stone replaced the original timbers and made Yaroslav's dream of turning Kiev into a city to rival Constantinople a reality. If the royal coffers managed it, of course. The lack of gold was a source of constant concern for the King of the Rus.

A huge wave of sadness washed over him. All of his father's aspirations, his desire for greatness, for Russia to be a power, none of it would come to pass unless something drastic happened. A sudden influx of cash, the means to continue on the path towards establishing an Empire. But from where? It saddened him to see what had become of those dreams. Drunken oafs sprawled out in a half-finished hall. What must any foreign dignitary think, he wondered, if one ever came to visit. Embarrassment, amusement, possibly both? Certainly not awe. Yaroslav sighed, threw down the goblet of unfinished wine and cut a path through the prone assemblage to the great doors. He pulled them open, grunting with the effort.

A blast of cold air struck him full in the face. Snow had not yet begun to fall, but soon this wild, barren land would lay buried beneath a thick, white blanket. He often looked forward to this time of year, the winter weather the most formidable defence system known, freezing the flesh and bone of anyone daring to venture into it. The intense cold kept the Normans out, deterred the Byzantines, and locked the Bulgars inside their own lands. But when the thaw came the dangers and threats of war would return. Spring, the harbinger of death. What to do then?

Yaroslav hugged himself tightly and gazed across to the rolling hillside and the thick black wall of forest beyond. Already the grass, tipped with frost, turned from green to white. Winter. Winter and gold: his two greatest considerations. Winter kept them safe, but nothing else was possible without gold. Defence, building, government, everything hinged on the yellow metal. With it, everything was achievable, including peace. Without it, the people would become afraid, grow restless. Rebellion would escalate and the crown would tumble. His father had taught him that all the goodwill and godliness in the entire world would not prevent the people from clamouring for a better lot. Bread filled bellies, not gold. But gold bought the wheat that made the bread. He sighed. If the King could not deliver, then he was doomed.

"Sire?"

Yaroslav whirled around, instinctively going for his sword, then stopped as he recognised Basil, his chief advisor. The man's eyes were thick with sleep, his hair bedraggled, a little snail trail running from the corner of his mouth to his grizzled chin.

"Dear God, you scared me Basil!"

"Pardons, Majesty," Basil bowed low. His thick robe was open to the waist, revealing his hardened torso, the stomach flat. A life of combat had honed his muscles into solid bands of steel. Yaroslav owed this man much, including his life. He was the only real friend he had and the trust he bore the man was absolute. He noted the dark cast across Basil's face and he knew something bad was about to happen. "A messenger has arrived, from the East. It seems that the Byzantine Emperor Michael the Fifth has been deposed."

Yaroslav gave a sharp laugh. "Damned Byzantines are always at war with themselves over who should rule." Yaroslav turned and looked out once more across the rolling plain.

"This is true, Majesty. But Hardrada led the uprising, at the head of his Varangians."

"Did he, by God?" Yaroslav chewed at his lip, considering this snippet of news. Hardrada's visits to Kiev had been frequent in the past, forging an alliance of sorts; Yaroslav's daughter, Ellisif, the mortar that bound it together, and the booty left behind in the King's safe keeping a guarantee of the Viking's return. Hardrada had designs on Yaroslav's daughter, but the lure of fame and fortune had drawn him to Constantinople. He had proved his mettle, fighting alongside the Rus against an insurgency by the Poles. A worthy ally; a formidable enemy. "Fortune always did favour him."

"If he is now all-powerful in the great city, Majesty, might it not be politic to consider pushing for the match?"

Yaroslav felt his stomach tighten, as it always did when Basil broached this subject. The gnarled, gigantic Norwegian, rough-hewn, uncouth and irreverent may not be the most welcome pairing for his beautiful Ellisif, but times were hard and Hardrada must have grown even richer by now. He shivered, but not from the biting cold. "Dear God ..."

"Forgive me, Majesty, I understand how the idea of your lovely daughter being tied to a man such as he must gall you, but he is brave, powerful and has ambitions." Basil stepped up closer to his king and Yaroslav watched him from the corner of his eye. "It would be a good match, Majesty. Agents assure me he has indeed grown rich, but the Empress Zoe has seized his wealth. If we could aid Hardrada in recovering what is rightfully his, he may well reward us."

Yaroslav stiffened. He had pondered many times on the possibility of plundering Hardrada's horde of booty. Only his innate sense of honour prevented such a move. But this ...

Basil plunged on, growing bolder. "It may not be honourable, Majesty, but we are in desperate need. Hardrada could be the means to buoying up our economy, of infusing it with a new vitality. His rewards would be significant, especially if he becomes the King of the Norwegians, as everyone knows he wishes. If we set the match, he may release his gold to us immediately."

"*If,* Basil." The King took in a huge breath and let it out in a long steady stream of steam. "If he does become King, then I will consider this proposition much more keenly. In the meantime, send an emissary to Constantinople, inviting our erstwhile friend to visit us, and reacquaint himself with Ellisif." He turned. "This emissary is to be accompanied by some capable guards, if you understand my meaning."

Basil bowed very low, "I shall see to it at once, Majesty!" He turned and disappeared back into the hall.

Returning to the landscape, Yaroslav felt the tightening of his shoulders, the bunching of muscles that always heralded the onset of a headache. A good match? A seafaring adventurer, with nothing to offer except vain promises of riches that might be. What if it were all a fairy story, what if Zoe spent everything before Basil's men could get their hands on it? She was more than capable of doing such a thing, having been the ruin of the Byzantine treasury more than once in her colourful life. However, if he could find a way to secure the already deposited booty and Hardrada were to become King of the Norwegians, what an alliance that would be, the promise of greater riches considerable.

Slowly Yaroslav's shoulders relaxed, replaced by a warm glow which settled in his stomach. He smiled. This was a chance, however slim, for his nation's situation to become very much better, very soon. A chance he would not forsake.

***

She caught up with him as he emerged from the barracks and strode across the wide Imperial Guard training ground. Most of the men were out of the city now, their duties sending them to far-flung borders of the Empire. A mere handful remained, for purely ceremonial functions. Now the Varangians had returned, the Imperial Guard was nothing more than a tiny shadow of its former self. Nikolias didn't care. His thoughts were with Leoni, and what he could do to protect her from the machinations of the General.

He saw the girl running towards him and sensed, even at this distance, that something was wrong. He stopped and waited for her to draw closer.

Recognising her, he relaxed a little. One of Zoe's servants, a young girl; small, short dark hair, sumptuous clothes of shimmering satin reflecting her high status.

She breathed hard as she approached. "You are a difficult man to find," she said between gulps of air.

"Well, you've found me now. What is it you want?"

"Not I – my mistress. The Empress Zoe. She demands your presence, immediately."

Nikolias instinctively brought his heels together. As an officer in the Imperial Guard, his allegiance to the Empress was beyond question. However, the General's eyes were everywhere, the tendrils of his spy network reaching into every corner of the city. Could this girl be a part of it, he wondered. Had Maniakes already caught wind of Nikolias's plan to ferret Leoni away and sent this girl to lure him into a trap? Or perhaps it was a genuine summons from the Empress? In this atmosphere of danger Nikolias no longer knew what to believe. He tipped his head forward slightly. "Then lead me to her," he said.

He knew the way of course, but he allowed

the girl to lead him forward. They entered the Royal complex, moving between the massive pillars, along the very corridors where Nikolias had first come across Leoni.

This time there was no hesitation, no creeping through the gloom and Nikolias's hobnailed boots clinked loudly across the marbled floor, the sound echoing throughout the vaulted halls. He grew aware of faces peering from darkened corners, hushed voices asking questions, wondering who this officer was, where he was going. The court, the extended royal family had emerged from the woodwork, returning to the life of richness and plenty they had basked in for so long, and which Michael had replaced with his own, unique take on how to rule. With Michael's fall, the rumourmongers had returned and with it Palace intrigue which, as ever, would find more store in gossip and speculation than the truth.

The girl gave him a self-conscious smile as she stopped outside the double doors of her mistress's room. A guard stood to the side, staring directly ahead. Nikolias, without hesitation, went in unannounced.

She sat on a chair, a thin silken robe cut to her midriff revealed her long legs, the right one propped up on a small stool. At her feet, another young girl, ebony skin shimmering, applied makeup to the Empress's toenails and did not flinch as Nikolias stepped forward.

"Majesty," he said, falling onto one knee, head bowed.

"Thank you for coming so swiftly," Zoe said,

not raising her eyes.

Nikolias took a quick, furtive look at her bronzed limbs. He felt a little shiver run through his loins. The woman was beyond doubt the most sensual he had ever seen. She shimmered with latent sexuality, her power oozing from every pore of her perfect body. A body that had known many lovers, conquered innumerable men, and now displayed openly for him.

The Empress of Byzantium.

Nikolias coughed, looked away and waited.

"I have a mission for you, Nikolias."

He frowned. "A mission, Majesty?"

"Yes. I want you to find Leoni."

Her words took him by surprise. His mouth dropped and without meaning to, he gave a little gasp.

Zoe's eyes widened and she studied Nikolias for the first time. "Ah ..." Then she smiled, no further words being required.

Nikolias looked nervously around the room. Apart from the two girls, they were alone. However, this thought brought him little relief. Either of the two handmaidens could be in the General's service. He needed to move with caution. He lowered his head further still. "I need to talk to you privately, Majesty."

Without a moment's hesitation, Zoe swept to her feet, ignoring the outraged look of the maid pedicuring the Empress's feet. "Get out, the pair of you." As the girls left the room, Zoe took hold of Nikolias's arm and brought him to his feet. "The balcony."

The view from the elevated position allowed

an interrupted view across the fabled city of Constantinople, the sprawl of the buildings disappearing into the distance; grey, shrouded mountains forming the backdrop. Nikolias sighed. The greatest city on earth, eternal, majestic. New Rome. Centre of the world. He looked down, aware for the first time that the Empress still had his arm in her hand. She looked up at him and smiled and his loins stirred again. He swallowed hard.

"So tell me," she said, her voice like velvet.

"The General," he managed, his voice constricted by a tongue thick with desire, "his spies, they are everywhere. And Leoni, she—" Her finger came to his lips and he stopped, almost crying out with shock. The Empress of Byzantium, *touching him!* His eyes bulged so much he felt sure they would explode.

"I know," she said quietly. "I know she was his agent, as well as his lover. She tried to hide it from me, but I am not as stupid as I appear." He tried to protest, but she pressed her finger harder against his lips. "Sssh ... I know what people think of me, that I am feckless, without substance, someone who only wishes adornment and grandeur. But the truth is so much simpler. Above all else, I wish for my people to be happy." She smiled, dropped her hand to her side and looked once more at the view. "I want you to find Leoni for me. I want her here, where she should be. I will deal with the General, so do not be unduly concerned about her safety." She gave him a sideways glance. "You don't hide your feelings well, Nikolias. I doubt you could hide them from her, even if you wanted to."

He blinked. Did she know already where Leoni hid? But no, that could not be the case. Surely to God this woman was not at the head of yet another network?

"A woman needs to know she is loved, Nikolias. So go to her, bring her to me and I will look favourably on your loyalty. Then perhaps you can make some plans for the both of you. You understand?"

He thought he did, but he didn't dare say. Instead, he bowed. "Majesty. I will endeavour to honour the faith and trust you have accorded in me."

"Oh, I know you will, Nikolias." She gave a little laugh and ran her fingers over his bare arm. "I have no doubt about that."

Seven

General Maniakes came over the rise, leading his horse down the pathway snaking between the fields to his villa. The cornfields cleared, the wheat gathered, his household carrying out their duties with their usual precision. He allowed himself to relax, the sweet early autumn air filling his lungs, transforming him from the rough, unforgiving soldier he was in the great city, to a more pliant and passionate individual. The promise of tranquillity afforded by his estate, a haven in which to rest and recuperate always did this. His wife was there. Helen. She was fair enough, a little heavy around the hips now, but she kept herself to herself, filled her days with the accounts, running the household. Their physical closeness was nothing more than a distant memory, but he needed her to keep everything moving smoothly. His land, his life. No other place brought such promise of peace and release from the responsibilities of power politics.

One blot on an otherwise unblemished panorama besmirched the vista. His neighbour's estate.

Maniakes growled, unable to suppress his growing temper. It was always like this. The first view of his lands, the rolling fields, the broadening sky filled with the promise of so much goodness ... all shattered with one single glance.

He stood on the other side of the fence, as if he knew. Perhaps he did.

Romanus Sclerus.

As Maniakes drew closer, straining to keep his eyes from burning away the flesh of the man, Sclerus stepped up to the fence and draped his elbows across the top; nonchalant, amusement in every line of his face. A man dismissive of Maniakes's power and influence. Rich, obscenely rich, and vain as only the most privileged can be. He waggled his fingers in mock greeting as the General rode by and shouted, "We have a problem."

Maniakes reined in his horse and turned his glare upon the man. Dressed in the finest silken robes hemmed with strands of pure gold, his thinning hair interlaced between the jewel-encrusted band he always wore, he appeared like a throwback from Rome, signalling to all his affluence and power. Maniakes resisted the urge to sneer. "What sort of problem?"

Sclerus pressed his ample belly against the woodwork. "Your men cut a furrow and diverted the stream. When I confronted then they said it was to irrigate the bottom field."

The General shrugged. "I don't see how—"

"They came onto my land to do it." Sclerus pushed himself away from the fence, holding the General's gaze, inviting the rebuttal, the outrage. When none was forthcoming, Sclerus laughed, a single, sharp bark. "I tanned their arses and sent them back to your side." To give effect to his words he rattled the wooden boundary between their respective farms. "I put them over this and gave them a thrashing. They won't cross over again, not if they have any sense."

Maniakes bristled and swallowed, forcing back the bile rising into his throat. He pressed his tongue against his bottom lip and forced himself to breathe calmly. His voice, when it came, was low, menacing. "You *tanned* their arses – my men?"

"Aye." Sclerus eyes narrowed. "The next time I catch them on my land, I'll cut off their bloody hands!"

The General, no longer able to contain his anger, made a grasp for the hilt of his sword, but the sudden movement caused his horse to react. It whickered loudly, stamping its feet with alarm, and the General struggled to keep it from rearing on its hind legs.

Sclerus chuckled. "My, my, that is a nervous beast. New, is she? You should have one of your men break her in for you, General. She might throw you, and then where would the Empire be with its favourite son lying in the dirt with a broken neck?"

Maniakes gripped the reins, leaning forward to smooth down the horse's mane, whispering words of reassurance in its ears. When at last it grew quiet, he turned his eyes to his hated neighbour and glowered. "You touch my men again and I'll kill you."

"Pah, you're full of hot wind, you old fart!" Sclerus laughed, contemptuous. "You may be something of a lord in the city, but down here, in the pig shit, you're no better than anyone else. So come down from your throne, *General*, and tell your men to stay on your side of the fence!" His face grew serious. "Or they'll know the consequences."

Sclerus turned and strode off, his formidable bulk disguised within the voluminous folds of his robes. He chuckled as he went, while Maniakes watched him, rage smashing against his chest, the hot blood pumping through his veins. Damn the man and his arrogance. In Constantinople, he would have his head served up on a plate – but here, here it was different. The outlying lands were becoming more desirous of controlling their personal affairs. Everyone knew the pressures from external enemies, so the landed gentry took the opportunity to extend and entrench their power, no matter how detrimental such moves might prove for the Empire. Whilst Maniakes fought against Bulgars, Turks and Rus, men such as Sclerus feathered their nests, preferring soft beds and pillows to the danger of campaign, never giving any thanks to the soldiers who risked their lives to maintain Byzantium's security. It was time such arrogant selfishness changed.

Maniakes ground his teeth. Perhaps, he

mused, before he relinquished his status he should ensure those changes came sooner rather than later.

***

Summoned to the residence of the Patriarch Alexius, Andreas paused at the steps to the magnificent villa set in the centre of the Royal enclave and tried to settle his thoughts. A herd of wild animals stampeded around inside his head, setting up a cloud of indecision and confusion. Rarely had he felt like this, set adrift with no clear view of the end in sight. One thing alone determined his actions; the knowledge that one day his blade would slice through Hardrada's throat. Nothing else mattered to him except the Viking's death.

The girl from the forest, Analise, gave him a brief glimpse of happiness, a tiny moment, a fragile insect's wing in the vast landscape of existence ... but a beautiful moment nevertheless. Hardrada took it all away by murdering her.

When he spotted the vile Monomachus beating and attempting to kill the young girl down at the harbour, all his pent up rage and hatred had rushed to the fore in a single, uncontrolled moment, the memories of Analise and her suffering proving too much. He wished his blade had flashed through the air, and destroyed the man's eyes, in a vicious repeat of Emperor Michael's fate. Blinded. Sent into the eternal darkness of fear and despair. Better than death. Andreas experienced neither guilt nor remorse for what happened. Rather, a sort of elation rushed through him, and how much more so when Hardrada fell under his knife? The thought filled him with unrestrained joy, far greater than anything he experienced when beating the fat oaf on the dockside. It would be heavenly.

Andreas counted the marble steps, shimmering in the glow of the sun. Each one led closer to the centre of intrigue. How he loathed it. The duplicity, the lies. Even from God voice on Earth.

The General warned him the summons from the Patriarch would come as soon as Andreas fulfilled his orders to prepare for Lady Theodora's return. He fitted out her private apartments with the finest furnishing available; teak tables from the Orient, glass bowls from Italy, vibrant embroideries from the north of Europe. Hastily employed servants stood ready, ceremonial robes and other state trappings gathered. Nothing remained except to prepare for her actual arrival, a troop of armed men already waiting to escort her to her new residence. He allowed himself a small smile, believing Theodora would present the General with a glowing report and have his faith in Andreas restored.

He climbed the steps, his heart light. The other things could wait. Time enough to deal a deathblow to Hardrada. Time enough to see the warm blood of the Viking running over the blade of his knife. Time enough to consider what would happen afterwards, when the reason for breathing had – what – gone? Gone, or changed? He didn't care which. Memories of the girl endured, engraved into his mind: what they shared, the warmth, the love. Hardrada took the promise of a life together away. For that, he would die.

"Ah, Andreas!"

The young officer blinked, bringing himself automatically to attention. Lost in his thoughts, he had wandered into the Patriarch's residence and now stood before the great man. Andreas lowered his head. "Holiness."

Alexius drifted closer without appearing to take a step, his long, flowing robes gliding over the floor, concealing everything beneath. "I have had a communication from the General," he began, a broad smile splitting his face. "Interesting man, the General, don't you think?"

Andreas frowned. What sort of a question was that? He gave a small shrug. "He is ... my commander, Holiness."

"Yes, quite right. You are loyal, Andreas; a worthy trait to possess in such troublesome times." He nodded, his smile so disarming, so beguiling. "Which is why I am entrusting you with a difficult task. To escort the Lady Theodora to visit her sister, in her chambers."

A further frown. Andreas, confused, shifted his weight. "Holiness, General Maniakes has already instructed me to—"

"I know all about the good General's instructions but there is no need. Her Royal Highness, Empress Theodora, is here."

Before he could voice further questions, the Holy Father turned and with a theatrical flourish of his arm beckoned someone to step forward.

Andreas gasped.

Theodora, small and thin, almost waif-like, a tiny head resting upon slim shoulders, with hair short, cropped close, emerged from the shadows. Her single robe, a plain garment of rough-spun brown wool, hung heavy and long over her slight frame. At first glance, without knowledge of her royal heritage, she appeared plain and poor, and almost ugly. Andreas had to remind himself she was the Empress Zoe's sister; she was as different to the glorious Empress as a lowly house sparrow is to a peacock. In truth, there was no comparison at all.

***

A sumptuous meal awaited on the table; platters filled with unleavened bread and humus, mountains of fried vegetables, roast fowl, fillets of sardines and tuna. Sclerus spent a moment surveying the feast, licking his lips in anticipation, silently thanking the hard work of the many cooks. He smiled across the table to his wife, who barely stirred.

"Something of a celebration," he said, settling himself down as a servant poured out the wine.

His wife, Drusilla, gave a small grunt. "As you are pleased with how well your little games with our neighbour went, I thought it only natural I should invite over some friends to wallow in your glory. They will be arriving shortly."

"Well, I thank you for your consideration."

"No consideration, husband." She leaned over and pulled off a few grapes from the spread of exotic fruits tumbling over a large, silver plate. She popped a couple into her mouth and munched them down, "The General has returned, and you are happy with the outcome. Nothing more."

"Mmm." Sclerus sipped at his wine. "This is good," he said and swirled the ruby red liquid around the goblet. "You know, once we have the General's lands, our vineyards can be expanded and we will be rich."

"We are already rich, husband."

"Mmm. *Richer,* then."

They sat in silence until the servant returned and announced the arrival of the guests. Soon the room resounded to laughter and pleasantries whilst servants spooned out the first course, a mix of figs, rice and nuts. From his place at the head of the table, Sclerus watched his wife picking at the food, barely acknowledging the man next to her as he gushed with ill-concealed devotion.

She had been a true beauty once, but the years had taken their toll, the lines around her eyes and across her forehead deep. Her bare arms sagged, her once full breasts appeared flatter, and recently he noted how little spots of dark brown had appeared on the back of her hands. She was old. No doubt she felt the same about him, but that was of no matter. His mistresses paid homage to his body, as it should be. He had needs, needs his wife failed to fulfil. Life followed a monotonous pattern of dampened sexual attraction and lost love. If ever love had existed.

He'd married her for her wealth, her good looks an added bonus. Never one to indulge too vigorously in anything physical, Drusilla took to managing the estate whilst he found satisfaction in others. Content to fill her quiet moments with tapestries and art, much to Sclerus's relief, she never commented or complained about his excesses. And when he paused from rutting between the legs of his mistresses, he put the remainder of his considerable energies into accumulating wealth. The General might prove an obstacle to further expansion, but not an insurmountable one. Sclerus's schemes for eventual success rivalled the General's for their outrageous effectiveness.

He thrust out his goblet and a servant instantly recharged it. "I saw the General stabling his horse," said a buxom woman, her hair stacked up over a laurel wreath tiara of silver and gold. "What a magnificent animal."

The man across from her pounded the table with his wine goblet and exploded with laughter, "What? The horse or the General?"

"I have heard it said," declared another woman, much slimmer, with the fullest lips Sclerus had ever seen. She leaned forward, shooting her eyes left and right as if about to divulge the most terrible of secrets, "that he is an amazing lover. That he beds all of his servants, and that none of them ever wish to lay with any other man after he has finished with them!"

The laurel wreath woman turned scarlet and the men roared.

Sclerus drained his wine. "It won't be long before he realizes that his position is hopeless out here in the sticks. Then we can think about how we can advance our ambitions in the city itself."

Mutterings of agreement wafted across the table

"Yes," Drusilla managed a small smile, "it would be good to be in Constantinople, amongst the elite. To share our good fortune."

"More social gatherings, you mean?" Sclerus cast his eyes over his guests and beamed. "Parties. Dinners. I know you too well, wife. That is all you hanker for."

"What I hanker for, husband, is a life."

"Ah." He smacked his lips, sat back in his chair and winked at the woman with the full lips, "Yes. A life. Of pleasure, laughter and ..." he reached out and patted the woman's arm, "fornication."

The laughter erupted and Sclerus winked again, her returning smile coy.

Later, with the meal demolished, he saw his guests to the door, cupping the woman's buttocks unseen, whilst her husband stepped out into the night and almost stumbled, drunk and unaware. She turned, her lips parted, and he pressed his own against her ear and whispered, "In the rear garden, after you have put him to bed."

He watched them go and returned to the dining room and tarried a while, savouring the last of the wine. He too was a little drunk, but he didn't care. A servant came in to clear the remnants, but Sclerus ushered him away and went through the house towards the rear. The night was thick and warm, the air alive with the sound of buzzing insects. Stars twinkled brightly and he took in a deep breath, savouring the isolation.

A footfall, very close and he turned and there she was.

"You were quick," he said, crossing to her.

"He collapsed in the solarium, so I left him, drunken pig that he—"

His fingers curled around her arm and he pulled her across the gravel towards the stable block. She giggled and at the door, he kissed her. She responded, coiling her hands around his neck, moaning. When she pulled her mouth from his with a gasp, her eyes grew wide.

"God, you're desperate for it, aren't you?" He put his foot against the door and pushed it open, then swung her around and threw her into a huge pile of straw and hay in the corner. The horses had long since been sold off to the army, at a good price, so the smell was somewhat ripe. She seemed unconcerned and laid back, opening her robe as he stood over her, ripping away his own. She licked her lips and he fell onto her, eager to spill his seed.

Afterwards he returned to the villa, flopped down into a couch and closed his eyes. Satisfied and happy, the evening had gone better than he could have wished. Drusilla was always so thoughtful and that woman, the one he did not know the name of, had proved a good fuck. He'd have to make a point of servicing her on a much more regular basis. As his loins pulsed with the memory, he allowed himself to drift off, imagining how it would all pan out. With yet another mistress and Maniakes removed, life was set to get even better.

With a start, he sat up and looked around the room, returned to its usual tidiness by the servants. A single candle guttered in the far corner, its feeble, sickly glow unable to penetrate the gloom to much effect. Sclerus squinted, aware someone stood in the corner; he gasped when the figure moved out of the shadows. "You!"

The figure eased itself into a nearby chair and picked an orange from a newly stacked platter. "You need a bodyguard," he said and peeled away the skin.

A cowl covered his entire head, hiding his face within the deep folds, but Sclerus didn't need to see the man's features. He knew exactly what lay there. The hard, set mask of a man used to extreme violence, eyes like beads, a thin mouth, flat nose. He studied the man's hands, as great as stone mattocks, the frightening strength lurking there apparent in the thick fingers, the calloused knuckles.

"I don't need a bodyguard," breathed Sclerus, reached for the jug and groaned with disappointment when he found it empty. He would have liked something to do with his hands; the man's presence disturbed him, made his stomach growl with fear, the threat of violence ever present. "I have you."

The man grunted. "I'm not a bodyguard. I do my job, and you pay me. That's the sum total of our relationship."

Sclerus considered his words and nodded his head in agreement. A man like him, a killer, was not the sort of person he wished to languish around his home. No, better to keep him at a distance, dealing out his gruesome business far from sight.

"Which reminds me," the man continued, putting the orange on the table, "you owe me."

It was Sclerus's turn to grunt and, without a pause, he stood up, went over to the far side of the room and pulled open the door to a large cabinet. He extracted a small, wooden box with a hinged lid, opened it, turned and threw over a small bag filled with coins. The man caught and weighed it in his hand before slipping it inside his robe.

"Aren't you going to count it?"

The man gave a laugh. Sclerus wished he could see the man's expression. "No need. I trust you. Besides, if it were short, I'd have to come back, wouldn't I?"

Sclerus shuddered at the thought, flexed his shoulders, put the box back in its place and returned to the dining table. "The plan has worked reasonably well so far, for which I'm grateful, but some loose ends still remain."

"True; they almost killed each other, but the Scythian is dead. I tracked him for days. A resilient individual – at one point I believed him dead when the Norwegian knocked him from his horse. Their final battle inside the city was truly something to behold. Hardrada is an awesome warrior."

"No one so much as suspected you were close?"

Sclerus could almost imagine the man's sneer. "Please. No one *ever* suspects." He pulled apart a sliver of orange and popped it into his mouth. "I am certain before long the others will also be dead. Perhaps my work will be done for me."

Sclerus thought back to the news he'd first received about the brutal death of an innocent girl, murdered, but by whom? He shook his head. "Hardrada can wait. We must first turn our attentions to the General."

"A difficult man to get to."

"Not here in the country, surely?"

"He has guards, even here. In Constantinople, it is impossible."

"So it will have to be at his villa?"

"Suspicion may fall on you. Your animosity is well known."

Sclerus knew this. He'd lain awake at night, trying to think of a way to remove his rival without the finger of suspicion pointing at him, but no matter how many times he ran it through his mind, he knew people would whisper and gossip, as they always did. "I will think of something."

"Perhaps you will. But think of it soon, because I must strike soon. I understand that he returns to the great city the day after tomorrow."

Yes, everything had accelerated. To have the General removed from play, and allow himself greater dominium to achieve his goals, he would need witnesses to prove his innocence. Another party, but far grander than this night's, a gathering of the great and the good, tongues used to wagging, voices others would *believe.*"I will need some more time, to arrange things. I will host a party, whilst you do the deed. There will be no proof to link me with the General's death." He grinned, pleased with his plan.

The man grunted again. "More time ... very well, perhaps the next occasion the General visits his farm. Unfortunately, we have no way of knowing when that might be." He shifted in his chair. "Of course, I could arrange a little something to facilitate his return at a time of our choosing. A disturbance, a robbery?" He raised his hand and pointed over to the far side of the room. "Some water?"

Sclerus bridled. The effrontery of the man! He struggled to refrain from commenting, stood up and crossed the room to the water jug. He stopped, frowning hard. How could the man possibly know the jug was here? The room was too dark to notice such details, the cabinet deep in shadow. Sclerus shrugged. No matter. He clicked his tongue when he found the jug to be empty and, lifting it, turned to inform his uninvited visitor, and almost cried out in surprise.

The man had disappeared, like a phantom into the night.

EIGHT

Through the mountain pass, the warriors moved in a long, straggling line that stretched far into the distance. In the vanguard a mounted column of heavily armoured men, helms crammed down on mailed coifs, spears held upright, kite shields slung over backs. To the rear, two hundred foot soldiers sweating under hauberks, ahead and to the flanks, scouts on wiry ponies combed the area for any pickets that may have been set out by the nearby encampment.

The reports came back.

Nothing.

Gerald de Brie allowed himself a smile when he received the news. These damned Byzantines were arrogant and complacent in their approach to war. How they managed to maintain such an enormous Empire, and for so long was a mystery to him. Like the Romans before them, they had allowed their guard to drop, their vast territories impossible to protect. With the coffers almost bare, mercenaries were ill-paid and thin on the ground, garrison troops stretched wide and far, protecting the Empire's borders proving a nightmare. The time was ripe for change.

He held up his mailed fist and the column slowed in a gradual halt. A group of riders came over the rise and halted a few feet away, breathing hard. "Lord, we have surveyed the camp."

Gerald turned to the scout, a young, wiry individual, his beige jerkin soaked in sweat. Even now, with the rolling time of the year and the sun a pink smudge on the horizon, Sicily was surprisingly warm.

"Tell me."

"At the gatehouse, two light troops. Along the walls, several more, but not the numbers we expected. The remainder sleep in their beds, my lord, oblivious to the danger. No horses mounted, no fires alight. They expect nothing, lord."

"Strange they did not post pickets."

"If they had, they would now be dead."

Gerald smiled again. The lad was of a particular mind. Brutal. Unforgiving. As only a good Norman should be. "Very well." He stretched himself up from his saddle, "Sergeant Guille!"

A massive man trotted up, his wide shoulders bristling with muscle under the chain mail of his hauberk. His face almost totally enclosed by a heavy iron helm, the nasal bar flattening his features and adding to his menacing look, eyes wild and black, jawline set. A man as hard as the land that had cradled him. He brought his horse close to Gerald's and slammed his right hand across his chest in a salute. "Aye, sir."

"Send forward the archers, with flame arrows, spearman behind. Instruct the Bretons to hold fast with the scaling ladders – they may not be necessary if we can breach the gate once it burns."

Guille grunted and turned his horse around to pass on the orders.

Gerald let out a long breath, then eyed the scout once again. "Ever been in a scrap, lad?"

The young man's face reddened. "No, my lord. At least, nothing like this."

"Well," said Gerald, "Just keep your head down, your eyes open, and stick close to me. Get yourself a shield whilst you're at it."

"I'm a scout, sir. I have no shield."

"You'll need one today, lad. Trust me!"

***

At the same time as the attack on the Byzantine outpost began, Nikolias oversaw the changing of the guard at the royal palace, then headed across the wide, open square towards one of the many gates to the centre of the city of Constantinople.

He moved quickly. At this time of day few people were about, so he threw away his usual caution. He had lain awake all night, thinking of Lady Zoe's words. She required Leoni to return to her. He had to obey – he had no choice – but how to protect the girl from the machinations of the General. When Maniakes discovered she had returned to the service of Zoe, he would want to ensnare her once more in his plots and schemes. Nikolias's stomach twisted into a tight knot; the thought of her being with the General almost made him baulk. There must be a way to follow out his orders and keep her safe.

By the time he reached his mother's home, a vague plan had formed in his mind. Leoni would have to agree of course, and his mother. Nikolias hung his head, overwhelmed by the impossibility of it all. His mother was too old for any of this, her life winding down. She needed peace and quiet, not the stress and strain of moving to another place. Would she even consent to leave?

He pulled off his helmet and dragged the back of his hand across his brow. Why had he allowed the situation to become so entangled; what had happened to his usual cautious nature? He never acted impulsively, always weighed up the options, be it in battle or in love.

Love. There was a word. He doubted he had ever known love. Affection, yes. Caring, naturally. There had been women in his life: some had been special. None of them, however, had made his heart sing the way Leoni did. And the wildest thought of all – he barely knew her. He had seen her walking in the corridors of State, eyed the curve of her hips, imagined the soft, sweet touch of her body. Lustful whimsies, nothing concrete or certain.

Now, with her under his roof, everything had changed. The closeness of her, the uniqueness of spirit he found irresistible.

Physically she was extraordinarily attractive, but the sensations that raced through his body whenever he breathed in her perfume went far beyond mere physicality. What lay beneath her loveliness moved him in a way no other woman ever had. And every time the image of her face came into his mind, a warm, comforting glow spread through him. Perhaps this was 'love'. Whatever, it proved irresistible and totally consumed him, clouding his judgement, causing him to be light-headed, almost child-like.

And then there was his mother. He put his hand across his face. She would have to come if she wished to remain alive. Convincing her might be another matter. Leoni too might refuse, reluctant to trust him. He sighed, dropping his hand to his side, where it brushed against the hilt of his sword. Reminding him of his duties and how the future hung in the balance, on the whim of the General. Crossing him would mean a death sentence.

In the end, did he have a choice? If he wanted Leoni, then the answer was clear.

He pushed the door and stepped inside.

The entrance gave way to a covered exterior, with stairs leading off to the upper storey. He could see the two of them sitting at the large table, the early morning sunlight trickling through a threadbare canopy, which afforded some shade. The year had moved on, the air chill, but the sun still battled to ward off the lowering temperatures. Soon, sitting outside would have to give way as the winter bit cold, replaced by nights next to the fire, fur coats pulled tight.

Nikolias stood and watched them both. They were engrossed in some needlework, a piece of decorated cloth, or blanket maybe. Cream coloured, large. Both women sat opposite one another, working away at the material, concentrating on their labours, not noticing him at all. They looked so content, so normal; a sudden surge of something new raced through his heart. A pain, true enough, but wholly pleasurable. He smiled to himself and went to turn away, anxious not to disturb them.

He was too late. Leoni's voice pulled him up sharply. "Niko!"

Again that stab of pain. Niko? His mother called him that, from when he was a little boy, running wild through the olive groves of their farm.

Leoni came up to him, her hand on his arm. For a moment, their eyes locked.

The moment would stay with him forever.

***

Set upon a slight hillock the outpost gave good command of the surrounding forest. Behind its wall, a covered stable yard and central keep. Room for a hundred men-at-arms, ready to rush to the defences and beat back any attack. To achieve this, a wooden palisade enclosed the open bailey, hyphenated by two stout towers, affording effective protection against assault, except from that most feared of all weapons: fire.

Archers scurried forward, keeping low, their

canvas shoes making no sound upon the dry, baked ground. Still amongst the trees, they settled themselves, one eye on their sergeant, his hand raised. When at last it dropped, they loosed off their first shower of arrows, black darts streaking through the white sky of the morning. The Byzantines at the gatehouse and the adjacent walls had no warning, becoming pincushions as scores of arrows thudded into their heads and other unprotected parts of their bodies. So sudden was the attack not one made a sound as they died. One man nearest to the gate managed to stagger towards the supporting wall and the alarm bell hanging there, but before he gripped the cord, a shower of arrows hit him and he pirouetted back along the walkway, pitching face down into the ground.

A silence settled. From somewhere far off, birds began their welcome calls to the dawn, but within the outpost, nothing stirred. All at once, erupting from the tree line, foot soldiers raced across the open ground to the palisade and the barred gate. They hastily piled up prepared hay bales, soaked in oil and pitch, against the blackened timbers. A sergeant-at-arms waved them away and before they had returned to the forest, archers loosed off burning arrows towards the silent pyre. Within a few seconds, the blaze caught hold, sending up a terrific cloud of black smoke, the sound of crackling amplified alarmingly in the quiet of the morning.

Some way off, Gerald, sitting astride his horse, signalled the Bretons to move forward.

"Damned smoke," he rasped, "it will be seen for miles. Guille, send in the men to scale the walls. Quickly, man!"

Soon, a swarm of infantry emerged from the surrounding forest, struggling with a profusion of roughly knocked together ladders, whilst others laden down with weapons, ran alongside. At their head, Guille urged them on, speed their one ally, any hesitation losing them the advantage of surprise. The fire at the gate raged, flames licking up the walls, engulfing the dry timber, belching smoke spiralling upwards in great, black plumes – too quickly. The lack of rain over the previous months reduced the outpost to one huge tinderbox, the heat so intense it beat back the men, who had to search for other parts of the wall to scale.

Guille watched in despair as above the furnace he heard the peal of alarm bells, the cry of men roused from sleep. In the confusion of smoke and flame, no one could predict the outcome, but a deeper anxiety gripped him. The great pall of thick smoke acted like a beacon, seen for miles around. Other outposts, alerted by the black clouds, would react and send reinforcements, nullifying any surprise, superiority in numbers spelling an end to the Norman incursion.

"Too much damned oil," shouted Gerald, riding his mount up to his sergeant-at-arms as Breton spearman retreated to the comparative safety of the trees, their efforts to break through the burning palisade proving too dangerous."Who in the name of God is responsible, Guille?"

Guille blanched. "A man named Tomas, Lord. Under my instructions, but ... perhaps he became overly enthusiastic? And the dryness, lord. No one could have expected the wood to catch the way it has."

Gerald pulled down his mouth. "Don't look for excuses, Guille. The man is a fucking idiot. Find him when this farce is over and execute him ... in front of the men. Do you hear me?" He struggled with his horse as it shied away from the blaze. Even at a distance of one hundred paces, the heat hit them like so many blows. "This is a damned bloody disaster!" He squinted towards the spiralling black column, wishing against hope the smoke wasn't as bad as he believed. The wish did not come true. "Bloody stupidity has lost us this day. God curse the lack of rain. God curse this bloody place, and *God damn the fucking Byzantines*!"

The flames licked around the towers flanking the gate. Within seconds, the entire structure burned with a frightening intensity, defeating the best efforts of any defenders brave enough to approach and attempt to beat down the raging fire. Gerald watched, gnashing his teeth, torn between urging his troops forward, or sending them back into the depths of the forest. As he debated with himself, one of the towers crumpled in a tremendous blast of shattered, burnt timber. Without hesitation he roared, *'Charge!'* kicked his horse's flanks and pressed forward, accompanied by the great mass of armoured cavalry, spears and javelins poised, mounts screeching, their voices raised in war cries.

Smashing through the burning remnants of the wall, the Normans closed with the confused and terrified defenders, most of whom were still stumbling from their barracks, sleep clogging their eyes and reactions, few with time to pick up weapons or don armour.

The slaughter became furious: horses wheeling around bunches of desperate men, Norman spears plunging into Byzantine guts, swords lopping off heads and limbs, the screams of the dying mingling with the roar of nearby flames.

Gerald's men were good, he knew that much, but only one Byzantine need escape to alert the whole Empire.

He needn't have worried. Any Byzantines who managed to reach the other side of the wall found themselves summarily dispatched, by either Bretons or archers. None would be telling anyone about what happened this day or any other.

As the last enemy soldiers hit the earth, Guille rode up to give his report. Gerald listened with detached indifference, glancing over to the remains of the outpost as flames embraced the wooden keep. The stench of wood smoke filled his nostrils as he spoke, "Withdraw, and assemble the men outside the ring of this infernal place. It was too damned close, Guille."

"Aye, my lord, but we have succeeded in putting the entire garrison to the sword."

"But not how I wished it. Alerted by the smoke, they'll send in scouts and once they report what has happened here, the response will come swift and merciless. Withdraw the men to clear ground and be quick about it."

Guille saluted, pulled his horse around and shouted at his men, many of whom waited,breathless, helmets off, soaked in sweat, eyes streaming from the smoke.

Gerald cantered over to the tree line and accepted a goatskin of water from one of the archers. He drank it down greedily, thankful to slake his thirst and cut through the gravel in his throat. All around him soldiers arrived, either on horse or on foot, muttering and mumbling, and Gerald waited for them to fully assemblebefore addressing them, anxious they should know without delay what lay ahead. "Men, this is the first of many outposts that the Byzantines have positioned along the borderlands. It is my intention to take them, one by one. This will mean that the campaign will be long and hard, and not always as easy as this one. Resilience, men, and a firm belief in God is what I require of you. Gird your loins, and prepare for battle."

"My lord," said Guille as Gerald made to turn away. "I have Tomas, my lord. Found him cowering amongst the Byzantine dead."

Gerald waited and watched a small knot of armoured foot soldiers dragging between them a whimpering black-eyed youth, face streaked with the blood from a cruel gash across his forehead. Without a pause, Guille dropped from his saddle and drew his sword.

"Incompetence cannot be tolerated."

The sergeant-at-arms surveyed the gathering of men. "We came within a breath of disaster, all because of this idiot." In one easy movement, Guille swung the heavy blade and cut through Tomas's neck before the assembly fully appreciated what was happening. A collective gasp issued from the men as the head flew from the shoulders, accompanied by a great spurt of blood, and then the body keeled over, crumpling to the dirt. The head rolled across the ground and stopped a few feet away, the eyes still open, mouth gaping.

Gerald viewed it all without a blink. He wondered, not for the first time, if some moments of consciousness remained before the black veil came down, but he dismissed the notion. A hard-boiled warrior met death with indifference, as part of his trade. Fanciful thoughts made one weak, indecisive, so he reined in his steed and turned in the direction of the next outpost. What was done, was done. It was pointless to tarry, the lesson taught.

***

General Maniakes rose late and breakfasted on a thin meal of dates and olives, with little appetite for much else. He had passed a restless night, grateful at least that his wife slept in her private apartment. Sclerus and his infernal meddling played around in his head; when would the bastard ever cease? Perhaps if the man had offered a decent price, Maniakes might well be inclined to negotiate, but all this aggression and strutting only served to get his back up. So, he had decided. The man could go and piss in the rain; Maniakes would not sell, not at any price. The dispute would continue and no doubt Sclerus would grow ever more adventurous, violent. Maniakes chewed a last mouthful and called his guards to his dining room.

"I want you to be extra vigilant," he said to the six men before him, chosen from the Imperial Guard of the royal palace of Constantinople. "My neighbour is becoming … how shall I put it? … obstinate and malicious. He wishes to take this land from me, hoping I will give in to the pressure he is applying. But I will not. It is your task to protect what is mine and you must be diligent and alert in your duties. I leave for the city this afternoon, so I expect my commands to be carried out, *to the letter*. If anyone crosses into my property, for whatever reason, you are to kill them. Understand?"

The guards all brought themselves together to attention as one.

"Will Her Ladyship need extra protection, sir?"

Maniakes thought, smiled, dabbed at his mouth with a cloth and stood up. "She'll be fine. I don't think Sclerus has any designs on her. It's my land he covets, not my wife." He stretched and grinned broadly. "If he wants a fight, by Christ he will get one!"

***

When he left his villa, some hours later, Maniakes did not give the farmstead a backward glance. He had barely spoken to his wife during his brief visit, passing her briefly on the terrace before he went to saddle his horse. She was a detail of his life, in the same way that other things were; his duties, his rosters, the minutiae of his daily work as General in the Imperial Army. She held no more significance in his mind than any of those, and he gave not one thought to her as he rode away.

It had always been his dream to retire one day, live out his days in solitary peace and quiet. However, he knew this was nothing but a fantasy, as likely to come true as a man sprouting wings and learning to fly. He was General George Maniakes, champion of Byzantine Rome. On his shoulders rested the responsibilities of security, the welfare of an Empire. He knew such a job would only cease with his death. The farm, the villa, they were nothing more than occasional distractions. As indeed was Leoni.

He pulled up his horse and stared out across the distant fields, the wheat now gathered in and the winter vegetables planted. The land, ploughed and prepared, was brown, an indication summer had ended and the rains and, later the snow, would soon make this landscape bleak and unforgiving. There would be little to lighten his mood, save perhaps the company of his lover. As images of her young, lithe body succumbing to his lovemaking sprang to mind, his loins stirred with a yearning that had for too long been dormant. As part of the plot to ensnare the foul, disgusting slug Constantine, she played her part well but had since disappeared, perhaps running into the arms of another. It irked him to think of her lying with someone else. Serving the Empire was one thing, but he wanted to monopolise her thighs for himself and tiny pinpricks of jealousy jabbed into the nape of his neck. He would launch a search as soon as he returned to the city. He needed her body and, he decided with a broadening smile, he would rid himself of his wife, turn his back on the whole stinking lot, and marry her.

Feeling much brighter, he spurred his horse and, as soon as he reached the main road which led uninterrupted to the great city of Constantinople, broke into a gallop.

NINE

Easing the door closed behind him, Alexius, Patriarch of the great city, moved away from the royal apartment with a heavy tread and headed towards one of the many sumptuous reception rooms nearby. Theodora and Zoe had met, for the first time in years, and their initial reaction had been like ice.

Theodora, forever the chaste saint, looked down her nose in disgust at her vibrant, ravishing sister who wore, no doubt on purpose, an almost transparent gown of gossamer thin white silk. As she moved, her full breasts strained against the material, nipples prominent, the dark patch between her legs visible to all. They could not have been two more contrasting individuals and it was hard to believe the same parents had conceived them both. But whatever their thoughts for one other, their ill feelings needed to remain buried if Byzantium was to survive.

So, he'd said the words, smiled the smiles

and left them, both bristling with indignation, to talk alone, without any interference. Perhaps it would prove to be the wrong decision; perhaps, when he returned in a little while, they would be at one another's throats. However, he doubted it. Both longed for the trappings of royalty: Zoe for the riches it would deliver and Theodora for the certain knowledge that heaven awaited her. Two decidedly different women, one anxious to retain, even extend her royal privileges, the other pious, quiet, contemplative. Together, they were irresistible.

He entered the great room of state, his sandals slapping over the marble tiles, and stepped out onto the balcony. It was late evening, the setting sun sending broad streaks of purple and orange across the sky. The city sprawled beneath him, smoke from the many houses belching upwards. Winter drew ever closer, the air now cold. If he allowed himself, he could almost imagine the city was on fire; the setting sun, together with the smoke combining to create the illusion of a huge conflagration. He shuddered. Was this a portent, a glimpse of a future event? He drew in a rattling breath, his stomach turning, feeling faint. Forced to hold onto the balustrade running along the balcony wall, he steadied himself as frightful images of death and destruction danced before his eyes. Dear God, surely not. The great city would endure, as it always had done, eternal and magnificent. He turned his face skywards. Dear God, surely not ...

A sharp cough caused him to start, and he swung around, wide-eyed with surprise.

A soldier covered in dust stood before him, out of breath. Alexius eyed him. The man, face drawn, sweat running in rivulets through the grime of his face, appeared terrified. Alexius frowned, the images of a Constantinople burning, overcome by some unknown force, now forgotten.

"What is it, man?"

"Holiness," the man dropped to his knees, lowering his head. His voice trembled as he spoke. "I have ridden like the wind, Holiness. Two horses dead underneath me ..."

Alexius blew out his breath, "Get to it, man!"

"Russians, Holiness. Half a day's ride away."

A lump developed in the Patriarch's throat. "*Russians?*"

"Aye, Holiness. They ride towards us, carrying the standard of truce. I believe they are messengers of some sort."

"Messengers? Are you certain? Not some raiding party."

The man shook his head, his eyes still turned to the ground. "No, Holiness. There are but ten, or a dozen of them at most. No more."

Turning, Alexius narrowed his eyes towards the horizon. The bright blaze of sunset now diminished, a tiny trace of dark purple all that remained of the glory of only a few moments before. He settled his breathing, tried to relax. Darkness slowly descended, lights beginning to burn within the sprawl, his fears of all-consuming fire mere fancy, replaced by a new very real danger drawing closer.

Russians, bearing messages, but of peace or war? He could not decide which.

***

Haldor's condition had grown worse through the night. His skin had taken on a yellow tinge, his eyes sunken, his mouth a thin, blue line. When the guards had come to unlock the door and escort Hardrada and his comrades to the palace of the Patriarch, Haldor did not stir. Going to his friend's side, Ulf put his hand on the man's brow and sighed. He turned to Harald, who frowned, trepidation etched into every furrow of his forehead. "He is in a deep fever, Harald. We need a doctor to discover the cause of what ails him."

"The blow he took in the side," Hardrada said, moving closer. He brushed away the guards and crouched down beside his old friend, noted death's pallor, a thin sheen of sweat covering the tightly drawn flesh. Haldor's breathing rattled in his chest like a mouse in a cage. "How many times have I seen this," he said, in a voice low, querulous, "Men, wounded in battle, walking from the field, their wounds bandaged, seemingly well, only to collapse and die some days later, racked in the pain of a terrible fever. Why?" He shook his head, reaching for the nearby blanket with which to cover his friend. "I've witnessed men cut in the arm or leg, who laughed, drank and ate heartedly, to then fall under the shadow. But Haldor's wound is different, and it troubles me." He gently pulled away the cords of Haldor's jerkin and drew back the material. A widening smudge of purple ran across his body, and when Hardrada drifted a finger over the angry welt Haldor moaned, back arching. "It is as if in some curious way the blood is leaking out *beneath* his skin, but how is such a thing possible?"

Ulf rocked back on his heels. "Damn that Scythian dog. You did well to cut off his head, old friend." He swung round and barked at the waiting guards, "Get a doctor, you morons! As quickly as you can – *now*!" As they rushed out, not daring to argue, Ulf ran his hand over his face and gazed into the distance. "I hope we are not too late. Damn his hide, why did he not tell us he was so sick? He said he was feeling well ..." His lips trembled as the words caught in his throat.

Hardrada shrugged his massive shoulders. "We have to face it; he is dying."

Ulf almost choked as he spluttered, "*Dying*?" His face took on a wild expression and Hardrada did not think he had ever seen his friend look so close to breaking as he did that moment. Ulf pushed past to cradle Haldor's head, as if he were a child in need of comfort. "He can't be dying. Nothing happened to him – a nick in the side, nothing more. How can he die from that?" He turned his face to Hardrada, eyes pleading, desperate for a sign, a few words.

Hardrada turned away, not wishing to witness any tears his old friend might shed. He knew Ulf, who had been with Hardrada through so much, always by his side, to know the giant Viking witnessed such a show of weakness, might never be able to overcome the shame. The unspoken code of fighting men, born into battle, hardened by death demanded resolve and silent acceptance of misfortune. So Hardrada dragged himself over to a nearby wall and sat, knees drawn up to his chest, gazed at his feet and waited. And Ulf did not weep but remained with Haldor, tugging the blanket tight against the cold, clammy flesh, holding his friend close.

After what seemed an eternity a small weasel of a man, engulfed in a thick, flowing red robe lined with grey fur, appeared, accompanied by two armed guards. He acknowledged no one, moving straight to Haldor to check his pulse before pulling a face. 'He has been in a fight?"

Ulf grunted and with deliberate tenderness pulled aside Haldor's shirt to reveal the wide blotch of purple that covered his friend's side.

The visitor drew a sharp breath, laid his fingers over the smudge and applied pressure.

Haldor squirmed, a guttural, almost animal sound coming from somewhere deep within him, lips drawn back in a grimace despite him remaining unconscious. The visitor frowned, continuing to prod the raised bruising. "He has been struck with something blunt and heavy."

"He fought, you are true," said Ulf, eyes never leaving Haldor's face. "He fell from his injuries, but nothing ..." He brought his face up, and the tears were in his eyes. "I believed him winded, a few cuts and scrapes, nothing serious."

"He bleeds inside," said Hardrada quietly.

The visitor nodded, "Yes. I am a junior doctor in the household of his most majestic Patrician, Constantine Monomachus, recently arrived in the City, and I am well trained in the subtle arts of healing."

"I don't know the man," said Hardrada, "but if you can help my friend I will forever be in your debt, and your master's."

The visiting doctor lowered his head and gestured to the guards to move closer. "Fetch a padded divan for this man." He looked again at Haldor as the guards rushed to do the doctor's bidding and spoke almost to himself. "He needs rest and hot, herb infused wine. I have a concoction which I can add and an ointment to apply to his wound. For it *is* a wound," he looked meaningfully at Ulf. "A wound inside. The ribs have broken and have pierced his lung."

Ulf gasped and turned ashen, his voice reaching breaking point when he said, "Will he die?"

"Today and the next are the most critical. I will apply an incision to drain off the blood and afterwards, it is imperative he remains quiet; if we can do this, he may survive. But he will need constant care. I will fetch my assistants to tend him."

The man stood up, inclined his head towards Hardrada and went to move, but the Viking's hand came down on his shoulder and stopped him. "Why are you doing this for us?"

The doctor shrugged. "Our orders are very clear, Harald Hardrada. From the Patriarch Alexius himself. To keep you and your friends alive and provide you with whatever you require."

"Then we have much to thank Alexius for."

"Certainly for your friend's life ... God willing, he will recover."

He turned and left, without another word.

Hardrada stared at the open door. "It seems we are mounting up our debts."

"Odin's teeth," said Ulf, "if Haldor dies ..."

He allowed his voice to trail away and Hardrada breathed hard, barely able to consider the likelihood. *If Haldor died* ... no one to blame, no one to seek for recompense or revenge. Or perhaps ... the swine Crethus, the man who wounded Haldor, may well lie dead, killed by Hardrada's blade, but Andreas, on the other hand, survived. If Andreas had not launched his attack when he had, none of this would have happened. With his interference came Haldor's wounding, the bastard Byzantine forever figuring large in the story. Responsibility, guilt, all of it on his shoulders.

To have a focus for revenge always made Hardrada light-hearted, almost giddy. If Haldor died, two reasons existed to kill the hated Andreas; Hardrada smiled in expectation of the violence to come.

Ten

The following day, Alexius addressed a hastily assembled Senate. There was much to tell, not least the arrival of eight heralds from the court of King Yaroslav of Kiev. Beside him stood the Kievian captain, silent as a pillar as Alexius waited for the press of dignitaries, lawyers and landed gentry to become quiet. A heavy helm masked the man's features, the dark, bronzed armour encasing his massive frame lending him a sinister air. Behind black eyes lay a simmering intelligence, which Alexius noted almost as soon as the man presented himself to the Patriarch earlier in the day.

The captain had pulled off his helmet, holding it in the crook of his arm as he lowered himself to one knee. "Most holy and gracious of all men in this most wonderful and sublime of cities," he began, face lowered to the ground, "I have a heartfelt appeal from my most glorious majesty, King Yaroslav."

The man's Greek was impeccable and

Alexius smiled, impressed that the Russian had mastered the holy tongue so well.

He'd listened to the appeal and as the words sank home, his mind swelled with thoughts of a new, strategic alliance, securing the vast northern borders of the Empire could lead all the way up to the ice-bound realm of Hardrada himself.

And now, here he stood to address the Senate with his plan.

They listened and responded with warm, almost relieved applause. The marriage of Hardrada to Yaroslav's daughter: the sealing of a diplomatic pact that would bring a new era of peace and understanding to Byzantium. The trade of the entire known world flowed through Constantinople, making it the richest and most powerful city on earth, but its enemies were jealous and looked with envious eyes upon the amassed riches. Forces gathered in each direction, all intent on hacking away great chunks of Imperial territory. What the Empire needed was foresight, leadership, direction. Zoe and Theodora could provide neither. Zoe, despite her pronouncements of devotion to duty and love of her people, was enraptured with dream of riches and fine clothes, whilst Theodora lost herself in prayer. Between them lay the road to disaster. Alexius's answer was simple.

Constantine Monomachus.

A great moan sprang from the throats of the assembly, Senators bristling with horror and indignation. One or two stood, raising their concerns over the clamour of the others.

"He is nothing but an idle good for nothing," shouted out one, "a man whose own brother cast him aside due to his vile habits."

Another, "Aye. He lounges in Lesbos with his lover, caring nothing for the Empire. What makes you think he will change?"

A clarion of agreement swelled as confidence grew. Another Senator waved his fist, "We don't want another Michael!"

Alexius raised his hands, his patience growing thin, but the voices of dissent continued unabated.

Amidst the cries, "Their Ladyships have the support of the people. Can you not let it be, Holiness? With this new alliance with the King of the Rus, we have no need to worry! We have no need of Monomachus."

Alexius waited, allowing his eyes to roam across the gathering, waiting for a pause, but none came. Instead, a single, rasping question from someone near the rear of the hall, "And what if Hardrada refuses?"

A sudden silence fell upon the assembly, necks craning to see who had spoken. The man responsible for the question rose and spread out his hands. "Has anyone considered that? The great Varangian, the saviour of our illustrious city, to champion us once more at the moment of our greatest need. Not with his sword this time, but with the pledging of his heart to a princess. But has he even met her? Does he know anything of her nature? We all know Hardrada to be a single-minded and ruthless captain of men ... but what we expect of him here goes far beyond anything demanded before. Tell us, Holiness, has the great man been consulted at all in this matter?"

Murmurings of agreement grew in volume and Alexius had to shout to be heard, "Wait, Senators, please listen to me!" He waited, gesturing with his hands for them to be still. They gradually settled. "Your misgivings are justified, Senators. I have not been idle these past days. Monomachus is no longer on Lesbos." Gasps, the stirring of further criticism. The Patriarch rushed on. "He is under the tutelage of trusted men, experts. It is my belief that within a short time you will witness such a transformation that even your most base, yet justified fears, will be put to rest."

"Who are these experts?"

"Please," Alexius smiled, "I ask you to trust me. I have prayed long and hard over these decisions and am convinced of God's hand in this." Murmurings, exchanged looks. "Monomachus will prove a most able choice. He is by no means another Michael." He raised a hand. "As for Hardrada, I ask you to wait and consider the advantages of this match, please." He smiled at the Kievian emissary captain who stood, grim-faced. "This man has travelled many miles to deliver a most gracious and well-considered proposal. I would not have called you here if I thought Hardrada would decline this offer." He held out his hand and the captain reached into the canvas bag hanging from his shoulder. He brought out a rectangular item wrapped in embroidered, purple cloth and handed it to Alexius, who held it with great reverence for a moment before carefully pulling away the fine covering. His eyes widened as he took in the image before him, created in the classic style of an icon. An exquisite portrait of a young girl, hair finely dressed with gold and jewels, a face of stunning loveliness, large, almond eyes, slim nose and full, slightly pouting lips. Yaroslav's daughter, the portrait an honest testament to her loveliness.

Alexius lifted the icon, turned it to the Senators and allowed them to gawp at what they saw, men at the rear straining to catch a glimpse. They approved, gasps and beaming smiles mingling with the palpable relief that rose from the throng, for no man could hope to resist such a beauty. Alexius struggled to prevent his face breaking out in a beam of triumph. The Senate convinced, as Hardrada himself was, of course, for he knew the girl already, meeting her when first he arrived at the court of king Yarolsav years before. But Alexius decided to keep this knowledge to himself, for now.

How he adored the intrigue of Court.

Eleven

The almost imperceptible knock on the door made her heart leap and she ran over to pull back the secret panel separating her apartment from the outside world, panting with expectation. She gave a tiny cry of relief as her lover slipped inside, his arms already snaking around her waist, pulling her close. She moaned as his mouth ran over the soft flesh of her throat, his hands gripping her buttocks. She surrendered to his caresses, her body melting as he lifted her off her feet and carried her to the bed.

They fell with a sigh onto the soft, down mattress, his hands already pulling away at her thin robe. When her breasts spilled out, he sat back to savour them for a moment before his greedy hands kneaded the erect nipples. "By Christ, Helen, just the thought of you."

She stretched out her arms, relishing exposing herself to him and watched him pull out his engorged manhood. She licked her lips, always marvelling at the way it arched up from beneath the folds of his belly. It was no matter to her that he was somewhat overweight. His body retained the memory of his former athleticism: the powerful biceps, the pectorals solid. Above all else, however, the sheer delicious feeling of guilt overwhelmed her, causing her sex to ooze with desire. Here she was, about to be ravaged by her husband's greatest enemy, the thought filling her with red-hot lust.

He pushed aside her soft thighs and buried his tongue into her, seeking out the very nub of her wantonness. She squirmed beneath him, clawing at his hair as he probed and licked. Then, without warning, he shifted position and rammed into her, her wetness giving him easy entry. She gasped, wrapping her legs around his muscular thighs, gripping him as he ploughed into her with long, powerful thrusts. She was alive only to the feelings burning within her loins as he manfully made love. Or was it love? She doubted she had any such feelings for this man; she used him, as he used her. Revenge, all the more exquisite because it was so totally gorgeous.

Sclerus groaned loudly and Helen allowed full vent to his lust, lifting her legs back over her shoulders to give greater access. He responded, reaching new heights of speed and depth, and soon the bed was in danger of collapsing under the ferocious assault of his loins.

If any servants heard, Helen no longer

cared, lost in the moment, mounting waves of pleasure flowing through her, the thrill of betrayal stronger than any drug. If only the General knew, if only she had the courage to tell him. The hated Sclerus, coupling with the wife of the great Maniakes. Such lasciviousness; such abandon; such exquisite humiliation.

A great bellow signalled the end of their lovemaking and Sclerus collapsed over her, snorting through his nostrils like a stricken bull, his body awash with sweat. She held on to him, not wanting it to end, clamping her hands across his back, keeping him close. He had done himself proud, but a tiny pulse of frustration coursed through her. Only a few moments more and she too would be satisfied. She bit her lip as he spasmed inside her, accepting no matter how divine the sensations, it would always be so. So she remained quiet and waited for the man to calm himself, for his breathing to return to normal. At last he rolled from her and lay on his back, chest rising and falling, a forearm draped over his eyes, sated.

She sat up and swung her legs over the side of the bed. His semen dribbled over the covers but she paid no heed. The servants would do their duty and their mouths would remain shut. They all knew the General no longer warmed her bed, that he sought his pleasures elsewhere. Why could the same not fall upon her? She was still a beautiful woman, desired by so many. One day, who knows, she might even find a man whom she could love.

Sclerus's ardour was satisfying, but the man's extreme selfishness meant she could never have a place in his heart. It mattered not, for she too would take everything from him and later, spit him out with as much emotion as she might a grape pip. In the end, in some way or another, everyone was used. Why not enjoy it if she could?

"I need wine," he mumbled.

Without a word she stood up, rearranged her robe, and went outside. She listened out for any movements from the depths of the villa and heard none. Puzzled, she walked barefooted towards the rear, a tiny frown creasing her otherwise unblemished face. A light breeze wafted through the azaleas, and insects buzzed around the ornamental arch forming the barrier between the garden and the house. Life continued as it always had, a gentle meander, long idle days followed by mild untroubled nights. And yet ...

Far away, perhaps coming from the cellar, she thought she heard something. A moan; an animal, possibly injured, trapped inside. "Phillip?" she called and waited for her manservant to answer. Nothing but the emptiness of the house came back to her.

As she moved forward, the shadow crossed her eye line and for a moment her entire world ground to a halt as terror solidified muscle and petrified thought.

***

The room stank of sweat and something akin to rotting food. Hardrada screwed up his nose at the smell and leaned against a marble pillar, arms folded, and waited. The summons had come early, without warning, not long after they had taken Haldor away to an infirmary.Ulf, who marched off towards the old Varangian barracks, had made a face, whilst four armed guards brought Hardrada to this place, leaving him to wonder what would happen next. And when he might see his companions again, if ever.

He studied the room, with its faded ruby-red wall coverings, worn upholstery on the couches, a table covered by a thin film of dust. His eyes fell on a partially open door at the far end and he decided to investigate further.

The annexe opened up into a wide, high-ceilinged bathing-room, dominated by a sunken bath in the centre; a puddle of stinking water the only memory of what had once been an opulent and luxurious place to while away the quiet times.

This had been the eunuch John Orphano's private apartment, Hardrada realised at last. Now, with the man himself having fled the city, these rooms, left to rot, left behind the foul odour of a life drenched in excess.

"The plan is to clear it out," said a voice.

Hardrada turned to see the grand Patriarch, Alexius, standing before him. The man had the most disconcerting way of gliding across the floor without making the slightest of sounds. Hardrada tried hard not to show his surprise. "Clear it out?"

"Yes," said the Patriarch and whispered past the giant Norseman. He stood and surveyed the empty bath. "When I think of what went on here, it turns my stomach."

Hardrada had to agree. Orphano, albeit a eunuch, enjoyed pleasuring his retinue of young, lithe boys. He wondered, as he sometimes did, if the stem of Orphano's manhood had been removed, would there still be desire. And if so, how he could be satisfied.

"I see it does the same for you."

Hardrada blinked, taking a moment to realise what Alexius meant. When he did, he smiled. "Yes. I try not to think about it too much."

"Wise decision," said Alexius. "I suggest we walk in the garden, Harald. The air without is much *cleaner*."

Alexius's words rang true. The early morning sun had barely begun to kiss the leaves of the acacia trees when the Patriarch led Hardrada through the gravel-covered avenue of the eunuch's extensive gardens. Some steps behind, two enormous armed guards strode, spears on shoulders, hands on the hilts of their swords. The Patriarch was taking no chances this day.

They strolled along the meandering path, passed lemon and lime trees, to a small orange grove and a stone bench, flanked by statues of water nymphs tipping out jugs of water into a derelict fountain. Weeds had taken root within the cracks, and here the air was thick with the aroma of ripening fruit, a pleasant relief from the oppression of Orphano's private chambers. Alexius sat, lifted his head and took in a deep breath.

Hardrada eyed the guards and wondered if they had brought him here to kill him, in secret, with no witnesses. Nothing would surprise him, and he calculated the odds of breaking the old man's neck before the guards brought their spears to bear.

"Sit down, Harald, and stop being so damned suspicious."

Hardrada smiled. Damn the old man's perceptions. "You know me too well."

"Aye, that I do. If I wanted you dead, you'd already be floating face down in the Golden Horn."

Hardrada grunted and settled himself down next to the Patriarch. "Strong words for a man of God."

"I do whatever I can to ensure the continuance of the Empire, Harald. You would do well to remember that."

"I do." He put his hands on his knees, counting the number of prominent citizens who would do all they could to ensure their *own*continued existence. He was unconvinced that the Empire would figure so large in their thoughts, more the size of their money chest. "So tell me, Holiness, what all this is about."

"The last time you served the Empire, you came to lead the Varangians from the north and save the city from the clutches of Michael the Fifth. You saved my life, Harald. And the Empire's too."

"You're too gracious, Holiness. I did what I did because I had no choice. The good and Godly Maniakes stitched me up good and proper."

"Godly is not a term I would use for the General, Harald. The man is a viper, as well you know."

"Aye, and he is also the greatest general Byzantium has known for a hundred years."

"Or more."

Hardrada smiled again. "Yes. And more."

Alexius clicked his fingers and one of the guards came forward. He held an object, wrapped in silk and the Patriarch took it, weighing it in his hands. He dismissed the guard with a curt nod. 'I think you might like this."

Frowning, Hardrada took the parcel and slowly unwrapped it. For a long time, he stared down at the lovely face staring back at him before covering it again with the silk. "This is supposed to mean something?"

"An emissary from your good friend Yaroslav brought it, more to convince the Senate than to remind you of her loveliness."

"That doesn't answer the question." Hardrada kept his voice low and controlled, once more estimating his chances of survival if he chose to attack now.

"No. But it worked. The Senate is convinced the match would serve both Empires well. With you guarding our northern borders, you could be an effective block to Norman expansion."

"So, you're willing to let me return to Norway, unhindered. Is that it?" He patted the wrapped icon. "And this is what? A threat? A guarantee of my unwavering service to the Empire? If I do not serve as you wish, you will tell Yaroslav I am dead?"

Alexius shook his head, "You have a fertile imagination, Harald. I do not wish you *dead,* in fact, nothing would grieve me more." He put his hand on Hardrada's arm.

For a moment, Hardrada almost laughed. Such a show of affection, however muted, was not in keeping with this stern old man's persona. "Then tell me what it is you want."

Alexius sighed and stood up all of a sudden. The guards flinched, coming to attention, but he waved them away as he strolled over to a nearby orange tree and casually plucked one from the branches. Closing his eyes, he breathed in the sweet perfume. "Life is all around us, my friend. This great city, its people, the Empire ... we are the cradle of the world. The New Rome, the keeper of arts and sciences, mathematics and literature. In the West, we are looked upon as weak and feckless, but the reality is almost the total opposite." He swung round to face the giant Norwegian. "We protect you all from those who long to destroy us. Normans, Slavs, Russians, Pechenegs ... and from the East, new enemies with murder in their hearts grow stronger with each passing day. I wonder if there will ever be a day when the world will stand up and call out their thanks to God for what we have done." He shook his head and slowly returned to the bench. "Perhaps when we are nothing but dust, then they will say, 'Ah, if only Constantinople still shone as the jewel in the crown that is God's world.' Do you believe in God, my friend?"

Shocked by the sudden question, Hardrada's throat went dry as he struggled to give the expected answer.

"Do not fret, my friend. Once a Viking, eh?" He gave a short laugh. "I think there is probably more Christian love in your heart than there is in most of my bishops!"

"I doubt that, Your Holiness."

Alexius shrugged. "Harald, you have served us well, but now I must ask you to serve us again. News has reached the City that the Normans have begun once more to encroach on our borders. We require you to lead your men west, as only you can, and strike at the Norman heart in Sicily."

Twelve

News came as Gerald took his breakfast and as he read the despatch, his appetite left him in an instant. He screwed up the parchment, his head hung low, whilst he mulled over the words.

"Is it ill news, my lord?"

Gerald eyed his lieutenant from beneath his brows. "You could say that. Gather together the officers and have them meet in my command tent."

"Within the hour, my lord."

"At this very moment."

He threw back his chair as the man scurried out and waited, bristling. Damn them all with their hare-brained notions, their constant manoeuvring and plotting. A soldier belonged in the field, doing what he knew best, not trapped within the confines of the debating chamber. The point of a sword solved problems, not mealy-mouthed debates over who should have what and when. He put his fist in his mouth and bit down hard. Damn them all.

By the time he'd dressed himself in his coat of mail, the officers had begun to arrive. They shuffled and muttered, none of them at all sure why they had been summoned, but when Gerald stepped out from his inner tent silence settled.

"I'll not tarry," he said, "I have received news from our Lord William. Incursions are to cease. Immediately."

The murmurs began again, exchanged looks of bewilderment, questions forming on lips.

Gerald held up his hand. "It seems there is to be a great council meeting at Melfi, in southern Italy. Our Lord William is to meet with their lordships, Drengot and Guaimar."

"Meet?" A large captain shifted position under his heavy hauberk. "Meet to discuss what? We are deep in Byzantine territory. If we suspend our actions, we will be cut off, surrounded and hacked to pieces. We must press on."

Stirrings of approval rose from the group of grizzled officers, men who had fought long and hard through the island of Sicily, carving out territory for their lords and masters. They had tasted victory and liked it, a far more digestible feast than defeat could ever be. And defeat at the hands of Maniakes had not been easy to keep down. They wanted revenge and got a taste at Montemaggiore, where they drove the Byzantines to the sea. Now they wanted more. Gerald knew it.

"We have been ordered to lay down our arms," said Gerald, "By Lord William, 'Iron

Arm' himself. We have no choice but to comply."

"We interrogated one of the survivors from yesterday's attack, my lord," broke in another."He told us that as soon as they spotted the fires from our first assault, news was sent to Constantinople. That was days ago. We are in danger of being annihilated if we follow these orders."

Gerald stepped forward, "You would have me disregard the words of our liege lord?"

The two men levelled eyes at one another whilst around them the other officers grew silent, the tension squeezing in all around.

"If it means we live, then aye."

Gerald reeled backwards, his hand going to his mouth in unsuppressed disbelief. "Dear God, what you suggest is treason!"

"What I suggest, lord, is life. Our lives. We cannot roll over and let the Greeks cut our throats."

"Gerald," Guille, his second-in-command put a hand on his lord's arm, "you can plead ignorance. Deny you ever received the despatch, or that you received it late. But you have to give our men a chance to counter any Byzantine threat. If we lay down our arms, we will be executed, each and every one of us."

"No," Gerald shook his head, "William would not allow that."

"William is a thousand leagues away. The Byzantines will want their revenge as they always do."

"They have pledged themselves to this council meeting."

"And they lie, as well you know."

Gerald tore himself from the man's grip as his heart hammered in his chest. He leaned on his breakfast table, still littered with the remnants of his unfinished meal. Everything had been so easy up until that point. The attacking of Byzantine outposts, one by one, step by step, the eroding away of their borders, driving deep into the heart, loosening their grip on the island. And William had charged him with the responsibility. The Normans were in the ascendency and Gerald would receive rewards in land and titles they could only have dreamed about a few months ago. And now this, the duplicity of greater men, their personal ambitions clouding judgements, disregarding the fate of their subjects. "You're right," he breathed. "Of course you are. William doesn't give a damn about us and changes his mind as the fancy takes him. As long as his coffers remain full, why in the name of Christ should he give a fuck about what happens to us?"

The assembled officers agreed with his words, grunting with satisfaction, the tension already dissipating.

"Difficult words, lord," said Guille, "but wise ones."

"Wise?" Gerald shook his head and turned to face his men. "Not wise, Guille. Treasonable. No matter what my personal thoughts are, I cannot ignore my lord's orders, my old friend. None of us can. Bound by loyalty and service, we have no choice. Call the men to arms and have them paraded for inspection. I will speak to them."

The collected group gaped at him as one; all except Jerome Bogarde, a young officer who had not long joined the force of Normans in Sicily, leaving his home in northern France to serve with his kinsmen in the Mediterranean isle."Lord Gerald is right," he said, ignoring the wild eyes turning towards him. "We have no choice. We are pledged to obey, no matter how difficult those orders might be." He slammed his fist against his chest. "I will arraign my men, lord."

He turned, but one of the others blocked his way.

There were eight men in the confines of the tent, including Gerald. Seven highborn and trusted Norman officers, serving the Dukedom with zealous piety. Until now. Gerald's throat grew tight. "For the love of God, try to understand. We are but one unit, far from home. If we do press on, we will not only have Byzantines to deal with, but our own brothers too. We will be outcast, rebels. All of us."

"Not if we delay," said Guille through clenched teeth. "See the sense in it, for God's sake! A few days, a week. Get the men in a position of strength."

"Aye," spoke up another, "there is a stone keep some twenty leagues from here. We can take it under darkness, make that our stronghold. From there, we will be able to defend ourselves against Byzantine attacks."

"It will take longer than a week to overcome a stone keep."

"If we are caught in the open, we will

perish."

"All of us," said Guille. "We will march to the keep this very day, take it and hold it. By then, we will know more news from the north."

"There's sense in what you say," said Gerald, his voice low; defeat etched into every word. He slumped down on his camp stool. "Guille, what you ask of me is beyond anything I have ever done before. To go against the express wishes of my liege lord ... I cannot."

"You must," insisted Guille, stepping closer. "We have known each other for many years, old friend, and I have been loyal in everything but this ... this is stupidity. If William seeks a truce, then that is all for the good, but all of us here know the Byzantines will honour it only when their sense of justice has been served. They will not accept a renegade band of Norman troops loose in their lands. They will send an army to destroy us, Gerald, and, unless we prepare ourselves, they will succeed."

Gerald held his friend's gaze. "God help us if William learns of our decisions here today."

"None of us shall tell him."

Gerald turned to stare into the youthful face of Jerome Bogarde. "I pray to Christ that is so."

Thirteen

A cold wind cut through the bare stone walls, howling along the corridors and spiralling up the many steps that weaved in every direction throughout the keep. At the uppermost level, braced against the battlements, Edward looked out across the land towards the sea. Wrapped in an ermine-lined cloak of dark blue, almost black in hue, he closed his eyes against the elements and let his long hair whip across his face. He did not care. Events had troubled him, and he swallowed down the bile, trying to still his heart. They thought him pious, a man of God, so devout many believed him a priest. And yet, what he had done could never be called godly. The murder of a King. He shuddered at the thought.

Two months ago, Harthacanute had lain stricken, as he had often done, and nobody asked why. The court, used to their King taking to his bed for long periods, continued as normal with Edward taking up the mantle, his mother beside him. England flourished, her riches grew, her people content, the rule of Danish Kings slowly transcended by Saxons. And no one complained, with the possible exception of some areas in the north, areas which still saw the Norse as their saviours, a fact Edward could never completely come to terms with. His mother's machinations had so far produced good results, both for the realm and the royal treasury. Her latest plot, hatched when it became evident Harthacnut was dying, meant to secure the country under Saxon rule. In the face of threats from Norway, it seemed good at the time. Now, Edward, consumed with guilt, was not so sure.

He hurried down the steps and wound his way to his chambers. The guards at the door stiffened but he ignored them and went inside.

His bed lay as he had left it, blankets thrown about as if struck by a maelstrom. Many a night he had spent in a whirlwind of nightmares and ghosts. Haunted by the face of his dead King.

He remembered the night it happened. A great feast, as Harthacnut always demanded; tables piled high with mountains of food, whole boars, suckling pigs, haunches of venison, swans, ducks and herrings flowing over large platters, ale and mead to accompany them. How the King loved to sup. Beside him, Emma, laughing heartedly, meat juices drooling down her chin, grease spattering the front of her gown. Edward watched, disgust rising from the pit of his stomach. She was his mother too, but her ambitions galled him. No sooner had the earth fallen over his father's coffin than she set sail for England, to marry the great King Cnut. Not a thought for Edward. Not a thought for anyone else.

There she sat, her mouth agape, her laughter raucous. A beautiful woman, even now, with the years rolling on, but Edward knew what lay beneath the lascivious exterior. She worked hard to secrete away royal treasure, and Edward's spies worked equally hard to bring him their information. As soon as the crown rested upon his head, he would banish her, together with her lackeys. The time for firm, authoritative rule had come now that Harthacnut lay dead.

Edward watched him die the night of the last great feast.

The poison took its toll at last. Emma had turned a blind eye to the systematic adding of drops of Belladonna to his food for months, his coughing and vomiting heard throughout the royal castle at Winchester almost every night.

And now, as he rose to bring the tankard to his lips, his eyes rolled and he fell, as if struck down in battle by a poleaxe, landing flat on his face on the hard stone floor.

The feasting hall erupted into a wild mass of crying as guards and earls rushed to the king's side, all of them too late to prevent the inevitable. Harthacnut, king of England, had died, and now Edward, his half-brother, ascended the throne.

He remembered the look in his mother's

eyes, that flash of victory. Her son, murdered. When she had first voiced the idea Edward sent her away, but it wormed his way through his brain, eating away at his sense of justice. Harthacnut's meeting with Magnus of Norway brought fear into everyone's hearts. He never spoke of what had passed between them, but Edward suspected they had agreed upon some form of treaty. A treaty that would hand the throne of England over to Norway on Harthacnut's death. His mother held the same suspicion, and her heart had turned cold towards her son.

Edward slumped down on the edge of his bed, his face in his hands, and fought to push from his mind the look on the dead King's face when they turned him over. The eyes, black as night, set in a face so pale it seemed carved from alabaster. But the teeth were the thing that haunted him. Clenched, giving him a wild, hysterical look, the lips drawn back, pain etched deep.

"Dear Christ." Edward's hands dropped and he sat and stared at the ground. Could he ever assuage the guilt? Perhaps some great deed, a monument to God, a celebration of his devotion. With exterior pressure mounting from across the North Sea, he needed to act fast, secure the throne, and make good his position. By cementing his religious fervour with the building of a great and magnificent minster, the people would see he was true and honourable and the rumours would fade. Acceptance. His most longed-for wish.

From beyond his door he heard the guards

slapping fists against hauberks and he waited, knowing whose approach it was.

There she stood. Emma, his mother. Wife of Ethelred and Cnut. Mother of children. Purveyor of death.

She barely gave him a glance as she went to the far corner and tipped wine into a silver goblet. "I've come from Godwin," she said without turning, drinking slowly.

He studied her back, the loathing mounting. His mother. Where was the love he should hold for her? Had it ever been there, hidden deep inside? If so, he had no memory. Nothing remained of his youth, his time with his brothers and sister. The innocence, the laughter. None of it stirred in his mind. Buried deep, deeper by far than images of the dead Harthacnut. His memory would always be there, to torment him until Judgement Day condemned them all.

With a shock, he realised she was staring at him, her presence dwindled by his reverie into the dark recesses of the room. Now, her eyes brought him back to the present.

"Did you hear me?"

"Godwin," he managed.

"We have spoken, at length."

A gaggle of thoughts, none of them good, brought nothing but confusion. He rubbed his forehead. "*At length?* You spoke with him without my knowledge, without my being there?"

"You're a frightened little boy, churned up by guilt and self-abasement. As you dither, Magnus grows bold. So Godwin has sent emissaries, to parley and avert disaster." She crossed the room with a sudden rush of determination and gripped him by the front of his tunic. "If Magnus invades, all is lost. We are not strong enough. But, thanks to Godwin, we will be given time."

He dashed away her hand and spun round, his body rigid with anger. Clenching his fists, he wrestled with himself, not daring to show her the depth of his despair. "Every step you take ensures the continuation of your own position, nothing more. I am king now, and by Christ, I'll no longer put up with decisions being made behind my back."

She gripped his shoulder and twisted him to face her again. "Then know this. Whilst you languish in your rooms and cry yourself to sleep, Godwin and I work tirelessly to secure this realm. We will make good your claim and Magnus will be persuaded to hold back from any rash decision. The line of Wessex will prevail, despite your ineptitude. "She smiled. " You are your father's son. And like him you are spineless and weak, and if you think I will allow you to—"

"My *father* was a great man! And before he was cold in his grave, you took Cnut for your husband, bore him sons, and forgot everything of who you are."

"Don't dare preach to me!"

"I'll do what the hell I like. I'm *King,* damn your eyes!"

"And you're King because I put you on the throne, you heartless, ungrateful child. I should have left you here for Harefoot's crows to eat you alive."

"Like you did Alfred?"

She struck him, hard and sharp, across the side of his face. He staggered back a step, but did not raise his hand to the pulsing pain or to stop the tears spilling from his eyes. "Godwin gave my brother to Harefoot," he said without looking at her, "and condemned him to death. And he would have done the same to me, to all of us. And now you sidle up to him as if he were some ally, some *friend*. You have no shame and you have no honour."

"I am your *mother*!"

"You stopped being my mother the moment you slid between Cnut's sheets. I want you gone, do you hear me? You and Earl Godwin both. Whatever this agreement you made with the King of Norway is done, you will leave."

Her face drained of colour. "You cannot."

"Yes, I can." Only now did he look at her, the strength surging through him. "And I will."

FOURTEEN

"The sad truth of it is," said Maniakes as they wended their way through the throng of citizens swarming amongst the many stalls of the buzzing marketplace, "we did not do enough."

Hardrada grunted. Alexius had set up their meeting but, always suspicious, the giant Viking insisted on it taking place in an area in full view of witnesses. Not for him the knife in the back, or the garrotte around the throat. Assassins lay in wait, of that he had no doubts.

"No sooner had we left than the Normans regrouped. They made mincemeat of us at Montepeloso, bettering your Varangians and causing the Empire shame."

"That is not how it will be remembered."

Maniakes snorted, "You think? We may have been heralded as saviours for overcoming Michael, but overall history will judge us harshly. We can wipe the slate clean with another campaign, and kick those bastards out of Sicily once and for all."

"We're not strong enough. Whilst Michael fucked everything that walked, the Empire grew ever weaker. We will be hard pressed to overcome the Normans now."

They stopped to watch a group of street conjurers performing some incredible tricks with ropes and serpents. Swollen with shoppers, eager to search out the newly arrived wares since the re-opening of the ports, the market throbbed with the hubbub of street chatter. Amidst them, the two men stopped to watch as a small group gathered to gasp as a tiny boy climbed a thick piece of hemp towards the sky.

"You see that?" sneered Maniakes. "Some Eastern mystic fills our people with awe and wonder and they lap it up like greedy pigs. We're assailed from all sides, old friend. Normans to the West, fanatics from the East. We cannot stand back and allow Byzantium to become a harlot, as happened to Rome."

"Have you found God all of a sudden, General?"

"I've come to the realisation that what we need is a man of intelligence on the throne."

A sudden collective cheer erupted from the crowd and Hardrada snapped his eyes to the rope as it collapsed in a heap on the ground, the boy nowhere in sight. People flapped their arms, spun around, searched everywhere, but the boy had vanished. The conjurer in charge rubbed his hands, grinning as the appreciative crowd threw coins into his collecting basket.

Maniakes took Hardrada by the elbow and steered him away as people pushed past, jostling to get a better look as word went around of what had happened. Hardrada allowed the General to take him out of the market place, to slip along wide boulevards flanked by spacious villas and dotted with lime trees. Life was returning to the city once again, citizens here and there, a revived sense of optimism evident in every smile and every laugh. The people, invigorated that Zoe had returned, saw nothing but good on the horizon; Hardrada wished he shared their view. But nothing could chase away the terrible foreboding which gnawed at the very core of his being.

They came upon the athletes' training ground, positioned some distance from the bustling streets, an enclosed area hidden behind towering ranks of cedar trees. Moving down the approach road towards the great double gates, flanked by sentry towers, Hardrada shifted his gaze and scanned left and right. No one appeared. No archers with knocked arrows, no javelin men or slingers hiding in the tall grass, nevertheless he felt their progress being studied with keen interest.

"You shouldn't be so suspicious," said the General as he stepped up to the doors and pounded them with his fist. "If we wanted you dead, you'd already be—"

"Lying face down in the Horn. Yes, the Patriarch said much the same thing. Curious that, isn't it?"

Maniakes smirked and was about to hit the door again when from within, the sound of a bolt drawing back, followed by the grating of rusty hinges, heralded the opening of the entrance.

A massive man filled the open doorway, his bald head glistened with sweat and exposed belly bulged over baggy satin trousers of deep red, held up by a wide purple sash. Thrust inside the sash was a scimitar, the favoured weapon of the east. He bowed and motioned both men inside with a theatrical sweep of one massive arm.

Hardrada stepped past him. From his height advantage, he could look down on the man's red-blistered pate. "You've been working hard."

The man's eyes narrowed into mere slits and held the great Viking's gaze. "You mock me, Viking?"

Hardrada snorted and turned his gaze away towards the huge arena spread out before them. It was a gigantic dust bowl, a flat expanse of hard, gritted earth baked by the sun, offering no shade or escape from the heat. On three sides, rows of stone seats afforded spectators a grand view of athletic and gymnastic events. Once, centuries before, gladiators fought here, such practises now confined to the history books. Citizens no longer paid to see men fight to the death, the pagan ways of old replaced by newer, more enlightened pastimes such as wrestling and boxing. Occasionally, however, re-enactments were staged, re-fighting of ancient battles, but with soldiers brandishing wooden swords and spears, the worst injury sustained might be a broken arm or a split face. A far cry from the excesses of Rome.

In the centre of the area a small group of men practised, the one in the centre deflecting spear thrusts and countering with measured blows, conserving his energy, ensuring each attack struck home.

Somewhat apart a brawny individual studied the skirmish, offering advice and encouragement, his voice calm but authoritative, echoing across the empty arena together with the crack of the wooden weapons. "Faster, boys, faster. Test him to the limits." He chuckled, folding his arms, enjoying the spectacle. Then his voice changed, becoming harder, sterner. "I said *faster!*"

The men responded and the one at the centre became hard-pressed, lost his composure, swung wildly with his sword, missing more times than he hit. He backed away, his face awash with sweat as blows rained in from every angle. A cry. A spear thrust home, followed by another. The defender buckled and a shaft struck him across the neck with a dreadful thwack and he fell to his knees, sword spilling from numbed fingers. As he attempted to rise, a butt slammed into his guts followed swiftly by a blow across the side of his head and he toppled over and laid still, a trail of blood drooling from quivering lips.

Maniakes sniggered but Hardrada remained

quiet. Over half a lifetime of battles, scrapes and barroom brawls, he'd watched any number of fighting men give of their best; some able to prevail, most ending up with their guts spilled in the dirt. This one, however, seemed different. He was flaccid, loose, his body not quite honed to the rigours of combat. A man whose pleasures had made him soft, a man who had probably never lifted a sword before in his life. "What is the purpose of this?"

As the spearmen set down their weapons and lifted the unconscious figure, dragging him away across the arena towards a sliver of shade on the far side, Maniakes looked askance at the Viking and grinned. "We came a little too late. A pity we had not seen the combat from the start, then you might have been somewhat more entertained."

"Seeing men fight has never entertained me, General. *Killing* entertains me, but not this type of circus act."

"It's no circus act," said the overseer of the fight, stepping closer. Almost as tall as the Viking, his bare chest and abdomen rippled, a body sculpted out of marble, as smooth and as strong as the finest statues found anywhere in the Royal Palace. He reminded Hardrada somewhat of Crethus, the gigantic Scythian whom he had despatched, but not without some difficulty from what he could remember. Perhaps this man was the same. Perhaps he was better.

"Then what is it?"

"It's a training regime, for a man too long in

his cups. A life of lethargy has left him slow and cumbersome. It is my job to bring some life into his bones, some solidity to his muscles." He thrust out his hand. "Marcellus Flavius."

Hardrada looked at the gnarled hand, the scars across the knuckles and frowned. "A fighting man, but not one whose favoured weapon is the sword." He grinned and took the man's proffered hand. "I am—"

The grip was firm and assured. "No need for introductions, Harald Sigurdsson. Your fame precedes you."

A tiny tingle played around the nape of Hardrada's neck and he grinned. "Not many call me by my family name."

"Would you prefer 'The Ruthless'? That is what your name means is it not, in your native tongue?"

"I'm impressed," Hardrada released his hand. "Not just a fighter, a scholar too."

"I'm a Roman. From the *old* school. That means I had a private tutor, learned my numbers and letters, read the classics and the histories. Together with Scipio Africanusand Constantine the Great, I learned about you and what you achieved in Sicily and beyond."

"And trained your body in between?"

Maniakes coughed, "Marcellus is the most renowned boxing champion of the Empire. No man has ever defeated him, and now he works at a very special project. Don't you Marcellus?"

"I do indeed, General."

"Perhaps you'd like to explain to our great

Captain of the Varangian Guard just what the project is?"

Hardrada held up his hand before Marcellus could speak. "What did you call me?"

Maniakes smiled. "You didn't mishear, Harald. You're reinstated, at my behest. You shall take up your command shortly, within the next few days. The Empire has need of you and your men. Just like Marcellus here, we each have our particular duties to perform to ensure Byzantium stability and endurance."

"Better Pecheneg curs than Varangian women-beaters."

Hardrada slowly turned and with cold eyes measured the immense individual who had greeted him at the entrance.

"This giant is Victorious Paulus Vendt," explained Marcellus, "from the boiled plains of the Magyars. When he heard of your coming he expressed his desire to meet you, and see for himself if the legends spoke true."

"Tell *Victorious* to keep a civil tongue in his fat head."

Marcellus chuckled, but Paulus stood ramrod stiff, unmoved by Hardrada's barbed words. "Victorious Paulus Vendt is not a man to be trifled with, Viking. He is the strongest man I have met, and I have known many I can promise you."

"Perhaps we should go," said Maniakes sounding tired, "Time is pressing and we have much—"

"I've heard it said that your prick was so

limp a Muslim dog replaced you in the Empress's favours."Vendt grinned, expectant.

"Did you now? And what else did you hear?"

"That you sleep with boys and when you rise in the morning your body is so racked with pain you can hardly move, so you call for your boys and they rub you until you grow hard."

"You're mistaken."

"Am I?" His hand crept to the hilt of his sword. "You call me a liar, do you?"

Hardrada smiled. "I call you *confused.*" The man frowned. "You've just said my cock is limp. Now, it's grown hard again. Which is it?"

"Limp for *girls,* but hard for boys." He laughed.

"This is tiresome," breathed Maniakes. "Can we go?"

Joining in with the laughter, Hardrada swung towards the General, beaming, and Maniakes showed his teeth. An icy chill fell over them as Hardrada said, "This is your doing."

The stillness settled for a moment, the laughter dying in that single breath; with a sudden explosion of speed and power Hardrada rounded on Vendt, slammed his elbow into the man's head and sent him crashing to the ground.

Before anyone could react, Hardrada sprang forward, pulled out the stricken man's scimitar from its scabbard and turned in a half crouch to face the others, his breath hissing through clenched teeth. "Was this your plan, Maniakes, to lure me here and murder me, well away from prying eyes?"

"Don't be so damned ridiculous," spat Maniakes, his hand hovering close to his sword.

"Or the Patriarch's perhaps? One of you plots to have me killed, of that I'm certain. Perhaps I should simply kill you all, and put an end to it?"

"Harald," said Marcellus, who still stood a little way off, his body relaxed, "I know nothing of any plots, I give you my word."

"The word of a Roman?" Hardrada shook his head. "Don't make me laugh." He put the point of the scimitar against Vendt's throat as the man groaned, recovering from the awesome blow. "This snivelling shit played his hand too soon so now you will tell me why the hell you brought me here. Before I cut off your heads, tell me who the flabby one is who got himself beaten up?"

"His name is Constantine Monomachus," said the general, "and he is to be the next Emperor of the Byzantine Empire."

The words stunned Hardrada, more forcibly than any blow from Marcellus's fists, and he straightened his back and frowned. "Are you serious?"

"Never more so. Marcellus will spend the next month training him before presenting him to the Empress Zoe. They are to be wed, then crowned."

"What has any of that to do with me?"

Maniakes shook his head, "Nothing."

"So why try to murder me?"

The General sighed, "Why does everything

have to revolve around you? For Christ's sake man, put away your sword and listen to what I have to say."

"Tell me first."

"Very well." The General pulled a face and looked at Marcellus. "Monomachus has nought to do with you, but as you're here ..." Marcellus shrugged and Maniakes turned to Hardrada once again. "The Normans are back, attacking fortified outposts throughout Sicily, and you and I are charged to go and beat them back."

"As we did before."

"As we did before. We sail within the next two weeks. Provisions are being gathered and ships prepared as we speak. It only remains for you to drill your Varangians." He swept his arm through the air. "And you'll do it here, well away from the army training ground. We do not want any spies wagging their tongues and getting word back to William Iron Arm."

"Within two weeks?" Maniakes nodded, and Hardrada allowed his sword arm to drop to his side. "Why the rush?"

"We received word only yesterday. The Normans have stormed two positions already, with great loss of life. We need to act swiftly to prevent further incursions because if they take Sicily, they control the main shipping lanes into the Western Mediterranean, threatening our trade routes with the rest of Italy, the Moors, Portugal and beyond. We no longer have the ships to adequately defend our merchant fleet, so we must defeat the Norman threat once and for all, on land."

"Not an easy task. When we embarked on the campaign last, we had twenty thousand men. How many this time?"

"Half that number. And a substantial number of them your Varangians."

"They won't take kindly to returning to that bloodied island, General, as well you know."

"Consider it an opportunity to avenge their defeats. I'm sure they will gag to get their hands on Norman throats."

"Ten thousand altogether, you say?"

"As near as damn it."

"It won't be enough."

"The Normans are not the force they were. I doubt they can sustain their attacks for much longer, so we strike them now, and send them back into the sea."

"So, it'll be you and me, together once again, eh, General?" Vendt rolled over and remained on his knees, palms flat on the ground, taking in rasping gulps of air. Hardrada eyed him and chuckled. "I hope the next one you send to kill me will be more of a challenge."

"I told you, I did not—"

"The trouble with you, General, is you tell so many lies I do not think even you know which is truth, or which is fantasy."

A voice wheezed to his left. "I'm going to kill you."

Hardrada frowned at Vendt, whose face had taken on a deep crimson hue. "And how do you propose to do that, my friend?" Hardrada hefted the scimitar in his fist, "I've got your pretty sword."

"You caught me off guard, you bastard. Next time won't be so easy."

"Victorious Paulus is so named because of his many victories over any number of opponents in the fighting ring at Hadrianapolis," explained Marcellus.

"Has he ever stood in battle?"

Marcellus tilted his head, thoughtful. "I'm not sure ... Paulus? Have you ever fought in battle?"

"Bugger that. I'm a man of the streets, not some bow-legged whoremonger who pisses himself in a field when he sees Bulgars riding towards him."

"What do you know of Bulgars?"

The man sneered at Hardrada, "I've killed enough of them. Man-to-man, with nowhere to hide. Can you say the same?"

"I put you down."

"By trickery." He pulled himself up. "Now I'll show you what fighting is really like."

A collective moan spilled from the throats of the others as Hardrada slipped the scimitar's blade deep into Vendt's belly. This could have been difficult, given the blade's curvature, but the edge was razor sharp and with a slight twist from Hardrada's wrist, it suffered no impediment. Vendt gasped, utter astonishment crossing his face; he looked down at the blade buried inside his flesh and mumbled, "Bastard," before Hardrada withdrew the sword, the action accompanied by a soft plop as metal left flesh before smoothly coming around in a wide arc to slice off Vendt's head.

Fifteen

Inside her private apartments, the Empress Zoe lowered herself into the sunken bath, sighing loudly as the fragranced water enveloped her. She closed her eyes, moaning in pleasure as she abandoned herself, aware only fleetingly of another body moving up close. She opened one eye and smiled. The nubile young slave girl smoothed cleansing lotions over the Empress's breasts with a large piece of natural sponge, paying particular attention to the hardening nipples. Zoe arched her back. "Just there," she whimpered, and the girl complied, plunging the sponge between her mistress's legs, delving deep, probing the giving, yearning flesh. Soon, her fingers took over the task, gently stroking her mistress until she writhed and groaned, gripping the sides of the bath, knuckles white beneath the tanned skin. "Oh, dear God," she gasped, her body going into a series of tiny convulsions, the water churning around her hips. "Dear God, I'm going to *come...*"

The slave did not cease, two fingers exploring

Zoe's inner sanctum, slow, gentle, incessant. She put a hand under her mistress's buttocks, lifting her, giving greater access, and Zoe responded with heavy, deep throated moans of pleasure, muscles in her stomach going into spasm, her body raised out of the water, back arched, mouth open, screaming, "*Christ!*"

***

In the adjoining room, the Lady Theodora knelt in silent prayer, eyes closed, hands clasped to her bosom. Next to her, gazing out across the balcony to the sprawl of the city stood the *Exarch* to Alexius, Simon Psellos. A tall, gangly man who constantly stooped to prevent his head from cracking against cross beams, he wore a permanent scowl as if to persuade those who bothered to look, that here was a man of serious intentions. For the most part, it worked. Those who met him commented on his piety, his intelligence and deep humility. As Alexius's deputy in the Church, Psellos remained with Theodora throughout her self-imposed isolation. She listened and trusted him, and he repaid her with duty and guidance in all things spiritual. Now, back in Constantinople, Psellos spent much of his time in silent contemplation, either alone or with Theodora. As now. Whilst she prayed, he thought. And to everyone who met him, those thoughts appeared to be chiefly on how best to serve Byzantium.

He moved across the room and stared at the adjoining entrance to Zoe's private apartments. He smelt the thick waft of perfume through the solid oak door and turned down the corners of his mouth. "Is it always like this?"

His voice, though low, caused Theodora to open her eyes, raise her head, and sigh. "I'm afraid so, Your Holiness."

His features grew dark. "As you know, Theodora, I am a faithful servant of His Holiness Alexius. During your prolonged absence from the city, we exchanged correspondence and he kept me informed of the terrors of Michael's reign." He closed his eyes for a moment and a shudder travelled through him. "Such outrageous, perverted incidents. His Holiness strove to rid the Empire of such wanton excesses and I supported him every step of the way, even in his employment of the heathen scoundrel Hardrada. But this," wringing his hands, glancing again to the closed door, "this is too much. I understand she is your sister, but—"

"We are as unlike as coarse hemp is to silk, Your Holiness. I will not attempt to convince you which of us is which." She smiled and stood up, smoothing down the front of her gown. "My sister took the path of licentious living long, long ago. As I studied, she pursued men. Whilst I took my vows, she bedded lovers. Our paths rarely crossed, until now."

"You must accept, surely, how wrong it would be to reinstate her to the Holy throne? The Emperor – or Empress – is God's divine representative on earth. Such a woman makes a mockery of the office." He flushed, turning his head away slightly. "Forgive me, she is your sister and you love her. I apologise for my words."

"Holiness," she went to him, fingers brushing his sleeve. "She *is* my sister, my blood, but in no way does that infer I excuse or even understand her behaviour."

"So tell me," he said quietly, his mouth a thin line of concern, "why does His Holiness continue with his plan to place her on the throne?"

"I *believe*," she said in the same conspiratorial tone, "his plan is to put Monomachus on the throne, with Zoe as his wife, thus linking him to the purple."

Psellos sighed. "Another pervert."

"Perhaps. I know he is a capable administrator, his skill with figures beyond dispute."

"But not a military man."

"We have the good General Maniakes for that, Your Holiness."

"And the Viking."

"Of whom I know little, other than what happened between him and my sister."

"He spurned her, so I understand, for another."

"Our niece, Your Holiness. The details I have yet to learn, but from what I do know, Hardrada wooed my niece whilst he was still bedding Zoe. She discovered his infatuation and threw him into jail. Michael then took his chance, murdered the Varangian Guard in the city, and became absolute ruler." She chuckled. "We are nothing if not a resourceful and imaginative family."

"Not the words I would choose, my lady." He tilted his head. "Forgive me for being so blunt."

She waved him away. "There is little about my

family about which I feel proud, Your Holiness. My sister least of all. She is weak and wanton, ruled by her lusts."

He turned to the door to Zoe's room. The moans and groans from within had ceased and he allowed his shoulders to relax. "And yet the people adore her."

"Yes. They respond favourably to a pretty face and a well-turned ankle." She winked. "And a swelling bosom."

His face reddened and he crossed the room to a cushioned couch and eased himself into it. "My mind is troubled. I have meditated and prayed for many hours, seeking guidance, answers ... I am lost."

"Lost? Please, Holiness, for so long you have been my rock, my constant support. Through the love of Christ, we have both found a kind of peace. What my sister does, what she *continues* to do may be repellent and sinful, but we cannot change her. She is who she is and in her own way, she too has found a kind of peace in that."

"How can you excuse her excesses?" He looked hurt, his face creased up, old.

She went to him, as she might a troubled child, stooped down and took his hand in hers. "Holiness, she has chosen her path. But we, we have greater journeys to travel. More difficult. Longer. The road to restoring Constantinople to its rightful position as the cradle of Christianity, in the glory of God, our father."

"It is that which I have thought on for so very long, my child. The more I think, the more I come to the same conclusions." He stared down at her hands. "Theodora, only you can bring true faith back to the Empire. Through your grace, humility, and love of God. The obstacles, however, are huge and we must be strong if we are to prevail."

"I do not understand."

His head came up, and the tears tumbled from his eyes. "My devotions to His Holiness Alexius have been tested, beyond imaginings. I see in his recent decisions the beginning of a misguided and unholy desire." He squeezed his eyes shut. "He covets the throne, my lady. Of that, I am convinced. For his own sake, not for Christ's."

She sucked in her breath, rocked back on her heels, her hands dropping from his. They stared into each other's eyes. "Can this be?"

"I am certain of it. He brings Monomachus into the fold, to marry Zoe, and for what? To secure the Empire, or to see it cast into chaos? He surrounds himself with vipers. Maniakes, Hardrada ..."

"I dare not believe what you say is true, Your Holiness. I *cannot!*" She slumped down beside him, gripping his hand, wide-eyed with the pain of disbelief. "The Patriarch is a man of God, and he loves our land. He would never do anything to besmirch it."

"I thought it true, my lady. But I see through his dealings with the General a deeper ambition, an earthly one. He wishes for Hardrada to travel again to Sicily, at the head of an army, and crush the invaders who ravage that island. A just decision? Perhaps. The chance to glorify himself in the eyes of the people? I am sure of it. When Hardrada returns as the victor, as he undoubtedly will, the people will see Alexius as the saviour. They will clamour for him to be Emperor, to serve them as their lord. Not Zoe and her new lecherous husband."

Theodora's legs grew weak and when she went to stand, her strength failed her. Psellos reached out and held her, guided her back to the couch, their positions now changed, with him standing over her, his face serious. "This is all too much," she managed, her voice a forced croak. "If it is so, Your Holiness, you have proof?"

"I have prayed. I have no doubts, my lady."

A low moan emitted from deep within her and she crumpled into the couch. "This is beyond reason ... a man such as he ... what are we to do?"

"We have little choice. We must thwart his plans."

"And how are we to do that? And have we the right, Your Holiness?"

"We have every right if it means the continuation of the Empire."

She nodded, knowing his words were true. Theodora bore no doubts, knowing this man to be one with God. For many years, similar suspicions stampeded through her mind and she grew to believe Psellos, not Alexius, was the rightful Patriarch of Constantinople. Daring to voice her thoughts, however, was quite another matter. Now, from listening to him, a new certainty developed. They were being guided. By God.

"So tell me what we should do and you shall have my full support."

He smiled, sat down beside her, and laid out his plans before her.

***

Sometime later, the Deputy Patriarch of Byzantium finished his light lunch of chickpeas, olives and tomatoes with a long drink of water; he dabbed at his lips with a napkin as he gazed at the soldier standing at attention in front of him."So," said Psellos, throwing down the cloth, "you believe the General has taken him off to watch Monomachus train?"

Andreas nodded. "He took him through the market, Your Holiness, and it was there that I lost them."

Psellos sat back, folding his hands over his stomach. "Not a good start. His Holiness Alexius gave you a duty, Andreas. To keep the Viking safe."

"Yes, Your Holiness."

"For all we know, Hardrada might already be dead."

"Yes, Your Holiness."

"Whilst you were charged to keep him out of harm's way – to keep him *alive*."

Andreas pulled in a breath. "A charge made by the General, Holiness."

The small dining table shook violently as Psellos brought his fist down with a slam. "You know full well all orders come from His Holiness the Patriarch!"

Andreas stiffened, brought his heels together, and snapped, "Yes, Holiness!"

"So, you believe him to be dead?"

"It would take more than the General and a

few of his hired hands to kill Hardrada, Holiness."

"I know that. I'm asking you your opinion."

Andreas didn't know. He grew edgy, shifting his eyes from side to side and made a tiny whimper. "Holiness, I'm not ... I'm not certain of anything."

"You attempted to better him, so I understand, and look where that got you."

Andreas, the heat rising to his face, longed to turn and flee but he knew he could not. Instead, he stood and sweated and longed for this humiliating meeting to end. The Deputy Patriarch, however, appeared to be enjoying himself and he stood up and came around the table with exaggerated slowness and bore his eyes into Andreas, unblinking.

"The man is a monster," said Andreas at last.

"A mad dog."

"Yes, Holiness. Exactly." He averted his eyes for a moment. "He ... he wronged me, Holiness. It is personal between us."

"I heard something, Andreas. Something about a girl?"

"More than a girl, Holiness. Someone I believed was special. And Hardrada *murdered* her." He closed his eyes, struggling to dispel the images rearing up of that awful day.

"So you would not mourn his passing?"

Andreas, struck by the absurdity of the question, allowed himself a tiny laugh. "*Mourn?* I would celebrate it, Your Holiness."

"Mmm." The Exarch moved past Andreas and opened the door. He peered down the long corridor. "Go down to the port, Andreas, and inspect the fleet. I want you to hand-pick a team of oarsmen for Hardrada's flagship. Men who will not shirk in their duties, or disobey their orders."

"But Hardrada will have his own men, Holiness."

"Yes. Which is why you will replace them with men of your choosing."

Andreas, remaining in front of the now vacant dining table, struggled to understand what any of this meant. "Holiness, I'm confused. Replace Hardrada's men with my own?"

"That is what I said."

"But ..." He turned around.

"It's quite simple, Andreas. Now set to it."

"Forgive me, Holiness. These are the wishes of The Patriarch?"

"I am His Holiness's faithful servant, Andreas. Our wishes and our commands all emanate from the same source." He turned and smiled. "God."

Andreas snapped his heels together and slammed his right fist over his heart. "I will strive to do as you command, Your Holiness."

"And unlike your miserable attempts to keep Hardrada under your eyes, you will *succeed* in these orders, Andreas. Orders which are to remain secret." He waved his hand towards the corridor, "Gather those men, Andreas and send word to me when it is done. I shall then inform you of the next phase in this particular duty."

Andreas marched out, eyes set ahead, and Psellos watched him go, the smile never leaving his lips.

Sixteen

They took her into her room and laid her down on the bed, one of the servants cooling her face with a large fan of peacock feathers. In the corner, arms folded, Sclerus looked on, a vacant expression on his face, concealing the turmoil of emotion within. Around the grounds of the villa, the guards sent by Maniakes lay dead, their throats slit. Inside, they found Phillip, the head servant, in the kitchens, trussed up like something ready for the pot, feet and hands lashed together behind his back, an apple in his mouth, and a note pinned to his forehead, *'See how easy it is?'*

Sclerus clutched the paper in his fist. This was not what he had wanted. Not to harm *her.*Sending a message was one thing, perhaps even killing the guards another, but to frighten Helen half to death and murder her faithful servant, the man had overstepped his mark.

Within the hour, the apothecary arrived and

administered a drinking draft. She spluttered as he poured it into her mouth, drop by drop, slow and steady. She swallowed, her eyes rolled, sleep came.

Sclerus paid the man and led him to the door. "She will recover?"

"A dreadful shock she has suffered, my lord. She needs rest, complete rest. I will send word to the General, let him know of—"

"No." Sclerus guided him through the door. "I will inform the General, never fear."

"*You,* my lord? But I assumed—"

"Never assume. There leads the road to misfortune." He smiled and closed the door in the man's face. He leaned back and let out his breath.

Damn the assassin for acting so precipitously! All very well to show the world exactly what he was capable of, but to do so in such a manner ... The servant lay dead, the guards too and Maniakes's wife, Helen, distraught beyond words. Now it would be up to Sclerus himself to set things right, look after her, make the required enquiries, none of which he wanted to do.

He walked back to the solarium, took wine and gazed out across the villa's extensive, manicured grounds; vibrant plants and assorted shrubs surrounded a central fountain, inlaid with marble tiles of purple, green and blue. A weak sun poked its face between wisps of cloud racing across the great arc of the sky and if he wanted he could close his eyes and wish it all away.

Some time later, after checking she was

sleeping, Sclerus slipped back to his home and climbed into bed. His wife did not stir from her room. He gazed at the ceiling, counting the cracks. He was sick with tiredness, his eyes gritty, tongue thick and dry, the tension around his neck bringing on a headache. He knew he should drink some water, but every limb was as heavy as lead so he remained supine, tried to clear all thoughts and allow his eyelids to close, wishing sleep to come.

Within a heartbeat, he heard a movement, like something soft gliding over the bare floor tiles. A cushioned sole on the hard stone. Startled, he sat up and listened out for a second footfall. For a few moments, nothing but the empty room echoed back to him and he wondered if he had slept for a moment and nightmares invaded his frayed mind. He put his fists into his eyes, rubbed hard, and heard the tiny chuckle. He snapped open his eyes, whirled around and saw him.

By the open balcony entrance, a man stood in the shadows, the long, heavy drapes that hung on either side flapping around his lower body in the breeze. Sclerus glared and the man tipped his forehead with a finger before rolling over the balcony edge and dropping out of sight.

Sclerus threw back the sheets and rushed across the room, angry, determined to challenge him, demand why he had entered Maniakes's home, startled his wife, murdered soldiers and the servant, Phillip.

Sclerus leaned over the balcony edge and

scanned the grounds, edged with orange and lime trees, the morning advancing, and saw nothing.

***

The training ground rang out with the sound of steel on steel as ranks of armoured soldiers wielded axes and swords, the screaming of officers accompanying the clamour and often rising above it.

Hardrada went through his regime, blocking, parrying, counter striking as two heavily built Varangians pressed in on him. He turned, dodged, ducked, struck shields, smashed through defences, kicked and pushed. With gritted teeth he deflected one mighty blow, slammed his shoulder into his opponent and threw him to the ground before he swept the legs from under the second and the fight was over.

The sweat ran down his face from under his bronze, spectacled helmet, stinging his eyes, wetting his beard. He leaned forward on his sword, gulping in the warm morning air and grinned as the two Vikings climbed to their feet, rubbing bruised limbs. "Same time tomorrow, boys?"

They exchanged sullen looks and trudged away, subdued and beaten. His eyes moved past them to the other groups of men engaged in mock skirmishes, and he saw Ulf, swinging his axe, roaring out his battle cries. One soldier had not been quick enough and lay on the ground clutching his arm, blood seeping out between his fingers. Hardrada sighed. Unless attended to, the wound might fester causing the man to die within a few days. He could ill-afford the loss of a single soldier.

The news arrived earlier in the day. He slept in the barracks, a simple curtain separating him from his men, the only consent to his rank. He belonged with his men. He fought with them in the fields of death, so why not share with them life as well? When the cough came from the other side, he pulled back the blood-red drapes and took the proffered note from the out of breath officer of the Imperial Guard.

Some twenty years or more ago, Hardrada had learned to read. Warriors, he knew, had little time for books; they memorised stories of heroes and brave deeds which came from the mouths of travelling storytellers. Hardrada, however, yearned for more and sought out one of these men, begged him to reveal the secrets of the strange symbols that travelled across the rolls of parchment from which they recounted myths and legends of the past. Over the weeks and months he took every opportunity to practise, and the best way so one such storyteller informed him, was to write his own words.

So he did.

And now, years since, he still found time to scribe a few simple lines of verse. These he kept secret. If Ulf or any of the other rough, hardened Varangians found out they would chide him with sarcastic remarks, tempers would fray, and fists would smash against jaws. Perhaps worse.

Now, the guardsman stood, eyes ahead, as

Hardrada took in the words. Orders from the Patriarch himself. To appear at the Sophian Harbour two days hence and prepare to embark for Sicily. He was to take a detachment of one hundred Varangian Guardsmen, a force supplemented by further detachments from the borders. A total of three thousand men.

He screwed up the paper, sucked in his bottom lip and looked at the guardsman, "Who gave you this?"

The man's head snapped upwards, "General Komones, my lord."

"I'm not your lord," said Hardrada and stood up, dressed in his thin night garb, his muscles straining beneath the flimsy material. Sometimes he longed for the cold, to feel the ice on his skin, the frozen stiffness of his hair. The warmer climes of the great city made him soft, the constant heat draining him of energy, every movement a struggle. He reached across for his undergarment, shook it out and raised it to the open window. There were too many holes, he mused. Perhaps some hag in the market place could stitch it up. Or perhaps he should put his hand in his pockets and spend some money on a replacement. "Where is Maniakes?"

"I know not, my lor—" The man wilted under Hardrada's hard gaze. "Sorry, *sir*. As far as I know, the General is travelling back from his country estate and will not be here until this evening."

"So who gave Komonos this command?" The man shook his head. "Very well," snapped

Hardrada, growing tired of the man's ignorance. He waved him away, pulled off his nightshirt and readied himself for the day.

On his way to the port, he made a long detour to the hospital, which stood beyond the Palace Wall, squeezed in between the impressive Church of Saint Irene and the massive splendour of Saint Sophia. Monks waddled by, shrouded in robes of black, heads lowered, humble as the dust. None gave Hardrada so much as a passing glance, even when he stepped into the airy opening of the hospital itself. The walls echoed to the sounds of voices and when he strode down the central aisle, Hardrada's hobnailed boots shouted out his steady approach.

A withered old man, enveloped in a voluminous robe, shuffled out of a doorway and stopped, head tilted, studying the massive Viking as he approached. "You'll be Hardrada," he said and stepped aside, gesturing for the giant to enter.

A small room, the sweet smell of jasmine clinging to the sparse furnishings, greeted him as he dipped his head and entered. Two beds, opposite one another, pressed against the walls; an open veranda at the far end looked out across the city. Airy, light and fresh, the kind of room to rest and contemplate. And recover.

In the narrow bed lay Haldor, blankets tucked under his chin, his face grey and drawn. He did not stir as Hardrada stepped close. For a long time the Viking stood and gazed down at his old friend, bombarded with images of how they met, their adventures, their scrapes with death. Everything blurred into one and Hardrada struggled to place events in the correct order and he frowned hard, becoming uneasy at his inability to piece together the past. Since first standing in battle at the age of fifteen, his world had remained one of violence. The normal everyday experiences of a human being seemed to have passed him by.

True, there had been brief moments of kindness, a touch or a kiss, but nothing ever managed to penetrate the wall of unfeeling hardness he built around him. Except for friendship. Haldor was one such friend, a man who gave him counsel, who often angered him, but never betrayed him. A man of truth, of good judgement, of unceasing support. And now, here he was, laid out like some corpse awaiting the burial rites. Is that what now awaited him? Would he ever recover, return to his old self, stand by Hardrada's side and push back his enemies?

"Harald?"

Hardrada blinked open his eyes, shrugging off the memories, and smiled at his old friend whose own eyes twinkled with a distant impish glee.

"Is that a tear I see for your old friend?"

"What, for an old bastard like you?" Hardrada forced a laugh, but he knew it was true. The thought of Hal's death was too painful to contemplate.

Haldor's hand snaked out from beneath the blanket and gripped Hardrada's own. "I'll be fine, they say." Hardrada frowned again, with curiosity this time, the disquiet leaving his body. "The monks. They have potions and medical knowledge, my friend, such as you could not imagine."

"I thought it was too good, the hope I had you would wither away and die."

"Not yet," Haldor grinned, but almost at once his face changed, growing serious. "But ... Harald, this *brush* with death, it has made me think ..." His grip grew tighter around Hardrada's fist. "We have been through much you and I. Ulf too. We have stood and fought shoulder to shoulder and ..." His other hand went to his forehead, trembling. Tiny pinpricks of sweat beaded across his flesh and he wiped them away with his palm. "I must sleep, my friend."

"I understand." Hardrada turned to leave, but Haldor's grip tightened. Hardrada frowned, sensing Haldor's inner conflict. "Tell me what is on your mind, Hal."

The smile returned. "You're the greatest of men, Harald. The finest warrior in the world. Your fame will spread and you *will be king*. It is your destiny, your *right*. King of the Norse. But I will not be there to see you crowned."

"Nonsense! You yourself said that—"

"No, Harald. I'm sorry, my bestest of friends ... it is time for me to go home."

Seventeen

Cold bit deep, penetrating to the bones and Yaroslav took yet another fur and pulled it tight around his shoulders. With no immediate effect, he ordered his servants to bring more wood and stoke up the fire in the hope of warding off the violent shivering which refused to stop.

He sat on a rickety stool, huddled over, eyes gazing at the floor, aware of the heat from the fire but not feeling it.

Some days before, with fever taking hold, he'd sent for his physician Bartholomew, who prodded and poked, mumbled for the king to make a motion, studied, screwed up his face and shook his head. The physician had hobbled away to his private rooms, re-emerging hours later, a great, dog-eared tome in his hands, wrinkled brow and serious eyes. "I shall have to bleed you, my liege."

The fever gripped harder that evening, tendrils of ice spreading throughout his body. Since then, the cold had grown worse until now, no amount of heat or thick clothing deterred its slow creeping course through every sinew and muscle.

The servant returned, struggling under a pile of rough-hewn logs. He groaned as he bent down, stacking the wood beside the grate, throwing three or four into the flames before stepping back. His face glowed red before the blaze and Yaroslav stared and wished he were a servant right now, or anyone at all. "I feel weak," he said. "Fetch me some wine, warmed through, with spices."

"You wish me to call the physician my lord?"

Yaroslav smirked. "What, so he can bleed me again? I have more cuts on me from that bastard than from all the battles I have ever fought! No," he sniggered, "bring me the wine, that will suffice."

He wanted to stretch backwards, but the stool had no backrest, so he rubbed his stomach, which rumbled, gathered his furs around him, and stood up. His joints screamed, feeling more like rusted iron than bone. If he could open up his knees, pour in some cod-liver oil, perhaps that might fix them. Age. Soon he would be in his fifties and the thought terrified him; there was still so much to do. He turned and lifted his blouse to warm his backside and for a moment, a wave of exquisite pleasure spread through his lower body, the heat penetrating the hard flesh, easing the pain a little.

He smelled the first signs of burning and stepped away, saw the edges of his fur cloak smouldering and laughed. "Wouldn't that be a way to go?" he muttered to himself. "Hero of a thousand battles, consumed by a household fire. I wonder what they'd say about that in their sagas?" Still chuckling, he sat down again and waited for the wine.

The door opened and Yaroslav looked up to see not the servant carrying the wine, but his son Iziaslav, face set hard with concern, the lines around his mouth deep. He strode forward, swathed in a thick goatskin coat and fur-lined boots. His head bare, long strands of limp black hair hanging around his face, he settled the tray he carried on the long table, poured out steaming wine into wooden goblets, and handed one to his father.

"You need a physician."

"That is what my servant said, and I'll give you the same answer and—"

"You *need* a physician who knows what he is doing. That ingrate Bartholomew lacks the skill and the knowledge, so I have sent riders to Miklegard to request they send one of their own."

Yaroslav stirred, arched an eyebrow, "You have sent riders? But they are already gone, emissaries, to present the—"

"The suit with Hardrada, yes, I know, Father." Iziaslav drew up a chair and slumped into it, letting out a long breath. "I have sent others. You need to be made well, in preparedness for the wedding." He looked troubled, drained his wine and Yaroslav studied every line of his son's face. "All being well, when Hardrada returns, he will bring a physician of repute with him."

"They will cross, my son. My emissaries left days ago. They must already be at the city. They will not tarry long."

"Perhaps Hardrada needs time. We can but hope, put our faith in God. I have prayed long and hard, father. We need you well. The kingdom, the people. We all need you."

"It is but a bout of ague. It will pass."

"You say that, but for how many days have you lay stricken? Five?"

"Four."

"*Four*? I thought it was longer." He went over to the wine and poured himself some more, looking askance at his father, the King, "Drink up. It will warm the bones."

Yaroslav did so, sipping at the piping hot mix of wine and spices. Its work began almost on the instant, spreading through his stomach into his chest, pushing away the sensations of cold. "I'm getting old," he muttered, feeling the truth of his words. "You speak true, my son. I need to be strong for the wedding. It will prove a good match, as Hardrada's treasure is vast and we need it, together with his force of arms."

"I have fears."

"Fears? How so? Fears about me? You need not concern yourself, I'll recover, albeit it more slowly. Age does that, you know. The body. It takes its time with the advancement of the years."

"I mean with Hardrada." He leaned forward as he sat, rolling the wooden goblet between his hands. "What if he does not come? What if he refuses Elisif?"

"Refuses? He will not refuse! He has met her and they have exchanged gifts, token of love. All those years ago, you remember?"

"I remember she was but a child."

"Aye, and him too. When he came here, he was nothing but a boy. And I took him in, and he returned my kindness with service. I watched him stand with me in battle, remember that too."

"I hardly remember anything. I was not much over ... damn it, I cannot even remember how old I was. Ten? It was half a lifetime ago and he has done much since. Elisif may have remained faithful to the promises made, but can the same be said for him? The Norse are well known for their infidelity, you know it is so." He drank, smacked his lips. "I have heard many tales of that man. How he wooed the Empress's niece...What was her name, Maria?"

"I know not. So many stories circulate, most of them preposterous. I heard her name was Sarah, and she was not a niece, but a servant of some admiral."

"Well, when she discovered the Viking's impropriety, Zoe had him thrown into prison."

"Aye, and I've heard it said she threw him into prison because she wanted his gold."

"No doubt the truth shall never be revealed. But my fear is, will Hardrada honour his part of the bargain? I am not convinced. There is much about this man I do not like, nor trust. He will forever do whatever he wishes, and love will not feature in his plans."

"The suit will give him security. It is his wish to be king of the Norse. With our friendship, his borders will be secured to the east."

"You play the same tune to the Greeks. Our friendship secures their borders."

"You know what my real tune is as far as

those Greeks are concerned. But I need Hardrada's gold, and I will have it. If he refuses to come, then I shall send more men and they will drag him back here in chains."

"You think it that easy?"

Yaroslav slammed his fist down on his knee, the wine slopping over the side of the goblet. He swore and stood up, throwing off his extra fur. "Damn your hide, boy! I'll not be questioned, you hear me? I am still King in this house, and when I give orders they are obeyed, or heads will roll."

Iziaslav paled at his father's outburst, and his lips trembled as he spoke, becoming like a little boy again, "Father, I never meant to question *you* or your wisdom, merely that this pact with the Viking is fraught with uncertainties."

"I am aware of the uncertainties." Yaroslav took in a deep breath and with the strength returning to his limbs, strode over to the table and tipped out the last of the wine. He drained the goblet in one and leaned forward with his palms on the table. "I have a plan. Something that will bring Hardrada back so swift his feet will burn."

"May I ask what the plan is?"

"No." Yaroslav turned and held his son's gaze. "Not yet. But soon the world will know, and when Hardrada returns, he will marry Elisif, and we make preparations to strike south. I have thought long on it, my son. There is no other way. But Hardrada will come, of that you can have no fear."

Eighteen

Nikolias found the Kievian Rus at the army stables, preparing their mounts for the long return journey. He had gone straight there after his meeting with General Maniakes. The General, not long in the city after his arrival from his estate, sat in his command tent, engrossed in a pile of tightly written communiqués that had long awaited him on his desk. Maniakes preferred a tent to the more permanent apartments set aside for a man of his standing. He told Nikolias it reminded him of when he fought on campaign, and if anything made him happy, it was fighting.

Nikolias stood before the great man, one arm cradling his officer's helm, the other clasped around the hilt of his sword. "I've been away two days and it as if the world has gone mad." Maniakes looked up from his papers and scowled. "I want you to tell me everything that has occurred, Nikolias. Do not omit a single thing."

Nikolias nodded and launched into the details of what he knew. The arrival of the emissaries from Kiev, the icon of Elisif, the mustering of the Varangians for the attack on the Normans, Hardrada's training. When he finished he stood, holding his breath, certain nothing had been left out.

"I have heard Andreas arranged for mercenaries and cut-throats to man Hardrada's flagship. I've also heard Andreas met with the Deputy Patriarch, Psellos. You know anything about that?"

"No, sir."

"And you, you have spoken to His Holiness, Alexius?"

Nikolias frowned. Where in the name of God did this man come by all this information? His network of spies and informers must permeate every pore of the great city. "His Holiness has instructed me to return to Kiev, General. To deliver a letter pledging Hardrada's hand in marriage to the Princess Elisif."

"I see. And since when does an officer of the Imperial Guard take orders from a priest?"

Nikolias's stomach turned. "It is a service to the Empire, General. I assumed it came from the Empress herself."

"*The Empress*? Do you seriously think she would allow Hardrada to leave unmolested?"

"I ... sir, I am not privy to the machinations of government. I do as I am told, sir, nothing less."

"I see. But you are an officer in the Guard, yes?"

Nikolias found his frown deepening. "Sir?"

"And as a *soldier*, you take your orders from superior officers. Would I be right in that assumption?"

An unbearable urge to run his fingers under his collar took almost all of his attention as the temperature inside the tent began to rise. "Sir. Of course, sir, but I could not refuse—"

"But you could not refuse a man of God, correct?"

Nikolias swallowed hard. "Yes, sir."

"Then, you should not." The General stood up. In the confines of the tent, he appeared huge and seemed to relish the effect he had on the young officer of the Imperial Guard. "Nikolias, you will travel north with the emissaries of Yaroslav and you will give him a token of our esteem." He went over to a darkened corner and after a quick rummage, returned with a fair-sized casket of olive wood, inlaid with ivory bands. He settled it upon the table with great reverence, flipped the catch, and lifted the lid.

Nikolias sucked in his breath. He gazed upon the heaps of gold coins and precious jewels stuffed inside the box, the light playing across the surface of diamonds, sapphires and rubies. His jaw slackened.

"There is more wealth in there than you will ever see in your lifetime, Nikolias." The General grinned and dropped the lid shut. He produced a key, placed it in the lock and turned the tumblers. He held up the tiny key. "I am entrusting it to you."

With his mind reeling, Nikolias could not

find the strength to speak. What he had here was the means to escape, to take Leoni to the farthest reaches of the world, begin a new life. Everything he had ever longed for, every hope, every dream fulfilled. He caught the General's stare and blinked. "G-General ... I am overwhelmed by your trust." He shook his head, his eyes threatening to well up. Yes, the means to a new life, but also the affirmation of the General's belief in Nikolias as an honourable and honest man. He looked at the proffered key and took it, folding his fist around the tiny piece of metal.

"You will deliver this casket to the King of the Rus as a token of our esteem, gratitude and love," he pressed his lips together, the final word seeming to cause him some difficulty."You will also deliver the contract of marriage, together with this." He produced a roll of parchment, sealed with a blob of red wax, stamped into which was the royal seal of the Empress Zoe. "This, my dear Nikolias, is worth considerably more than what is kept in that box. You guard it with your life and ensure it is presented to the King alone."

***

Nikolias strolled out of the confines of the Great Palace and wandered through the boulevards beyond the wall. He passed the glistening churches of Saint Bacchus and Anastasia, unaware of the people around him, the sights and sounds of the bustling markets and warehouses, the beating heart of the city emerging once more from its period of stagnation. The smell of the sea lightened his mood and when he reached the port of Sophia and gazed upon the many galleys and merchantmen unloading goods for a moment, he experienced an overwhelming sense of melancholy. In his mind, he had already planned to leave this great palace, to set north with Leoni, escape and leave everything behind. Seeing it like this, the sparkling water of the Sea of Marmora lapping gently against the harbour walls, seabirds dipping and diving, their calls filling the clear air, and the sky a gorgeous light blue, unblemished by clouds, he wondered why he would ever leave. So many people throughout the Empire only ever had dreams of Constantinople, few experiencing its beauty for themselves. His privileged position allowed him to breathe it in every day of his life, and now he meant to leave.

He passed the gleaming lighthouse, the constant fire in the tower smouldering dimly in the morning light, and edged his way through dock workers, porters and scribes, the air filled with the clamour of trade. Cranes strained with the weight of produce, slaves within the treadwheels awash with sweat as taskmasters urged them to further their efforts with the crack or flick of whips. Carts rumbled by, packed high with bundles of silk and other cloth, leather, metal, horn and bone. Laughter, orders barked, yells, squeals, the crash of broken crates, the creak of thick ropes as berthed ships struggled to set themselves free of their moorings.

Nikolias watched it all, a kind of awe

overtaking him. Could there be anywhere else in the entire world where such riches came and went, the well-oiled machinery of Byzantium, serving the people as it had for seven hundred years, displacing Rome itself as the centre of the universe. He doubted it and seeing the profusion of endeavour around him, guilt played around inside him, the idea of Maniakes entrusting him with such a responsibility. He patted the cloth bag slung over his shoulder, bulging with the casket, the rolled parchment. Leave all of this, the cradle of the world, his life, his dreams and memories, and his duty to God, to Empire. All for the love of a woman.

He blew out his breath and continued, passing one of the many taverns that stood a little way from the dockside. A profusion of narrow streets branched off into the depths of this area of the city, not a place Nikolias frequented as his rank forbade any such visits. He knew what happened here, of course. The whores, the drunks, the range of services provided for the many sailors from a hundred different lands who came and went, none of it causing him the slightest desire to experience such things for himself.

A great roar from a nearby alehouse snapped him out of his thoughts and from an open doorway a large man exploded into the street and hit the ground hard, sprawled flat on his face. He groaned, blood seeping from smashed bone and Nikolias instinctively went down on one knee to check his injuries.

A swarthy man, dressed in a crimson

waistcoat and voluminous yellow trousers, his hair braided, he moaned, attempted to lift his head before collapsing once again. Nikolias rocked back on his heels, the stench of wine and ale overpowering. As he rose to step away two brutes erupted from the alehouse, savage looking men with wild, black eyes, snarling teeth, beards covered with trails of spittle and blood. When they latched onto Nikolias, recognising his uniform as that of a soldier of Byzantium, their snarls turned to lurid grins.

"Well, what have we here," said one, rotating massive shoulders bulging with muscle.

"I'd say it was a poxy wallflower come to report back to daddy about what we've been getting up to," hissed the other, the mood changing, crackling with tension. The second drew a long knife from the scabbard hanging from his belt.

They appeared European, their faces ruddy, their skin coarse, hair stiff and bleached by the sun, and their Greek harsh, heavily accented, but effective. Nikolias had no doubts what was in their hearts and he stood up, moving one hand to the hilt of his sword, aware of their eyes settling on the bag at his side. "This man needs attending to." He toed the unconscious hulk at his feet.

"You attend to him then," said one and cackled. "And let us have what's in the bag."

Nikolias tensed as a further two brutes rolled out into the narrow street. They clamped their hands on the shoulders of their comrades, laughing, eyes rheumy, faces awash with sweat, their early drinking already well advanced. "What have we here," spluttered one, swaying as he spoke.

"Bastard," said one of the others.

"Here to spy on us," said another.

"Making sure we're doing as we're told. Look at him, with his pretty white tunic and his lovely little helmet. He'll look good when we splatter his brains all over the street. A real hero of Rome, eh?"

They all laughed at that.

"Yeah, they'll make him a hero, stuff him with vine leaves, put a javelin up his arse and carry him through the hippodrome before the first races begin. Bastard."

Without warning, the man with the knife charged.

He was hefty, squat, with shoulders almost as wide as the door from which he had emerged and as he charged, he roared. No doubt such a tactic had served him well: the many scars across his face and upper body, straining beneath a torn, open jerkin of grey linen, attested to the many scrapes he'd been in. However, Nikolias was a trained officer, a soldier of the Empire, the Royal Bodyguard itself. In one fluid movement of strength, balance and expertise, he gripped the man's collar and using the attacker's forward momentum, twisted and threw the great oaf over an outstretched leg and smashed him against the opposite wall.

Within a blink, Nikolias followed through with one, two, three solid punches into the man's kidneys and a final snap-kick into the back of his knee and he crumpled to the ground, whimpering.

The others stood frozen with shock, their grins fading as Nikolias hefted the dagger in his hand and chuckled, "Now, perhaps you should tell me, who is it I'm supposed to be spying on, and by whose orders?"

All three rushed forward, a stampede of human muscle enraged beyond imagining, screaming, hands thrust out ready to destroy. Nikolias closed, the dagger taking one in the throat, followed by his sword streaking from its scabbard to hew off another's arm. The third caught him, slammed him against the wall, a knee ramming towards his groin. But Nikolias's own knee blocked the blow, striking into the soft flesh of the man's inner thigh; his head butt, given extra effect by his helmet, broke the man's nose with an audible snap. And then his blade buried itself up to the hilt in the man's gut.

Sucking in the air, Nikolias backed away a few steps. Others emerged from the alehouse, curious, confused, some angry, most incredulous and uncertain what to do next. Squeezing between them with gruff authority came a man Nikolias knew. By the look of him he appeared at once alarmed, angry and shocked. An officer in the army himself, bareheaded, wearing no armour, only a buckled-up belt and sword, the chain of his rank hanging loose from his throat. A man the assorted collection of mingling bruisers and drunks seemed to revere as they shuffled aside to allow him through.

He came closer, casting an eye over the fallen, ignoring the screams of the one who had lost his arm and now lay huddled in a corner, blood leaking from the vicious open wound where his forearm had once been. He shook his head, put his hands on his hips and glowered towards Nikolias. "What the *fuck* do you think you're doing?"

Nikolias held the man's gaze and slowly sheathed his sword. "I could ask you the same question."

Grunting, the officer twisted around and barked, "Get back inside, the entertainment is over."

With much murmuring of disappointment, they slowly obeyed, trooping back inside the alehouse.

"They're to be my crew," and he turned and smiled at Nikolias. "Perhaps I should explain everything over a drink, seeing as you're here." He motioned Nikolias to follow as he moved towards the alehouse door, and Nikolias complied and followed Andreas inside.

***

Much later, Nikolias left the alehouse and headed immediately for his family church.

Nikolias had planned to visit the Church of St Thomas even before the incident outside the alehouse, now he had a more urgent need. As an officer in the Royal bodyguard he, like every other soldier in the Byzantine army, had a true sense of piety and love of Christ. The delicate balancing act between doing one's duty – being prepared to fight, kill and die, if need be – and obeying the tenets of the Church often gave rise to tension and stress. To kill was wrong. Everybody knew as much. And Nikolias had killed and now, with the blood still fresh on his hands, he knelt in prayer, begging his Lord for forgiveness.

A lone monk glided across the cold, bare marble floor to the far end and set a taper against a bank of candles. He turned, saw Nikolias and bowed his head before moving on.

Making the sign of the cross, Nikolias muttered a final few words of supplication and turned to go.

A shadow moved at the far end. Thinking the monk had returned, Nikolias paid it no heed and went down the aisle towards the main doors. With nobody else inside, his hobnailed boots echoed throughout the building, a strangely sad sound which seemed to reflect his sense of loneliness and despair.

At the door, he took up his sword and buckled it around his waist. He gave one last glance around the church. The shadow remained, a single figure clad in the black habit of a monk, the cowl disguising the owner's features. A slight, slender individual, silent and still. For a moment, Nikolias thought it might raise an arm for it moved slightly towards him, a tiny ruffling of the garment, a movement from within the folds. Almost as soon as it had begun, the figure returned to its stillness and Nikolias went outside.

***

One of the Rus threw a thick bedroll over the back of his horse and Nikolias blinked, returning to the present. He chided himself for thinking too deeply, of being too concerned over so many permutations. There would be stress enough without adding to them with thoughts of what to do with Leoni, why the figure in the church seemed to be studying him and what to do with the news Andreas had given him. He sighed as he checked his saddle bags. A crew, assembled to man Hardrada's ship, to take him across the sea to Sicily and set him down on the beach. And then what? To abandon him? But why, the man served the Empire, had proved his worth more than once. Why concoct yet another scheme to destroy him when the greater threat was the Normans, the very force Hardrada was being sent to destroy.

A stable-hand shuffled by, face creased as he hefted Nikolias's saddle and threw it over the back of his mount. Time enough to think and time enough to worry on the journey north. For his mind was made up. Andreas and his revelations settled it all. No more apawn, no more a player in a mindless game of intrigue borne of hatred. He'd leave it all behind, and take Leoni with him.

Nineteen

A rough shaking of his shoulder brought him awake. Monomachus sat up and instinctively dashed away the offending hand. Used to the pampering of servants, a glaring brute reminded him, if he needed any reminding, his former life had gone, replaced by a new regime of meagre food and tough, physical training. For the better part of a week he had been subjected to daily runs, lifting of weights, stretching, flexing, sweating. Weapon training, boxing, grappling. His body screamed, every joint and muscle locked in agony. After the first day, he truly believed he would die. This morning, however, proved the first time he could stand without his thighs buckling beneath him.

The manservant glowered. A squat, grizzled beast, more bear than human, grinned, revealing a fine set of broken, blackened teeth. "Master wants you."

Monomachus grunted, went over to the basin and threw tepid water over his face, ignoring the insects floating upon the surface. Wiping himself on the end of his shirt, he pulled on his breeches and motioned for the brute to lead the way.

They crossed the training ground, weaving through the sparring posts where wooden manikins stood to receive blows from practise swords. Little plumes of dust swirled around his bare feet. No one was allowed sandals. The brute, whose feet were wide and splayed, seemed not to notice, but Monomachus continued to suffer; the calluses and developing bunions a constant source of misery, far worse than the night cramps and the burning muscles. He gritted his teeth and teetered onwards.

At the command tent, the brute threw back the entrance flap and jerked his head. Monomachus pulled in a breath and dipped inside.

The gloom made distinguishing details difficult. Somewhere in the far corner, a shape moved; Monomachus squinted until a flame flared and a candle brought much needed relief from the darkness.

Surrounded by the yellow halo, Marcellus stepped forward, bare-chested, muscles shiny with sweat. He set the single candle down on a low table and poured out wine from a clay jug. "How long have you been with us?"

Monomachus frowned, his mind doing a quick calculation. "Six days."

"Six days ..." Marcellus drank wine and tapped his teeth with the rim of his goblet. "We don't have much longer."

"I don't understand."

"The General wants you ready in four more. I don't think we can do it."

"Ready? Ready for what?"

"You'll have to ask him."

"I'm asking *you.*"Monomachus, suddenly angry, took a step forward, breathing hard. "Damn your eyes, I've suffered enough of your insolence. I am of noble blood, you hear me? You have levelled upon me such indignities, such hardships that I feel I could—"

"What? Kill me?" Marcellus chuckled. "No, you're nowhere near ready to do that, my friend." He moved forward, pushing Monomachus in the chest with the goblet. "You're fitter, some of the flab has gone, but you're still as slow as a leech. And a leech you are, sucking the life blood out of everyone you meet. Two days ago you demanded the youth Dressus fetch you wine and dates for your breakfast."

"He is a servant."

"No. He is a circus fighter. You know what that means?"

"A sort of gladiator, I guess."

"Correct. He is fifteen years of age. Big for his age, isn't he?"

"He's enormous."

"I ordered him to ensure you were awake every morning, to provide you with bread and water. Nothing more."

"Hardly a crime, asking for wine."

"It was not what you asked for, but the *manner* in which you asked. Or should that be ordered? You deny it?"

"Deny what? For the love of Christ, you haul me out of bed at this ungodly hour to berate me over *this*? Are you mad?"

Another shove forced Monomachus to stumble backwards. Alarmed at Marcellus's strength, he threw out his hands, "For God's sake, man, I meant nothing but—"

"It's lesson time."

Before Monomachus could fathom the meaning of the words, a rough hand seized him by the collar and hauled him outside. Monomachus, thrown off balance, fell to his knees into the dirt and winced. He wiped his mouth with the back of his hand and turned his face to see a half-armoured youth standing before him, scimitar in one hand, small oblong shield in the other; his chest open, his lower body covered in thick, padded pants of deep blue and shin-high boots of stout leather. He wore an open-faced helmet of bronze which shimmered in the morning sun, encasing a hard face, black eyes unblinking and alert.

Dressus.

The youth seemed even more huge if that were possible and fear twisted his gut; he snapped his head left and right as Marcellus and the brute moved forward to flank him. "What is this?" he managed.

"Training day," said Marcellus. "You've done enough sparring, enough play-fighting. Now is the time to test your skills, the skills you've been learning for eighteens hours a day, every day." He sniggered. "It's time to put it all to good use. Fight him."

"I can't!"

"You will, or he will kill you."

The brute chuckled as Marcellus drew his sword and pressed it into Monomachus's trembling hand, who gazed at it, wide-eyed, as if it were some strange, unknown object. "If you refuse to fight," continued Marcellus, "I'll kill you myself."

Monomachus felt his throat tighten as panic and terror solidified his body. His mouth fell open, panting like a dog, his tongue thick and eyes moist. "I cannot. I am not ready."

"You'd better be." The brute grinned and reached for his belt to pull out a thin, sharp-bladed sword of Eastern design. "Or I'll slice open your gizzard."

Whimpering, Monomachus lifted his sword. He swayed unsteadily, watching the silent Dressus. "Dear Christ," he whispered, "all those mornings, the things I said, they were all in my nature. I never meant to insult you."

"This is not about insults," said Marcellus, withdrawing a few steps, "this is merely a test. To see how well you have learned your lessons."

"But I cannot *fight*, damn you!"

"You've trained with the sword, you've learned to thrust and parry ... now we take it to the next level. *Begin!*"

Dressus roared rushing forward, the scimitar raised high above him, already coming down in a blur as Monomachus screamed and retreated, slashing wildly with the short sword. Metal clanged against metal and the brute guffawed, his mouth wide with delirium.

The youth pressed on, the scimitar flashing, hitting only hot air as Monomachus continued to retreat, dodging, ducking, weaving. The sword dangling heavily from his hand, limbs unable to bring it up, no strength in his muscles, brain confused, paralysed. He whimpered, spittle spraying from quivering lips, as his knees gave way and he hit the ground, the sword falling from numbed fingers. "Oh, sweet Christ."

Dressus kicked him hard in the chest and he fell backwards with a grunt. Another kick in his ribs bent him double; he cried out, in fear and shame, *"Please, dear Christ, please don't kill me!"*

A hand gripped him, hauling him to his feet, and the youth sneered, "Kill you, you shit? I wouldn't waste my fucking time." The youth's knee snapped up and erupted into Monomachus's groin. A great sea of nausea swept over him and he gagged and crumpled, hands clasped to his genitals, the vomit burning through his throat.

Aware of distant laughter, hands clapping in applause, appreciation of a job well done, Monomachus rolled over and saw them, in a huddle. The three of them, Marcellus and the brute congratulating the youth with back slaps and peals of amusement.

Monomachus's head cleared at that point. Shame, indignity, rage, all combined to return vigour to lifeless limbs, direction to his thoughts. He spat out the last clump of vomit, swept up his sword and charged.

It happened so quickly that neither the brute nor Marcellus had time to react. Before Dressus knew it, the sword plunged into his back, the blade biting deep, bursting out of his midriff; he whimpered, blinked, and fell.

Monomachus stood as the youth's body collapsed, its weight allowing the sword to slide from out of the flesh, leaving the blade to drip blood as Dressus hit the dirt, face down and dead.

No one moved; all of them too stunned to do anything except gape. Monomachus, the first to recover, threw down the sword and spun away, heading for the lonely billet where he rested.

The day's lesson was over.

Twenty

Sometime during the afternoon, Ulf found Hardrada sitting in the Royal Gardens, crouched over on a marble bench, studying an orange as if it were the most amazing thing in the entire world.

He sat down next to his old friend and breathed in the thick perfume of jasmine. "I often wish we could take this with us."

Hardrada raised his head, "Eh?"

"This place. I wish we could put it on a ship and sail it back home."

"The winter would kill it."

"Aye, but the summer, Harald ..." Ulf shook his head. "Of all the places I have been, this is the one I will forever keep in my heart."

"You sound like a poet."

"Do I? I thought that was you? I've seen you writing, scribbling down words whenever you've a moment, in the aftermath of a battle or ... a love affair ... that's when you write."

Hardrada sighed and sat up. He tossed the orange a few times, catching it in the palm of his hand, studying it closely. "If people don't remember me for my exploits, perhaps they'll remember me for my words."

"You think they are more memorable?"

"I think they have more worth, old friend. Anyone can kill, even love. Not many can write."

"An artist. Is that what you are?"

"I'm not sure what I am anymore." He pressed his thumb nail into the orange and broke through the skin. A thin spray of juice hit his face, but he paid it no mind as he attacked the flesh and peeled it away. "Haldor is going home."

Ulf let out a long breath, "I know. I've just come from his sick bed. He said you'd been, and you'd talked."

"I don't know what I'll do without him. He's been my conscience these past twenty years. Whilst you," he gripped Ulf's knee, "you've been my rock."

Ulf's cheeks reddened and he turned away before Harald noticed the tear tumbling down his cheek.

"He has pledged to accompany us home, before he sets off for Iceland. I am honoured, Ulf, for without his counsel I am not confident of how best to proceed."

Ulf sniffed, running his hand over his face before speaking, "It is that which brought me here." He held his friend's gaze. "I've been to the harbour. The preparations are well underway. Perhaps three more days. But ..."

"Tell me, Ulf. I sense your uncertainty. There is bad news?"

"More than bad. Our men, the crew of your flagship, have been replaced."

"Replaced? I don't understand, why would anyone wish to—"

"By Anatolians and Bulgarians."

Hardrada's face drained of colour. "Who the hell ordered this?"

"I know not who *ordered* it, but I know who commands them."

The silence yawned between them before Hardrada breathed, 'Who?"

Ulf did not blink. "Andreas."

***

They marched down to the harbour together, neither speaking, faces set hard. Hardrada had his great axe over his shoulder, in the crook of his arm his bronzed, spectacled helm. Ulf, hand-and-a-half sword lashed to his back, gripped the short sword at his side, almost needing to run in order to keep up with his striding friend.

The many people who thronged the narrow streets parted as the two Vikings made their way towards the Harbour of Sophia. Alarm rippled through the people, exchanged glances and mutterings of panic, even dread. Clearly these men were on a mission: violence oozed from every pore of their tense, taut frames.

At the dockside, Hardrada pulled up and laid a hand on Ulf's shoulder. Nodding towards the waiting ships, the giant Viking growled. "I don't see any of our men. Not a one."

"They were billeted in that training ground."

"Were? What the hell does that mean?"

"It means, Harald, they have been moved. They're back in their barracks, awaiting further orders."

"Who from?"

Ulf arched an eyebrow. "Who do you think."

"*Maniakes.* Damn his eyes. I knew he schemed something, the bastard. I'll carve his heart out before this day is ended." He swung his axe from his shoulder and hefted it with both hands. "Let's find out what's going on here."

The flagship lay long and proud on the surface of the crystal waters, the great dragon-headed prow proclaiming to the world this was a Viking vessel, primed and ready for war. Over its deck swarmed a small crew of men, arranging stores and equipment for the voyage. From the look of them, swarthy, black-haired and squat, it was clear these were not Norsemen, but Eastern Europeans. One or two glanced over as Hardrada and Ulf stepped on board.

The ship was long, at least thirty strides and the banks of rows with spaces in-between allowed for upwards of a hundred men to man it. Hardrada went straight to the stern and stepped onto the raised platform from where, during the voyage, he could view his warriors and the direction they took. Behind, the tiller and in the centre a single mast, the great sail furled. He put his axe blade down upon the decking and leaned on the shaft. "Where is your commander," he said, his voice booming above the clamour of the men as they continued to work.

They stopped, as one, and all eyes turned towards the giant. No one spoke.

"I'll only ask you once more. *Where is your commander?*"

Ulf stiffened beside him and gripped his friend's arm. "He comes," he said, loosening the sword in its scabbard.

Hardrada watched as an armoured officer of the Byzantine Imperial Guard, accompanied by half a dozen soldiers armed with spears, clambered up the gangplank, pausing to remove his helmet.

The Viking bristled and straightened his back, the axe coming up in his hands. "*You.*"

"Hello, Harald. Seems like we can't keep away from each other." And with that, Andreas stepped onboard and pulled out his sword.

Twenty One

He knew something was wrong even before he pushed open the broken door.

The street stood too quiet, no birds sang, and when he came around the corner he stopped, the frown biting deep. The atmosphere pressed around him, a dreadful sense of foreboding seeping into his very soul. A crash from a nearby shutter as it closed caused him to whirl, but all that followed was the slam of cross beams, the shutting out of the world.

He edged forward, on high alert, ready to defend himself from any attack but as he drew nearer to his mother's house, he realized nobody lurked about. Nikolias took a breath and went inside.

Groaning at what he saw, he cast his eye over the scene of violence within. Ransacked, the place a maelstrom of broken artifacts and torn clothes. Furniture lay shattered and thrown about, as if struck by a tempest. A cooking pot, contents spilt across the floor, had rolled into the corner where a single rat scurried away with a large chunk of par-boiled meat clamped in its jaws. The silence crushed him, the horror overpowering.

His voice, when he found it, was small and feeble, little more than a croak. "Leoni?"

No reply came. She was not there; he needed no confirmation.

Nikolias drew his sword, but already he knew what awaited him. Holding his breath, he crept through the strewn remnants of a life once shared with his mother. In the rear room he found her, draped across the truckle bed, her throat cut, the blood dried, soaked into the bed clothes.

The strength left him at that moment, and he collapsed against the door frame, sword clattering to the ground. He slid, the sobs racking his body, and nothing else mattered, not anymore. The great weight of despair came down and at that point the burden proved too great, the floodgates opened and he cried, without shame, without any care. His mother lay dead. How could he not?

Some time later he went outside again, as if in a dream, no feeling in his body, lifted his head and cried out in total despair. A long, mournful sound poured from him and then he pitched forward, the blackness engulfing him.

**

When he awoke, the pain pulsed through his face; he rolled over, realising the impact of his fall may have broken his nose, or at best smashed his mouth. He blinked, the dried blood tight over his flesh, and sat up. Alone, he pushed down with his palms and levered himself to his feet. Reeling, he staggered down the street, keeping close to the wall, one thought burning through his mind.

The figure in the church, sent to spy on him. The absence of Leoni. The murder. Only one man had the power to enact such horrors.

General Maniakes.

In some impossible way, using his network of informants, he had learned of Nikolias's abduction of Leoni, of his plans and he had acted, as only he could. Perhaps even the attack at the alehouse had been orchestrated by him, Andreas too. The man's revelations; how they planned to kill Hardrada, set him adrift on the beaches of Sicily to be overwhelmed by the waiting Normans. All of it, every word etched with the signature of Maniakes.

And Nikolias had fallen for it. The ignorant, noble officer of the Royal bodyguard, sworn to preserve the life of the Emperor, how naive could he be? How pitiful.

He continued on through the streets, moving with renewed vigour, every step bringing strength and determination to his stride, motivated now by a burning desire for revenge.

To kill General Maniakes.

***

The two pieces of news reached General Maniakes as he was about to leave his command tent, pitched a few paces beyond the walls of the Imperial grounds. The rain, which had broken an hour or so before, fell even harder. Maniakes sat, huddled under his cloak, head down, immersed in a lengthy report, his first indication of someone approaching an urgent call of, "General!" He stopped and stared at the grim-faced soldier pounding towards him. As he drew closer, Maniakes could see the drawn features, the breathlessness. The man dropped to one knee, as if Maniakes were royalty. "Sir, forgive me ..." He swallowed hard and thrust a rolled piece of parchment, "News, sir."

"Stand up, you buffoon, and pull yourself together." Maniakes snatched the roll and turned away to read it.

His eyes noted the words, but within a few sentences they blurred. He looked to the sky, more stunned than shocked, his mind unable to register the enormity of what he had read. So he tried again, more slowly this time. There was no mistaking the meaning, and he crunched the roll up in his fist and glared at the messenger. "Who gave you this?"

"It arrived this morning, sir, before you had—"

"I asked you *who* gave you this?"

The man's face paled to chalk white. "A messenger, sir. From your estate. He had ridden through the night."

"And where is he now?"

"At His Holiness, the Deputy Patriarch Psellos's apartments, sir."

"Psellos? Why was he taken there?"

"I don't know, sir. But if you wish it, I can—"

Maniakes dismissed him with a snapped

shake of the head and pushed past him. The man fell in behind, needing to half-jog to keep up with the striding general. "General, sir ..." the man continued, voice hesitant and uncertain.

"What is it, man?"

"There is something more, sir."

"More?" Maniakes stopped, and the bustling soldier almost collided into him. "More news? Tell me."

The soldier wrung his hands, unnerved at the General's words. "Sir. News has come from the training ground, sir. Constantine Monomachus, sir. There is a problem. Marcellus sent a runner to inform you, sir."

"By Christ, can no one ever get anything done without my constant fucking presence?" he steamed, shoulders rising and falling as his anger intensified. "What the fuck has happened?"

"The runner did not say, sir, and I was about to come to you when this other news arrived. And I'm sorry if I have not—"

Maniakes held up his hand. "Shut up." He studied the man for a moment, his bedraggled appearance, the rain soaking through his clothes. "You came here straight away?"

"Yes, sir, as soon as I..." He frowned as Maniakes pulled off his cloak and handed it to the soldier.

"Take this," said Maniakes, "and go immediately to Psellos. Tell him I am leaving for my estate and I shall not return for the next three days. He is to inform His Holiness Alexius, you understand?" The soldier nodded, staring down at the cloak in his hands. Of royal purple, edged with gold thread, it was a plain and heavy garment proclaiming the General's rank. "I am going to the training ground and see what the hell has happened." He sniggered. "What is your name, soldier?"

"Victor," he whispered.

"Well, *Victor,* put the damn thing on. I'll go back to my tent and get myself another. The rain is hard, and you are soaked through to the skin."

Victor forced a smile and was about to say something when Maniakes turned and strode back to his tent. The man's shocked, stupefied reaction would stay with him for a long time.

***

The rain hammered down. It was often this way, prolonged days of clear, crystal blue skies, pulsating heat, followed by a sudden, unlooked-for deluge. Now was one of those moments, and Victor drew the cloak tighter around his throat. He wore a felt turban, the off-duty dress many soldiers donned when not on active service; his thick trousers lashed tightly with leather thongs around the calves. Well-protected, he nevertheless hated this weather and he bent himself against it, and hurried through the open ground towards the palace complex.

When the figure stepped out from the space between two statues, he paid it no mind. Even when it fell in behind him, Victor ignored any possible threat. The rain smothered noise, masked the footfall, the sing of the sword as it rasped out from its scabbard.

Too late he reacted, managing a half-turn as the blade struck home, sinking into his lower back, slicing through kidneys and beyond. He screamed, a high-pitched shriek, whipped away in the downpour. As he pitched forward, the sword came across his neck in a blur, the killing blow, half severing his head.

Nikolias pushed the body over with his foot. And stood and stared.

Despair enveloped him, the groan emanating from deep within, lost in the rain.

He staggered backwards, watching the blood from the dead man soaking into the dirt. And the face, staring lifeless. Not a face he knew, not a face he wanted to see. How did he make a mistake? The cloak.

For the body was not that of Maniakes; Nikolias was beside himself with indecision. To continue and find the General, or flee?

Approaching voices made the decision for him, and he slipped away, using the downpour to disguise his flight. He slipped into a narrow side street, heart pounding, grief too great to even consider what direction to take.

Twenty Two

The Empress lay back on her padded couch, arms hanging down the sides, legs open, naked save for a thin, silk shift draped across her midriff. Around her, handmaids attended to her body; one delicately painting her eyelids with thick, black liner, another smoothing lotions over her legs, cooing, "Mistress, you have the body of a young girl."

Zoe knew it was not so. Her morning ritual of studying her face, arms and legs revealed the relentless march of age. The creases under her eyes grew deeper, the muscles in her thighs and arms more slack, but she refrained from chiding the girl. She enjoyed the attention, the girl's fingers sending delicious waves of pleasure through her flesh.

Soft hands smoothed cream into her cheeks, circular motions relaxing muscles, easing stress. And Zoe had stress, despite the news she had received earlier.

Two hours before, she'd lain in bed next to her lover, propped up on one elbow, studying his strong, lean body, her hand gently lifting his long cock to examine it. He was no Crethus, the magnificent Scythian captain who had taken her body, conquered it with his manful lovemaking, but he served a purpose. Crethus had given her everything she'd ever wished for in a man: attention, endowment and, perhaps most important of all, absence. Since the death of Crethus, the one thing Zoë no longer yearned for were the attentions of a lover who shared every moment of her life. She now preferred solitude and quiet, only needing a man when the urge became too great. Crethus proved the perfect match, offering her a chance for love, companionship, before the bastard Hardrada killed him and hardened her heart. Her breath rasped; the very forming of the Viking's name brought a new bout of burning hatred to her very being.

The Viking had come into her life some years before, lusted after her and she, the idiot she was, had succumbed and allowed him to put his great cock inside her. Many, many times. How she rued that day, for it was not long before his lecherous eyes settled on her adopted niece, Sarah. She remembered the Viking coming into her apartment unannounced, his arrogance breathtaking, seeing his eyes settle upon the young girl as she stood combing through Zoe's hair. She should have realised then, of course, what would happen. She'd chosen to put any suspicions out of her mind but when she'd found them in bed, drawn by the moans filling the room with such urgency the whole damned palace must have heard, she'd ordered the guards to seize him. They had bundled him away to the prison tower close to the church of St Hagatha. As for Sarah, Zoe had packed her off to a nunnery, to lament, consider her actions in much gentler surroundings.

She still resided there. A young girl, life's adventures ended before they had barely begun.

Zoe felt no remorse;certain circumstances required such actions. And Hardrada's contempt needed punishing.

And then, after Maniakes had released the bastard, he had killed Crethus. So when the opportunity arose to rid herself of the man, once and for all, she'd seized it with both hands.

For now, one hand seemed enough as she stroked her lover's cock to full hardness. He groaned, arching his back, and she lowered her mouth over him and drank him in, her tongue causing the groans to grow louder, more urgent.

She mounted him without warning and rode him vigorously, pounding down on his hard body, taking all he had. And, when he emptied himself into her a few moments later, she rolled off him and stared at the ceiling whilst he whimpered like a child, muttering how wonderful she was, how exquisite. She closed her eyes, trying to summon up images of Crethus. When the Scythian mounted her, it was she who proclaimed her infatuation, her disbelief at his prowess. The man beside her did not cause stirrings within her, memories brought these. And as those memories swirled around in her head, she placed her fingers into her sex, found the tiny button of nerves, and swiftly brought herself to orgasm.

He, the fool, believed her gasps were for him, and he caressed her breasts and nibbled at her ears as her hips ground into the bed before her body slowly became calm.

Snapping her eyes open, she studied his face and pitied him, weak fool that he was. To allay any concerns, she smiled, and his body relaxed.

"I am your captive," he whispered, running a finger along the outline of her jaw. "I never believed such feelings lay within me."

"You're a man," she said, trying her best not to sound too derisory but when his finger stopped its gentle caress, she realised something had struck home. She ran her tongue across her bottom lip, "But what a man you are."

His eyes bulged, "You mean it?"

So much like a little boy, she mused. An endearing feature, in many ways. The man had declared his virginity when she had first lured him into her bed. The prospect of devising a plan to suit her needs, to use a man of God in such a delicious way to achieve it, caused the most divine sensations to stir inside her stomach. "Of course." To emphasise the point, it was her turn to stroke his cheek. Not an unpleasant body, his enthusiasm and eagerness to please were alluring, and his face, as it glowed above her during their coupling, comely.

Taking his virginity had been wondrous. Watching him struggling to keep himself under control but once he gave way, the sheer ecstasy in every line of his features brought a sort of peace and contentment to her. The knowledge she still possessed the physical weapons to ensnare and subdue men in order for them to carry out her schemes gave her more pleasure than the act of coupling. Now she used her charms to launch her latest plan.

The final destruction of Hardrada.

"Are you sure," she continued, "everything is in place?"

"Everything, my love. All of his men have been replaced and even now they are preparing the flagship before its launch. Hardrada will have no choice, even if he demands his men replace the crew Andreas has put in place."

"And you are certain they will abandon him?"

"They owe no loyalty other than to their paymaster. Me."

She breathed out through her nose. "To be more accurate, my sweet, that is *me*. You have done well so far, and only one thing gives me concerns. I will need proof he is dead."

"Andreas will provide the proof. His ships will remain offshore, observe the destruction of Hardrada, then the agreements with the Normans signed, he shall return. The General will be unable to do anything about it and will have no choice other than to accept defeat."

"Whilst the Empire loses Sicily."

"We placate the Normans, Hardrada is dead, and we no longer need to concern ourselves with our western borders. From what I understand, the threats to the east are by far the more urgent. It is a sublime plan, one which will ensure stability for generations to come, and one for which your future husband will receive most of the credit."

She sat up, pushing his hand away, and swung her legs off the bed. Naked she walked over to the open balcony and looked out towards the city. A cool evening, the distant trickle of fountains mingling with the chirping of numerous insects.

She tensed as he came up behind her, his hands snaking around her waist, pulling her towards his erect cock. If anything, his constant desire to ravish her body brought her a kind of reassuring warmth.

His lips pressed against her neck. "You are glorious," he said, his voice thick and unsteady. "How can it be I have lived my entire life without experiencing someone as delectable as you?"

He turned her around, plunging his mouth to her breast, tongue exploring her nipples, fingers kneading into the swell of her buttocks. She arched her back to allow him greater access and lifted a leg, wrapping it around his own. No Crethus, but a man nevertheless. Once Hardrada lay dead, she would spit this one out like a discarded pip from a grape. A few moments of pleasure as a reward for undertaking her plots. Nothing more.

"I want you again," he murmured.

"You never stop wanting me."

"Does that trouble you?"

"Of course not. I love it."

He grinned, swept her up into his arms and carried her to the bed, laying her down gently on the mattress before stepping back to expose himself to her; his long cock arching back towards his belly, glistening, ready to service her need once again.

"A man of God such as you," she said, her tone mocking, shaking her head, smiling. "You'll never go to heaven."

"I am already in heaven," Psellos said and slid between her thighs.

Twenty Three

The room stood foetid, the stench of stale sweat permeating every fold of material, every splinter of wooden floor. Even the walls dripped with it. Andreas sat on the single, rickety bed, face in hands, searching for some sign, an inner voice, a message to guide him through, along the twisting path of treachery before him.
Nothing.
He allowed his hands to drop and slowly drew his sword, laid it across his knees, and stared at the sharpened blade.
On the ship, Hardrada had stood like a solid pinnacle of granite; the men had shied away, terrified by his presence. None of them so much as took a step when the Viking levelled his axe at Andreas and bellowed, "I want my men back on this ship by nightfall, or your head will be floating in the dock."
Andreas would have liked to kill him then. The bastard Ulf had laughed. Two of them, vicious, brutal killers. How many would have

lost their heads if Andreas had chosen to fight? His hatred for the Viking knew no bounds, but his loyalty to the Empire was paramount.

This was the song he sang, to convince himself, to assuage his anger, even shame. Any other time he would have fought, but so many orders ran around in his head, so many conflicts, and none resolved. To ensure Hardrada sailed to Sicily to die, was what Psellos had commanded. Yet Alexius and Maniakes seemed to declare the opposite. The Empire needed Hardrada, they said. Only he could guarantee the loyalty of the Varangian Guard, so who to believe, who to obey? Psellos promised all Andreas's superiors spoke with one voice, the ultimate commands coming from the Empress herself. Andreas, if he questioned any of it, may well lose his position, his freedom, perhaps even his life. So Psellos had said.

But did the Deputy Patriarch lie?

He stood up, swinging the sword through the air, practising a few moves, in an effort to unfreeze muscles, reinvigorate his body. He recalled how Hardrada stood and glared, "I'll command *my* men to prepare," he said and then left. What was Andreas to do now? Inform Psellos, admit defeat?

A sudden whirl and he struck with the edge of the blade through the mattress of the bed, parting it in two with one mighty blow. It smashed asunder, goose feathers billowing up in a small shower, and he fell to his knees, consumed by self-doubt and confusion. The blade clattered to the ground as he pressed his hands to his breast, muttering his prayers, "Dear Christ, help me."

***

Marcellus tipped a pitcher of water over his head and stood, breathing hard, allowing the cool liquid to ease away the heat from his aching body.

All morning they had trained, pummelling Monomachus's body, pushing him to the very limit of his endurance. They had taught him moves that no one else knew; tricks to stand him well against even the most determined attack. "Now you've killed," grumbled Styrias, the brutish assistant to the legendary Marcellus, "you won't have any problems holding your own."

Marcellus watched, criticised, offered advice, joined in to instruct. True, Monomachus's body responded well, the fat dropping off him, his muscles hardening, but the man had partaken too long of rich wine and good food. The man moved quickly; he now *looked* as if he could fight, but the flabbiness would take weeks to remove.

With the session completed, everyone retired to their rooms just as the heavens opened and the rain poured down. Inside his tent, Marcellus rubbed himself dry with a towel and picked up a fresh tunic as Maniakes came through the door, out of breath and eyes like a wild cat's, soaked through to the skin.

"Where is he?"

"He's safe, General."

"Dear Christ, he'd better be."

The General went directly to the wine and poured himself a large gobletful. Marcellus smirked. Another member of the royal household, fattened by wine. Damn them all. Effete Greeks with nothing between their legs but soft dough. How in the name of Christ had they conspired to rule the world?

"Your informers are quick to tell you bad news, General," said Marcellus, sitting down on a hard-backed chair. "Perhaps if they had waited a moment or two, they could have told you the whole story."

"You set him against a gladiator? Are you a total idiot, Marcellus?"

The boxer straightened his back, body taut. "Don't tread too hard, General. I'm not one of your soldiers to order about."

"And don't mistake me for some half-baked oaf who has not stood in battle, fought men, and killed more times than you could ever imagine."

Marcellus scanned the man before him, the taut frame, the heavily packed muscles, thick ropes bulging in neck and forearm. He saw the truth in the General's words. The man's fame preceded him. A worthy opponent, not simply a man to circle around in the dust of the hippodrome, but a man whose blade ran with blood. "Constantine Monomachus is perfectly well," Marcellus said at last, releasing the tension, leaning back in his chair. "I know what I'm doing. Prepare him, you said, as if for the arena. Well, that is what is happening, General. Do not fret over what might happen, for nothing will which will endanger his life."

Maniakes gnawed away at his lip, then drained the wine. "I'm going away, tonight. I have received news. Apparently, someone broke into my home, killed one of my servants, and terrified my wife."

"You know who it was?"

"Oh, yes, I know." Maniakes tilted the wine jug to pour himself another measure. "I want your man, Marcellus. I need him to guard my home whilst I am away."

"My man?"

"The thug who is always lurking about."

"Styrias? I need him here, to help me with Monomachus. We have less than a week to get him fit."

"I need him too. Whoever broke into my house did so to send me a message. That I could be reached, you understand?"

Marcellus spread out his hands, "In that case, why not simply send some of your men? A few hand-picked Imperial Guardsmen? Or even those Varangians you seem to have a soft-spot for."

"No. I want this done anonymously. No one must know. Fetch Styrias and have him report to my command tent within the hour. He is to bring enough provisions for a day's ride, you understand?" He smirked. "Do not worry yourself, Marcellus. You'll be well compensated." To emphasise his point, he brought out a small leather pouch and threw it onto the table beside the boxer. "A little something to get you through the next few days."

Marcellus stuck out his bottom lip and

picked up the tiny bundle. He hefted it in his palm, the clink of coins inside clearly discernible. "Music to my ears, General."

"I thought as much." Maniakes looked around. "Have you a coat? I must return and do not wish for another soaking."

Marcellus stood up and searched through a pile of clothes in the corner. He found an old goatskin jerkin, big enough to cover a horse, and threw it across to Maniakes, who sniffed at its coarse fibres, pulled a face, but nonetheless gathered it around him. He grunted, and went out into the night.

Marcellus stood and stared. Losing Styrias would be problematic. Without his trusted deputy, all of the training regime would fall to him, and Marcellus hated the idea of being with the loathsome Monomachus more than need be. Since the killing of Dressus, the man had become even more unbearable, boasting of his prowess, forgetting all of his former tears and cries for mercy. Only one point in the whole dreadful affair gave Marcellus a focus on which to find some solace.

The money.

***

Through the sodden city streets, a lonely cart pulled by a forlorn-looking mule wound its way towards the Constantine Gate. The darkness and the weather helped to disguise the figures; one on the seat, bent over, flicking the mule's rump with the reins every so often, and amongst some bales of well-wrapped wool, the other, swathed in a large, thick cloak. If a guard's eyes were to look closely, he might have noted the ropes fastening the cloak, preventing the figure from moving. However, under the stone ramparts, not one did, and a miserable-looking soldier waved the drover through with an impatient gesture. As thunderrumbled and lightning arced across the sky, he dived back inside the guard block to find warmth from the fires within.

The drover urged the mule on and the cart rumbled along the Mese road towards the Gate of Charisius. He kept his eyes down, allowing the animal to find its way, the slow, relentless pounding of its hooves a comforting sound amidst the constant buffeting of the rain. Somewhere over to his right, lights flickered in the many houses and other buildings he passed, but nobody ventured outside, not with the weather so foul.

Behind him, the other moaned and the drover strained to peer and check that all was well. The figure huddled still deeper within itself and the drover, satisfied, turned again to face the front.

From out of the darkness, a pair of riders clattered by. The drover barely gave them a glance, not that he could recognise much in the gloom, but he guessed they were soldiers. The big one at the lead wore a helmet with a larger plume than usual. Perhaps a commander of some sort, but he cared not. The journey he had before him was a long one and the opportunity to gain any rest unlikely. So he hunched his shoulders against the rain and settled himself once more as the mule lumbered on to the Walls of Theodosius.

Twenty Four

"It is not like you to show such concern."

Sclerus turned from the balcony and stared at his neighbour's wife sprawled naked across the bed. Her lithe body gleamed in the pale moonlight trickling through the open window. Her lovemaking proved vigorous and accomplished; a woman well used to having what she wanted. With a rich husband and now a lustful lover, it was no wonder her smile beamed broad. "I'm worried," he said, eyes never leaving her.

She rolled over onto her stomach, curling her leg backwards. "You fuck her more than you do me."

"I've known her longer."

"Ah, yes. Of course." She smiled coyly. "But is she better than me?"

"I doubt I have had better than you."

Pleased, she cooed and rolled over, black eyes boring into him. "Leave her then, monopolise me. I'll give you everything you could ever want."

"I know that ... but there are other considerations."

"Yes. I thought as much. Your feud with the General. Everyone knows how much you hate him, but nobody knows why. You resent him, perhaps? His prowess between the sheets is well known."

"Dear Christ, you believe I am not good enough? I don't hear you complaining."

She shrugged, "Truth be told, I've had better, if you must know. You're enthusiastic enough, but ..."

He crossed the room at a rush, seized her by the throat and forced her head into the pillow, his face twisting with rage. "Damn your heart, you whore! One word from me and your husband will know of your infidelities and he'll hang you out to dry."

Nothing flickered in her face. "He knows already, you fool. He's always known. Whenever he's sober, he manages to get it up for a few seconds, but he knows I need more. So he turns a blind eye. What he doesn't know doesn't hurt him ... his very words, Lord Sclerus. So take your fucking threats somewhere else where they can be more effective."

"You bitch," he cocked back his fist ready to strike.

"Hit me, and he'll cut off your balls. Don't underestimate my husband, he's a man with powerful connections. More than you, I'd warrant."

His grip relaxed as her eyes mocked him; her thin, cruel mouth curled into a sort of smile, her skin ... her skin ...

He clamped his mouth around her sweet breast and gnawed at her nipple whilst her hand crept to his naked buttocks and kneaded the flesh.

"Yes, that's it," she murmured gently, "take your fill of me. Fuck me with all your strength, and I'll make you the finest lover in all of Byzantium."

He drew back, gasping, "God, where have you been all my life."

Her hand found his semi-erect cock, "I've been waiting. No more threats, silly boy. You understand?" He nodded, breathless. "You can't use and discard me like a camp whore. I'm highborn, resourceful and rich. But I want more. I want *power*. I'm well aware of your ambitions." Her hand worked at him, drawing back the flesh of his manhood, squeezing, tugging, moulding it ever harder, "I know you have ambitions too and I wish to be part of them."

"God, you are magnificent." He plunged once more to her breast, urgent now, desperate to consume her body once again.

She played with his hair as he continued to chew and lick, "You are my good, brave boy." He scooped up her legs under the thighs and pushed them back over her shoulders as he plunged into her. "Oh God," she rasped, closing her eyes as he began to thrust. He powered on, putting all of his lust into his efforts, and beneath him she responded. "Yes, that's it. Harder, my lover. God, Sclerus, I have mistaken you ... you are ... so ... fucking

... good!"

He gritted his teeth and increased his speed. As he drove into her, he studied her face, her eyes dilated, lips plumped with blood. She was a glorious beauty: her lithe waist toned and bronzed, her thighs slim and supple. As much like Helen, but more so. A curious, mysterious allure, irresistible; such wantonness, such control. He loved it, the thrill of her, the way she dominated him, taunted him with her words, contemptuous of his lovemaking, yet so responsive when he was inside her. As now, his flanks heaving, reaching further heights of effort and speed asshe squirmed beneath him, open and alive.

He loved fucking her. He squeezed his eyes shut, the sweat rolling down to sting them and when she cried out, he accelerated, their bodies a blur now, the bed groaning beneath them. Soon he would be spent, and she would lie there and mock him again, telling him he needed to do more, and his erection would grow. She knew it, played on the fact, capable of bringing out the very best in him. And now the revelation of her real ambition. She wanted to be his concubine, to share in the wealth and influence found nowhere else but behind the walls of Constantinople. Well, if that was what she wanted ...

"Oh dear God," she bleated, clawing at his back, nails raking through flesh. "I've never ... known you ... to be so ... Dear Christ ...

He threw back his head and, with his final thrust going far deeper than the others, he flooded her, kept himself there, eyes clamped shut, the heat surging through him, the passion overcoming him. He shuddered and cried out before finally collapsing on top of her, both bathed in sweat, hearts pounding, unable to speak.

"Sclerus ..." she said at last, her voice shaky, exhaustion almost complete, "My God ... I thought I knew ... But you, you are beyond ..." She bit his shoulder and he moaned, rolling off her, his limp cock wet as it plopped from her sex. She laughed at his heaving belly. "You think you can do that again?"

"Almost certainly," he grinned, a hand groping for her flat abdomen. "Make me into the finest of lovers, you said."

"You're almost there, my sweet."

"But your words ... you're cruel, Sylvie. Cruel."

"You know I don't mean it. I shame you because I know it causes you to try harder."

"Ah. Yes. To try harder." He sat up, ran a hand over his face, and sighed. "I need wine, then I'm going to visit Helen."

"Why not stay here?"

"I wish I could, but I must ensure she is well. Someone left early yesterday morning, one of the cooks. I think he may have gone to inform Maniakes."

Her fingers trailed down his back, "Are you fearful of his return."

He tensed, shrugging away from her caress. "Not *fearful*. The man holds no fears for me. Contempt is the only thought I have for him, remember that."

"Still your passion, my sweet. Reserve all of that for me." She pressed herself close to him, putting her cheek against his shoulder blades. "We could make a plan, put Maniakes into an uncompromising position. If we could devise a way to shame him, to cause dishonour ..." She let her words hang in the air.

"I'm already devising plans, the likes of which you would not believe."

"Oh, I do believe it my sweet. You are an ambitious and resourceful man." Her hand snaked around his bulk and sought out his flaccid manhood. He groaned. "Come back to me as quickly as you can, my body already yearns for you."

***

He went to his private apartment and scribbled down the few lines already conjured up in his mind. The servant hovered by the door, shivering in the cold of the early morning, the sun still some hours away from revealing its face.

Satisfied, Sclerus rolled up the parchment and placed it inside a thin leather wallet. He fastened the cord and motioned for the servant to approach.

"Ride, as fast as you can, and deliver this to my sister. Give it to nobody but her, you understand?" The man nodded and took the message, slipping it beneath his jerkin. "You must press upon her the urgency of her coming here. She must abandon everything, you hear me? *Everything.*"

"You can rely on me, my lord."

Sclerus grunted. He had little choice. Events were moving faster than he would have wished, all because of the assassin's presumptive strike. Damn the man, damn them all.

He pushed past the servant and paused to pull on a thick over-garment. "Go now. And stop for no one."

"My lord."

The man rushed out and Sclerus stared at the open door. From somewhere deep within the villa, the sound of his wife's snoring meandered through the emptiness. If she knew of the plots would she remain silent? Could she? Their match had been a good one once, before her parents had drowned in the Aegean ten years ago, while travelling across the sea to Constantinople; their flimsy vessel no match for the wild and sudden storm that broke upon them, smashing them to pieces. The bodies, white, bloated and purple veined, washed up on the shore had already provided food for carrion birds before someone recognised the remnants of their faces. That day had brought all of his dreams crashing down, a day when the reason for his marriage died. To live in idle luxury, fuelled by his in-laws' wealth. Well, now he had to make his own way. His estates struggled, whilst Maniakes's flourished. He clenched his fist. The tide had turned, but he must hurry before the General regrouped and again thwarted Sclerus's scheme. A good scheme, but a dangerous one. He needed to proceed carefully, with intelligence and fortitude.

Disaster almost followed with the assassin's ill-conceived actions, but a chance remained to regain the initiative, to take new, necessary steps. And his sister would play her part and bring everything to its rightful end.

She was to seduce Constantine Monomachus, rule his bed, addle his brain, and place the germ of an idea that only Sclerus could bring prosperity. And Monomachus would understand the logic, once Maniakes lay dead.

Sclerus smiled. A small set back, but one easily overcome. Of that he felt assured.

Twenty Five

Nikolias reached the command tent too late. He realised this even before he drew back the canvas flap, sword in hand, and looked through the dark interior, to find Maniakes long gone.

Sheathing the sword, he stepped back into the cold air. The rain had eased and across the sky, long streaks of black cloud separated, allowing the moon to poke through and give some light to the dark. Enough to navigate his way through the Palace complex, and help him make for cover if patrols passed his way.

He considered that the General might be in the barracks, perhaps returning to the palace itself, where Leoni once served as the Empress's handmaid. In truth, Nikolias knew he could be anywhere. The soldier he had mistaken for the General, a curious turn of events ... to wear the General's cloak, abroad in the dead of night ... Nikolias rubbed his chin. Maniakes certainly would know Nikolias's response to the death of his mother. A trap, premeditated, to lure in Nikolias? He could not begin to understand why. Nor did he want to. The act proved enough, and Maniakes had to die. Reasons and understanding would come later, perhaps in Heaven. Or hell. Whichever awaited them both.

No one troubled him as he crept between the sprawling buildings of the palace complex, passing through the Royal Gate, giving a brief nod to the guards. They recognised him and made no comment, coming to attention in time-honoured fashion. The rain dripped from their bronze helmets and he grinned, saying,"Get yourselves inside, boys," before he marched through.

Once out of sight, he checked around the Chalke Gate, the ceremonial entrance to the palace, its bronze gates running with rain. Beyond were his quarters, set inside the royal bodyguard barracks. Nevertheless, he took his time, not wishing to draw attention to himself by rushing headlong to confront the general.

Passing through the idealised statues of the Christ, he ducked inside and took a moment to shake out his cloak. In the corners, and against the partition walls, candles burned, giving off a warm, honey-coloured glow and he turned his mind to wishing all of it were a dream. If, only for a moment, to turn back time, stay at home, defend his loved ones. Grief, like a massive weight, bore down on him and his body crumpled with a spasm of despair. He waited, wiping the burning tears from his eyes with the heel of his hand before moving on with a brooding, heavy step.

He gazed at the soldiers positioned at every doorway, pristine in bronzed hauberks and helmets, hoplons resting against quilted pants, spears erect. He recognised one of the men as a personal shield bearer to himself and stepped closer. "I'm looking for the General. Has he passed this way?"

"Not tonight, sir."

Nikolias tried hard not to reel at the news. He'd banked on Maniakes being here, searching for Nikolias himself. Or at least his assassins. "Not one sighting?"

"Rumour has it he has left the city, sir."

Nikolias turned his head to the other guard who had spoken. "Left the city? Are you certain?"

"Like I say, sir, it is only a rumour."

Nikolias swung away, unconsciously gripping the hilt of his sword. Damn the man. Having ordered the vile deed, he had fled. No doubt with Leoni. But where to?

It did not take long for Nikolias to find out. Within the complex, the second tier of barracks proved virtually empty. The great days when the area buzzed with the sound of hundreds, if not thousands, of armed guards had long gone now. Michael's mismanagement and distrust had seen to that. Now, a mere token strength remained. But within the quarters lay the personal apartments of the General Komonos himself, a man considered to be the next leader of the Byzantine forces, both here in Constantinople and at every far-flung border post. He'd earned his spurs in the windswept plains of Anatolia, proving himself a master tactician on the field of battle. So far he had kept himself to himself, not indulging in the sort of power-politics that made Maniakes such a dangerous and unpredictable opponent. Where Maniakes lusted for power and glory, Komonos seemed content to carry out his duty and nothing more. A pious man, never partaking of wine or good food, his Spartan lifestyle endeared him to the Holy Church, which saw in him the promise of leading the Empire to a more religious state.

Knowing the hour was early, Nikolias nevertheless went into Komonos's outer apartments, roused the slumbering guard, and demanded they wake Komonos. Startled and mumbling a string of apologies, a guard disappeared through the great bronze door of the inner chamber and almost instantly returned, scratching his head, looking bemused. "He's not there, sir."

***

Outside, the rain now ceased, Nikolias was at a loss what to do next. He found a marble bench and sat down, shivering beneath his sopping cloak. Another hour and the dawn might ease his conscience. The death of the soldier in Maniakes's cloak played around inside his head. He had the urge to visit his chapel again, but how could anything wash away the frustration, the brewing hatred, the desire to plunge his sword deep into Maniakes's heart. No amount of praying, or begging for forgiveness could ever make him whole again.

At the sound of hobnailed boots crunching over the gravelled gardens he turned to see Komonos striding, determined, towards him, flanked by fully armoured guards. Nikolias, stomach churning, knew the moment had come, orders made, Maniakes sealing the trap. And Nikolias had allowed himself to walk straight into it, a blind, stupid oaf. He stood, legs quivering, and lifted his sword, knowing it was futile, that they would seize him, flog a confession out of him, perhaps condemn him not only for the murder of the soldier, but of his mother too. Maniakes, damn his hide, had won.

"Nikolias," boomed Komonos.

"General, sir," Nikolias shuffled his heels together and brought himself to attention. "Forgive me, but I did not—"

"The Lord General Maniakes has placed me in charge of the City whilst he is away. We are on high alert, and you are entrusted with a hundred spears to make your way to the port of Theodosius. At once."

Nikolias heard the words, but they jumbled around inside his head, making no sense at all. "The port? Why ... General, I'm not—"

"Pull yourself together. There has been an attempt on the General's life, made this very night."

"An attempt on his life?"

"Aye. One of his men, stabbed to death in the streets. He wore the General's cloak, so it is clear who the real victim was meant to be."

Nikolias's stomach lurched, his throat growing constricted.

"We are rounding up all potential suspects. You are commanded to go to the port and arrest the chief amongst them." He pulled himself up straight. "Harald Hardrada."

Twenty Six

By the time Nikolias and his force of well-armed soldiers arrived at the Port of Sophia, Hardrada was nowhere in sight.

Andreas, defiant as always, stood amidst the dockside workers who laboured at the start of a new day, together with the remnants of the crew sent to man the Viking's flagship. The ship itself remained tied up alongside the harbour wall, the gently lapping water rocking it with an almost hypnotic motion and Nikolias gazed at it, wondering why events had conspired against him with such venom.

"My mother is dead."

"Eh?" Andreas leaned forward, straining. "What did you say?"

Captivated by the water, its depth, the promise of a soft embrace, warm and comforting, Nikolias's voice barely rose above a whisper. "I went home and she was dead. Someone ... I thought ..."

"Nikolias." Andreas stepped closer, placing his hand upon the bodyguard's arm.

Nikolias pulled around, ripping his arm free, his eyes wide with alarm, bulging with surprise and bewilderment. "*What?*"

Andreas took a step back, his hands raised. "My friend, I don't understand ... your mother? What happened to her?"

Ignoring the question, Nikolias pushed past him, jerking his head for the armed escort to follow.

"Where are you going?" shouted Andreas, but Nikolias no longer listened. Orders needed following, personal problems and issues put to one side; his loyalty and duty as an officer of New Rome unquestioned.

He became aware of a man running alongside him. Nikolias strode along, his eyes boring into anyone who dared stand in his way. Only when the man managed to get ahead, waving his arms, did Nikolias stop, mouth open, breathing fast.

"Sir, where are we going?"

Somewhere, far away, the cry of seabirds. In their song, the promise of visits to distant lands, the freedom to range far and wide, independent, masters of their future. He gazed upwards, picked out the graceful flight and the pristine white plumage and wished to God he was anywhere but here.

"What have I done?"

"Sir?"

The rest of the escort promptly came to attention, a few exchanged murmurings, muttered questions beneath the rim of helmets.

"I thought it was him, you see." Nikolias stretched out a hand and leaned against the opposite wall. A series of images flashed across his eyes. Leoni, his mother, sitting at the table, consumed by their needlework, faces split into wide grins. Sunny days, rolling hills; Leoni running in a thin white dress, caught by the breeze, her young body naked underneath; his mother calling, 'Niko, you will be a good boy, won't you? Niko? You will, promise me you will.'

Voices from far away seemed to call him as a great heat rose up from his throat, across his face. Dimly aware of people, all of them jabbering, jabbering on and on, like a pack of wild dogs hungry for the feast, snapping at his heels, bringing him down. Down to the ground, where it was cool and still; where voices grew soft and the darkness offered so much, welcoming him, rescuing him from all of the worries and anxieties of a world gone mad. He went with it freely, the ground rising up to hit him solidly in the face and the world went black.

***

Hardrada and Ulf cut across the city, keeping to the backstreets, hoping that their attire and weaponry would pass unnoticed in the dark. On the way, Hardrada laid out the plan to his friend, one which had been fermenting inside his mind for some days now. The encounter with Andreas gave added impetus to his thoughts.

"This bodes ill," he said through gritted teeth. "They replace our men with hired mercenaries, cut-throats every one of them. How long into the voyage will it be before our throats are cut?"

"I don't understand," said Ulf. "Why kill us when only the other day Maniakes charged you with leading an expedition to Sicily? Why would the man change his mind so swiftly? He knows the Normans are a threat, and you are one of the few men who know the topography of the island, and who has knowledge of Norman tactics. To kill you ... *us* ... it makes no sense."

"Aye." They talked as they walked, keeping voices low, airing thoughts in the rain. Thoughts that had played like wild beasts in Hardrada's head. "I believed Maniakes lured me to the training ground to kill me. Away from prying eyes. But the more I thought about it, the more I realized none of that was true. If he wanted me dead, plenty of other opportunities presented themselves. Then, at the port, replacing our men ... why would Maniakes do that?"

"Then if not Maniakes, who?"

"Someone who could not be blamed, whose blood-stained hands would forever remain hidden. A person so desperate to appear blessed, righteous and holy. A person who has already caused the deaths of more than one Emperor but who needs the people to believe no such charges could ever be laid at their feet." He shook his head and grinned. "The Empress herself."

Ulf pulled up sharply and Hardrada took two or three further steps before he realized his friend no longer walked beside him.

The rain came down in an endless stream, blacker than the night itself. But Ulf stood beneath the torrent as if it were not there. "Why would she do all of that?"

Even the few spaces between them meant Hardrada had to shout to make himself heard. "Simple. She wants my gold."

***

Skirting the Severan Wall they slipped through the Pisan Quarter, shying away from those few brave enough to venture out into the chill of the early morning, and rested close to the Church of St Irene. They broke pieces of hardtack, munched and washed them down with warm water from a goatskin gourd. Ulf stretched himself out beneath the eaves of the entrance whilst Hardrada kept his eyes on the streets that led to the church steps. An iron-grey sky, streaked with slivers of silver promised some respite from the rain and he took out a whetstone and lazily honed the edge of his great battle-axe.

Ulf finally stirred, shaking himself like a great dog, to find Hardrada already going through a series of practised moves, swinging the axe, blocking and cutting imaginary attackers. People averted their eyes, none wishing to incur any wrath from the gigantic warrior, but Hardrada felt no threat. The people of the Pisan Quarter were renowned for their friendliness and generosity towards Byzantine citizens, their friendship crucial in maintaining Imperial control across the Mediterranean.

"I'm famished," said Ulf standing up, groaning loudly as he stretched out his arms. "Dear Christ, my poor bones."

"You shouldn't blaspheme on the steps of the Lord's House, you ignoramus."

As if noticing it for the first time, Ulf turned and lifted his head upwards, taking in the enormous entrance doors with the intricately carved pillars flanking them. A massive, ornate marble arch, hyphenated with grim sculptures of cowled faces, glaring down at any sinners seeking forgiveness within. "Bleak," he said and came down the steps. "I can't blaspheme. I'm not a Christian."

"Pagan ignoramus then."

"That's more like it." Ulf coughed, hawked and spat into the dirt. "Now, any chance you can tell me where the fuck we're going?"

Hardrada grinned, "What's the matter, you don't trust me?"

"That goes without saying. I'd just like a little insight into the shite that runs through your head that's all, shite you call intelligent thought."

"Ah, I see." Hardrada waved over to his left. "We're going to the port. I know someone there, an old seadog who might be able to sell me a ship or two."

"Sell you a ship? What the hell are you talking about, we've got a ship. More than one, over in Sophia."

"Aye, and we've also got a treacherous crew ... and that fucking Andreas with murder in his heart. No, we're not going to Sicily, or anyfuckingwhere these miserable shits order us to go." He looked about, checking that no suspicious passers-by listened. "Go to the barracks, muster the men. Have them gather together in the training ground, understand? I want one hundred and twenty of our best, lads, and we're going to drill them."

"Drill them? Harald, I don't get any of this. Talk plainly."

"Very well," he said and leaned close to Ulf's ear and told him the entire plan.

Twenty Seven

Being woken so early was not a common occurrence. Feverish, quick to anger, and a man of considerable strength, William Iron Arm threw back the bedclothes and glared at the man standing over him. "This had better be good."

The soldier, dressed in hauberk and coif but no helmet, snapped to attention. "He was insistent, my lord."

"Well, whoever he is he'd do well to remember who I am." He snapped his fingers. "Get me a robe." He stood shivering in his long nightgown. The fever had raged for two days now, and although still powerful, William sweated, white flesh tinged with blotches, and stooped forward. He hugged himself until the soldier returned with a thick ermine-edged robe of deep crimson and swung it around his lord's shoulders. William snuggled under the material and nodded. "I'd like warm wine. Spiced."

Nodding, the soldier withdrew to prepare

the drink whilst William shuffled over to his waiting panoply, pushed away the pieces of armour and took up his sword. He fastened it around his waist. Better to face a messenger armed. In these times, nothing was ever certain. Not only that, his bouts of fever were becoming more common. The first bout had seized him on the eve of Montemaggiore, but he had still managed to lead his cavalry against the Varangians on the following day and smash them. A good sword often helped when doubts surfaced on the faces of courtiers and visiting emissaries. All would do well to remember the moniker he bore with such pride. 'Iron Arm'. Not something he had come to lightly.

"My lord?"

He turned and took the proffered steaming goblet of mulled wine. Sniffing it first, he grunted and took a sip. Hot, well-spiced and sweet. The soldier had missed his vocation.

"Who is this messenger that so insists on an audience?"

"Jerome Bogarde, my lord."

William paused in the act of taking another drink and instead blew a trail of steam across the surface. "Indeed. Is he alone?"

"He is hot and sweaty after a forced ride, my lord."

"'Is he alone?', I asked."

"He is my lord."

And so he was, standing there with his back to the shuttered main window in William's great hall. He stiffened as the Iron Arm strode in and William smiled at that, noting the tension creasing the man's features.

"So." The Iron Arm drew closer, ran his eyes over the man's attire. "A long ride my man said."

Bogarde dipped his head. "My lord. I have ridden from the port of Bari, where my ship is docked. It awaits my return, before I am missed."

William frowned, "Before you are missed? Who by?"

"Gerald de Brie, lord."

"He has his orders, damn it. To stand down, whilst the council convenes; so what the hell brings you here, Bogarde? Your place is in Sicily, with Gerald's men."

"He is hard-pressed. We are all hard-pressed. When your message arrived, my lord, informing us of the forthcoming council at Melfi, Gerald's men believed they would be side-stepped, left to the Saracens or the Greeks. They came close to open revolt, my lord. Only by my insistence and my Lord Gerald's fortitude, was open fighting between the factions prevented."

"Let them be sidestepped? You mean, they believed I have abandoned them?"

"Aye, lord." He turned his eyes away for a moment. "And Gerald too, my lord. He has come to believe it."

"This cannot be so! Gerald de Brie is my most trusted Lieutenant. How did this base rumour arrive, tell me."

"Many of the commanders felt this way, my lord."

"Then I'll have their heads, damn them! If I

cannot have loyalty in my ranks, I am lost." At that moment, the strength left his legs and he teetered, a mist descending over him, causing him to reach out. A strong arm took his own, guiding him to a seat, and he fell into it, watching the floor swirling around before him. He put his finger and thumb into his eyes as a waft of heavy spices invaded his nostrils. Hot, sweet, someone tipped a little between his lips. At once the warmth returned, bringing with it a kind of relief.

"You are not well, my lord."

William blinked, dragged a hand across his eyes and saw Bogarde kneeling before him, the soldier behind. "Damn fever." He shook his head, took more of the wine. "I had a surgeon. A Saracen. A man of great wisdom and resourcefulness. They killed him."

"My lord?"

"Someone accused him of poisoning my food, but … no proof. They killed him. Since then, this damnable fever will not shift." Another mouthful. Slowly, he felt able to rise and, with a little support from Bogarde, gained his feet. "I often wonder if someone else poisoned me." He pulled in a huge breath and held Bogarde's concerned stare. "Don't fret, lad. I'm well. Well enough to keep my wits. Listen, I shall order my scribes to pen another message, an *order* this time, giving you full command of my forces in Sicily."

Bogarde's face drained of colour. "My lord! I cannot, I am merely a—"

"Damn it, lad, you've risked your life coming here this day." He leaned forward and gripped the young soldier's forearm. "I've always had suspicions about him and his cur of a Sergeant at arms. I can trust no one, but you ..." He grinned. "I knew your father, did you know that?"

Bogarde nodded, his eyes growing moist.

"Your mother too, truth be told. I'll not lie to you, lad. She was a comely wench, and your father did not stand in my way." He nodded, holding Bogarde's look. "Aye. There it is. He was strong your father, and loyal. Even after I'd bedded her, he swore his fealty to me, just as Gerald de Brie did."

"I have heard say it was Gerald himself who took my mother ..." He swallowed hard, "Who took my mother to his bed. And that afterwards ..."

"Aye, lad. You did not know of it, the truth?" Bogarde shook his head. "Well, best not tarry over things we cannot undo. He took her, and she resisted. A bad night, lad. Things we shall not speak of, not this day."

"I had suspicions, but ..." He dragged in a breath. "What are your orders, my lord?"

"I'll give them to you, in writing,lad, together with a contingent of men. That'll add a touch of iron to the words you'll convey. Then, I'll have Gerald back here, with Guille too. I'll not have my commands ignored, lad. You understand me on that? *Never.* You tell Gerald he's a bastard, and I'll roast his balls before I cut off his head. That'll set his guts to churning, and you'll enjoy the spectacle of that I'll warrant."

"That I will, lord."

William grinned. "But you, lad. You must hold in Sicily. It's not safe, not yet, not until the council reaches its decisions. And, besides, you have another service to perform."

"A service, my lord?"

"Aye. Unfinished business, lad." He chuckled. "Now, get yourself a new horse and prepare to take up your new command."

Twenty Eight

A thickset man hunched at a table, his huge rounded shoulders making him appear as if he had no neck, pored over a dog-eared map, his stubby forefinger tracing the line of a river.

Hardrada stood in the entrance to the man's ragged tent and waited for the huscarle beside him to announce his arrival. He gave the mail-clad warrior an icy glare, and the man responded by trumpeting, "Lord Sigurdsson would seek council, my lord."

The big man sighed but did not at first give any other indication he had heard. Eventually, after stabbing at a point on the map several times, he leaned back in his chair and regarded Hardrada keenly. His battered face bore the scars of innumerable battles, a single eye of piercing blue studying the towering Hardrada with scant indifference. Where the other eye should have been, only a red-rimmed black hole remained, an angry white line bisecting the crater, a token of an axe or sword blade.

"I've considered this ill-thought-out plan of yours," a low rumble announced, "to strike out into the Hellespont and make good your escape. I like it not." He dismissed the huscarle with a sharp wave of the hand. Hardrada waited a moment before stepping fully inside, dipping his head through the goatskin flaps of the sweat-filled inner sanctum. He wrinkled his nose but remained silent. "Have you lost your mind, perhaps? Two ships, manned by your Varangians, but piloted by me?"

"No one knows the channels better."

"Aye, and there's good reason for that. Everyone else is lying at the bottom of The Horn."

"I need to get away, Master Mariner, and I require your help in order to do it."

"To escape the Empress's clutches."

"My plan is not only for that. You know it full well, Master Talen."

"Bah!" Talen reached across the table for a pewter jug and poured himself a goblet of golden coloured liquid. "You promised me gold. That is my only interest in you or your fucking high ideals. To be King of the Norse," he shook his head and drained the wooden cup, smacking his lips. "I'm a Dane. I care not two fucking hoots for you or your fucking shithouse country, but I'm damned if I'll risk my life over such a pathetic plan as this." He pushed the map away. "It won't work. You'll never pass the chains."

"I have two crews who will be trained in a method, Master Mariner. I need from you two ships and your intimate knowledge of the tides. Leave the chains to me."

"Bah." He poured more drink. "If you manage to break out, where will you go? Eh? Answer me that. The good General Maniakes favours you, so I hear. The Patriarch Alexius also, although God knows why. You think they will simply let you go, waving you off from the quayside perhaps, whilst they shit in their pants over Normans and Bulgars?" He shook his head. "There is nowhere far enough for you to hide. They'll find you and cut your throat."

"I'll go where my desire takes me. The fewer who know that, the better."

Talen smiled. "Well, I know, you arse. North, that is where you head. Back to the frozen wastes."

"You'll not speak of it." Hardrada leaned forward. "I'll pay you well to keep your mouth shut. You understand?"

"Don't have it in your head to unsettle me, Norseman. I've killed bigger and better than you." He tipped the jug against the lip of the goblet and, finding it empty, cursed and hurled it towards the entrance. "You'll pay me two-thirds now, the rest when we reach the Dnieper." He prodded at the map. "I've worked out a route. It's hard, fucking harder than you'd believe, but we might succeed. You'll pay me the rest when we get there. *If* we get there."

Hardrada straightened, unsettled that the Danish mariner knew or had guessed the destination. "Half now, Talen. They are the terms."

"Then find yourself another pilot!" He nodded towards the map. "Although you'll be hard-pressed to levy a better sailor than me."

"Your fame precedes you, the reason I sought you out."

"Keep your lily-perfumed praises for your whores, Norseman. It's two-thirds, or you'll walk all the way to Russia."

Hardrada took in a deep breath. He wanted to kill him then, but he knew there was little choice other than the one laid out by Talen. He acquiesced with a curt nod and left the tent, his rage brewing.

Twenty Nine

Sometime after dawn, the rain finally stopped and she sneaked a look from beneath her covering of lambskins. The cart trundled on although the going proved laborious, the wheels forever sinking and sliding in the mud, but somehow always managing to pull free with great sucking sounds.

Every plank of wood, every spoke, every hinged and jointed section creaked and groaned alarmingly. Leoni felt sure if she moved too much the whole lot would collapse, dumping her into the stinking ground; she kept herself as still as possible, while every muscle screamed to stretch out and her stomach growled for food.

She could not remember when last she ate. Beside her lay a small goatskin gourd, long since drained of water, the only thing he had given her, this monster who had walked into her life and in a few horrifying moments transformed the world into one of pain and terror.

To look back at what had happened was too awful, but her mind refused to shut itself away from the memories.

Nikolias had barely left when the stranger came through the door, a slight man wrapped in dark clothes. Leoni had screamed and he'd backhanded her, sending her crashing against the far wall where she squirmed and whimpered, recalling in that one, dreadful moment the worst excesses of the vile Monomachus. Was the same about to happen again? She'd wriggled into the corner, bringing up her knees, looking on in disbelief as she saw him take Niko's mother by the throat and lift her off her feet. She'd made no noise and did not attempt to beat him off as he dropped her across the bed, the sound of his laughter, harsh and cruel, etched into Leoni's brain.

As long as she lived she would not forget that sound, laced with sadistic malice, triumph, rejoicing. He'd slipped out a curved dagger, straddled the old woman, and sliced through her throat, sawing the blade forwards and backwards, severing every tendon and vein.

Leoni had gasped at the sight of the blood leaking from the mother's throat, her legs thrashing like two strings of thin white thread. Such a tiny woman, so frail and dying as her hands clawed at the horrific wound. Even before she grew still, the murderer swung around and paraded himself before Leoni, thick trails of red gore covering his black clothes like ropes. He'd moved towards her and she'd screamed, squeezing herself into the corner of the room, knowing life was about to end.

But it hadn't.

Instead, he'd bundled her into his strong arms, dragged her outside and thrown her into the back of a cart. And here she remained, trembling with the cold, with rain soaking into the core of her being.

Around them, a profusion of trees of different shapes and sizes pressed in from all sides. Water dripped in a constant shower, almost as strong as the rain. Every time the mule knocked a trunk, a new deluge followed and she whimpered, made herself smaller, and wished to God she could find escape in sleep.

When the cart stopped, she held her breath, waiting for his hands to grab her and pull her to the ground. What his plans were she had no idea, but she felt sure that rape figured large in them. He had not uttered a single word since the attack, but one glance at his cruel, black eyes told her everything she needed to know. A killer, efficient and heartless. He would not baulk at having his way with her, so she waited and tried to steel her heart.

She heard him getdown, the cart yawning ponderously to the left, then slamming upright again as he hit the ground. A stifled grunt and his boots receded into the distance. A chanced look saw him striding towards a cluster of white-walled buildings, one more squat than the others, shutters open, door barely keeping upright, its hinges so rotted.

He went inside and from deep within came the sound of voices, one angry, the other low, menacing. She had no doubts to whom that belonged.

After a few moments he re-emerged, and she ducked down amongst the lambskins before he spotted her. She squeezed her eyes shut, listening out for his breathing, the cart rocking as the tailgate swung open and rough hands grabbed her and hauled her out.

Leoni stood, bent over, clutching her lambskin around her, fear gripping her limbs, contracting her larynx. She managed a tiny bleat when he put his hand under her chin and lifted her face. He grinned and in the shadows of the hood he wore, his eyes burned.

Inside the hovel, a fire crackled in the grate and an old woman swathed in black moved around with heavy pots held in two gnarled fists. She placed them on cast-iron stands over the burning wood and shuffled away into an anteroom without even a glance.

A man, a great lumbering hulk with an enormous barrel for a belly, replaced her; bald-headed, wisps of beard stroked his sweat-stained jerkin straining over his bulk. He dried his hands on a tattered cloth, surveying her with greedy eyes, a wet tongue lolling across his lower lip. She almost vomited at the thought of him, of what transaction had passed between this vile creature and her captor.

A heavy shove in her back almost toppled

her, and she floundered for a moment, her lambskin falling to reveal the thin silk shift, the lines of her body clearly visible. The big man groaned and she saw it, his erection tenting his loose, Arabian trousers. She recoiled, gathered up her cloak and covered herself. Finding a rickety stool, she sat down, hunched over, her eyes cast to the floor.

The old woman reappeared and stirred the pots, mumbling as she did. Leoni caught a few words but did not recognise the coarse, nasal dialect. It may have been Thracian, and if so, that meant they were many miles from the City. They had travelled most of the day and night, setting a good pace despite the rain. If Nikolias managed to follow, how could he know which direction to take, how far to travel? Despair crushed her: she pressed her face into her hands and wept.

A hand stroked her hair, and she snapped her head up. The old woman, face as wrinkled as a dried prune, cooed and ahh-ed, continued to stroke the blonde locks and smiled, toothless but kind. "Sweet," she said, more of a croak than anything. "Hungry?"

Leoni managed a nod and the old woman hobbled away, back to the pots, ladled out a bowlful of steaming broth, and came back with it. Leoni took the bowl and a wooden spoon, and stirred through the thick, orange liquid, the pieces of roughly cut vegetables and mutton bobbing to the surface. She took a tentative sip; the flavours burst into her mouth, almost causing her to swoon. Without further ado, she attacked the food, shovelling spoonfuls greedily into herself, eyes closed, enraptured by the taste.

After three bowlfuls, each wiped clean with unleavened bread, Leoni settled herself into her clothes, feeling so much better than before. Strength and awareness returning to every part of her, she studied her captor keenly as he too took mouthfuls of broth, but far more slowly than she. All the while his eyes scanned the room, alert for danger. She saw, for the first time where the folds of his robes parted, the sword at his hip and the dagger, the killing weapon, and she shuddered.

Her captor warmed himself by the fire, great clouds of steam rising from his clothes. She so wanted to join him, to feel the warmth seeping into her body, but when the owner of the dilapidated tavern blundered in again, rubbing his hands and gawping in her direction, she decided remaining sat on the stool would be the safer option.

Behind him shuffled the old woman, who elbowed the oaf aside, and waddled over to her, a heap of clothes in her arms. She smiled and nodded. "Sweet," she breathed. "Dry clothes. Come."She held out a gnarled claw and Leoni found herself, as if in a dream, gently steered out of the room into a dark, cramped space towards the rear of the building, with nothing more than a slit in the wall to allow in any light. The woman clattered around, moving the various bits of furniture and boxes to clear a space where Leoni could stand and remove her clothes. For this was clearly what the old woman intended and Leoni thanked her, stroking her bony shoulder.

The woman shook her head. "Sweet," she said and went out again, pulling the feeble door to as near to being closed as possible. The wooden slats joined haphazardly, with great cracks running their length, and Leoni took a moment to check outside. Nothing moved, so she went to the clothes and shook them out.

A full-length undergarment, thick pants and a jerkin. A pair of felt boots completed the collection. Grossly too large for her, they were nevertheless thick and warm and, most importantly, dry. Without a moment's thought, she shrugged off her still sopping lamb's wool robe and let it fall to the ground. Then she took the hem of her shift cross-armed and lifted it from her body.

She wished she had a towel to dry herself with and, as the goose bumps broke out across her flesh, she hugged herself, her teeth chattering.

The flimsy door crashed open and there he stood, chest heaving, the belly bulbous, the erection greater than ever. She yelped and stepped back, an arm across her breasts, the other hand stretched out towards him as he leered and drooled.

"*Sweet,*" he moaned and stepped into the room, his chubby little fingers working away at his baggy trousers, which fell to his knees, his stubby cock poking from beneath a thick thatch of curly black hair.

Leoni pressed herself into the corner, turning her head away. If she fought him, she would die. But if she allowed this hideous slug of a man to molest her, how could she ever take another breath without shame or disgust welling up inside? True she had taken all the Emperor Michael could give her, had lured him in with her tales of the General's prowess, feeding his perversions, capturing his heart. And in the end, his lustful enthusiasm, his desire and need for her brought a kind of calm, an acceptance of who she was. There could be no mistaking Michael's affections were real, and this had had a curious effect upon her. To be loved, if love it was.

But this, this was beyond anything she could ever accept. As she stared with bulging eyes at the man's approach, her mind closed, her body limp.

At a great explosion of smashing timber, collapsing crates, a bluster of movement, she snapped herself awake and saw the captor, his arm around the oaf's throat, watching the ensuing struggle.

Both of them blundered into the mess of the room, urgent and violent. The captor's forearms bulged with the strain, his teeth gritted in his efforts to squeeze the life out of the other. However, the man's enormous bulk, when he managed to turn, crushed down upon his attacker and they fell in a tangle of limbs, both squawking, desperate to gain advantage.

Leoni took her chance, swept up whatever clothing she could, and ran out of the tiny room and straight into the arms of the old woman.

For a moment they stood and stared, both of them alarmed. Leoni recovered first, pushing past her, and scrambled into the pants and jerkin she had found. As she suspected, they proved too large, and she frantically scrambled around for something to lash everything tight around her.

She fell on some twine and grabbed it, binding it around her waist, stuffing in the jerkin. Behind her, the fight continued, wood shattering, and screaming reaching new heights. The old woman skipped from one foot to the next, fists rammed into her mouth, whimpering like a wounded beast.

Waiting no longer, Leoni went back into the main room and made straight for the door. As she tugged it open, the sunlight burst upon her and she staggered backwards, blinking madly, arm across her face. Almost blinded, she stumbled outside.

The mule stood as before, chomping away at some oats someone had provided.

And beyond the animal, three men. Dismounted, their horses tied to an overhanging branch, they contemplated her with questioning looks. Armoured men, soldiers, hauberks freshly oiled, helmets shimmering in the sunshine.

Their bemused expressions turned to full, toothy grins and when they spoke, Leoni immediately recognised their tongue.

Bulgars.

Thirty

Sclerus knelt next to the bed, head in his arms, half conscious. The night had been long, but Helen slept soundly. When he had come to her, a slight fluttering of the eyelids told him she still lived. Fear had gripped him, thinking the murders had frozen her heart. Such things were not uncommon, and Helen was not young. Shock often proved deadly, so he left his lover's arms and crept into the General's villa to check on Helen's condition. Now, with the morning marching on, Sclerus knew he should leave. If the General arrived and found him this way, the cut of a sword blade would soon follow.

He stood up and she moaned, stretching her arms and legs. The blanket fell away from her body to expose her breasts and at once the stirring grew in his loins. He fought against the urge to plunge into her. When he forced himself to turn away, a woman stood in the doorway. A woman he knew all too well, a mocking glint in her eyes, her mouth curled up at one corner, knowing.

"You really are a bastard."

He grunted and moved past her. "There was an attack, in the night. I needed to make sure, but she seems fine." He watched her approach, languid, graceful, as slim as a stream and golden limbed. Why would any man need anyone other than her?

"I came as soon as I could," she said, the voice of honey rolling over him, memories of warm nights when he would slip into her bed and feel her arms about him.

"Things have accelerated," he said, glancing around for wine, or anything to slacken his sudden thirst. "But I'm glad you're here."

He found a jug, half-filled with ruby red, and he poured himself a goblet and drank it in one.

"My servants are at your home, stabling the horses," she said, taking the jug to fill her goblet. "I met a woman there, in your bed. She seemed annoyed."

"Ah." Sclerus moved over to the rear doors, which opened out onto the ornamental garden, the leaves of the many trees still covered by a fine film of rainwater. The heavy, musky smell of damp vegetation invaded his nostrils. Nevertheless, he stepped outside and sat at the table under the shade of a grape vine, lovingly threaded around wooden stations to create a cool, natural parasol. She joined him, her richly embroidered blue gown swishing across the ground.

"Who is she?"

"My neighbour's wife."

She gaped for a moment before recovering. "*Another* neighbour's wife?" He nodded and she chuckled. "Dear me, Sclerus, but you play a dangerous game. Bedding two married women. One for political gain, the other ... for vanity?"

"Drusilla no longer holds any attraction for me. I need companionship, so I seek it where I can."

"You need sex. Don't try to fool me, your own sister. I know you all too well."

He looked across to see her expression, that annoying, contemptuous look, all-knowing, all-powerful. "Scleriana," he said, feeling the tightness around his throat, "events have somewhat overtaken our previous plans. Someone broke in, killed Helen's guards, her manservant. She took to her bed and has remained there. The General is on his way."

Her eyes closed for a moment. "Wonderful. And you had no knowledge of this attack?"

"Of course not! Our man is a lunatic, out of control. I never ordered him to—"

"So you *did* know?"

"No, not this!" His fist came down hard upon the table. "Damn it, woman, you think I would jeopardise all our efforts by ordering such lunacy?"

"Well, you employed him. Tell me," she leaned forward, hair falling across her face, but her lips still visible. Full lips, so soft, so alluring. "Are you listening to me?"

He ran a hand over his face and when he peered at his shaking palm, he saw sweat. Of all the women he had known, and there had been many through the years, none of them brought such fire to his loins as his sister. The shame of it gnawed away at him constantly, but as he rutted above his many conquests, images of her always invaded his mind, the sensation always making his orgasms so much more powerful and satisfying. "Yes. I'm listening."

"You *employed* him, paid him well. You can dismiss him as easily."

"He seems intent on finding his own way."

"By attempting to kill the General's wife?"

"If he had meant to do that, it would be her grave we would stand over, not her bed. But he has played his hand too strongly, and now Maniakes will return and the truth will out."

She gripped his arm. "You stand firm, brother! We haven't waited all these years for you to throw it all away now, for one stupid mistake."

He rolled the goblet between his palms. Her words rang true. The years they had discussed and debated long into the night, poring over their schemes, knowing all along that circumstances would always stand against them. And then came Michael and suddenly there was a hope, a chance. Until the Patriarch Alexius saved Hardrada.

"Not one," he said, his voice low.

Thirty One

Nikolias stood, shame-faced, shivering whilst Alexius shuffled towards him. Despite the afternoon sunshine spilling in through the open windows, the cold bit deep. The Patriarch of Constantinople, aged, bent over, seemed to feel it more than the chaste officer of the royal bodyguard before him. Face ashen and drawn he now used a cane to aid his walking.

He sighed into a chair, shaking his head. His ceremonial robes hung heavy on his withered frame, and he ailedwith a mysterious sickness no one could explain. The physicians had done what they could, had studied the ancient texts, but no amount of blood-letting or purging eased his condition. Now, a rambling wreck, rumours circulated that his days were few. As the man's blue lips trembled, Nikolias saw it was true.

"I am troubled by all of this, Nikolias,"the great man said, his voice unsteady, thick with sickness. "Nothing grieves me more than the death of your mother, but, for the love of God, what were you thinking when you took that girl to your home?"

Nikolias wanted to shout out, to grip the Patriarch by the throat, and shake him, venting all the anger, frustration and loss on this sad old man. How could he ask such a thing? *That girl?* So much unspoken in those two simple words. "She is not a whore," he said when he found the strength to do so.

The old man shook his head. "You've fallen in love with her, and she has blinded you to the truth."

"No."

His eyes came up, and for a moment they blazed with a memory of his former power. "Don't doubt me, Nikolias. I may be dying but I still know the ways of this world, the tendrils of sin which reach out from a woman's body.

"That's not how it was. She was *forced*, holiness, by Maniakes, to become Michael's whore, but no one else's."

"So you say. And I do not doubt the General played a lewd game, but if everything else is true, you cannot blame him for your mother's death. It has no purpose, despite the girl's disappearance."

"He wanted her for his own. She told me as much. It is he who is in love, Holiness."

The old man's hands wormed around the top of the cane, modelled on the ancient Imperial eagles of Rome, crafted from pure gold. "The General has left for his country estate, Nikolias. Someone broke into his villa, assaulted his wife."

Nikolias's mouth slowly dropped open. "I don't understand. Why would someone do that? A thief, desperate for money perhaps, or ..." His words hung unfinished.

"The girl is not with him. Nor does she reside in his chambers. The Empress claims no knowledge, and her sister Theodora stays shut away in a sort of crypt, lost in her prayers ..." His eyes dimmed. "Ensconced with my deputy, Psellos. You might consider that to be a righteous thing ..." His shoulders drooped and for a moment Nikolias thought the man had fallen asleep. As he reached forward, however, Alexius stirred, taking in a sharp breath, his hand halting Nikolias in his tracks. "I'm tired, tired of it all, Nikolias. The intrigue, the deception. I believed that with Michael's removal the Empire might find a kind of peace, that through Theodora there might be a way. Then the General, he came to me and together we began to turn our minds to another way. Constantine Monomachus, a man of huge intelligence but the most sordid perversions. If in some way we could hone his mind and body, return him to the one, true faith, perhaps then we might be able to restore order. Wed him to Zoe, reach agreements with our enemies, and begin the slow road to recovery. And now this. If what you say is true—"

"It is, Your Holiness. I swear it."

"Then we are already too late. Other forces conspire to undermine us." He reached over and gripped Nikolias's hand with surprising strength. "It is not Maniakes who took the life of your mother, but another. An infinitely more dangerous and wicked individual."

"But who, Holiness? Who could have done such a thing, and to what purpose?"

"To cloud your judgements, my son. To send you into such a rage that you would thoughtlessly murder the General, thus removing him. An obstacle to their machinations. They would soil your hands with his blood, whilst I poisoning me. Hardrada too. That was why you were sent to arrest him. The way would then be clear, my son. Nothing could prevent them from seizing power."

"Who?"

Alexius blew out his breath. "If I knew that, Nikolias, do you think I would be sitting here pontificating over their dastardly crimes? They have recruited Andreas, that much is clear. I believe they wanted Hardrada to sail away into a trap."

"You cannot know that for certain."

"Yes, I can, my son." He pushed down on his cane and rose to his feet, sucking in his breath a few times, before shuffling across the room to a closed cabinet. He fumbled with a key and opened it. "The General entrusted you with a payment of gold, Nikolias. I hope you still have it."

"Of course, holiness, but ..."

The old man turned, clutching a piece of parchment. "Andreas wrote to me. Why, I am not exactly sure. He told me Psellos had ordered him to find a crew of trusted men, to take Hardrada to Sicily where he would be killed by the waiting Normans." He waved the parchment in his twisted fist. "It's here, signed."

"Then we must arrest them, every one of them."

"We cannot. To do so would reveal ourselves to those others who remain in darkness. The true enemies, the true perpetrators of this scheme."

"So what do we do?"

"Before you leave for Kiev, my son, you must take a detour and speak with the General. Tell him what has transpired, and warn him. Because I feel those who assaulted his wife are the same ones who murdered your mother, and we are all being lured into something terrible and sinful."

"And what of Andreas?"

Alexius shrugged. "Disappeared. Perhaps he has already taken his life, but his shame must be great. To have betrayed my faith, to have taken his lead from Psellos ... Lord have mercy on their souls, but I am fearful for the life of Theodora and for that reason I have one more deed for you to perform, before you leave for the General's residence. A deed that will cleanse you of all your sins, my son. For it will serve the Empire well, and could even save it. And as a payment, you are to take for yourself the casket the General gave you."

Nikolias heard his heart pounding in his ears, the only sound he believed to be real. The Patriarch's words were fanciful, pieces of nonsense. He was dreaming all of this, he remained face down in the street where he had fallen. All the rest, the waking up in the Patriarch's apartments, the cool hand of a nun stroking him to full consciousness. No, all of it mere fancy. A dream. The casket, the gold, the gems? *"For myself?"*

"Aye." Alexius came forward, holding Nikolias's gaze with his own. "And for that, my son, you must kill Psellos."

Thirty Two

They were burly men and brutish. Leoni knew she had little chance of escape, not now. They barred her way, arms spread out as if looking to grab hold of her as they crept forward, appearing to relish the game, laughing, exchanging comments in their guttural, gruff accents. She stood in the doorway, waiting and watching, wondering what to do.

Behind, her captor grappled with the innkeeper and God alone knew which of them had come out on top. Ahead, these three, their intentions plain on their face. Why had life conspired against her so brutally? Was this what she had always feared would happen? Punishment for her sins. The strength drained from her muscles; she fell to her knees, hands clasped in front of her heaving breast. If this were punishment, then let it be so. She decided not to resist, for perhaps with that came certain death. Better to allow these animals to use her as they seemed fit, then wait for an opportunity to escape.

One of them made a grab for her. A rounded man, body heaving against his coat of mail, right arm covered with a thick padded material, well protected against attackers.

But not the captor's blade.

It sang through the air as he stepped into the open, the blade cutting off the Bulgar's arm just below the elbow. The man screamed with a high, animal shriek and staggered backwards, blood pumping from the great wound.

Leoni shrank back, cowering against the adjacent wall to the door, watching her captor move like a cat, darting swiftly this way and that as the two other brutes drew their weapons, attempted to hack him down. But the captor, unburdened by armour, proved too fast. He cut, slashed and struck, sword slicing through the mail as if it were paper, stabbing at unprotected flesh, killing with a rapidity and grace that Leoni found terrifying and yet strangely mesmerising.

Breathing hard, the captor swung about, lips pulled back in a wild, animal-like grimace. "You bloody bitch," he snapped and was upon her in two strides, grabbing her by the throat and hauling her to her feet. "That's twice I've saved you and I'll not do it again."

He threw her down, sheathed his sword and went over to the dead men, before turning to the first of them, whose arm still pumped blood, lying in a tight huddle a few steps away, whimpering. Leoni watched him, wondering how life could change so dramatically, in a few simple movements. One moment alive, with nothing but lechery on his mind, then there in the dirt, watching his life draining away. Dear God, what had become of the world to make it so awful?

Satisfied any danger had passed, the captor went through the saddlebags, checking them for provisions. He grunted. "We must be on our way. We'll take these horses, leave the mule and the cart, that way we can make more time. You can ride I take it?"

She gaped at him, his nonchalance, his total disregard for what had just happened. He made no reaction, any more than he would to the rain falling again. Natural. Nothing to comment upon. She nodded. "Yes."

"Do it then. We'll take all three horses and ride as hard as we can."

She wandered over to the horse as if in a dream and stopped when the moans of the wounded Bulgar pierced her thoughts. "You're not going to leave him like that are you?"

"Why the hell not? He would have done the same with you after he'd finished." He swung himself up into the saddle. "They're murdering bastards and are now rotting in a fiery furnace, I shouldn't wonder. So don't waste any time worrying about them. We have to get on."

"But he's bleeding to death."

"Good. Perhaps it might afford him a few moments to contemplate his life, try to find some excuses to spout off to God when he walks up to the gates."

Leoni took hold of the reins and hauled herself into the saddle. The big mare stomped and snorted, but she managed to keep control. Many years had passed since she had last ridden, but her captor seemed as at ease as he had with the killing. "And what about the old woman?"

"She's inside with her husband."

"Her hus ... Holy God, you have killed them too?"

"Save your fucking graces, you dirty bitch! I know what you are, so don't come the fucking patron saint of lost souls just because it suits you to do so. You fucked your way through the royal family, so don't feign disgust with what I do."

"I never killed anyone ..." She bit her lip, knowing she lied. She had killed, stoving in the Scythian's head when he wandered into Constantine's chambers a hundred years ago. How could things change so totally within such a short space of time? She looked down at the dying Bulgar. The man would have gladly raped her, as would the innkeeper. Neither deserved her pity and yet ... "Where are you taking me?"

"Well away from this shit-hole. Now stay close and don't try anything stupid."

He kicked the horse's flanks and moved away, its companion tied up behind, and Leoni grudgingly followed.

They rode through the morning at an easy canter, despite the captor's insistence at them needing to make good speed. The countryside flowed by, rolling hills covered with cypress and larch and meandering streams. The land basked under a warm sun, the sky clear and bright. At any other time, Leoni would have enjoyed the stint in the saddle, but not now. She had no idea where they were going, or what awfulness awaited her. Of one thing she was sure – if the captor meant to kill her he would already have done so, a thought which brought her a modicum of peace. Whenever she allowed her mind to rest, however, images of the frightful bout of killing rose up once again and her mood grew dark and troubled.

Towards the top of the rise, she stopped to view the vista spread out before them, the glistening trail of a river wending its way through verdant plains. Here, no cities crouched in valleys, no sprawling farms or huddled villages. A vast, open stretch of uninterrupted countryside, the like of which she had never seen.

"The next city is Adrianapolis," he said without warning, leaning against the pommel of the saddle. "From here we veer west, follow the course of the river, and by this evening we shall be at Sclerus's estate." He turned, hawked and spat into the dirt. "You know Sclerus?"

Leoni studied him: the thin sharp features, the long nose. Sometime in the journey he had pulled back his hood to reveal a pale, stubble-covered face, chiselled as if from granite. When he turned to her, she looked away quickly and shook her head.

"He'll like you," he said, a touch of menace in his voice. "A great lover of women is our Sclerus."

"I'll not be another man's whore."

He sniggered, "Dear Christ, woman. I know all about you, how the General made good use of your body then shared you with the Emperor. You are what you are."

"The General ... I was his concubine."

"Oh, and there's a difference is there?" He looked out over the rolling fields and sighed. "When I was a boy, my father would take me up into the hills where we kept our goats and, on days not unlike this, we'd stand and stare. My father loved the land. But I always wanted more. I knew how great the world was and so, when I was old enough, I travelled down to Constantinople and signed up for the Varangian Guard."

"The Varangians? But you are not a Norseman, surely?"

"No. I'm as Greek as you. But they took me in and they trained me and I became better than most. I fought all across the Mediterranean, and in Sicily I served Maniakes and stood side by side with Hardrada." His eyes darkened. "I saved his life, the bastard. Killed two Normans who were pressing in from behind, and when I received a sword thrust under my arm for my troubles, he left me on the field to die."

For a moment Leoni thought the man might cry; his face drawn, the lips trembling. But it was not sadness that changed his features, she sensed it. "You hate him?"

"Aye, I do that. Maniakes too. They are the same those two. All they care about is their own glory. Bastards the pair."

"How did you survive?"

"I found a hovel and an old woman gave me shelter. She tended my wounds and when I recovered, I took a ship across the sea to Byzantium. By then the place was in turmoil. The old Emperor was dead, and Michael was already moving against the Varangians. So I left and met up with a man who made me a very tempting proposition. Sclerus. He had ambitions for power, his hatred for Maniakes driving him. So I offered myservices and the plan took shape. I watched you all, although none of you knew it. I spied, listened, learned. Sclerus wanted the Empire weak but could not move against Michael as Maniakes had him well and truly trussed up." He grinned. "With you. He loved you, I think."

"Love?" She shook her head. "I doubt if either man had the slightest idea what that word means. The General wanted to control Michael, and yes, he used me, and I did it willingly but ..." She allowed the words to fade, memories stirring, Michael's hands roaming over her, his voice soft, husky with desire. Now he lay in some stinking hermitage on the edge of the world, blinded and alone. "He wanted me to do the same with Monomachus. A vile, disgusting man, worse than any of them. I couldn't. I have had enough."

"Ah, the words of the recalcitrant. A sudden rush of piety is it, or shame?"

"Neither. Something you wouldn't understand."

"Ah, I might. I've seen you, my lovely. With the officer. The one whose mother got in my way."

The words slapped her across the face and the tears sprang forth; she held onto the reins and shook at the memory of the terrible moment when he came and killed.

"You're a whore, no matter what you say. And that boy, he no more loves you than I do." Another hawk and he spat out a thick globule of phlegm. "Jesus, I think something is wrong with me." He put the back of his hand against his mouth and coughed. "Love is a pile of shit, my lovely. I saw what love can do when I followed Hardrada on his sojourn to the north. The great oaf, Crethus, and that measly son of a whore, Andreas. Hardrada saved Andreas and I laughed whilst I watched them. Fucking idiots they are, noses stuck up their own arses. There was a girl, and she tended to them and when a war band came, she saved their lives again. Maybe she had a sense of duty, or did it all out of Christian good grace, but I saw the change in Andreas. And then she died."

"Died? How?"

He grinned. "You may know how to fuck, but you know nothing about life, do you? It's many faces. How, without warning, disaster comes a-calling. Well, I saw their fucking faces and I grew mad. You hear me? *Mad.* So I crept into the camp and found her, recovering from having the Scythian's hand around her throat. He probably thought she was dead." He chuckled. "Well, she soon was. I got down next to her and slit that beautiful throat of hers. Those bastards blamed each other. Still do. Their hatred has become legendary, and such knowledge brings me great pleasure." He sniggered. "So, we go to see Sclerus and he will use you with Monomachus once again. And when Nikolias, your innocent lover, discovers his mother dead and you gone, he will think it can be only one person. Maniakes. The whole plan is so sweet, so simple. And," he pulled himself upright, readjusting the hood to cover his face, "it's all worked out beautifully."

He kicked his horse and moved on.

Leoni watched his back for a few moments, her body racked with a mix of anger and hatred but also with an overwhelming feeling of sadness. Nikolias. He must be out there, somewhere. Searching, desperate and alone. Had he already tried to kill the general, been thwarted, killed himself? They had not so much as kissed, but the kindness in his face, the touch of his hand, the promise of a good, simple life ... she pulled in a ragged breath. This bastard had walked in and destroyed everything. If she had a knife, she would put it in *his* throat.

Perhaps she still could. All she neeDdo was wait.

***

Towards late afternoon, the captor reined in the horses and took out some unleavened bread, dates and hard cheese. Seated under an almond tree, they ate in silence; she nibbling at the corners of the bread, he munching it all down with relish. He gave her a gourd of red wine, which tasted sweet and strong. If she could lie back against the trunk, she might give herself up to rest. But no sooner had she closed her eyes than she felt him stir and stand. She eyed him, tendrils of fear spreading through her. He held his sword, his body taut and alert.

"Riders," he said, crumbs of bread falling from the corners of his mouth.

She scrambled onto her knees, her mouth open, and listened out for the slightest sound.

They came from both sides, three men in one group, four in the other. They bore shields and long lances, and she could smell them long before they came into view. Their horses whickered with tension and as they drew near, she saw they were exactly the same as the three at the tavern. Comrades at arms, those others perhaps sent ahead to scout for danger, and now their companions here to find out what had happened.

Some half dozen paces away they stopped, horses snorting, the men's eyes boiling from beneath the nasal bars of their helmets. Mail coifs, full hauberks, surcoats of earth brown, the lead man leaned forward in his saddle, the leather groaning, and he grinned. "Well, well, what have we here, two little lovebirds?"His Greek impeccable, without accent.

Leoni realised, with a sudden rush of hope, that perhaps she had mistaken them for foreigners when all the time they were compatriots. As she stood to begin her explanations, her captor stepped across and held up one hand. "She is my captive," he said, voice even, low, no edge of fear. "I am taking her to be tried for murder."

She gaped and was about to speak when the lead soldier swivelled around and roared, "Hear that lads, the little white dove is a murderer."

They all joined in, but their laughter held little humour, more a mocking resonance of contempt. "Ask him where Bertrand is," another grumbled.

The lead soldier nodding vigorously, smiled down at the captor. "Good point. You have seen Bertrand have you, friend?"

"I'm no friend of yours."

"Ah, yes, I can see that. I can also see dried blood on your sword blade." The silence stretched out and then, one by one, the soldiers lowered their lances, levelling the points towards the captor. "Explain that, can you?"

"We had trouble. At an inn."

"Trouble? Interesting." The lead soldier pulled himself up and adjusted his belt; the only one not bearing a lance, his air of ease clashing with the tense readiness of the others. "What sort of trouble might that be?"

"The sort that requires a sword."

"Ah." He smiled. "Now, let's just assume I believe you ..." He held up a mailed fist as his companions bristled and grumbled, "*Assume* I said. This inn ... small place was it, man and wife? Big fella, pot-bellied? Outside, a mule and a cart full of goods bound for market?"

Leoni's stomach turned to water. They *knew,* damn their eyes! They were playing some hideous, insane game, and in a few moments they would charge and death would follow.

"I'll kill more than one of you before this is over," snarled Leoni's captor. "And you, *friend,* you will die first."

The soldier sucked in a sharp breath, "Steady, friend. No one said anything about killing." He laughed, looked at his companions, shaking his head. "Lads, we have here something of a warrior. A man well versed in the art of killing. We had best not close with him, my lovelies, as he's bound to chop off our heads!"

"Well, in that case," said one of the men from the group on the other side, "we'd better not take any chances with the fucker."

Leoni screamed as the arrow struck the captor in the throat and he dropped to his knees, shock gripping every feature. He gagged, the sword clattering to the ground, and both hands tore madly at the shaft. The first lance hit him in the chest, the second through the back of the neck. Two more in his sides and he slumped forward, the breath rushing out of him in a single burst.

The lead soldier, still grinning, slowly slid from the saddle and went over to the dead man, toed him with his boot, and glanced across to Leoni. "The truth, girl, or I'll cut off your pretty little head."

"He killed them."

"All three?"

"Yes. The man and his wife too." She stepped over and spat at her captor.

"Bastard."

"It's true what he said? You're a murderer?"

"My name is Leoni, and I am the handmaiden of the Empress Zoe of Byzantium. This man kidnapped me in the hope of gaining a ransom. My mistress would pay a great deal for my safe return."

"Would she indeed?"

"Yes, she would."

"You don't look like a handmaiden," he stepped closer, flicked at Leoni's coarse jerkin with a mail-enclosed finger. "More like a cowherd."

She threw out her hands, her delicate, manicured fingers the only proof she required. He grunted. "No cowherd," he said. "A good price you say?"

"A fortune." She cocked her head, arching a single eyebrow. "But only if I am untainted."

"Ah, yes. Of course. Well, in that case my little lady, we'd better keep you safe, hadn't we?" He chuckled, took her by the elbow, and led her over to her horse. "Bit stupid denying you'd met up with my lads when you're riding their horses. Don't you think?"

"Aye," she said and mounted the mare. She looked down at the corpse of her captor. "But he always was stupid."

"Yes. And now he's dead. Who was he?"

"God knows. I don't think I want to know."

The man barked some guttural commands to the others, one of whom dismounted and rifled through the corpse's clothing. After a few moments he stepped away, muttered something indecipherable and got back on his horse.

"Well," said the soldier after a few moments of silent consideration, "we are in something of a fix. You say you do not know where he was taking you?" She shook her head. "Well, in that case, we'd best take you to camp, that way we can decide what to—"

"Take me back," she cried out.

The soldier gaped at her. "What? Where? To Constantinople? Are you mad?"

"Send word. A message, a demand. My mistress will pay you handsomely for my safe return."

"She's lying," hissed one of the others.

The lead soldier frowned. "Perhaps. Perhaps not. It is three days to camp, only one to the city." He rubbed his chin.

"I say throw her down and fuck her. All this talk about ransom, it's all shit, Egor. That's all it is."

The lead soldier, Egor, continued to consider the alternatives before holding her eyes and smiling. "Very well, little bird. Here's the deal. We'll take you back, send word to your mistress. And if the money does not come back with my man, we will fuck you under the walls of the city, then leave you for the crows."

"Fuck her anyway."

Egor chuckled. "It may well come to that." He licked his lower lip slowly. "It may well indeed come to that."

Thirty Three

A group of mounted soldiers clattered down one of the streets. Hardrada watched them go by, pressing himself into the shadow of a shop doorway. A difficult thing to execute, given his size, but the soldiers appeared too intent to give him so much as a glance. When they had passed, he stepped out into the daylight and marched in the opposite direction, making his way as quickly as he dared towards the Severan Wall.

Within the hour, he met up with Ulf who took him without a word by the arm and steered him towards a nearby tavern, deep within the sprawl of the Genoese and Amalfitan Quarter of the great city. An area that spread across the wall and brought together a rich and thriving populace of merchants and tradespeople from across the Mediterranean basin. Inside the place buzzed with the sound of a dozen different dialects, and both wine and ale flowed freely. Ulf found a corner and sat his old friend down, catching the eye of a serving wench. "English ale?"

She grunted and disappeared amongst the throng.

Hardrada wrinkled his nose. "This place stinks of putrefied fish."

"Aye, and not a Greek in sight." He leaned forward. "I went to the training ground, spoke to the lads. Ranulph is preparing two crews."

"You've done well."

Ulf sneered. "Not as well as I could have. They've split the guard, put over half in billets down by the Port of Theodora. Things are moving quickly but have been put on hold."

"Oh? Why, what happened?"

"Maniakes has left the city. Rumour has it he may not be back for days, perhaps even weeks."

"So, they stall? The expedition to Sicily, it must wait until the great General's return?"

Ulf nodded and sat back with his arms folded when the wench returned with the mugs of ale and slammed them on the table. She waited, glaring until Ulf tossed her a coin. She eyed it suspiciously, bit it, then disappeared again, satisfied.

"They wait, but not for the General. Orders are coming through thick and fast. Komonos, or even Kekaumenos may well take the lead."

"Both very able generals."

"Aye, and they want you, Harald."

"I know that." He picked up his ale and blew off the froth from the top before taking a large mouthful. "That bastard Andreas wanted to stitch me up, send me into a trap. You saw him down there, Ulf. Saw the burning in his eyes."

"Aye, I did. But it's not Andreas who makes the orders, Harald. And those orders have changed. It seems the idea of a trick has been overtaken with a real desire to crush the Normans. So we *do* sail, and we do fight."

"It's a load of shit. The Normans have regrouped, and they kicked our arses last time. It won't be easy. Better to reach some diplomatic agreement."

"That's what they're doing." Ulf drank, smacked his lips. "In the meantime, they want a presence on the island, in order to negotiate from strength."

"No. I've had enough of them. I'm going north, Ulf. I'll let them think I'm with them, but to hell with their plans and their fucking intrigues. Time to think for myself, for my own destiny. I'm travelling north and I'm will be king."

"That'll be harder than beating the Normans, Harald. Magnus is king. He won't step aside, not for you, not for anyone."

"I have my own plans, my friend. I've waited this long, I can wait a while longer."

"They won't let you go, you know that. Zoe, Alexius, even Maniakes. They'll stop you. And there's the great chain across the Horn. You can't leave from Port Theodora, nor from Neorion."

"I've struck a deal with Thelon."

"That turd? Jesus ..." Ulf drank again. "Can he raise the chain?"

"No one can, not without a small army to overrun the guards at the placements."

"Well, then. What do you propose to do?"

"The men Ranulph has, we'll train them. I've thought on it, long and hard, and there is a way. But the men will need to respond to instructions, as quickly as possible. That's where I'm heading, right now. To the training ground and Ranulph's men. I'll show them what needs doing, and then we're off, my old friend. Off home."

Ulf shook his head, sighing loudly. "It's not that easy."

"I know. But we will do it. All we need is time. Time and effort."

Ulf shook his head again, more emphatically this time. "My friend, I haven't told you the worst part."

As the noise of the inn receded into the background, Hardrada noted the change in Ulf, almost as if he were pressed into a corner, trapped. The look in his old friend's face, the hard stare, the thin mouth. Tension. Stress. Despair. "The worst part?"

"Aye. The Varangian Guard has its old commander back, and he's there, even as we speak, strutting like an elk before them."

Rancour pooled within Hardrada's guts and unconsciously his hand fell to the hilt of his sword. "I thought he was dead."

"So did we all. But he's not. He's been killing Bulgars in Anatolia and now he's back, and he's hungry for a fight." Ulf leaned forward, his voice barely a whisper. "And he wants it with you."

Thirty Four

Rising earlier than usual, Psellos partook of olives and oil-soaked bread in the solarium, leaning back in his wicker chair to watch the sun coming up over the sea of rooftops. No matter in which direction he turned, the city remained, a vast sprawl of humanity, houses, villas, mansions of every shape and size; punctuated with endless soaring spires of the many churches, abbeys and monasteries that made Constantinople what it was – the centre of the Christian world.

Word had reached the Patriarchs of the Byzantine Empire from the West, rumours of popes asserting their authority, of gruff voices, disenchantment and open resentment. But Psellos and everyone else knew the West had neither the resources nor the inclination to attempt any forced agreement between the two arms of the one, true faith. The Normans blustered, the Bulgars glared menacingly, but neither had the strength.

At least not yet.

Psellos considered the idea of an armed confrontation between them and dismissed it almost at once. Such a thing could never happen, at least not in his lifetime. For now, he had more pressing matters and he unconsciously turned to the far wall and the closed door leading to an anteroom. Inside slept Andreas, who had come in the night, informing Psellos of the clash at the port. How Hardrada had threatened, swung his axe, hewn two men with two strikes, and the rest, seeing such strength, had thrown down their bundles and fled. The news kept Psellos awake most of the night,his mind filled with alternatives. But of one thing he was sure. The incident proved to him, if ever proof were needed, that Hardrada must die. Nothing could ever be achieved whilst the heathen Norseman lived.

His servant came in after a tentative knock, head bowed, shuffling forward. "Forgiveness, Your Holiness, but there is a man at the door who wishes an audience."

Psellos snorted, popped the last olive into his mouth and grunted, "Send him in."

The servant retreated and after several moments the man appeared, a heavy grey cloak enveloping his slight frame. Psellos scanned him from head to foot, clicking his tongue at the bedraggled creature. "News?"

Closing the door gently behind him, the man threw back the cowl, revealing an ashen face, riven with deep worry lines and small, darting blue eyes, the thatch of black hair in stark contrast to his pallor."Holiness." His voice betrayed his origins; a man from the East, beyond the borders of Persia.

Psellos nodded to a chair in the corner, which the man brought over and sank into. He took a proffered plate of bread and oil and wolfed the few scraps down before Psellos could even take a breath. "You take your service to the extremes, Imrahn. I do not wish for a dead spy, but an effective one."

"If I did not live my life as a beggar, Holiness, I would have no life at all."

"I pay you well. I trust you are wise enough to store it away."

"Believe it, Holiness. I look to the future with relish. A smallholding, some sheep, maybe olive trees." He ran a forefinger around the plate and sucked off the last few drops of oil. "There will always be a need for olives."

"A good plan, Imrahn. I'm glad to hear you look beyond the present. Not many men do."

Psellos pulled in a breath, growing serious all of a sudden. "You have news?"

"His Holiness the Patriarch has met with the young officer, Nikolias. He travels north, with documents for the King of the Kievian Rus, Yaroslav."

"Documents? You know what they contain?"

The man shrugged, a thin smile spreading across his grizzled face. "I do not yet possess the skill to look through the seal of the Holy Mother Church, Holiness. He has another document, one given to him by General Maniakes. Quite the little delivery boy is our Nikolias. He is attending the funeral of his mother this very day …" He looked out from the solarium towards the morning sky, streaked with red and purple. "It might rain, Holiness. That would prevent him from making good time; an accident maybe, or trouble with his horse ... who knows." He turned again to the deputy Patriarch. "An opportunity to search his saddle bags."

"I do not want him harmed; such a step would be too great and may alert the Patriarch himself."

"He is already alerted, Holiness."

Psellos felt his throat narrow. Thirsty, he reached for the pewter jug of wine and poured himself a good measure. He gulped it down and sat, the back of his hand pressed against his lips, staring into the distance. "You know this for certain?"

"I sat beneath his window, Holiness. A beggar, sleeping in the shade. I heard every word."

"Tell me."

Imrahn did so, recounting everything that had passed between Nikolias and Alexius and with each new revelation, Psellos sank deeper and deeper into himself, becoming more anxious with every word.

When the spy came to the end of his recount, Psellos pushed himself to his feet and moved to the open window, leaned against the balustrade and contemplated the orange groves below.

"Holiness. If you wish it, Nikolias will never leave the city."

"My concerns lie not with him," Psellos managed, the words catching in his throat. He coughed. "How goes the poison?"

"My man tells me it is working, and no one suspects. Except, of course, the Patriarch himself."

"And yet he continues to take it."

"His manservant tastes all of his food, Holiness. Of course, the manservant knows exactly what to eat, as it is he who administers the dose. So, despite his suspicions, the Patriarch takes it."

Psellos swung around, his face hard, resolute. "Instruct him to increase the dose."

"Holiness, if we accelerate then real suspicion will surely follow."

"I don't care. I want him dead, you understand me. Dead. By the end of this day. Alexius will move against us all if we do not prevent him. You hear me?" His eyes narrowed and the bones beneath the skin of hishands, gripping the balustrade gleamed white. "Against us *all*!"

***

Nikolias learned from the stable-hand the Kievian Rus emissaries had already left the previous day. The news came as no surprise, the Rus visitors' patience growing thin as they awaited the young officer's return. The events of the previous day, and the night, were of far more import to him than any journey north. But now, standing there in the coolness of the Church of St Thomas, those events seemed as distant as the stars. The funeral canticles complete, the priest's rituals done, Nikolias made the sign of the cross three times across his chest and turned around, leaving his mother and his past behind.

He winced at the sun before positioning his helmet over his head, cramming it down, adjusting the chinstrap. He stooped to pick up his sword and belt and the shadow fell over him.

"The Patriarch seeks a final word, sir."

Nikolias breathed out slowly, straightened his back and buckled the belt. He eyed the man standing in the shadows, unable to make out his features, but knowing who he was. "Can you not tell me? I must leave, as His Holiness knows well enough."

"There has been ... an *incident*."

"Explain."

"His Holiness would prefer you to hear it from his lips, sir."

"Is it safe?"

"It is now."

Nikolias snorted and walked down the steps. At the bottom a sudden thought brought him up abruptly and he turned again to the shadow. "You're not coming?"

"My work is done, sir ... for now. I must return to my duties."

And with that, the man slipped around the entrance pillar behind which he had hidden and slinked into the side street running alongside the church building.

Nikolias shook his head. Damn them all, even the Church. Why did God allow them to employ such slithery eels to do their dirty work for them? Alexius, Psellos. They were all at it. Shaking his head, he stepped into the open plaza and hurriedly made his way towards the Royal enclave and the palace of the Holy Patriarch of Byzantium.

***

The main doors flung open, flanked by two guards, resplendent in ceremonial uniforms of bronze, red cloaks hanging from shoulders, hoplons glowing white. They stiffened as Nikolias approached and he gave them but a brief nod before stepping inside.

There were more guards, two holding a man between them, a third next to a dead body. On a low couch, shivering violently, Alexius and one of his older servants comforting him.

He looked ghastly but a light flickered in his eyes when he noticed Nikolias, and he pushed the servant away. "My son," he said, voice shaking, old.

Nikolias strode forward and went down on his knee. "Holiness. What has happened?"

The Patriarch nodded towards the man struggling between the two guards. "He came, hoping to find me dying." He pointed to the dead body. "My manservant. His task, to poison me."

Nikolias glanced to the corpse. "You suspected as much."

"Aye, but not from my own household." Gripped by a sudden bout of coughing, he held on to the man beside him. "Only Simon here remains loyal. Forty years, man and boy." He forced a smile and Simon whimpered. "Hush, you old idiot. I do not ail, thanks be to God. But I am old." His eyes lifted and met Nikolias's. "The creature over there is a Persian spy of my deputy, Psellos."

Nikolias stood up, moving a hand to the hilt of his sword. "We'll get him to testify, Holiness. Present this abomination to the Empress and—"

"No, my son," snapped Alexius quickly, "the

Empress must know nothing of this. We must shield her from all such concerns. Within a fortnight, she shall be married to Constantine Monomachus and you, Nikolias, must deliver my message to King Yarolsav. But I needed you to know, my son. Psellos is the agent of someone whose ambition is so great, they will do anything to succeed. This cur," he jabbed a finger towards the cowering spy, "has told me much, not all of it without some persuasion."

"Damn you, old man," spat the struggling Imrahn.

Without warning, Nikolias swung around, took a few quick steps and rammed his fist into the man's guts. With a great outrush of breath, the spy squawked and sagged in the arms of the guards, his body limp, gagging for air.

"*Bastard,*" hissed Nikolias and gripped the gasping man by the jaw, lifting his head. "Who killed my mother, you shit."

"Nikolias, *please,*" cried the Patriarch.

But Nikolias ignored him, rage engulfing him. "And where is Leoni? Tell me, you piece of shit, *tell me!*"

As his hand went for his sword, other hands took him by the shoulder and more guards filled the room, wrestling him to the ground where he thrashed and screamed, kicking out, frothing and cursing.

From beneath a veil of red rage he watched them drag out the spluttering spy and he grew quiet, allowing his body to relax, controlling his blood lust, his desire to kill. His breathing slowed, more shallow, tension dissipated from his muscles until, at last, they released him and he sat up.

"Nikolias," the Patriarch's voice came like a cool breeze from across the far side of the room.

Shame came then, overpowering him, and Nikolias put his face in his hands and wept.

From somewhere, he heard gentle orders, and hobnailed boots withdraw, and the door closing. But Nikolias remained on the floor, desperate to rid his mind of what had occurred, praying silently for forgiveness. When a hand rested on his arm, he gasped and turned. The kind, old face of Alexius smiled at him. "My son, you have suffered much. But there is no need to torture yourself."

"Forgive me, Holiness."

Alexius closed his eyes, shook his head. "Nikolias. There is nothing to forgive. Imrahn worked for my deputy, Psellos. A spy, seeking out information wherever he could. We are surrounded by opposing factions, all intent on one thing only – power. I am not alone, however, in having my own network. Psellos's manservant is my creature and it was through him I learned of Psellos's decision to end my life this very day. I had long suspected it, and bribed the manservant to bring me information whenever he could. He felt that today I should know the truth." He nodded at the body. "There it is. And Imrahn, he gave it all up, as I knew he would at the word castration."

"He needs to die."

"He is but a pawn, Nikolias. The real villain lies to the north and the estate of General Maniakes."

Nikolias felt the rage returned, "I knew it.

Damn his eyes, I knew it was him!"

Alexius's grip on his arm tightened. "No, Nikolias. Not the General. His neighbour."

Nikolias frowned, his thoughts jumbled, the Patriarch's words making no sense. "I don't understand."

"Neither do I. Not all of it. So, my son, you must take a diversion. Before you continue north, you must deviate and visit the General and find out what you can. For there you will also find your mother's murderer, and ..." he smiled, "Leoni."

***

From the open balcony of his solarium, Psellos saw the approaching soldiers, their hauberks glittering in the sun, and he knew.

He turned and leaned back against the balustrade. He should get word to Theodora, give her something of an explanation. She deserved as much. For years they had been confidants and only lately had that become meaningless as the need for Zoe's exquisite embraces became ever more urgent. Perhaps she should know first, but time had defeated him. Betrayed, not only by his servants, but by his own rash stupidity. He should have waited, been patient, not acted precipitously. Zoe would have counselled caution, but belief in his abilities overrode it all. And now, the royal bodyguard hastened, carrying an arrest warrant. He knew without needing telling. Alexius had survived, all plans thwarted, no doubt Imrahn spilling it all before he spilled his guts.

Damn them all.

Raised voices echoed from the corridors

beyond his chamber door and he crossed the marble floor and turned the key. The tumblers engaged with a heavy clunk and he stepped back as the first fists pounded.

"Open the door, in the name of His Holiness Alexius, Patriarch of New Rome!"

Psellos, tears streaming, walked backwards, his eyes never leaving the bronze inlaid timbers of the door, which shook with the relentless hammering. Soon they would bring axes or maces and smash their way in.

His back jarred against the balustrade, and he twisted his neck and looked below.

The voices louder, something heavy crashed again and again against the woodwork.

Alexius would not be denied.

Well, damn him to hell, he'd deny then all, except God. For God would wait and He would judge. Past, present and future. All of it there for scrutiny, all of it for weighing up. And at the final account, Psellos knew his place in paradise was assured. A good man at heart, all he had ever wanted was peace.

And the love of a good woman.

***

They burst through the door in time to see the deputy Patriarch throwing himself from the open balcony. Two soldiers rushed forward, hands outstretched, desperate to grab him. Too late, they slammed against the balustrade and watched Psellos in his final mad flight, hurtling through the air to smash on the stone ground below.

Thirty Five

The stable hung heavy with the smell of stale sweat and horse manure, but it gave Nikolias a sense of comfort. Although an infantry officer, he loved to ride, had done so since an early age. He adjusted the bridle of his mount, pausing, nuzzling the great beast's nose. For a moment, he drifted back to a time when he and his mother would wait with beating hearts for the return of his father from campaign.As soon as he appeared, the great red plume streaming from his battered helmet, Nikolias would burst into a run, pounding down the dusty lane, desperate to be in the arms of the man who meant so much to him.

How many times had he waited? How often did nightmares visit him with visions of his father lying dead in a distant field? The relief at having him back proved overwhelming, and Nikolias would cry and his father would chide him for being too sensitive. "If you wish to be an officer in the Guard, my son, you'd best toughen up your resolve!"

Those words echoed through the years as he stood and took in the aroma of horse and hay. There came the day, of course, when his father did not return. They brought his panoply and sword and laid it down on the table. He and his mother stood and stared, neither able to register the enormity of what it meant.

The men who came said the words. None of them meant anything. What good were words when one's own blood seeps into the earth and all you have left is a memory?

Nikolias demanded to see the body. He was fourteen. The men said it was impossible: his father's body lay in a ditch together with a hundred others. They couldn't even tell him what country they had fought in, but it was distant and barren, bleak and harsh. And the Patzinaks, or Pechenegs as others called them, were fierce and indomitable fighters. They raided the Empire's northern regions around the Balkans and proved a constant threat. On one such expedition, Nikolias's father had lost his life. The Emperor Michael had recruited such men, whom he called Scythians, into his personal guard, and Nikolias lost all respect for royalty. It rankled him seeing these animals roaming the streets, arrogant, without fear of reprisal until, of course, the Varangians under Hardrada destroyed them to a man.

And now, here he was, travelling to give tribute to a distant king in order for the same Viking to marry his princess and secure the north against future incursions. The machinations of diplomacy lost on him, he saw the sense in keeping strong men close, and despicable ones deep in the ground.

Like the man who had murdered his mother and taken Leoni.

He doubted he would ever find him, but perhaps the detour to alert Maniakes to what was happening would give him an opportunity. The road was long, arduous, and no one could predict what waited for him along the way.

***

"I am neither Greek nor Bulgar," he said, watching her as Leonie pulled her fingers through her hair in a desperate bid to untangle her locks. "I am from Kiev, and I am Rus."

She understood his words but gave no acknowledgement, eyes downcast, staring into the ground. Not so far off, the others busied themselves around a makeshift camp, their guttural voices hard and unfeeling.

"My name is Egor."

She fought against the urge to turn her face towards him. Feeling his eyes boring into her, she shifted uncomfortably, swivelled and stared out across the plain. They rested in a slight dip, shaded from the sun by a line of thickly packed trees. At this time of the late afternoon, the heat sucked everything dry, draining energy, making every movement slow, laborious. "I need to bathe," she said.

"There is the river," he said, standing. He adjusted his belt and stretched. "We will camp here, boys," he called to the others, who barely glanced across.

Leoni sighed. "The river might be dangerous."

He grunted. "There is an inlet, not more than a hundred paces. I'll show you."

"I'd rather not."

Egor smiled. "You think I'll take advantage of you? You yourself said the Empress would not pay for ravished goods."

For the first time she returned his gaze. "I spoke true,"

"I do not doubt it. I'd be a fool, wouldn't I, to squander the ransom before it is even collected?" He turned away. "We won't be long, boys." And with that, he motioned for her to follow him. After a brief pause, she did so.

***

They sat and followed Leonie and Egor with their eyes. The smallest of them, a slightly built, swarthy youth with a great mop of black curls framing his aquiline features, shook his head. "You think he'll fuck her?"

"More than likely." The largest, a huge, lumbering brute who wore his hair shaved on top but with thick ringlets hanging down each side of his face, prodded at the spluttering fire he had just managed to light. "But he's no idiot. I've followed him a half dozen years or more and never known him to put anything before personal gain."

The young man stretched back on the ground, both hands behind his head. "I've never been to Constantinople. Heard of it, obviously, but never so much as caught a whiff of its splendour."

"*Splendour?*" The brute snorted, rocking back on his heels. "I've seen many places, none of them splendid! I've been to Jerusalem, Baghdad *and* Constantinople. They're all shit heaps."

The third one of the group sat down with a loud expulsion of breath, brows bristling. "Constantinople is the eye of the world. It may not be a glittering jewel, but it is the greatest city on earth. There a man could make a life, be someone."

"Pah!" the brute turned and spat into the dirt. "You're a dreamer, Ahmed. You always have been."

Ahmed smiled, grim but silent.

"I can't believe you have visited those places," said the youngest, "and not been affected by them."

"I was *affected*." His face split into a wide grin, displaying a fine set of chipped and blackened teeth. "By the fucking stench!"

They laughed and fell silent, each lost in their thoughts.

A wind gathered from across the plain, sending up tiny eddies of swirling dust and, beyond the distant mountains, the sun made its inexorable journey below the western horizon. Already the air turned chill. The next day would see them arriving at the walls of the great city but a long night lay ahead.

"You think we will receive a good ransom for the girl?"

"Who knows," said Ahmed, voice low,

uninterested. "Whatever the total, it won't be enough. It's never enough."

"I'd like to find a place," continued the youth, staring at the purple, unsullied sky. "A farm. Not so big, just enough for me and a good woman. Live out my days in peace." He craned his neck to peer at the brute who stood, like a great bull, staring out across the plain. "That's not so much to ask for, is it?"

The brute shrugged. "I lost my family to a Norman raid half a lifetime ago and ever since then I've been on the road, selling my sword to whoever was willing. I've had a good life. Plenty of women, good food, wine. Dice." He screwed up his eyes. "Dreams? Dreams never come true, Julius." He held the youth's eyes. "Trust me. When you've witnessed as much death as I have, you'll understand the truth of it."

"The truth of what?"

"Life. We come screaming into this world through no fault of our own, and we leave it screaming with a stranger's knife in our throat. Everything in between, you seize for the moment and enjoy what you can."

"And afterwards?" Julius propped himself up on his elbows. "When the curtain falls, Victor? What happens then?"

The brute shrugged again. "I'm not one for God, if that's what you mean."

"No, maybe not God ... but you must believe in *something*?"

"Must I? Why must I? I've seen enough killing to realize that nothing is permanent in this world. Flowers grow, wither and die. Dogs and cats and goats and sheep, they all grow old, fall and die. Men too. In battle, I've watched life end, seen it spurting out in great red rivers. Heard the pleas, the cries for mothers. Nah," he shook his head, "life is hard and cruel and nobody gives a damn about you or anything about you. Take what you can, that's what I say. Because tomorrow, you are dead."

"But today is not yet done."

Both Victor and Julius turned and stared at Ahmed, who had risen to his feet and looked out towards the east where the incline reached towards a stony outcrop.

"What do you mean," said Victor, already reaching for his sword.

"I mean, where is Stavros?" Ahmed turned and looked to his two companions. "He is meant to be on watch."

"So where the fuck is he?"

No one spoke, but all of them felt the air change, the temperature drop.

***

Leoni gasped as she plunged into the crystal waters, striking out towards the centre of the sheltered inlet. Here, surrounded on three sides by craggy cliffs interlaced with an abundance of shrubs, which clung for grim life between the cracks and crevices, the air was still and warm.

Egor watched her from the bank, the pulse of desire surging through his loins constant. When she had stepped out of her jerkin and pants, her body gleamed like alabaster, unblemished, as smooth as marble, the muscles rippling through her thighs, the buttocks round and taut. She had glared at him, demanding he avert his eyes, and he had grinned, challenging her; she had responded with a look of arrogance on her beautiful face and let her clothing drop. Holding his stare, she turned and dived beneath the water. And now, he sat and wondered if he might dare take her for his own. She would resist, of course, but time would show her the intelligence of such a match. He had money, enough to make a life. Put away his sword, lie with her and fuck her every day. Together they could make something of this world.

"Have you a wife?" she'd asked him when they came to the place where the river divided and stood on its bank and watched the smaller tributary meander by. She swept a hand through her long hair, pushing strands behind her ear. "A family? Where do you come from?"

He laughed. "So many questions. Why do you need to know?"

"Because you're different. Not like the others. There's a humanity about you. I see it, hidden deep, but there all the same." She sighed and stepped down to the inlet's edge and tentatively dipped her toes into the water. Immediately, as if struck by something sharp, she snapped her foot back and gasped. "It's freezing!"

"The mountains are cold at this time of year. The summer has turned to autumn." He came up next to her. "When the winter comes, this place is brutal. There is so little shelter, and the wind screams across the plain, cutting you like a knife."

"When that man, that *monster* kidnapped me, I thought I was dead." She slowly sat down on her haunches. He followed her and they sat silence.

"Where was he taking you?" Egor asked at last.

"I think it was to General Maniakes. I was his concubine, his whore. But ..." Her voice trailed away, tinged with anger.

"You told me you were the Empress's handmaiden. Was that a lie?"

"No." She turned her face to his. "But Maniakes used me. Promised me riches and comforts, a place at his side. In return I had to seduce the Emperor himself, learn the secrets of his heart, his plans and schemes, make myself indispensable to him."

"And this you did?"

"I had little choice. When Maniakes first took me to his bed ..." Her eyes closed for a moment. "I'd never known such ... passion. Such desire he had. On and on, he loved me as no man had ever done before ... " She gave a rueful smile, "Or since. I was lost, unable to resist. If he'd told me to fuck with a jackass, I would have done it. Anything to please him."

"So he loved you?"

"*Love?*" She laughed aloud, "Dear Christ, no! I don't think he even knows the meaning of the word. No, there was never any fondness or care. He wanted my body, nothing more."

"And you gave it to him."

"Whenever I could, yes. The more he did it,

the more I wanted. Even when I was with Michael, all I could think about was Maniakes. And the bastard couldn't give a damn if I lived or died, as long as I did as I obeyed him."

"So why did you stop?"

"I found myself ..." A hand moved to her eyes, a hand that trembled. She sniffed as she pressed the heel of her palm to her eyes to stem the tears. "Michael. The Emperor, he was ... like a little boy. Kind and giving. All he wanted was to love and be loved. And I began to ... *change*. You understand?"

"Not really, but carry on."

"Michael was a monster, in so many ways. Ignored as a child, unloved, the Empress adopted him and groomed him to rule. But all the while Michael had different ideas. Yes, he wanted power, but he wanted *absolute power*. No more hangers-on, no more priests and bishops telling him how to be a good servant of God. He *was* God. But more than any of this, he wanted devotion and love. I gave him love, and he responded. Towards the end, my feelings towards him changed from revulsion to a kind of desire. I found myself thinking less and less of the General and more of the Emperor."

"And so you decided on another path? Another life. You whores are all the same. You fuck hard whilst all you ever do is count your money. To hell with tomorrow. Today I'm going to lie on silk cushions. You're no different from me and my men."

Her eyes blazed. "I'm not a whore, I was

forced. But by so being, I began to see that there could be another life. Michael promised me the same as Maniakes, but I believed the Emperor. I could see it in his eyes."

"Ah, yes. Like you could see the humanity in mine?" He snorted and stood up, kicking a large stone towards the river, the sound of it plopping beneath the rippling surface lost in the constant growl of the flow. "So what happened to these thoughts of yours, eh? Where have all these promises of a good life disappeared to?"

"Michael was overthrown, deposed and banished. As his concubine, my life could have been in danger, but the General came to me again and for a moment I believed he had done so because of me. Me." She shook her head. "The bastard had other plans. Always the plots, always the abuse. They brought Constantine Monomachus to the city to become a sort of puppet Emperor, and my job was to seduce him, find his weakness, and force him to be Maniakes's creature. I couldn't do it, so I fled. In the confusion of the fighting, it was easy to simply disappear."

"But you were found, by that evil-looking bastard, the one who killed my men. Who was he?"

"An agent of the General's more than likely. A spy, assassin, call him what you will. He must have been watching me for days, weeks. Perhaps months. He found me and he murdered Nikolias's mother and brought me here. The rest you know."

"Who is Nikolias?"

"An officer, in the Royal Bodyguard. He found me, helped me escape."

"Dangerous thing to do."

She smiled. "I think he loves me."

"Ah," Egor nodded, pursed his lips, smiled. "Such romantic sentiments you have. The whore turned devoted servant."

She flew at him with bared teeth. He caught her wrists, turned her over and dumped her into the earth, straddling her. She squirmed beneath him, but his strength proved too great and he pressed down on her and kissed her full on the mouth.

"God, you're a beauty," he said and moved back, unbuckling his belt.

She sat up, "You can't. If my mistress knows, she will not—"

"She already knows," he said, stepping out of his pants. "You fucked the General and the Emperor himself. She's not a fool. So now," he licked his lips, "you can fuck me."

"Wait, please." She stuck out her hand, palm forward, and stared at his long cock, hard and ready. "Please, I do not want you to—"

"You want it slow, is that it?" He leered, inclined his head and cackled. "A whore with preferences, eh?"

"Please. Let me bathe, and then we will lie together." She got to her feet and went to him, hand circling his hardness. He groaned. "I want you, but not like this. I will show you what lovemaking can be like, if you'll let me."

His eyes misted over, his mouth drooled. "Damn it, woman, but I need to fuck you!"

"And you will." She smiled, leaned into his neck and nipped at his flesh. Her hand took on a new urgency, moving along his length. "How could I not want you?" She breathed into his ear and felt his knees buckle. "I'm going to bring you to the height of pleasure, and you'll never want anyone else for as long as you live." Her lips floated over his. "But I want it to be good, for both of us. Not a two-minute fuck, with you grunting like a bull. I want us *both* to enjoy it. There will be plenty of times when you can simply bend me over and fuck me senseless. But today, at this moment, I want more." She smiled. "And I want to be clean."

"Go into the water again," he said, gathering his pants around him. "You'll soon get used to the cold, and you'll feel cleaner for it."

"Yes, you're right," she said and kissed him again.

She stepped over to the bank, pausing to consider the depths. He caught her and spun her round, his manhood rigid, pressing against her body. She slipped out of his arms and stepped away, an eyebrow arched. "Aren't you going to look away?"

He laughed. "Dear Christ, I'll never look away again!"

A coy curling of her mouth, eyes downcast, and then she went into the water.

***

They found Stavros a few paces from where he had stood watch, face down in the dirt, his throat cut. Blood tinged the hard, dry grass around his head and for a few moments all of them stood, too stunned to speak.

Victor reacted first, swiveling around in a low crouch, body tense, sword ready. "Be wary, there are assassins close by."

Julius pulled his bow from behind his back and notched an arrow whilst Ahmed jumped up onto the largest outcrop and scanned the horizon.

"Anything?" asked Victor, his voice low, legs bent, tense.

"Nothing."

Julius scrambled down the far side, moving at a steady pace, firm-footed. The incline was slight but even so, the loose ground made movement precarious. When he stopped and looked back towards Victor and Ahmed, he realised how exposed his comrades were, and opened his mouth to warn them.

Thirty Six

He stood in the centre of the training ground in full ceremonial garb, the breeze wrapping the hem of a scarlet cloak around his thighs. The hauberk was of Norman design, falling to his knees, his helmet Seljuk, the eclectic mix of the well-travelled mercenary. At his side he clutched the gold-banded hilt of his sword, the pommel also of gold, presented to him by the Emperor Constantine IX in reward for services rendered. He was the leader of the Varangian Guard, honoured and lauded throughout the Empire. And he appeared angry.

Bolli Bollason cut an imposing figure, with his long flaxen hair falling to broad shoulders from which bare arms bulged with muscles. His eyes glinted with a cold, piercing blue hue, and he tensed as one by one the surrounding Varangian warriors fell silent, everyone aware of the mounting tension as a single figure appeared at the entrance.

For a moment silence fell, filled with

expectation of what would happen. The two men faced each other, indomitable, assured.

Pulling in a breath, Hardrada strode across the gravel, head high, mouth set, his great battle-axe upon his shoulder. Without a helmet, his hair swirled in the breeze, draping across his face, masking the glare radiating with burning malignancy.

They had fought together in Sicily, where Hardrada, in the grim killing fields of that Mediterranean isle, had forged his reputation as the most feared warrior in Christendom. Others gazed in hushed awe as his great axe swung and hewed heads, cleaved bodies from shoulder to waist. Drenched in sweat and the brains of his foes, his teeth bared, the loud laughter ringing over the ranks of those facing him, no one dared draw too close as the realisation spread that here was a man against whom no one could stand.

And now, here he was again.

Some three paces away, Hardrada stopped. A head taller than the great captain of the Varangian Guard, he appeared at ease, one hand holding the axe loose, his face impassive.

"You're back."

Bollason rarely smiled, preferring a scowl and the uncertainty and fear it imbued in his enemies, something he tended to promote. This time, however, he made a slight upturning of his mouth. "Observant of you. How goes it with you, Harald? I hear they put you in a cell?"

"I heard you were dead."

"You shouldn't believe all you hear."

"Nor should you."

Bollason allowed his eyes to wander over the giant. "Still as arrogant as when you first came here, Harald. No doubt you were hoping to step into my shoes, thinking me dead?"

"It had crossed my mind. Events conspired to prevent me from doing much more than killing Scythians."

"You like killing."

"Aye. I do that." He dragged a hand through his hair to reveal eyes, hard and narrow. "So what brings *you* here?"

"A summons. To lead the Varangians back to Sicily." He leaned forward, the thin smile frozen. "To undo your bungling efforts, and throw out the Normans."

If the barbed remark was meant to rile Hardrada, bring him to temper, it failed. The giant merely shrugged. "They have already ordered me to go. However, I have some other business to attend to."

"Maniakes has left the city. Komonos is in command, and he has superseded all orders. I lead, Harald. You are to stay here."

For a moment Hardrada almost laughed. Such news suited him better than anyone could imagine. "I've set Ranulph to work to train a crew."

"So I understand. You planning on leaving us?"

"And how am I supposed to get past the boom? The links of that chain were forged in the bowels of hell, Bolli. No one can sail over it."

Bollason nodded. "So. You will remain here, with your men and when I return, we will speak again." He took a step forward and pressed a forefinger against Hardrada's barrel chest. "There can be only one commander, Hardrada. And I am he."

Hardrada looked down at the other's digit and grunted. "When you return, Bolli, I shall be more than happy to cut that off." Their eyes met. Neither blinked. "And then your head."

The sound of Bollason's breathing grew louder, the man's neck reddened. Then he swung away and barked an order, "Fall in, you miserable shits. Gather your gear and prepare to march." He swivelled to give one final look towards Hardrada. "We sail at first light. Try not to die before I return."

Hardrada watched the man march away into the distance, the regret of not having killed him there and then already developing deep in the pit of his stomach.

***

They sat in a dark, dingy tavern, the only other customers a group of gnarled mariners from the east. Ulf had his legs splayed out, a pot of mead resting on his gut cupped in both hands. "How many has he left us with?"

"One hundred."

"Barely enough to crew one ship, never mind two."

"Ranulph has told me they know what to do, have practised the moves over and over. Fifty per crew is fine, given what I have in mind. Anymore might make the ships too heavy."

"And what about your booty, Harald? How do you propose to get that?"

Hardrada wrinkled his nose and took a sip from his cup. "I have another plan, old friend."

"Care to let me in on it."

"Best not. It's something I'll do alone. Bollason sails at dawn, and we will wait another day before we do the same."

Ulf peered into his mug. "There's something I don't get. You and Bollason. Why such hatred between you?"

Hardrada pulled a face. "Other than him being a bastard, you mean?"

"I've fought with you in a dozen battles, my friend. Covered your back as you have covered mine. From the battle of Stiklestad to fighting the Scythians at the Forum of Constantine. But I wasn't in Sicily, so I'm guessing something happened there?"

"And you'd be right." He drained his mug, and slammed it on the table a number of times to get the attention of the barkeeper. The man waddled over, his ponderous belly sagging over the top of his pants. He took the Viking's cup and went back to fill it. "We'd taken something of a beating from the Normans. We were in open ground, pulling back to the coast when they hit us from the side. Hundreds of them, maybe thousands. It was early evening and they came with the sun at their back, their lances levelled, and they went through us like hot irons. By the time we'd recovered we were broken, in total disarray and those of us who could, managed to reach a dip in the hillside. We held them there but we lost greatly, my old friend."

He stopped when the barkeeper returned with the filled mug and plonked it onto the table. With a grunt, he drifted away again and Hardrada picked up the ale and took a large mouthful. "As night came on, we slunk off and travelled through the darkness to make the ships. It was there I came across Bollason." Another drink. "He blamed me for the loss of the men, telling me I should have put out scouts; he was wild, out of control, frothing at the mouth like some rabid dog." He leaned forward, his eyes burning. "I *had* put out scouts, Ulf. I'm not an idiot. Something happened. I don't know what. Maybe the Normans were too damned smart, I don't know. We'd beaten them, time and time again, but that night, fucking Iron Arm came on us like a demon. He knew where we were, Ulf. He *knew*."

Ulf frowned, taking a moment to digest Hardrada's words. He drank slowly before speaking. "Are you telling me you suspect betrayal?"

"Bollason is a mercenary, as we all are. He has no allegiance except to his own pockets. I'd amassed more treasure than he could ever have dreamedof. He wanted it. And the only way to get it was with me dead."

"But ... how could he find it?"

"Zoe knew."

"*The Empress?* How?"

"I told her."

Ulf croaked, mead catching in his throat, as

he racked in a bout of violent coughing. Hardrada watched him in silence, waiting for him to recover, sipping at his ale patiently.

"I ..." Ulf wiped his mouth with the back of his hand and took a few more mouthfuls of drink. "I don't understand. Why would you tell her, and why would she tell Bollason?"

"She wanted his help in killing her husband."

Ulf's eyes bulged and he sat upright, casting his eyes quickly around the room. The mariners were in a huddle, muttering in their strange, singsong voices. He looked at his friend. "So the rumours are true? She did kill him?"

"By slow, systematic poisoning, yes. The woman is a scheming bitch, longing for power for its own sake. The glory of being Empress means more to her than the blessed sacraments upon which she is supposed to devote herself. And wealth, old friend. Wealth more than anything. She craves it relentlessly. We'd been lovers, but I knew it was only so she could get her hands on my money, not my cock." He sat back. "She used me, and I knew it, but I didn't care. The woman is insatiable, and a bloody good fuck too." He laughed and drank. "When she introduced me to a friend's daughter, a young wench named Sarah, that's when things went wrong. She grew jealous, threw me in prison, and invented the story of me stealing money from the royal coffers."

"And Bollason?"

"He'd slipped off to fight the Bulgars, leaving us all open to Michael's mad antics.

But he always made it known, wherever he went, that I had been responsible for the debacle on Sicily. And I have always known he was in league with Zoe to get my money."

"He was her lover too?"

Hardrada nodded. "I saw them."

Ulf shook his head. "You ... saw them? Making love?"

"They didn't know it, of course. But I filed it away, planning on making use of it sooner or later. But then Bollason got his orders to move north, so ..." He drank. "So, I had my revenge and most sweet it was. I took Sarah to my bed and circulated the rumour that we were to wed."

"Which must have hit Zoe hard."

"As I intended it to."

"Jesus, you play a dangerous game, my friend. She had the power to cut off your head."

"Not without proof, Ulf. Even with her invention of me stealing the money, she couldn't make it stick without evidence. I had Alexius on my side, as he knew I was the only person left who could help the Empire. The same night we were arrested, Michael's men cut down our comrades, our Varangian friends. I am still not entirely convinced Zoe did not have something to do with that too. I thought she might release us ... as I said, I was a poor, blind fool because, despite everything she did, she still controlled me, Ulf. Such a woman she is." He shook his head slowly, eyes misting over. "I may even have loved her. Damn her eyes."

A final mouthful and he stood up, adjusting his belt. "We have one more day before we sail. We have to get Hal from his sick bed."

"He's coming with us? Is that wise?"

"He can't stay. If he does, they'll kill him."

Ulf threw down his mead and clambered unsteadily to his feet. "We might all end up dead anyway."

"Aye," said Hardrada, his voice distant. "We all will, one day. The manner in which we die is the important thing. And I plan to die as a warrior, not in some back alley or in a stinking cell. On the field, old friend, surrounded with the bodies of my enemies. That is my destiny, of that I am certain."

Thirty Seven

Her plan was a simple one, born out of desperation. To lure him into the water, seduce him, perhaps render him unconscious with arock, or a tree branch, then flee, taking his clothes with her. If she could muster the courage, she might even kill him with his sword. She had killed before, without hesitation. This might be different, and not solely because of the act itself. His companions, enraged, would seek her out with an urgent desire for revenge, her fate sealed. By then, however, she would be lost amongst the hills and trees. It would be days before they uncovered her, and the General's estate would be close.

If she knew the way.

Better, perhaps, to continue on to the city and take her chances with the Empress?

Her mind whirled with the many permutations. Whatever she chose, she had to do something. Egor stood on the bank, watching her, his mouth hanging open, his cock sticking out declaring to the world his intention. Whatever she decided, if she did manage to over-power him in some way, by the time he recovered, she would have made good her escape.

Leoni shuddered beneath the cool, gently lapping water of the inlet. She knew in that instant nothing of the sort would occur. They had her; they would use her if they wished, slit her throat and toss her aside. Egor would have her, and perhaps make her his own.

She stood up in the water, the plan developing. Yes. Perhaps there might be a chance after all ...

Stretching her limbs, she ran her fingers through her hair, pulling back the locks as the water dripped from her lean body. The late sun cast a golden light over her flesh, causing her to glow like burnished bronze.

She heard him before she saw him, surging through the waters; she gasped at his urgent approach, his hauberk and coat discarded, his torso hard, white as marble. Then, he was on her, his strong arms around her waist pulling her close, his mouth locking onto hers.

"Dear Christ," he breathed. "You are more than beautiful. You're a goddess."

His lips ran over her neck and she allowed him full rein, knowing this was the only way. To be his, to surrender to him, lure him with promises, then perhaps he himself might kill the others, and with only him to deal with, her escape would be guaranteed.

He lifted her, nothing more than a child in his arms, dragging his tongue over her stomach, her breasts, and she held onto him as he cradled her, realising that only after he was sated would she be able to carry out her plan.

***

Ahmed cried out when the arrow hit Julius in the side of the head, burying deep into his skull, pitching him over onto his side, where he went into a weird, jerking dance, hands flailing, desperate to pull out the dart. Ahmed stood rooted, watching his comrade in spasm, unable to react, his muscles atrophied with terror.

Victor moved behind him, roaring out a stream of oaths and Ahmed saw the assailant come out of the trees, low and fast, discarding his bow, the sword in his hand. And he saw him close with Victor. Victor, the man who had seen so much, had fought so many times, huge and strong and dangerous. And he saw the attacker killing Victor as if he were nothing more than a straw-filled manikin used in the training grounds. Then, unable to move as fear locked his limbs, the man turned, the glint of the blade, and Ahmed could do nothing but whimper and feel his bowels open as the blade sliced through the warm, evening air ... nothing at all. Not anymore.

***

Leoni led him by the hand from the water, his hand cupping her buttocks, kneading the flesh. The haze of the sun gave some warmth, but exposed like this, her flesh shivered. Was it merely the cold, or something else. Egor swung her round, resumed his attack on her body, nipping at her nipples, fingers searching out the nub of her sex. She groaned, arched her back, and for a moment resistance faded. Why not have a man such as him, strong, resilient. He would protect her, keep her warm and safe. There was a coarse, animal sense about him, so unlike Michael, so different from the General. The General cared nothing for her, using her as a tool for his own orgasms. Egor, so lustful, so ardent, seemed centred on giving her nothing but pleasure, putting aside his own desires until she was satisfied.

He gently lowered her to the ground, his lips seeking out every fold and crevice of her body, slowly delving into her sex, finding the inner sanctum of her need, boring into her, long, light, luscious.

Leoni cried out, his hands scooping up her buttocks, raising her to give him greater access. She clawed at his hair, eyes closed, lost in the indescribable sensations pulsing through her body. Never had a man loved her with such unselfishness. No longer able to centre on any thoughts of propriety, of right and wrong, of dreams and plans for escape, she opened herself utterly to his attentions. The simmering warmth of her orgasm grew until it exploded in fire, her loins alive; she dug her nails deep into his flesh and begged him to penetrate her, to soothe the flames.

Her eyes snapped open as Egor drew back, his eyes alive with desire, his cock rearing up towards his belly. He grinned. "You're coming with me," he said, his voice thick and trembling. "I'm not taking you to the city. You're mine."

"Oh God, yes," she said, reaching out to clasp him around the neck. "Take me wherever you wish. I'm yours."

He grinned wider still, "Aye. You are that."

He leaned towards her to guide his cock into her waiting sex.

Leoni gaped, saw, but did not believe. The hand, seizing Egor by the scalp, dragging him away, the blade cutting deep into him, the metal erupting from his stomach, the blood spraying out a wide fountain.

"*NOOOOOOOOO!*"

She scrambled to her feet, grabbing a piece of Egor's clothing, covering her exposed breasts, and blubbering in disbelief as Egor crumpled lifeless to the ground. The assailant stood, his sword dripping blood, his eyes so wild, and tongue lolling from lips drawn back over snarling teeth.

But not an assassin, not a wild tribesman, nor a robber or brigand. A soldier, protected with lamellar armour and a gleaming helmet of bronze. A soldier of Byzantium.

A member of the Imperial Guard.

Thirty Eight

Thunder rumbled, lightning picking out the details of the darkened streets. Hardrada, hood pulled over his face, shoulders hunched, moved swiftly along the slight incline towards the harbour. Some hours ago a meeting with a ferryman proved fruitful. At least for the ferryman. Hardrada, a bag of gold coins lighter, knew it was his only sure way to get out of the KontoskalionHarbour and cross the Marmara Sea to the island of Principus.

Although not late, the rolling time of year meant the Iron Gate, which separated the harbour from the city, had already closed. The guards, preparing a brazier against the chill, jerked their heads when Hardrada drew closer. As hands moved to swords, the gigantic Viking held out yet another bag of coins. "Evening lads."

"And where might you be going?"

Hardrada shrugged. "Some business, lads. With an old merchant friend. Something that can't wait until morning."

"You'll need a written permit," said one, voice bored.

"And we're not your *lads*."

"No offence," said Hardrada, wondering if he should strike now. There were three of them, well armed, with perhaps more on the far side. If they raised the alarm, all hope of remaining incognito would be lost. So he relaxed his shoulders and weighted the bag of gold in his hand. "It is important I get down to the harbour ... *tonight*."

A few exchanged looks, some licking of lips. Hardrada bounced the bag a few times and tipped out the money into the nearest proffered palm.

If any recognised him, none said. One turned away and drew back the great bar with a solid thump. The iron hinges groaned as the huge door inched open and Hardrada slipped through.

The smell of the open sea filled his lungs as he scurried down the winding lane to the waiting mass of bobbing vessels. A great flash of lightning revealed a huge assortment of ships and boats, anchored side by side in the shelter of the harbour, one of three on the western side of the city. Kontoskalionmay not have been the largest of the harbours, but in the cold half-light, it appeared the busiest. From any number of decks and cabins came the sound of men's voices, raised in either laughter or anger. A hundred different dialects from all across the known world, the crews manning ships from the very limits of the Empire's borders bringing with them goods and wares to sell in the bustling markets.

From over on his right, a sudden burst of outrage and three men spilled out of a nearby tavern, a desperate scramble of arms and legs. The screams of whores, the shouts of innkeepers, the sudden flash of a blade, then silence. Hardrada pulled his coat around his neck and moved away in the opposite direction.

He found the man huddled close to the harbour wall, gnawing on a hunk of meat, a miniscule iron pan beside him, piled with glowing embers, which hissed and spat dangerously. The man seemed not to care, and continued with his loud chewing as a sudden flash of lightning lit up the surroundings, giving his face a sudden eerie, ghastly glow. He stopped, turning his face to the sky, lips moving soundlessly.

As Hardrada got down on his haunches, a low, drawn-out rumble came from the direction of the distant mountains.

"You're late," said the man, then clamped his teeth into the meat and ripped off a piece.

"No matter, I'm here now." He rolled his shoulders. "Feels like rain, so we need to get going."

The man cackled. "We cannot go this night. The storm, it will be upon us before long and if we get caught out in the open sea, we'll—"

Hardrada reached out a huge hand, seized the man by the wrist and pulled it, and the hunk of meat, away from his face. "We leave now. Before the storm takes hold."

The man's eyes were vivid white in the

darkness. "It is approaching. You don't understand; out there in the Marmara, we'll be capsized. Can you swim?"

"Aye. I'm a Viking."

"That's supposed to mean something?" The man growled, pulled his arm free of the grip, and licked his lips. "Very well, we might make it. But," another cackle, "it'll cost you double."

Hardrada tensed, and in an instant threw back his cloak and reached for the hilt of his sword, "You mercenary dog, I'll cut out your tongue!"

"Do that, *Viking,* and you can row yourself over to Principus."

***

Sometime later it had still not rained, but the wind grew in strength, and the temperature dipped as enormous sheets of lightning lit up the sky to illuminate the shingle beach of the tiny island. As soon as the skiff beached, Hardrada swung himself overboard and struggled ashore whilst the ferryman pulled the tiny boat farther up over the shingle.

"We were lucky," he grumbled, his voice sounding as if in a cave, amplified due to the total stillness of the place. "We will have to stay here until morning."

"At first light we leave, tempest or not."

"God must have some plans for you, Viking."

"My plans are my own." He slowly slid out his sword from its scabbard. The ferryman flinched, stepping back and Hardrada laughed. "Be assured, ferryman. It's not for you. You stay here, find some shelter, and as the dawn rises, we return to Constantinople."

He turned and made his way up the slight incline towards a wall of trees.

***

Finding the convent was not as easy as he had expected. Although small, the island was a strange place for him, and the almost total darkness made it virtually inaccessible. He emerged from the trees as more thunder pounded from above, closer this time, and the first few spots of rain fell. He readjusted his hood, bent forward, and moved on.

In time, he came across a few squat buildings, silent and lonely in the night. But above them, a larger building silhouetted against the night sky stood on a raised hillside, several tiny beacons of light blinking from window slits. As he moved to continue, he tripped over something, perhaps a fallen tree or a protruding root, and cried out before hitting the ground with a heavy thud. He cursed, rolled over onto his backside and rubbed his knees, grinding his teeth with the pain. Within a moment an ancient door creaked open from one of the nearby dwellings and a figure emerged, lantern held high in one hand, the other holding a sword.

"Who goes there?"

Without hesitation, Hardrada climbed to his feet and slipped onto the narrow path, which wended its way up towards the larger building. He heard more voices raised in alarm, but by now the night was his friend, swallowing him up before any curious eyes could pick out his shape scurrying along the pathway. He broke into a jog as the rain became heavier; before he reached the large entrance to the building, it had become a deluge, forcing him to find shelter amongst the trees bordering the path.

He sat beneath the overhanging branches and drew up his knees, cursing his bad luck. God's plan, if the ferryman's words were true, seemed to entail causing Hardrada as many problems as possible. He felt under his thick pants, seeking out his right knee, and gingerly traced where the hard, impacted earth had broken his skin, now sticky with blood. He put his head back against the tree trunk and shot a glance to the leaden sky. A jagged fork of lightning lanced through the greyness, almost immediately accompanied by a massive clap of thunder. The ground shook and the rain poured down, hammering against the leaves. The water dripped and Hardrada cursed again, making himself as small as he could before slipping into sleep.

He awoke with a start, snapping his head around in all directions, tense and alert, able to pick out details as the dawn spread out across the far horizon. To his right, the white, red-roofed monastery beckoned him forward, quiet, solid and strangely menacing. A house of God, or the means to his destruction? Hardrada shuddered at the thought.

The rain had ceased, but he was wet through, the cloak soaked, his body numb with cold. Picking up his sword, he clambered to his feet, groaning with the effort, sucking in his breath as forgotten pain bit into his knee. He flexed it, the newly formed scabs cracking audibly and when he took his first step, he limped.

Pausing for a moment to allow the pain to subside somewhat, he took in more of his surroundings; the olive and almond trees forming a thick veil across the hillside, beyond which he caught glimpses of the sea, the lights of the city, the occasional galley gliding into the docksides. As the day marched on, soon the Sea of Marmara would teem with more ships than he could count and perhaps fortune would smile, and he could return, unnoticed, amongst the throng.

He shivered as the cold gnawed into his very bones, and his thoughts turned to the ferryman, waiting down below. If the man had already made his way back, all would be lost. Some way off, the first birds of the morning took up their welcoming song. Soon, the sun would warm the air, still the soul. The nightdone, the promise of the day dispelled his fears. Hardrada shook himself and strode up towards the doors.

Thirty Nine

In his private apartments, the Patriarch Alexius swathed himself in sumptuous fur-lined robes and waddled from his bedchamber into the adjoining study. A servant busied himself stoking up the fire and Alexius mumbled a greeting. The servant bowed with an accentuated flourish and beamed, "Your Holiness, I have some freshly grilled sardines awaiting you, together with orange juice and—"

"Not this morning, Peter. My stomach is not up to it. Some water will suffice."

"Are you unwell, Your Holiness?"

Alexius smiled at the boy's concern. "*Old,* Peter. That is what I am." He stepped up to the servant and patted him on the cheek. "Thank you, Peter, but do not worry. My bones are frail, my teeth crooked and my hair is falling out ..." He patted the boy again. "Other than that, I'm perfectly well. The poison has not done its work."

Peter breathed a long sigh and lowered his

head. "Water it is, Your Holiness."

The servant turned to scurry off, and Alexius held up a finger. "Peter, find out where they have taken the body, won't you?"

Peter nodded and went out.

The Patriarch contemplated the blaze of the fire for a moment, wondering if Psellos had found paradise or the gates of hell, waiting for him after his suicide. A mortal sin, how could there be any other outcome but endless torture and pain? Such hopes, such plans for the future; the steering of the Empire towards a new age. Theodora, wise, pious, without blemish, sitting upon the throne with her sister Zoe, tempering the vices of the court with grace and devotion to God. All now gone, smashed in that single instant of madness. But why had Psellos plotted against them all? Was it naked ambition, avarice, desire for riches, or did someone else's hands direct the play? With Psellos's brain dashed across a marble courtyard, the truth could remain hidden forever. Unless ...

Alexius eased himself into a well-padded chair, stretching his palms towards the flames, and tried to still his shivering body. Old indeed he was, with so much yet to do. He needed to summon his strength and officiate over the crowning of the two sisters. He had thought long of Monomachus's return, of the General's plans to place the man on the throne, but Alexius would have none of that. Not now. Such ideas had gone awry before, when Michael settled himself into the warm embrace of the purple. Power had corrupted a once beautiful and God-fearing young man, turning him into a reckless monster, intent on destroying everything and everyone around him.

Monomachus would be the same, Alexius felt sure. The man's improprieties were well known, his appetites a scandal. How could anyone contemplate placing such a creature on the Holy Roman throne of the Byzantine Empire? And why had he considered such a course, even for a single moment? The attempt on his life by poisoning had cleared his mind, made him see the folly of the General's ambitions. Ludicrous, that's what it was; unhealthy and vile and Alexius would play no part. Enough of perversions and immorality, the Empire required faith in God and the sanctity of the Holy Mother Church. Nothing else mattered.

The door wheezed open and Alexius waved the servant closer. "Peter, I am cold. Perhaps some hot spiced wine?"

A shadow fell over him and Alexius tensed, wondering why no answer or comment came to his command. He craned his neck and gasped with surprise. He went to rise.

"No, Your Holiness," said Theodora with a smile, laying a soft hand upon his shoulder. "Stay there. I shall bring a chair. I have much to say and you, my dear, dear Father, need only listen."

***

Zoe slipped out from under the bedclothes and sat on the edge of her bed, rubbing her thighs briskly. The open balcony glowed with the first rays of another golden morning but the cold still lingered. The year was advancing, the evenings becoming longer and colder, the start of the new day still tinged with a biting chill. She stood up, turned to survey the sleeping man who had shared her bed, and for a moment considered rousing him. His cock lay limp on his thigh, his body bronzed, lean and hard. A young guard who had caught her eye, drunk her wine, and taken her body repeatedly. A confident and competent lover but not a Crethus. Not a Hardrada.

He moaned and rolled over onto his side and a brief thrill raced through her, his taut, smooth buttocks and rippling thighs reminding her of what had been. But as soon as it came, desire left her. She reached down for her gown, the piece of clothing he had torn from her body with an urgency that had frightened her, and draped it around her shoulders.

She padded over to the balcony and stepped outside.

The cold air struck her face and she drew the gown closer around her, shivering in the fresh morning. An unsullied sky stretched towards the shimmering coastline and she spotted the two proud ships easing their way out of the port, sails unfurled, oars dipping, setting their course that would lead them eventually to Sicily.

A smile spread over her face. Revenge tasted sweet. The damned Viking, who had come into her bed and captivated her with his ardour, his need, and she, like the fool she was, surrendered. No sooner had he partaken of her willing flesh, his eyes had wandered. She should have known it, but her weaknesses allowed her little chance to resist. Soon, thoughts of Hardrada's betrayal had receded into the darker corners of her brain as the lustful Crethus replaced the Viking and became everything she had ever longed for in a lover. Hardrada had killed him too. Damn him, for all the pain and misery he had brought to her. Well, no more. Now he was sailing off to his death, and the knowledge made her grow calm, contented.

Strong arms wrapped around her waist, and the guard nuzzled into her neck, his manhood hard and ready against the material of the robe, pressing between her buttocks. She purred, arching her back as his hands slipped inside and caressed her flesh. She turned in his arms, his lips crushing her own, and he swept her up and carried her to the bed, a delicious wave of surrender cascading through her body. He lowered her gently to the bed and pulled apart her robe. She glanced down at his erect cock and moaned.

No longer would the spectre of Hardrada haunt her. For he was soon to die, forgotten and alone; the knowledge of the Empress's victory seared into his brain. Such sweet, divine retribution. The guard gripped her buttocks and lifted her as he pushed forward, and she cried out, more in triumph over Hardrada's defeat than the sensations caused by the guard's passion. But he wasn't to know that, and as he drove into her with greater urgency, she allowed him to think it was he, and not revenge, which brought her such glorious satisfaction.

***

Shivering with cold, Hardrada tugged at the bell once more and at last the door creaked open slightly. An aged face peered out from the tinycrack, curiosity mixed with anxiety etched into the many wrinkles, which spoke of a life interlaced with intense study and contemplation.

Hardrada, aware he must present a fearful sight, smiled warmly, dropping his head in reverence. "Sister, I beg leave of you. I am a weary traveller, washed upon this isle in the storm last night. My boat lies broken on the rocks and I beg you for some warmth, perhaps some food."

The crone nodded, taking in Hardrada's clothing. "You are a Varangian," she said and opened the door wider.

Somewhat surprised, Hardrada nodded several times, "You are knowledgeable, sister. I am a Guardsman, yes. My mission was to bring messages, but they are lost. The storm ..." He shrugged, spread out his hands. "Such is life."

"Come in. We have a large fire and hot broth. You can dry your clothes, warm your bones, and I will send a message to the village for a ferryman to return you to the city."

Hardrada stepped over the threshold and looked around him.

A formal garden, laid out in a geometric

pattern with a central fountain, stood before him, the heavy perfume of lavender mingling with an abundance of other aromas. A bright confusion of flowering plants, trimmed lawn, neatly laid out borders of darker green miniature hedgerows. In the far corners, vegetables and herbs, with already silent sisters tended them, gently working away at the soil with patient, concentrated strokes from rakes and hoes. The silence, broken only by the constant trickle of the fountain, brought such a sense of peace that for a moment, Hardrada forgot the purpose of his visit. Here was a place to linger and be still, to forget the many worries and stresses of the world, and contemplate a greater purpose.

"Come," said the crone, taking him by the elbow and leading him through the narrow, pebbled paths, which bisected the different areas of the garden.

He looked down at her wizened, bent frame. A tiny woman, enveloped in black robes and veil. How long had she lived here in this small tranquil place, separated from the rest of humanity. Had she any idea of what lay beyond the walls of this convent, he wondered? The dangers Byzantium faced, both present and future? That men died in order for her life to continue undisturbed? He should have felt anger, perhaps, but somehow such feelings had no place here, so he swallowed them and allowed the nun to take him into the main building.

Here, the coldness of the plain, white walls seemed to amplify the morning chill. His boots echoed over the hard floor as they made their way deeper into the convent. Not a vast place, nevertheless by the time they reached the far end, the light from the main door grew feeble, causing the interior to dim, as if cloaked by night. From somewhere, tiny candles fizzled into life as another sister put tapers to wicks, and the crone took him into a smaller annexe and he gasped.

The room, of small dimensions, lined with books and lit by dozens of candles, seemed to hum with warmth. A great fire, stacked with wood, crackled, and arranged in front, a series of hard-backed chairs upon which ancient women sat and moaned.

"These sisters remain here. Retired now from the rigours of work, they live out their final days in quiet and peace." She tugged at his arm and motioned for him to sit. "Please. Rest. Warm yourself, and I will fetch someone to bring you food."

"You are kind, Sister."

"I am the Mother of this house, my son. And you, you are Harald Hardrada, and I know why you have come."

Forty

The servant brought in wooden platters stacked with olives, cucumber and tomatoes. Sclerus, sitting back in his chair at the head of the table, drummed on the wooden surface with his fingers.And waited patiently for the man to withdraw before sending a scathing look towards his sister as she picked absently at the food.

"I do not understand your reluctance," he said. "You have been the man's mistress for, how long is it, two years?"

"Three."

"Three *years* ... and now, you suddenly have an attack of conscience?"

"It is not that, brother." She studied a sliver of cucumber before slipping it into her mouth. "The idea of continuing to bed Constantine is not my concern."

"His concubine, lodged in a sumptuous house in the Imperial enclave, all the comforts you could ever wish for ... I fail to see why such a proposal should—"

"The Empress," she said quietly. "How could you even contemplate such a proposition, knowing she would wish me nothing but ill?"

He sat forward, both fists slamming down on the table. "Damn it, do you know nothing? The Empress couldn't give two figs for Monomachus! All she cares for is the continuation of her role, to be swathed in fine silks, to bathe in expensive perfumes, to cover herself in jewels. The woman is shallow and mercenary and will—"

"And will grow jealous. As any woman would. And once she does, she will plot my downfall, perhaps even yours."

"No. Monomachus will convince her, have no fear. The General too, once I make him see the sense of my plan."

"The General?" She snorted, rolling an olive through a trail of oil. "He is your sworn enemy, you have always said as much. Now you propose to ally yourself to him?" She shook her head. "He hates you as much as you hate him. What makes you think he would ever agree to such an alliance?"

"He is greedy for power. He attempted it once, with Michael. He failed and only just managed to escape execution because nobody could link him with any treasonable acts. He cleverly made a peace with Hardrada and the Varangians, but did not foresee how Alexius used his position as Patriarch to undermine everything to return Constantinople to a more reverent, faithful city. Now, as his influence diminishes, Maniakes is eager to re-establish himself. He sees Monomachus as his vehicle to more influence at Court, and if, through you, I convince him that he will find a way to controlling the new Emperor ..." He grinned. "You are a child in such matters, sister."

"But not when it comes to fucking, eh, brother?" Her face reddened and she stood up, throwing back her chair with such fury it crashed to the ground. "You think it is so easy for me to prostitute myself in order for you to gain power? Damn you and your plots and schemes. I hate you, and I hate myself for what you have made me."

In contrast to her sudden outrage, Sclerusrelaxed and sat back to study her with an amused expression. "Such exemplary piety, sister. You fail to remember it was not me who forced you into Monomachus's bed."

"Damn your eyes, Sclerus, but it *was you*! You introduced us."

He shrugged. "I asked you to become his companion, not his mistress."

"Christ, but your arrogance makes me want to vomit. You *used* me, and now you want to use me again."

"Oh, grow up! You knew damn well what was proposed, and you went along with a willing heart. Aye, and willing body too! Don't attempt now to wrap it up as anything else. You fucked him because you believed he would shower you with riches, just as the Empress so believes. You're both the same. Both whores."

She flew like a wild cat, hurling herself across the table to grapple him about the throat. They crashed to the floor, Sclerus screaming with shock and fear as her nails dug into his flesh. Her strength terrified him and despite his best efforts to rip away her arms, he failed. Desperately he flailed, trying to find some leverage and break her grip. The blood boiled in his head, temples pounding, and eyes bulging. He kicked and scrambled, cried out, high-pitched, pleaded with her, with God, with anyone. Nothing worked, and a developing grey haze came down over his eyes.

And then, a sudden bright light overcame all, bringing with it instant relief from the pain and horror of his sister's attack. The weight of her body left him and he rolled over onto his side, gagging and spluttering, as somewhere far away angry voices raged. He gathered his knees under him and stood up, finding the edge of the table to steady himself.

His wife had her hands on his shoulders, her face creased with concern. "What in the name of Christ is happening here?"

Sclerus waved her away, picked up the chair and slumped into it. "Fetch me wine," he croaked.

Opposite, Scleriana was in the arms of one of the servants, red-faced, teeth bared, breaths coming in ragged gasps. "I'll see you dead, you bastard," she hissed.

Pouring the wine, Sclerus's wife trembled as she spoke. "What manner of wickedness is this that a man's own sister should say and do such things?"

Sclerus snatched the goblet and drank down the contents, wine spilling out from the corners of his mouth in his haste. He brought the empty vessel down with a smash. "The kind that refuses to recognise truth." He looked at his wife. "What are you doing out of bed? I thought you were sick?"

"I am. Sick of you and this existence you put me through. Now this." She shook her head. "I want no part of it."

"You're not a part of it, woman." He stood up and glared across the room at his sister. "You will play your part, damn you, and you will do it willingly. The rewards will be immense and you will thank me for it."

"*Thank you*?"Scleriana ripped herself free from the servant's grip. "Have you not listened to anything I have said? The Empress?"

"Silence," Sclerus came around the table, rubbing his rapidly swelling throat where the nails had broken the skin. He dismissed the servant with a scathing look, waited for him to leave the room, and then released a long sigh. "I am your opportunity to become powerful and rich, sister. Do not jeopardise it all with this ill-timed sense of self-righteousness. You went willingly to his bed, and there you will remain."

"You understand nothing. You call me *whore* whilst you, you do the same without any thought for those you use and abuse."

"My God, listen to you. Such godliness. It is a wonder you do not become a nun."

For a moment he believed she would attack again as her body tensed, and he held up his hand, forcing a smile. "*Please.* This does nothing to further our cause. And cause it is, sweet sister. We are close to becoming what we have always wanted to be. Rich."

"What you have always wanted. You have never considered that things may have changed."

"*Changed?*" He gave a short laugh, twisting around to look at his wife, standing there in her white nightdress, face aghast. "You heard correctly, wife. Rich. We will have a house in the city, a grand house. You can live the life you have always longed for." He turned to his sister once more. "And you. Don't dress it up into something it is not."

Her eyes narrowed. "I do not. You introduced me to Monomachus and we became close. Something you could never understand, for you life is base and holds only one goal. Money." She shook her head. "Well, I discovered something far more potent."

"What's this?" he asked, tilting his head, the mocking tone in his voice difficult to disguise. "Are we having an attack of conscience? After all this time, dear sister, you expect me to believe you have changed your mind, have grown guilty, ashamed, *noble?*"

"No." She sniffed loudly as tears tumbled down her cheeks. "The Empress, she may well hate me, but in the end she will have to accept me. I lied to you, Sclerus. It is not her I fear. It is the life you wish me to pursue. The life of a concubine, to be shut away, mocked, shunned. It is that which frightens me."

"I don't understand you. You've been with him for these past three years, living a life as his mistress. What would change when he becomes Emperor? Nothing, nothing at all."

"No, you're wrong. Everything would change. For I have *not* lived my life as his mistress, but ..." She shivered, dragged the back of her hand across her nose. "I wouldn't expect you to understand. For you, everything is simple. You're a degenerate dog, sniffing around in the shit, looking for scraps to fatten your belly. You'll do anything to further your ambitions, even use the ones closest to you. Well, things have changed, Sclerus. Beyond your understanding."

He frowned, bemused. "What in the name of Christ are you talking about?"

"I love him, Sclerus. I love him and I cannot let him go."

Forty One

They woke him early, shaking him by the shoulders and he lashed out, confused and alarmed, reaching for his sword.

"A messenger, sir."

He blinked and sat up. "How dare you disturb me in such a way as—"

"Begging your pardon, sir, but we had no choice."

Gerald threw back his covers and stood, stretching and yawning. "You'd better explain yourselves." He eyed the two fully armoured cavalrymen for the first time and frowned. "Quickly."

They exchanged a look, and then the first soldier spoke. "It is Jerome Bogarde, sir. He has returned with written orders."

"The snivelling wretch will feel the bite of my blade, by Christ!" Gerald pulled off his nightshirt, mindless of the cold, and pulled on his undergarments. "I already have all the orders I need. Muster the men and have them prepare for—"

"I'm sorry, sir," interjected the second soldier. "Jerome has already given the orders."

Gilbert stopped in the act of buckling on his sword-belt and swivelled his head towards the two men. "*What* did you say?"

As if in a dream, detached from reality, he saw them draw their swords and he knew then, if he hadn't already guessed, that life and fortune had turned against him. He swallowed hard. "This is the Devil's work."

"No, sir," said the first. "It is by the order of our lord and master, William Iron Arm."

***

They dragged him out into the morning and there, drawn up in a ragged semicircle, waited his troops. Guille amongst them. However, it was the armoured figure in the centre who took his full attention. Jerome Bogarde, arrogant, all youthfulness replaced by an aura of authority. Gerald's stomach turned to water, strength draining from him and the two soldiers held him fast in their grip before throwing him to the ground.

"You are deemed a traitor," said Bogarde without ceremony, "and are stripped of your command." He held up the orders, the seal broken. "I have presented these orders to Sergeant Guille and he has repeated them to the men. The situation has changed, Gerald. Our lord, William Iron Arm, requires men of devotion and unquestioning obedience to lead."

"Like you, you bastard?"

Bogarde took two steps and hit Gerald hard

across the face, knocking him sideways into the dirt. Breathing hard, Bogarde straightened his back and roared, "Men, we ride for the coast where we meet a Varangian host from Byzantium. We will strike them as they disembark and by the day's end we will have Hardrada's head on a pike. These are Lord William's commands."

"You're mad," spluttered Gerald, rising up from the ground with the blood dripping from his shattered nose. "Both you and William. We are not enough to fight a full-pitched battle, as well you know."

"You would do best to trust in Lord William's better judgements, Gerald. He is not a fool. He has entered into an alliance, which will not only assure him of control of Sicily, but revenge against the Norseman. It seems he is not the only one who wants the bastard dead. Now, we ride to the coast and you, Sir Gerald, you will sit on a hillside and watch me triumph over the Vikings." He grinned. "And then, I will cut off your head."

***

Hardrada sat over a steaming bowl of broth and spooned down mouthfuls, blowing over the hot liquid to cool it before eating. The nuns close by, of which he counted three, snoozed as the glow from the fire wafted over them. A tiny feeling of envy fluttered through his stomach. To spend days doing nothing at all, everything done for you, what a wonderful way to live out the remaining years ...

No sooner had the thoughts stirred than he brushed them aside. Life, for him at least, was a constant round of striving; his ambitions would not be thwarted, nor deviated from, no matter how strong the lure of a quiet, secluded life might be.

He chuckled to himself, mopping up the last of the broth with a hunk of bread. Without doubt, these religious personages lived a good life. Devoting oneself to God, study, contemplation, had alot to be said for it. Perhaps, when his time was close, he might reconsider and retire to a distant secluded monastery, somewhere cold. He liked the cold, longed for the biting wind of the fjords. Rain, that was something he could do without, as last night proved, but the sucking, relentless heat of Byzantium proved too much. He shook his head. If he thought about it long enough regrets could come. Regrets for missed chances, wrong turnings, ill-judged decisions. Coming here, to the east, perhaps the greatest of his misjudgements ... The money he had stashed away, now in the greedy palms of the Empress Zoe. God, how they had loved. Until his roving eye got the better of him, as always.

He sat back and stretched out his long legs, releasing a contented sigh. His eyes grew heavy and, before he dozed, he placed the bowl on the floor, clasped his hands over his stomach, and surrendered to the comforting warmth of the fire.

"I expected you much sooner than this."

He sat bolt upright, startled by the voice. She had come upon him as quietly as a ghost and now she stood there, in her nun's habit, nothing exposed except her face. And what a face it was. The same olive complexion, the huge brown eyes, the full lips.

"Sarah," he breathed and went to stand.

"No," she said, her hand pressing down on his arm. "Sit, Harald and tell me what it is you want."

"How ..." He allowed himself to slump back into the chair. Her gaze, as hypnotic as ever, quietened him, causing all of his anxieties to simply drift away. She always possessed that power. When first they met, a voice of liquid velvet drew him in and all at once all thoughts of Zoe left him. This girl, beyond beautiful, had captivated everything he had. From that first moment, he was hers. And she knew it.

They'd made love, but only after many secret meetings, and exchanged promises of devotion. Her body, a dream, sleek and slender, rolling over him, bronzed limbs, mouth enveloping his ardour. Young, full breasts, flat stomach, rounded hips and buttocks. He'd loved her each night, over and over, every time their coupling more intense and frenzied than the last. She'd clawed his back, bitten his neck, and he never tired, the passion always there. At night, alone, the memories would enflame him once more, and he brought himself to orgasm with the thought of her.

And then Zoe had discovered them, her rage uncontrolled, thrown him into a dungeon, his death plotted. She told the world it was because he had stolen Imperial gold, but both he and the Empress knew the truth. At least, he did eventually. Jealousy. How could anyone overshadow the divine Empress?

Sarah had, and still did. Even in those simple robes, the promise of her body brought the flames to his loins and he cared not who could see it. "How did you know, how did the Mother Superior know?"

"I told her on the day Zoe delivered me here. Everything. She comforted me, wiped my tears, held my shaking body. In no time, with the Lord's help, the memory of you grew dim as I devoted myself to my new life. A life of seclusion and prayer."

"I don't believe you. You couldn't forget what we had so quickly."

"Couldn't I? You did."

She went to an empty chair and brought it over, placing it next to him. The other elderly sisters barely stirred, their gentle snoring rhythmic and deep. Sarah sat down.

"I cannot lie, sometimes memories do return, but I no longer cry myself to sleep. I've learned not to care, you see."

"I've come to take you away."

She raised her eyebrows. "Really? And how do you propose to do that?"

"By picking you up, throwing you over my shoulder and taking you back to my ship."

"I see." Her face returned to its former impassiveness, his words seeming to cause her no alarm. "I think the Holy Mother would have something to say about that."

"She can say what she likes. No one is going to stop me."

"Your arrogance was always the thing I disliked most of all about you. I will not come with you, Harald. What happened between us happened to another girl in another world. I cannot go back. I will not."

"I'm not asking you to."

She tilted her head and studied him, a twinkle of curiosity playing around her eyes. "Then what are you asking me to do?"

"To come with me on my journey north. Zoe has my money and I want it."

"Ah!" She slapped her covered thighs with her hands. "So, there it is. The reason. You want to ransom me, is that it?"

"In one."

"Dear God, but you are a mercenary cur, Harald. It is not love which has brought you here, but simple greed."

"I did love you, Sarah. You know it."

"Yes. Perhaps you did, for a few brief moments. But you never came looking for me, did you? When you were safe, with Zoe out of the way, where were you then?"

He shook his head and turned away, abashed by her words. They stung him and he chided himself for being so weak. "Damn it, Sarah, if I could have done ..."

"Fret not." She patted his arm. "Your love was a brief flicker in your quest for blazing glory. I knew it then, and I know it now. You wanted me and you had me. But love was never your goal. More a manacle, yes? Tying you down, preventing you from achieving your ambitions."

"I cared." His eyes held hers. "I truly did care, Sarah."

"But not enough." She gave his arm a final

slap and stood up. "You had best leave, Harald. You're dead to me now and I have no intention of ever being a part of your awful schemes. Just go. Please."

"I can't. I need my gold. And Zoe will not release it, not for anything. Except perhaps you."

Sarah shifted to leave and he stood up, towering over her, tense, serious. "I'm taking you with me, Sarah. We will be gone for perhaps ten days. No more. Then you can return to ..." He scanned the room and smiled. "This *sanctuary*."

"I'm not going."

"You are. You can either come with me freely, or as I said. Either way, you are coming with me to the North."

The sound of shouting reached them, men's voices from beyond the walls. Hardrada frowned, a hand reaching for the hilt of his sword.

"The Holy Mother told me she would call for assistance. Seems like they are here."

Hardrada cursed under his breath, drew his sword and shot her a murderous look. He growled, "It didn't have to be like this," and left the room at a run.

Forty Two

General Maniakes closed the bedroom door with exaggerated slowness and crossed into the solarium. He stood for a moment with his face turned to the sun and took several deep breaths. His wife had not spoken, her face drained of colour, her body rigid with terror. In all the years he had known her, he had never seen her in such a state. And now, the sunlight bathing his face, he did not know what to do.

This was not battle, men arraigned in preparation for death. Tactics and strategy were his bedfellows; assassins in the night were not. Whoever the man was and whatever he wanted were mysteries, unfathomable. To hunt him down would prove too difficult and Maniakes had neither the time nor the means. So he stood and waited for inspiration, but none came and when he turned and returned to the dining room his body felt heavy, his mood dark.

He poured wine and sipped it, allowing the

warmth to spread within him. The combination of alcohol and sun should have made him feel easier. He knew, in that instant, nothing would ever be easier again.

He pulled off his boiled-leather breastplate and placed it on the table together with his helmet. As he went to unbuckle his sword belt, a movement over to his right caused him to stop. He reached for his sword and turned, preparing to defend himself against the intruder.

Sclerus smiled, "Steady, General. I come in peace."

"What the devil do you want here?"

"A few quiet words, that is all." He took a step forward, saw the pointed sword, and held out both hands. "I'm unarmed, General. I mean you no harm."

"Somebody did."

"Aye." Sclerus's face darkened. "So I understand. Helen is unharmed?"

"*Helen*?" Maniakes's sword hand trembled. "Take care, Sclerus. Your familiarity may cost you dear."

"Merely the question of a concerned neighbour, General. Whatever our differences, your good wife is not one of them."

"What the hell do you mean by that?"

A slight chuckle and Sclerus sat down at the far end of the table and reached out for the wine jug. He tipped a generous measure into a goblet and drank. "I take it then that she *is* unharmed?"

"Not that it is any concern of yours, but yes, she is unharmed. In some distress, naturally."

"Naturally. Have you any suspicions as to whom it may have been?" He motioned towards the sword with the wine goblet. "Do you mind putting that thing away? You'll have me thinking I'm not welcome."

"You're not."

"Well ... amuse me then, why don't you, and listen to what I have to say."

"If you know anything about happened then you had best—"

"I *know* nothing, but I have some thoughts. Whoever it was wants you, General. Dead. Clearly, such ideas coming out of my mouth may strike you as somewhat surprising ... after all nobody wants you dead more than I ..." He smiled and sat back in his chair, rolling the goblet between his palms. "However, to break into your house, murder a servant, terrify your wife? Hardly my style, General."

Maniakes snorted and sat down, laying the sword on the table. "I haven't stopped riding for two days, Sclerus. Tell me what you want to say and get out."

"In my humble opinion, there are three people who want you dead. The Patriarch of Constantinople, His Holiness Alexius." He waited. Maniakes simply stared back at him. "The Empress herself ... and ... Harald Hardrada."

Maniakes looked away and considered his armour, lying there on the table. A soldier born and bred, a man of the camp, loved by his troops, heralded as the finest general alive. Success and fame, however, come at a price. The envy of others. "Any one of them has good cause," he said, his voice sounding hollow even to his ears. Tired, he rubbed his face. Of course, the one who wished him dead more than any other sat not so very far away. Sclerus. Perhaps he was at the centre of the plot, if plot it was. He didn't know; he didn't care. Somewhere out there a lunatic roamed, a nameless, faceless maniac capable of the most dastardly of deeds. It may be time to take his wife back to the city and guarded by men who knew what they were doing.

"Towards that end, General," said Sclerus, cutting into Maniakes's thoughts, "I have a proposition for you, one which I believe you will find most appealing."

Maniakes never allowed his eyes to leave his sword and armour. "I doubt that."

"Trust me. It is something I have planned for, something which has been fermenting for many months."

Interest piqued, Maniakes frowned. Slowly he turned to his neighbour, the man he loathed. "Planning for many months?"

"Before his enforced banishment, I was in communication with Orphano, the Emperor's administrator and confidant—"

"Michael had no confidants."

Sclerus pulled a face, somewhat amused, "Well, we all know that isn't true. He had *one*, installed by your good self into his bed."

"The girl? She was nothing but a plaything, someone to tease out information ..." He sat up, wintery tingles seeping through his limbs. "How in the name of Christ do you know all this?"

Another smile, more of a leer this time. "I know much, dear General. As I said, I had been in communication with Orphano and together we devised a quite splendid scheme. All in secret, of course. Nobody knew. In fact, with Orphano laying the seeds, so to speak, you probably thought it was all your idea."

Maniakes went through the many machinations of the previous months. Whilst Michael sat on the throne of New Rome, desperate to ensure his authority, Orphano, the Patriarch Alexius and he all worked towards his eventually fall. Now, Sclerus introduced another level of intrigue. Had he been party to the plots? Plots of his own design? Maniakes shook his head. "I don't believe you. I would have caught wind of it."

"No, my dear General, we were too careful. But when Michael moved precipitously and sent Orphano away, I knew I had to begin our work." He tipped out the last of the wine and swirled it around the goblet. "Monomachus, General. Brought to Constantinople to be schooled and prepared torule. Orphano's idea. Not yours, not His Holiness Alexius's. Orphano's. The very same man banished to a distant isle, to live out his days forgotten and ignored. But, together with me, the architect of a plan to restore Byzantium to its former glory. For hundreds of years, our Empire was ruled by men of strength and insight; not simply politicians of consummate greatness, but strategists who prepared for the future. Men of vision, men of God."

"You sound like a bishop, Sclerus. Who are

you trying to convince? Me, or yourself?"

"I do not need to convince anyone, my friend. The Empire began to break when that bitch Zoe murdered her first husband."

"You do not know that is true. None of my investigations uncovered the slightest piece of evidence."

Sclerus shrugged, drained his wine. "Be that as it may, I feel sure she was responsible. For her second husband's death also, I am certain. The woman is a viper."

"But beloved by the people, as Michael discovered to his cost. Is this your plan, Sclerus? To *replace* Zoe by your creature, Monomachus."

"*Our* creature, General. Together, with Monomachus under our control, we can gain more power and influence than we ever imagined."

"I envisage Monomachus and Zoe married, to rule jointly. Alexius believes the same."

"Alexius has changed his mind, General. He wishes Theodora to ascend the throne."

"Then he is a fool. A woman cannot rule, not without the assurances of the army and the army adore Zoe."

"The army too can be controlled."

"You forget one thing. I'm commander of the Imperial army. I could crush you all. I merely have to give the order."

"Yes." Sclerus smiled. "Yes, I know that, my dear, dear friend. Which is why I have other things to tell you. Things that will ensure your compliance."

"Don't fence with me, Sclerus." Maniakes let

his fingers fall onto the hilt of his sword. "I could destroy you in the blink of an eye."

"Yes, no doubt you could. Your reputation for violence precedes you, dear General. But if you kill me, or oppose me, then the girl, the one you used so gratuitously against Michael, will be arraigned before the Senate, to give evidence of your duplicity."

"Leoni? Pah, you expect the Senate to believe the words of a simple girl scorned? They would laugh her out of the Senate House, as they would you."

"Yes, no doubt. But if her evidence is supported by that of your wife?"

Maniakes felt his mouth fall open of its own accord and for a moment his mind whirled.

"For months now, my dear friend, I have been bedding her. And in our moments of passion, she told me all. I have it all signed, my friend. Documents, evidence, the words of a noble woman used and abused by her great, yet overly ambitious husband."

From somewhere, Maniakes managed to find his voice. "I don't believe you."

"Believe what you like. My hand reaches far, my friend. I could destroy you as easily as my man broke into this house and came within a breath of murdering you in your bed." He held up his hand. "Yes, I admit it. It was not my idea to strike so early, but I must say that by so doing my man has worked a wonder. You are here. Exactly where I want you."

Throwing back his chair, Maniakes leaped to his feet, sword in hand. His body trembled, gripped by anger and disbelief, the heat rising to his face, his heartbeat pounding in his temples. "I knew it, you bastard. I knew you were at the bottom of this. You're a fool, Sclerus. Telling me everything like this. *A fool!* I'll have your head on a spit before the day is out, and I'll break all your plans, all your pitiful schemes. I care nothing for the girl. Your evidence will not hold up. You've overstepped your mark, and now you're going to die."

"Think carefully, General. If you kill me, the truth will out. I have made my arrangements. My man, who even now is in the City, will deliver papers to the Senate, to the divine Empress and to Alexius. They implicate you on every level, my friend, of conspiring against the royal throne. It will be your head on a spit, Maniakes."

"You're bluffing."

"Am I? If you believe that, then kill me. But with my death will come your fall, as certain as tomorrow the sun will shine once more. Best to sit, dear friend, and allow me to tell you how we are going to make Byzantium great again."

The smile on the man's face, so arrogant, set off a series of internal earthquakes within the General's body. Rage spewed out and he threw down his sword, gripped the edge of the table, and shook uncontrollably. If the man spoke the truth, doom would indeed fall. Worse than death, worse than any nightmare or demon, sickness or malignancy. Shame.

He staggered over to the open veranda and looked out across his estate, the breeze stirring the leaves and branches of the endless rows of olive trees. Soon it would be time to harvest the crop and he would need men to work, ensuring another year of profit. If he wished hard enough, perhaps he could change the present, already find himself retired, sitting and watching the rolling seasons idle by; all of Sclerus's words a distant nightmare, forgotten. "Very well," he sighed without turning around, "tell me of your plan, Sclerus."

He heard the scrape of his neighbour's chair, the soft footfall of his approach, and then listened to his words as he told him how they were going to become the most powerful men in the world.

Forty Three

Jerome Bogarde sat astride the destrier, re-adjusting his iron helm, the nasal bar causing considerable discomfort as it pressed against his bulbous nose.

Next to him, Sergeant Guille peered out across the grey, gently rippling waters, took a quick glance towards the assembled troops, and blew out his cheeks. "You are certain of your intelligence, lord?"

"Intelligence? What the fuck does that mean?"

"Your *spies*, lord. You can rely on their information?"

"Of course. Everything is at hand. Psellos has arranged everything, with all the intricacy of the loathsome snake he is. Hardrada is sailing to his certain death and on this day the Byzantines will rid themselves of their greatest threat and we will have Sicily."

"I understood Hardrada was their most able of captains? Their hero?"

"He betrayed the Empress, Guille. Nobody

does that. It is her wish that he dies, and her influence which has procured the establishment of our power base here. It's a happy day, Guille. Gerald should have trusted our Lord William. If he had, he would be sitting here in command of our forces. A fool he was, and his death will be the reward for his stupidity and blindness."

"And you, lord? What will your reward be?"

Bogarde gave a wry smile. "To see Hardrada's head on a platter as I deliver it to William Iron Arm. I will have estates here on the island. My future is assured." He winked. "Yours too, Guille, as my trusted lieutenant."

Guille bowed his head briefly, about to speak when an outrider came up the hill, his mount snorting with the effort. The scout reined in his horse, struggling to keep it under control as it kicked and stamped at the soft sandy earth of the low hill. The man clearly had been riding fast; sweat poured down from beneath the rim of his soft fur cap. "Ships sighted, lord," he said breathlessly.

"How many?"

"Two so far, lord."

Bogarde gave a tiny cry of elation, "So it begins, Guille! Just as Psellos promised. Two ships, a total of one hundred and twenty men, and Hardrada amongst them," He slapped the side of the destrier's head. "Ready the men, Sergeant, for today we kill ourselves some Vikings!"

***

There were three of them, encased in lamellar armour, bronze helmets and grieves. They bore swords and shields and Hardrada smote them in the entrance to the small convent. One had managed to land a blow, the blade slicing through Hardrada's unprotected forearm before the Viking's blade ended his life. With the fight over, Hardrada reeled back inside, clutching the vicious wound as it leaked blood through his fingers. Lightheaded, he paused, supporting himself by leaning against the inner wall, breathing hard.

Before him, the mother Superior surveyed himself with unblinking eyes, her features set hard, any thoughts of disappointment well hidden beneath her perfect mask."You are a murderous cur," she rasped and whirled around, disappearing into the confines of the main building.

Hardrada watched her go and couldn't help but smile. Such hypocrisy, he mused. Another of God's servants prepared to countenance violence to ensure the preservation of the faith. He knew little about God or Christ; only that holy writings preached understanding, acceptance and forgiveness. The old ways were better, more honest. Destroying enemies brought glory, not in the turning of the cheek, but in the heat of battle. These damned Byzantines lauded themselves as so self-righteous whilst pursuing ambitions in the most ruthless and brutal of ways. They were no more Christian than he was, and the Mother Superior had shown them all up for who they truly were. Romans. Cruel and unbending. Well, to hell with them all. He steadied himself and strode back inside to find something to bandage his arm and take Sarah down to the shoreline and the waiting skiff.

***

From the crest of the hill, Gerald, hands bound in front of him by thick, coarse ropes, gazed down at the beach and watched the Vikings coming ashore. A huge commander, swinging his great axe, barked orders and the men spread out to engage the Norman horsemen as they poured down from the sandy slopes. From this distance, the cries and shouts were nothing more than muffled squeaks, but he knew what those noises meant. Fear. Despair. Caught in the open, the Vikings fought, broke and ran. Gerald frowned. This was not their usual way. He had fought them many times, knew them to be hardy fighters and, in such a situation, they would stand and die. Not so these men. Already they were throwing down their arms and raising their hands in surrender, whilst amongst them the giant commander cleaved heads before he too fell, overwhelmed by numbers.

"Look at them," muttered the guard at his side gleefully. "Poxy turds the lot of them."

"They're not Vikings," said Gerald without taking his eyes from the skirmish, so soon ended. The defeated warriors already bundled into small groups, Norman spearmen keeping them quiet.

"Varangian scum," spat the other guard, leaning on his spear. "They've forgotten how to fight, living the good life in Constantinople they've grown soft, effete."

Gerald narrowed his eyes and shot a look to the guard which he hoped held as much venom as he harboured inside. "You ignorant bastard, they are *not* Varangians!"

The other jabbed his sword hilt into Gerald's kidneys. A blinding pain shot through him; he gasped and fell, clenching his teeth, desperate not to fall into unconsciousness. "You watch your mouth," he heard the guard snarl. "The only ignorant bastard here is you, and you'll be dead soon enough. Together with your Varangian friends."

***

Those 'Varangian friends', bundled together in groups of twenty or so, stood bound with leather cords and ropes. Their heads downcast Bogarde regarded them with a mix of confusion and anger. At his shoulder, Guille breathed into his ear. "These are not Vikings, lord."

"I can see that."

The truth of the situation screamed out at him with every eastern European face he saw. Not a Norseman amongst them, they were Bulgar mercenaries for the most part, with the odd Turk thrown in for good measure. A motley crew indeed, ill-fitted for battle against hard, professional Norman cavalry. What in the name of God was Psellos playing at, he wondered. And how had Hardrada been duped into believing these men could aid him in recovering Sicily? Were there other ships heading this way, with more men, this time better able, and better led? It had to be so, Bogarde told himself. How else to explain this insanity?

He rounded on his sergeant, "Bring me Hardrada. I want to know what infantile game this is."

Guille saluted and strode off. Bogarde tore off his helmet and sighed, relieved at last that he could breathe more easily. "Bring me some wine," he snapped at nobody in particular and walked over to a nearby outcrop of rock, sat down, and looked out to sea. It stretched unsullied towards the horizon, not a bird, not a ripple. More importantly, no more ships. None of this tasted right. Grateful for the low casualty rate, nevertheless he found it hard to understand why Hardrada would come so unprepared. Had he lost his edge, or even his wits?

"Lord."

His head snapped up and he snatched the goatskin from the hand of the waiting soldier. He took a long drink, gasped and wiped his mouth with the back of his hand. "How many have we captured?"

"Nigh on a hundred, Lord."

"And our casualties?"

"Low. Less than ten, with three dead."

"I want pickets posted. Keep watching the sea, there are bound to be more." He shook his head, "This has to be the vanguard. To scout out the land. The main invasion force must be close behind, and then we shall have a real fight on our hands."

The soldier slapped his fist against his chest and went off through the sand to make good Bogarde's orders. If the remaining force came, Bogarde planned to attack them with archers as they disembarked. He knew he would have little hope of containing them for long. The last time they had come, over ten thousand Byzantine foot soldiers, together with three thousand Varangians and as many cavalry had pounded up these beaches. Maniakes at their head, urging them on. The hero of New Rome, with Hardrada beside him. Bogarde did not fight them then, but he knew the stories. Over campfires, veterans had regaled him with tales of death and glory, how the great Varangian axes had swung and cut deep into the flesh of Norman men and horses.

Those images ate into his very brain, kept him awake at night. And now this. His hopes for immortality little more than the grains of sand he now picked up with his mailed fist and allowed to filter through back to the ground. Like dust. Nothing.

He jumped as a body dropped at his feet, blood-spattered, wheezing in pain. Bogarde stood up, reaching for his sword in alarm.

"It's not Hardrada," said Guille, palm outstretched, calming the moment.

Bogarde gaped at his sergeant. "What the hell do you mean, it's *not* Hardrada?"

Guille motioned for the accompanying soldiers to turn the wounded and broken warrior over onto his back.

The man groaned, teeth clenched in agony,

and Bogarde saw the numerous sword cuts, the split hauberk, the blood running, seeping away in the sand in tiny rivulets. He got down on his haunches and peered into the man's wild eyes. A face gripped with pain, deeply wrinkled, bearded, his grey hair plastered to the flesh. "Who in the name of God is he?" His eyes fell on the golden-hilted sword still unsheathed at the man's hip. "He is a Varangian commander, but this is not Hardrada. He's too damned old." He stood up, the rage erupting from every pore of his body. He raised his clenched fists and beat out at imaginary enemies, lifting his head to the sky, "Dear Christ, why do you forsake me so?"

"Your Christ truly has forsaken you, Norman dog," said the wounded man, his voice low, barely audible. And as Bogarde struggled to understand the meaning of what had happened, the wounded man began to laugh.

Forty Four

With the sun less intense than it had been, Monomachus found the slight chill something of a welcome change as he pounded around the final circuit of the training ground. In the centre, Marcellus stood, his great tree-trunk legs rooted to the spot, tapping out the rhythm of the run against his leg with a reed cane. The man's grin, a permanent fixture that morning, urged Monomachus on, to prove the despised Roman wrong.

Almost a month ago they had brought Monomachus here, subjected him to a frugal diet, a hard floor for a bed, and constant physical exercise, shedding the pounds and turning flab into the makings of muscle. No longer the man he was, at least in shape, he harboured a deep hatred for the man who grinned and waited and tapped.

Crossing the line for the last time, Monomachus shuddered to a halt and doubled up, breathing hard, watching the sweat roll from the tip of his nose to a spot in the dirt. Thank God for the chill. Thank God he had survived.

A hand clapped him hard on the back, but he did not stir. "Well done, at last," cried Marcellus with barely contained glee. "It's been a long, hard road, but you've done it. Your training is done, and you are ready."

Monomachus neither felt ready or in the mood for celebration. All he was aware of was the burning stitch in his side and the desperate need for water. He straightened himself up, wincing at this final exertion. "We really are finished?"

"Aye, we are that. I'm proud of you, man. Look at you," he struck Monomachus's midriff with the reed cane, "you're fitter and stronger than you've ever been, I'll warrant. From this point on, you watch what you eat, do your daily squats and lower the volume of drink. That way you may prevent yourself from further visits to my little pleasure house!"

He laughed. Monomachus scowled. "I won't be coming here again, have no worries. You've enjoyed seeing me suffer and I won't forget it."

Marcellus's eyes narrowed, the laughter swiftly disappearing. "I did as ordered, Monomachus. There was nothing personal in it."

"You're a sadistic bastard, as are all Romans. What you forced the boy to do," he shook his head, "I shan't forget that."

"A test, nothing more."

"Which resulted in his death. A child."

"Aye, and his blood is on your sword."

"But on your soul."

Marcellus grew tense and for one terrifying moment, Monomachus believed the Roman would attack. No sooner had the moment come, however, than it dwindled, leaving Marcellus smiling. "You test me, Byzantine. As I tested you. But now it is done, so let us go our separate ways. I have other duties and responsibilities which require me to leave Byzantium, so I wish you well."

Monomachus snorted and whirled around. He strode across the training ground towards the collection of small, squat buildings in the far corner. There he could clean the sweat from his body and wash away the memory of this detestable place forever.

He went through the dilapidated door and pulled off his thin linen jerkin. He threw it in the corner, picked up an old rag and wiped his face. Outside, behind the building, a well provided water and he needed water desperately, his throat parched, the stench of stale sweat rising from every pore. He turned and almost cried out in alarm.

Framed in the doorway, the sunlight from behind her revealing the outline of her body through the thin shift she wore, a girl stood, head tilted, clicking her tongue. "You look as if you need a bath," she said.

Monomachus did a double take, not knowing what to say or how to react. He coughed, looked around for something to cover himself with, and then gasped as she took a step towards him. So close, he could smell her perfume, take in the smoothness of her skin, the voluptuous lips, almond coloured eyes, hair that fell in shimmering strands to her bare shoulders. She ran a perfectly manicured nail across his chest, tongue darting between her lips. "My, you are hot aren't you?"

He ran his hand around her back and pressed her body closer. Her mouth opened and he kissed her, long and passionately. She pulled her head back, "My God, I've missed you."

He grinned, "It's so good to see you, my love." He kissed her again before swiftly pulling away her thin dress and attacking her breasts greedily with his lips. She purred, grabbed handfuls of his hair, and allowed him full rein over her body, which he consumed with gusto.

He had her on the floor, entering her without ceremony, thrusting a half dozen times before coming with a roar of complete satisfaction.

They lay side by side staring towards the ceiling, the only sound that of their laboured breathing.

"An animal," she sighed.

Monomachus chuckled and patted his stomach, a great deal of the flab now despatched. "What do you think, my lovely? Am I more of a lion than an ape?"

She rolled into him, snuggling up close to him, "You were never an ape, my love. But yes, you are certainly ... *different.*" She traced the length of his flaccid cock, "But here is the same." She sighed and sat up, gathering her flimsy robe around her shoulders. "We need to talk, my love. I have news, from my brother and the General Maniakes."

"A pox on him." Monomachus climbed to his feet and stretched. "I need to wash, get rid of this stink. Then we will talk."

Scleriana rose to her knees. "Listen, please. They plan to use you, my lover. They have a scheme in mind, a plot. They wish to use our love for one another and hold it over you as a threat."

"A threat?"

"Yes. Once you are married to the Empress and become Emperor yourself, they will move against you. Undermine you, inform the Empress of our affair and Zoe will move for an annulment ... *if* you do not do as they wish."

"Become their creature?" He smiled. "I always knew it, my love. Do not fear, I have ideas of my own."

"But you must be careful. Maniakes is powerful. If he wanted to he could—"

Monomachus stooped down and took her face between his hands, "You must not concern yourself with the ways of power, my love. I have waited long for this time and I am not going to let it slip away now. I am to be Emperor, and once I am, all men will know what I am capable of."

He smiled and drew her close to his chest, "You are my love, Scleriana. I may be a vile, disgusting bastard who takes whatever he wants, but I only ever have you in my thoughts. I am not some base fool who underestimates my enemies. I have made mistakes and done some loathsome things, but that man has gone now. For that I have to thank Maniakes, for bringing me here to this place and introducing me to Marcellus and his harsh training regime. But every day, lying here in this pitiful place, I have meditated long and hard over who I was and who I want to be."

He pushed her face back and kissed her. "I have much to do over the next few days, my love. You, you must come with me to the Patriarch Alexius. I will present him with my own plans and you will see how great I have become."

She gazed into his eyes and slowly her mouth turned upwards. "I trust in your intelligence, my love. My only thought is for your safety. My brother, he is a vile, contemptible creature. I despise him, wish him dead."

"There will many more deaths before these next few days are out, my love." He cupped her breast and lowered his mouth to her swiftly hardening nipple. "God, I've longed for this."

"Slower this time, my love," she breathed as he pushed her back down to the ground, throwing open her gown.

"Oh yes," he growled, "it will be. My bath can wait, for now all I want is you."

Forty Five

There were choices to make, and as he walked through the orange groves of his estate, the autumn sun warming his bones, Maniakes sifted through what he could do. When he sat astride his horse and surveyed the field of battle, his forces arraigned, the tactics distributed to his lieutenants, the world proved a simpler place. Battlefields and the screams of the dying, all his bedfellows. This, this was something far more complicated, even disturbing. The hated Sclerus presented intoxicating possibilities. But to continue, to take the final step, he did not feel certain at all. All his life he'd served the Empire, given it everything he had, but in the end were the rewards enough? He'd schemed with Alexius and Orphano to topple the deranged Michael V, and what advantage had he gained? Perhaps the things Sclerus offered would lead to exactly the same conclusion. A man of honour, courage and foresight, the saviour of the Empire. They might even erect a statue in his honour.

Images of Leoni came into his mind. Her nubile body yielding under the prowess of his cock. She had proven a good pawn in the game he played. Useful, willing, pliant. Now, she was lost, and his wife bedded by Sclerus. None of it had come to mean anything. A waste of time and energy, to be so close to seizing the ultimate goal, the throne of Byzantium, only to be thrown once more into the mix. He was better than this. He deserved more.

He laboured throughout the day, writing and re-writing the orders. They needed to be precise, to leave no misunderstanding. With a final perusal, he called for his servants, the remaining ones, and gave to each of them the sealed documents. They were to ride, with all haste, to the eastern reaches of the Empire and deliver his commands to the officers billeted there with their men. The time was nigh. No more prevarication, the die cast. As he sat in his solarium and watched the servants ride off into the distance, a moment of anxiety gripped him. He put his fists into his mouth and leaned forward on his elbows, wondering if his chosen course of action might prove his undoing. Well, if that were so, then so be it. His life had been one of hardship, decision and struggle. No more would he allow himself to wait. Whatever the outcome, he had made peace with his conscience.

He stood up and poured himself wine, drank slowly, knowing there was no turning back. Sclerus, Alexius, Zoe. Monomachus. All would soon realise.

From within his wife called his name.

She too. Betrayer of his trust. True, he had bedded many, Leoni included, but the knowledge Helen had surrendered herself to Sclerus brought him such revulsion, his body shook. Decisions made.

She sat in front of a steel mirror, running fingers through the tangled knots of her hair; he came up behind her, pressed his fingers into her shoulders and squeezed.

She purred. "Mmm, I love it when you do that."

"As you love me, my darling."

He felt her tense under his probing fingers. She soon relaxed again, giving a small laugh. "Of course. I'm feeling somewhat better today. I wanted to tell you, so you needn't worry." She swivelled around on her stool and smiled. "You could return, if you wish. To the city."

"I have yet things to do. I have arrangements to make. And you, you need a new servant."

"I can do that myself." Her eyes twinkled, her hand slipping underneath his thin linen shirt. "I've missed you."

He leaned his head towards her. "You have? And why is that, my sweet?"

A tiny frown, a moment of anxiety. It flickered across her face and her eyes glinted like steel. "I ... I do not understand your question. It is you who have had no feelings for me these passed months. Years." She sat back, considered him. "My love for you may have matured, become less physical, but it has never faltered. Despite your many liaisons with whores and serving wenches, I admire you for the great man you are."

"You seem to know a lot about what I do, my sweet."

She snorted. "The whole world knows it, George! I have no need of spies, unlike you."

"I have to protect my back."

"And what about me? Where were your protectors when that animal broke into this house? Tell me that."

"You could well ask the same of your lover."

The atmosphere changed, glacial, and she hurriedly got to her feet, sweeping up a brush to attack her hair as she strode into the corner, back turned, hiding her features. The anxiety, fear even, was plain to see, her agitated movements proving it so.

Maniakes stepped up to her once again. "I know all about him." He turned her by the shoulder.

Her lower lip trembled, her eyes becoming moist. "How could you?" she whimpered.

"Because he told me."

The fight went out of her and she almost collapsed, knees buckling. He supported her around the waist, staring into her eyes, and slipped the dagger under her breastbone and into her heart. She shuddered in his grip, a look of total disbelief crossing her face before the lights dimmed and she sagged, a dead weight in his grip.

He allowed her to fall to the ground, heavy and lifeless. Her blood billowed across his shirt; he looked at it, then at her. So quick. One moment there, no fears, no worries, concerned only with how she looked, how she needed to untangle her hair. And now this. A corpse.

Maniakes bent down and wiped his blade on her shift. Her lifeless eyes gazed out at him, pieces of black, dull glass. How different from when they had first met; her parents influential and rich, securing him a position in the highest echelons of the army. To rise so dramatically, and to love her with more ardour than she had ever known. He knew it from her cries. But then, as the years moved on, life and duty took him to distant parts, and nubile bodies. So many nubile bodies. He had feasted on their flesh, and Helen became nothing but a means to an end. General George Maniakes. Hero of Sicily.Commander of the Imperial army. Destined for greatness.

"What in the name of Christ have you done?"

A strong, urgent hand pushed him aside, and Maniakes fell backwards, and saw Sclerus as if in a dream, the man picking up Helen's body in his arms, holding her close.

He watched in silence before getting to his feet, to stand swaying, unable to understand what had happened, or why. His wife. Dead by his hands. The lines truly crossed now. No hope of turning back.

He considered plunging the knife into Sclerus's exposed neck, to sever the carotid artery, to send him into the darkness together with Helen so they could stay forever entwined. Lovers,bonded for eternity.

But he did not. Instead, he padded out of the room and returned to the orange grove to stand and gaze at the sky. A sky so very blue. Endless.

Forty Six

It was cold in the skiff, exposed as they were in the open sea. The city spread out before them; a huge, imposing smudge upon the horizon, the many churches, towers and walls black against the white sky. Hardrada trailed his hand in the water, studying the tiny wake as his thoughts turned to the next step. In front of him, huddled in a thick blanket, Sarah sat white-faced and silent. Since taking her from the convent she had fallen into a deep depression, seeming to age before his eyes. That vibrant beauty, the bronzed limbs, all hidden beneath her nun's habit, but even so there was something else.

A dryness, bitter and chill, emanated from every pore of her body. This was not the girl he knew, the one who had folded her mouth around his cock, begged him to make love, to bring her once more the height of pleasure. Willingly he had obliged, and often. Their lovemaking urgent, desperate even, and he had rutted and roared like a wild beast as her young, soft limbs gripped him, urging him on. God, how she had loved him.

And now, here she was.

Married to Christ.

He turned away, disappointment mixing with rage. He should have taken her with him, before Zoe caught wind of their affair. If he had followed his heart, he could have made good his escape, left the city and all of its foetid abuses behind. Instead, the Empress moved first, caught him in the trap, seized his gold, and threw him in prison.

And put Sarah away.

He splashed his face with a handful of seawater and craned his neck to eye the ferryman easing the skiff forwards. The man had said nothing when Hardrada and the girl found him cowering in a tiny cave just up from the beach. Frozen and soaked through to the skin, the man nevertheless went to his duties without complaint; now the only sound he made was a rhythmical grunt as the oars cut through the waters, taking them all ever closer to the great city.

A figure stood on the quayside, a big man, square-shouldered, dressed in mail hauberk and iron helm. Resting on one shoulder was the shaft of a battle-axe, his right hand holding the butt.

"Ho, Harald!"

Hardrada beamed, anxiety and anger falling awaythe instant he recognised his old friend. The skiff bumped in between anchored galleys and the ferryman tied it up next to the wall, Hardrada already helping Sarah to her feet.

"Watch the ropes," he said as she staggered towards the ladder dropping down the side of the wall. "It's slippery."

She moved as if in a dream, her features betraying no emotion. Hardrada watched her from the boat as she ascended, saw Ulf helping her as she reached the top. His old friend grinned down at him. "You took your bloody time."

"I had some issues," Hardrada lifted his bandaged arm, stained brown with blood. "The Mother Superior arranged a welcoming committee."

"I hope you killed the bitch."

Hardrada chuckled. "Now, that would be a mortal sin, as well you know. And I am not a sinner, my friend."

Ulf laughed and led the girl away as Hardrada turned and looked at the ferryman. He tossed him a bag of coins, which the man caught and weighted in his palm. "God damn your eyes, Viking."

"Thank you. May the blessings of the Lord Jesus Christ be upon you too."

"If I'd have known you were going to break into that convent and steal that girl ..." He shook his head. "You've damned me by your actions, you heartless bastard. What will you do with her? Rape her, give her your child? Is there no depravity you will not indulge in?"

"By Christ, you're a pious old bastard aren't you?" Hardrada grinned. "I'm sure God knows of your innocence in all of this, so don't be afraid of losing your place in paradise. You've earned your money, that should make you sleep soundly."

"It's blood money, you bastard! You blighted that holy place with your presence, and I did nothing to stop you." He squeezed fingers and thumb into his eyes. "Cursed am I."

"There is something you could do, to make it right."

The ferryman lifted his face. "What? There is nothing. Even a decade of prayers will never wash away the guilt I feel."

"Deliver a message. To the Empress." He pulled out the sealed parchment, enclosed in a thin leather pouch, tied loosely with string. "I had planned on giving this to her myself, or letting one of my men ... but, perhaps if you ... listen, give this to her and I'll offer up twice as much gold as you have there in your hand to a church of your choosing. How about that?"

The man's eyes widened. "You would do such a thing, for me?"

"For your soul, ferryman. If you give your word to deliver this to the Empress."

Without a pause, the man reached forward and snatched the pouch from Hardrada's grip. "Damn you if you do not give that money, Viking."

"Damn you if you do not deliver it."

And with that he scaled the rope ladder.

***

They kept to the side streets, following a twisting route through the maze of tightly packed houses, moving from one quarter to the next. Curious looks did not linger long. Too often people from all walks of life wandered these thoroughfares, so questions consisted of nothing more than a furtive glance. It was all to the good. Hardrada may have been an unmistakeable figure, but no one appeared in the least concerned. Even the occasional soldier paid them no mind. Indeed, the farther they went into the city, the less their presence seemed to attract attention. Tiny groups gathered on street corners and babbled on about the latest news. Market stallholders, crying out their wares, paused to indulge in conversation. All around an urgent excited buzz filled the air.

"What's going on?" asked Hardrada, pulling up before a tired looking tavern.

"I don't know," said Ulf. I've been over on the far side, well away from all of this. A marriage perhaps, or some religious thing. Games maybe."

Hardrada frowned and peered down at Sarah. "Is it a festival? In honour of some saint?"

Her eyes remained blank, lifeless.

Hardrada gave a sharp exasperated sigh. "Shit, she hasn't spoken a single word since we left the island."

"Do you blame her? There she was, living a lovely, comfortable life, then you arrived. I think even my tongue would be locked in my mouth."

"You'd do well to keep it that way right now," he said with exaggerated seriousness. Ulf grinned and Hardrada motioned to the end of the street, "Well, whatever it is, it might do us some good. Whilst they are all indulging themselves, we can make good our escape."

Ulf pointed to Hardrada's bandaged arm, pink where the blood had soaked through. "That looks nasty."

"The sisters put some herbs on it. It'll heal well enough."

"So, even in a convent you managed to get into a fight?" Ulf shook his head. "And what will the Empress do when she hears about what you've done?"

"I've sent her a message. If it goes as I plan, our route to the north will be a smooth one."

"I see. You think she'll take the bait?"

"Let's hope so," he said quietly, not daring to look in Sarah's direction. If Zoe did *not* 'take the bait', he had little idea what he would do next.

***

In her royal apartments, the Empress Zoe applied a final few spots of cream to her cheeks, then sat back to admire herself in her mirror of polished steel. She turned first one cheek, then the other, pursed her lips and smiled, pleased with the effect. The Patriarch may be a man of God, but he was a man nevertheless. Anything to soften his heart, and send a flicker of desire through his cock would be well worth the effort.

Guards fell in behind her, escorting her through the broad corridors of power. Outside, the air was cool, summer now something of a memory. Soon the rains, like the one of the previous day, would become more of a feature and life would change. No longer gentle strolls through avenues flanked by larch and limes, but prolonged hours huddled before fires, listening to the constant drivel of a hundred courtiers and government officials. How she loathed the minutiae of rule. How she longed for someone else to take the reins and steer Constantinople towards something akin to calm, order and peace, allowing her time to indulge in good food, good wine, and an abundance of lithe young men.

Mounting the steps of the Patriarch's palace, guards and senators alike bowed deeply, some mumbling blessings and prayers for her continued good health. If only they knew how hard she laboured to ensure the continuance of her beauty; the many creams and concoctions applied in a daily ritual, which took up most of her mornings but left her feeling refreshed and ready to face the world. Image was everything and the lingering looks from men from all sections of society, low and highborn alike, sent flutters of happiness and satisfaction through her. So many men desired her; so many longed to feel the warmth of her shadow, the radiance of her smile. A goddess to so many.How she loved it.

Guards announced her arrival and the great double doors of the Patriarch's assembly room wheezed open, the heavy aroma of sweet incense wafting over her in an instant. She blinked, fighting back the urge to wipe her moist eyes. To smudge her make-up would not do, not at this moment.

Through the clouds of perfumed smoke, a plump and smiling priest arrived, shuffling forward, bowing low. "Your Grace, His Holiness the Patriarch was not expecting you. He is in—"

"Inform His Holiness of my presence, and instruct him to meet me in his private apartments." She levelled a hard gaze upon the priest, who wilted under her stare, "At once!"

The priest bowed even lower and hurried off without a word. Zoe sighed and looked to her guards. "Wait for me outside. I'll send for you when I'm done."

The men snapped their heels together, saluted and left with rigid formality. Zoe, who knew the building well, swept over to the far side and made for a thick, leather-padded door. A guard opened it without a pause and she went inside.

A fire crackled in the grate and wine and olives waited on the small ebony table standing next to a sumptuous couch, covered with silk cushions. She eased herself down, took an olive and bent one leg, allowing her robe to fall open to reveal the bronzed flesh of her thigh. She put her head back, closed her eyes and waited.

She did not have to wait long.

The door opened and in shuffled Alexius, looking so much older than he did in their last meeting, the strain etched deep in the lines around his eyes and mouth. He allowed his eyes to wander over her for a moment before he bowed. "Highness."

Zoe swung her legs around and stood up, smiling. "My dear friend," she said, voice as thick and slick as olive oil. "I trust you are well?"

He took her proffered hand and kissed it, looking at her from beneath his brows. "I have been better. The cold creeps into my bones. This winter, I fear will find me—"

"Yes," she said, gliding across the room to the fire, "I'm quite sure. Come and warm yourself, and tell me of your plans."

She watched him over her shoulder, saw his frown, the hesitation. "Plans? I do not ..." He forced a short laugh.

"You must not think me deaf, or ignorant, Holiness. I have my own means of discovering what happens within the confines of *my* palace. I know you meet with my sister. I know you talk."

"Highness, if you believe me to have been—"

"Psellos's death was unfortunate, was it not? Your deputy? A capable man, in so many ways."

"Highness ... Psellos took his life. Your *agents* must have informed you."

"Took his own life ... yes, I suppose that is the official line." She thrust out her palms towards the fire as Alexius shuffled next to her.

"If you think I have in any way conspired against you, then you are mistaken, Highness. I have been your supporter since the very first. But, I have struggled with certain ... *decisions*. This plan of Maniakes's, to see you wed to Monomachus ... I have misgivings."

"You and I both, Holiness." She caught his surprise and laid a hand on his forearm. "However, the Empire needs to be guided towards a better future. I cannot do it alone. Monomachus is the best choice."

"You agree to marry him? I ... the man is a notorious womaniser and I am unconvinced our future will be secure under his stewardship."

"Stewardship? He will be *Emperor,* Holiness."

"Highness, I have prayed long on this matter. It is true that initially I agreed with the General's plan, but the Lord has given me guidance, Highness. I feel the better course would be for you to rule in conjunction with your sister. She is most able, a woman of high esteem, beloved by the people. Intelligent, pious, the very epitome of the Byzantine ideal."

Zoe struggled to quell the simmering rage inside. Damn them both, Theodora and this weasel of a man. "Alexius, I am Empress. I make the decisions."

"But together, you would be so much more able, Highness. Monomachus will bring nothing to the Empire except division and ill feeling. The Senate will never accept him."

"The Senate will do as I tell them."

"Highness," he reached out to her with both hands. "I beg you, think well on this course. Maniakes has erred. I have prayed long over this and I know it is so. Together, you and your sister will restore our fortunes I am certain."

"And militarily, Holiness? The people may be happy to see my glorious sister parading herself around the Hippodrome like some saint, but in the meantime the threats to our borders continue to grow."

"How can you know such things? You are nothing more than a—"

"Than a *woman*, Holiness? Is that what you were about to say?"

Alexius turned away, moving over to the couch. "Forgive me, Highness, I did not mean to criticise." He slumped down, a huge sigh exploding from his lungs. "I am weary, Highness. Sometimes my mind is not as sharp as it once was, but ..." He raised an index finger, giving weight to his words, "I understand your concerns about the borders. I have a solution."

"A solution? Monomachus is the *only* solution, Holiness. Together with Maniakes we can ensure not only our safety, but our prosperity too."

"Forgive me, but that is not so. Maniakes will use Monomachus as a puppet, nothing more. The General is consumed with his ownambitions and if we do not curb them, we will be in mortal danger. Not from perceived threats at our borders, but internally. Maniakes has greater ambitions than any of us ever perceived possible."

A cloud came down over her, so thick that for a moment she could neither see nor think. The Patriarch's network of spies and investigators was notorious. Better, perhaps, than even her own. She swung over to him and sat down. "If what you say is true, and I have no proof either way, perhaps you should tell me of your solution?"

"Hardrada."

She gaped at him. "Are you serious?"

"Never more so. He is as capable a commander as Maniakes, has proved his mettle more than once, and is a loyal and faithful servant to the Emp—"

"*Faithful servant?*" She blazed with anger. "Are you mad? You spout your condemnation over Monomachus and yet you dismiss that vile Viking's excesses? You've lost your reason, Holiness, as well as your energy."

"Highness. You must hear me out. If, as I feel sure, Maniakes is openly plotting against the throne, we have little choice but to rely on Hardrada. He has the loyalty of his men. He came to our aid before, when Michael threatened to remove us all. Whatever your differences, you must put them aside for the good of the Empire."

"I'll not do it. And you cannot know what is in the General's heart. He has served us as well as anyone, certainly better than your damned Viking!"

Alexius shook his head, put his hands on his knees and pushed himself to his feet. He crossed the room to his desk and unlocked a small casket. He turned to her, a rolled parchment in his gnarled fist. "I received this from one of my people only this morning. I meant to bring it to you, as soon as my meetings with the holy bishops were concluded. As it is, with your coming here, perhaps you should read it."

She eyed the roll, her throat dry. "What is it? Tell me."

"Orders. Written by Maniakes, commanding his army to assemble and prepare to march on Constantinople."

The same cloud grew closer, overwhelming

her. "It ... it cannot be genuine."

"It is, Highness. His signature ... it is his death warrant."

She snatched it from him and scanned through the words. Before she even reached the end, each letter twisting like a knife into her heart, the tears welled up and blurred the remainder of the order. She put it aside and sat, her body shaking.

"I am sorry, Highness." He returned to her side. "If we put Hardrada in command, with the able General Kekaumenos at his side, we will prevail."

"No." She shook her head. "We cannot."

"We *must* Highness. The longer we prevaricate, the more Maniakes will be able to consolidate his position. With your command, I can inform Hardrada of his appointment and we can face Maniakes in the field, with overwhelming force."

"Holiness. You do not understand." She raised her head, the tears flowing unchecked now. "If only you had trusted me, if only you had come to me and spoken to me ..."

"My child," Alexius smiled and sank down beside her, holding her hand in both of his, "What's done is done. We must move. We must stop Maniakes before he can—"

"Holiness. We cannot. Hardrada is dead." His look, so downcast, so broken, she wanted to draw him close, to hold him. A devoted servant, a man of God, but so innocent, so ignorant of all the intrigues of government. He professed to know, his network of informers bringing him whatever they could, but the simple fact was he did not know what to do with the information he gathered.

She shook her head, the sadness gripping her. "I'm sorry. It is my fault. I hate him, for what he did to me; his betrayal, his dishonour. When you took him under your wing and convinced him to lead the Varangians against Michael, I kept quiet. But inside I raged, Holiness. I knew I had to have my revenge, and as soon as Michael was defeated that is exactly what I have done. He has gone to his death, leading an ill-fated mission to Sicily, believing all of our forces would join him. Like the fool he is, pig-headed and full of his own greatness, he fell into my trap and now lies dead. I'm sorry."

"And I am too, my child." Alexius squeezed her hand. She narrowed her eyes, mouth opening, but unable to speak. "It was not Hardrada you saw sail away to his death, but Bolli Bollason, former leader of the Varangian Guard. A Viking, but hated by Hardrada and no friend of mine."

She shook her head. "You ... You cannot speak the truth. How ... how could you know?"

"I am old, my child, but not as dim-witted as you would believe. Hardrada lives and shall be our salvation." He stood up, crossed to the ebony table and poured himself wine. He drank it down in one and turned to her again, a new light burning in his eyes. "And Monomachus will not rule. Not as long as I remain Patriarch of Constantinople."

***

She returned to her royal apartments in silence, walking in a daze, reeling from the Patriarch's words. Alone, having dismissed her guards, she stood on her balcony and looked out across the sea, the late afternoon sun throwing a diluted, hazy light across the gently rippling surface.

Hardrada, alive? How could she have been so out-manoeuvred? To have all of her hopes dashed so completely ...

She held onto the balcony wall, steadied her breathing, and tried desperately to formulate a plan to get everything back on course.

The courtier coughed softly behind her; she whirled around, sending him such a scathing look he recoiled, bowing so low his head almost touched the ground. "Forgive me, Highness. The guards did announce me."

Had they? She knew not, lost in her thoughts. A herd of wild beasts could have rampaged through her rooms and she would not have noticed. She sucked in a breath. "What is it, man? Speak out!"

"Highness." Still bent double, he thrust out his hand and the leather document wallet he clutched. "An old ferryman insisted, Highness. Said these were words you must know."

"*Must know?* Damn your eyes, man," she took the wallet, ripping away the string, and pulled out the piece of parchment. She read. Held her breath. Re-read and then, before any thoughts came to mind, the great black cloud descended again, swallowed her up, and delivered her into darkness.

Forty Seven

The sea seemed calm enough as Hardrada oversaw the embarkation of his men. Guards, posted to warn of any enemy approach, stood tense, eager to leave. But Hardrada took his time and as some men helped Sarah on board, he turned to Ranulph. "When we have reached the Black Sea," he said, "I'll not ask anything more of you, old friend. I've given you a good measure of my gold and you can return here if you wish, make a life."

"A pox on that, Harald. I've had enough of serving these Greeks. I've got a woman in the north. I'll set myself up with her, grow almonds, or brew ale. Something."

"Grow old."

"Aye. That too."

They laughed, clapped each other on the back and then, when the last of them had boarded, Hardrada signalled for the guards to join them.

Hardrada was the last to walk up the gangplank. He nodded to Ulf and Haldor, then raised his voice to the men as they prepared themselves to begin rowing the ship out into the bay. "Remember the drill,lads." Hardrada reached over for the war-horn and raised it aloft. "Two blasts to begin, then a long single blast to get back to positions." He looked at Talen who leaned over the prow, gauging the depth of the water. "All is well, pilot?"

A low grumble and Talen turned, his face etched with misery and anger. "Fuck you, Viking. Just get the fucking thing moving. I'll tell you when."

Ulf, standing close by, leaned towards his old friend and whispered, "When we're clear, I'll spit him like a pig."

Hardrada grinned. "You're so ungrateful, Ulf. Without the services of that bastard, we would not be able to do this at all." He slapped his old friend on the back and went to the stern, raising his arm to Ranulph in the second ship. When the response came, Hardrada turned, lifting his voice to roar, "Row, you bastards! Row for all you're worth!"

They eased out into the bay, making good progress through the various merchant ships and galleys tied up close by. Not as busy as the southerly ports, nevertheless the Neorion Harbour bristled with boats and ships and it took some careful negotiation from Talen to lead the ships out into open water.

From here, with the port behind them, orders were screamed for the oarsmen to double, even triple their efforts.

Men groaned under the strain, muscles bulging, bodies breaking out into a sweat as the men gripped and pulled back on the oars. The pace increased as with each stroke the ships surged forward, lancing through the waters with growing momentum. Teeth clenched white in faces drenched with perspiration, wild eyes peering forward, everyone waiting for the order to come.

Hardrada ran forward, leaned over the side next to Talen and watched the distant shore of the Galata peninsula streak by. At its head, the Megalos Pyrgos, the great tower, stood like an accusing finger, at the northern end of the Golden Horn, warning the Vikings to desist. Within this tower resided the mechanism that raised or lowered the great chain across the entrance to the Golden Horn. In times of danger, it prevented the passage of ships into the northern expanse of open water. Right now, the chain guarded the entrance, pulled taut. The Empress Zoe's orders had been rapid and immediate. Hardrada grinned. Just as he had expected.

He saw the great chain before Talen turned, serious-faced, menace in his features. "On my command."

Hardrada swung around, bringing up the horn. "Ready yourselves, lads," he shouted, and the rowers responded, putting their backs into their efforts. The ship increased speed as the men gritted their teeth, sweated and toiled, heaving back on the oars, eating up the distance between them and the chain.

"Soon," breathed Harald, heartbeat thumping in his temples. Soon.

He caught sight of Ranulph's ship,

labouring somewhat behind. Hardrada felt the first prickle of panic. The ships should be together, next to each other. For the plan to work, they needed to be as one. He raced to the stern, gesticulating wildly with his arms, breathing with relief to see the oarsmen responding. Ranulph, his voice lost amongst the sound of sea and surge, the straining sinews of the men, urging them on to even greater efforts.

And then Talen screamed and Harald lifted the horn to his lips and gave two huge blasts.

It worked, like a well-oiled machine, the men racing to the stern as one. Sarah hysterical, as eighty or more burly men swamped her in a mad, screaming rush.

The ship lifted, its prow leaving the inky black waters, propelled forwards by the enormous speed the rowers had set. It passed over the great chain, raised to prevent unwanted ships from reaching this part of Constantinople. But this day, it could not hold back Hardrada, who blew another blast and the men, like one great, incensed beast, rushed forward again to the bow. Some took hold of Sarah and carried her, her arms beating at them in wild confusion to no effect.

With a great splash, the ship hit the water hard, throwing out a massive wave as the stern rose up into the air, missing the chain by a body's length.

Still carried forward, the ship settled, listing erratically from either side, and the men returned to their benches to renew their rowing, and bring the ship under control.

Sarah whimpered and Hardrada held her close and for once, she did not pull away.

Then he looked to Ranulph's ship, and disbelief mingled with horror.

Ranulph's ship, slower, not as able, its men perhaps not as strong, seemed to pause in mid-travel, and the chain caught its underbelly. The awful, sickening splinter of the wooden hull reached across the water to Hardrada's ship and every man stopped and turned and watched.

Surreal, almost as if in a dream, everything slowed to a walking pace. The groaning, splitting wood, the dreadful tearing apart of the ship's entrails as it broke open like an over-ripe fruit, spewing forth its contents. Men, screaming, floundering, falling into the churning sea to be devoured in an insane fury of foam and cold and death.

Hardrada screamed to his crew to turn about, but Talen seized him, shaking him. "It's no use, damn it! We cannot turn, the chain will not allow us."

Hardrada tore himself free and ran to the stern, leaning out, wild-eyed with denial at what he witnessed. At his shoulder, Ulf, crying out, "*Ranulph!*"

But Ranulph was nowhere to be seen, only the mass of desperate men drowning in an unforgiving sea.

***

They waited on the farthest shore, not far beyond the walls of Galata. No one spoke, not even Talen, who sat still and silent, all of his usual sarcasm and insults gone, lost in his thoughts.

When Ulf returned, accompanied by a group of Varangians steering a cart loaded up with wooden chests of various sizes, and bundles of bulging flax sacks, he jumped down and shook his head. No other words were necessary.

Hardrada watched Sarah walk away, the three Byzantine guards at her side. She did not look back and he felt grateful for that. Sarah was part of the world he was leaving behind, a world he no longer wanted or needed.

Ranulph had been part of that world also. A man of courage, honour. A man whose only wish had been to live out his remaining years with his wife, in a simple farm, living out a simple life.

Now he lay at the bottom of the Horn.

Zoe had ordered the chain raised, to prevent Hardrada from breaking free of her yoke. He had succeeded; she had failed. But in the process, at the moment of victory he had lost so much and he did not know if he would ever feel whole again.

Forty Eight

In the far distance, the sound of a melancholy bell, rhythmically calling the faithful to prayer, cut through the mist and Bolli rolled over onto his back and wondered if he had woken up in Heaven.

But if this was paradise, then why was it populated by black crows and bent-over hags rifling through the fallen corpses strewn across the sand?

He shook his head and sat up, wincing at the pain stabbing into his side. Gingerly placing the flat of his hand against the rent in his tunic, he felt the dried blood, hissed in a breath and tried to stand.

His legs buckled and he fell again, groaning aloud. A figure loomed over him, the face of an old woman, toothless, rheumy-eyed filled his vision. She mumbled something, which Bolli did not understand, and then a goatskin gourd pressed against his lips and he took in a large mouthful of spiced, sweet wine. Strength ebbed into his limbs almost at once, the alcohol warming frozen joints, and he managed to sit up again, coughing as the wine caught the back of his throat. She offered him more and he took it, nodded his thanks and she spoke again in a language he vaguely recognised as Latin, or Italian, or something similar.

She levered his elbow and helped him to his feet and he looked along the shoreline, the dead stripped of clothes, bobbing like corks in the ebb and flow of the waves. The Normans, underlining their reputation for ruthlessness, had slaughtered the entire crew. And there, amongst them, stuck on the end of a large pike with its face looking out to sea, a man whom Bolli thought he might know. By his haircut, a Norman. Beside him, another. Both, with eyes open, stared out into the endless sea of time before them, executed and parade, a lesson for all to remember.

Others began to crowd around. "You are with the Greeks?" one asked, and Bolli experienced a surge of relief that at last he could understand what someone said. He managed a nod, gestured for more wine, and drank the gourd dry. "We watched it all from the heights," said the crone, waving her hand in the vague direction of the surrounding sand hills. Bolli followed her pointed fingers and grunted. "They herded these poor unfortunates together, gave them food and water, then killed them. These two," she motioned towards the hideous symbols of Norman retribution, "they dragged them to the water's edge and hacked off their heads. They cheered at the first, but laughed as the second screamed and struggled."

"What did he say, did you hear?"

"Aye. We all heard. Like a wild thing he was, 'Damn your eyes, William will know of this.'" She shrugged. "The other, the one now in charge, he said, 'William already does' and then they all laughed as this man swung his sword and took off the other's head."

"William? Are you sure he said William?"

"My French is as good as my Greek, young man. I was a nun once. Before you were born." She cackled and rubbed her nose, "Before I met a young man and realised what I'd been missing." She repeated the phrase, as far as Bolli could tell, to the others who all joined in with a chorus of ragged giggling. One by one they drifted away to resume their frightful searching of the dead. The old crone remained, holding Bolli's stare. "We can offer you some food and shelter in our village, if you are able to walk the distance." She frowned. "You are badly wounded, and I can tend to that."

"I thank you."

"I have no love for Normans, but you are clearly not one of them."

"I am Norse. From Iceland originally. Far, far away." His eyes glazed over, memories of home rushing into his mind.

The crone coughed, touching his arm. "Who might that William be?"

Bolli blinked and shrugged. "There is only one I know of, for certain. William Iron Arm, Liege Lord of the Normans in Italy. I have crossed his path before." He nodded to the heads. "He is ruthless and violent. No man crosses him and lives."

"You lived."

"Aye." Bolli forced a smile. "But I was not the one they expected."

"I do not understand."

"Neither do I. Not fully. But I will." He again touched his side. "You are right, my wounds need tending before they begin to go bad. Too often I've seen men die from wounds not cleaned sufficiently. So I'll accept your kind offer, old woman. And thank you."

"You can thank me once we know for certain those damned Normans will not be returning."

"I doubt they will, not now. Their plan, whatever it was, did not go well, and these men have paid the price for failure. Whatever happens, I intend to stay alive."

He passed over the empty gourd, which she took, and then slowly led him away from that fearful place where the sea lapped over the bodies of the dead and the crows feasted on the flesh.

Forty Nine

Constantine Monomachus stood in the huge entrance to the Imperial palace and took a moment to breathe in the rich perfume of power. Soaring columns reached to the great arched ceiling, covered in an array of frescos detailing the many and varied exploits of past Emperors, enemies being defeated, God smiling with pleasure. And everywhere the glitter of gold.

Guards lined the walls, resplendent in lamellar armour and bronze, helmets topped with red plumes, spears and shields shining. A herald stood before him, a small round man, beaming as he bowed, a dramatic flourish of his hand preceding his declaration, in a surprisingly loud voice, "Welcome most gracious majesty. The Empress awaits."

Monomachus tore his eyes from the glorious decorations and looked askance at Scleriana. "This is the moment I've dreaded."

"You will soon be Emperor, my love. Do what is necessary."

"Even if that means bedding the Empress?" She smiled. "You can think of me whilst you do it."

He squeezed her hand. "A villa for you, my sweet. On a cliff top overlooking the Adriatic. With sweet wine and olives, and more gold than you can count."

Scleriana closed her eyes for a moment. "I need to be close to you, my love." She turned her face to the vast expanse of ceiling. "I wish to live here, as your concubine."

"That might take some selling to her divine Empress."

"You will succeed, my love." She leaned forward and kissed his cheek. "As only you can."

Monomachus caught the herald's perplexed look and smiled, squeezing Scleriana's hand again. "Yes, my sweet. You could be right. But for the moment, wait here. Enjoy the ..." he swept his hand through the air in the general direction of the ceiling, "decorations!" Then he released her hand and motioned for the herald to lead the way into the depths of the imperial enclave.

***

Two officers of the guard bowed low as Monomachus neared the huge leather and gold inlaid doors of the Empress's private apartments. Other soldiers snapped to attention as the herald proclaimed, "His gracious majesty, Lord Constantine Monomachus, purveyor of all that is good and righteous, in the name of Lord God Almighty, Light of the World, seeks audience with her most divine Majesty, the Empress Zoe of Byzantium, Daughter of the World and Queen of Justice."

All about bowed low as the doors, as if of their own volition, swung inwards and there she stood, majestic in silver and gold encrusted robes, her headdress glittering with diamonds and emeralds, her lips ruby red, full and sensuous, eyes lustrous, skin burnished bronze. Monomachus felt his loins respond. She was as everyone had said, as beautiful as the morning in springtime, as seductive as the most glittering of jewels. A woman lusted after by every man who breathed, peasants and priests alike. A goddess. Empress Zoe.

He stumbled forward as if in a dream, drinking her in. Dimly aware of the doors closing behind him, he watched as if in a dream as she approached, mouth parted in a slight smile, her tongue licking her full lips. She took his hand in hers and the warmth of her touch sent a thrill through him, bringing him to full erection. "My sweet," she said, and leaned into him and kissed him, those soft lips enveloping his own, tasting of sweet cherries. He closed his eyes, relishing the moment. "I heard you were big," she said, her eyes widening as her hand cupped his erection tenting his robe, "but I thought they spoke of your girth, not this." She squeezed him and he gasped. Slowly her hand moved over his stomach, across his chest, and along the length of his arms. "Big. But not flab. You have become more of a man, Monomachus."

"For you, my queen."

Her eyes closed for a moment. "I have longed for a man these past weeks," she smiled at him, "and here you are, at last."

In a rush, he took her around the waist and pressed her to him, kissing her mouth with a new urgency, "My God, you are more lovely than I ever imagined."

She expelled air through her nose, laid her palms against his chest and pushed him away a little. "Patience, my sweet. We are to be wedded and crowned on the morrow. All the arrangements are complete."

"I have news," he said, battling to regain some of his usual self-control, forcing himself to turn his eyes from the swell of her breasts. "Sclerus, a most able and loyal son of Byzantium, has informed me of a dastardly and terrifying plot against our royal persons by the cur George Maniakes. We have to prepare a force to march against him. A force led by Harald Hardrada, as counselled by His Holiness Alexius."

A dark look fell over Zoe, the former expression of ardour replaced by a scowl and she turned away. "I have spoken to Alexius, at length. He refuses to support our marriage and has dug his heels in over our coronation."

"In that case perhaps we had best delay and—"

"There shall be no delay," she snapped, her eyes blazing as she swung back towards him. "Already an entourage from the Patriarch of Hadrianapolis is approaching the city walls. I have not been idle, as many would think I am."

"You mean His Holiness?"

"I mean my *sister,* Monomachus. She is the main obstacle against us, always has been. Why Alexius brought her back, I shall never know."

"How can anyone know the machinations of such a man? But right now, the problem with Maniakes is the most pressing. If he assembles his troops, then he will march on Constantinople and we will have to face him. We must inform Hardrada and make ready our army."

"Hardrada is of no use to us now, Monomachus. Trust me."

"I know of your animosity towards the man, and I appreciate how loathsome it must be to countenance his help, but we *need* his services."

"Then you had best look to the north. For he has gone, and his treasure with him."

Monomachus felt his stomach lurch. "*Gone?* What in the name of Christ do you mean?"

"He has fled, making his way back to his homeland and leaving us to fight our own battles." She stepped up close and laid a single, superbly manicured nail on his chest. "And you, my lovely, sweet husband-to-be, will lead our forces and crush Maniakes before he is within a hundred leagues of this glorious city."

Monomachus gaped at her, growing light-headed, and he almost fell before she held him, drawing him close, breathing into his neck. "Do not fret, my sweet. All will be well. Tomorrow we shall wed, and then I will take you to my bed and show you more love and pleasure than you ever thought possible. The following day we will address the citizens in the Forum of Constantine, and assemble the greatest army this Empire has ever known. You will be a hero, my love." She nipped his ear, and ran her tongue around the lobe. "Imagine. My husband, the Emperor, saviour of the Empire. You will be proclaimed throughout the known world, and our love shall become a legend." She arched her back and looked deep into his eyes. "Constantine Monomachus, Son of God, and the finest lover in all Christendom!" Her hand delved between the folds of his robes and sought out his limp cock. "And tomorrow, you shall begin to prove it."

***

That night Monomachus lay in bed, staring into the darkness. His room, situated well away from Zoe's private apartments, separated by a maze of twisting, corridors, was small but comfortable. Scleriana and he had feasted on roasted quail and tomatoes before retiring and making love ardently until she wilted under him, unable to do anything other than lie back and allow her lover to partake of her body in however many ways he wished. And he did partake, repeatedly, having her in any number of different positions, roaring out his orgasms, on and on until she begged him to stop.

Spent, she collapsed and fell into a fitful sleep whilst he remained awake, thinking of Zoe and the words she had spoken. To lead an army? Even with the help of General Katakalon Kekaumenos, an awesome responsibility indeed. And what if Maniakes prevailed? What terrible retribution would he bring to those arraigned against him? The prospect was too awful to contemplate, but he was trapped, with nowhere to go and nothing to do except hope and pray all would be well.

Sclerus had brought him news of Maniakes, but Sclerus was not trustworthy. Could this be part of yet another plot? Was it Sclerus, and not Maniakes, who posed the greatest danger.

With heart pounding in his throat, Monomachus dragged himself from under the covers and made his way to the far table and the remnants of the feast. He poured himself wine, drank it down, and picked at a few scraps of uneaten quail. They had played him for a fool, every single one of them. Zoe especially. But he could do nothing about her. Maniakes, if God willed it, defeated in the field of battle and Sclerus ...

He squeezed fingers into his eyes and knew he must act swiftly. All would be well. Trust in God, he said to himself, and victory is assured.

But God might not approve of what Monomachus had in mind.

***

The day broke warm and glorious and already people crowded into the streets and avenues of the great city. The news had been posted, the announcements made on every corner. And now, the expectant buzz filled the air.

Trumpets resounded throughout

Constantinople and those citizens close to the magnificent edifice that was the Church of Saint Sophia, stopped mid-track to turn their faces towards the imposing basilica. Even in the more distant areas of Constantinople, a preternatural hush settled over everything. This was an event of significance, and not one to ignore or be unconcerned about.

The bells rang out their plaintive peal and, hidden for the most part from the eyes of the many, the Empress Zoe made her slow way through the subterranean passageway that led from her private apartments into the great church proper. As she emerged, the trumpets blew again, the noise soaring up into the far reaches of the gold illuminated ceiling. From the surrounding walls, the many frescos of past rulers gazed down with benign eyes on her magnificence.

And she was magnificent. Clothed in heavy robes of purple and pure gold thread, her headdress draped in layered plates of the precious metal, her face painted with all the artistry and skill of the finest handmaidens available. She radiated beauty and as she glided past, the many courtiers and dignitaries gasped in awe.

This was the Empress of the world, God's chosen ruler of the greatest city on Earth. The central pillar of a civilisation that went back six hundred years, loved and universally adored. And here, on this day, she would marry Constantine Monomachus and rule with him for as long as God granted her the breath to breathe.

Already the artists had worked furiously to disguise the name of her previous husband on the enormous fresco which dominated the far wall of Saint Sophia. Michael IV's name obliterated, replaced by that of Constantine IX. The man groomed by John Orphano, the eunuch, and delivered to the city by the agents of General Maniakes. The man, trimmed of flab, made an imposing figure and he stood at the altar, as he had done for many hours, and beamed at his new wife's approach.

Some distance away, standing radiant in sumptuous ruby-red robes, with hair interlaced with gold and silver bells, Scleriana stared in silence. Monomachus did not acknowledge her, but everyone knew who she was. News did not travel slowly in the streets and avenues of New Rome.

Priests swung incense, a choir took up an ancient chant, and Zoe swept up to the altar, took up Monomachus's hand and waited for the Patriarch to approach.

As suspected, the Patriarch was not Alexius. The Patriarch of Hadrianapolis stood in charge, arms spread out in supplication, voice booming across the assembly. It was he who gave the couple God's blessings and, if anyone thought ill, no one said a thing. It was all in God's plan, and that was good enough for everyone.

The steady, monotonous thrum of the great bells reverberated through the Patriarch's apartment. Kneeling in the gloom, two candles flickering in their sconces above his private chapel to the Holy Mother, Alexius clasped his hands against his chest and sought some meaning from his Lord. Always he had strived to do his very best to ensure the stability of the Empire, his counsel always actedupon.

No longer. Zoe, who until only recently was his greatest admirer and confidante, had changed. Something had come into her thoughts, forcing her to distance herself from her old and trusted friend. Alexius, of course, knew why. And in the shadow, a dark unmoving shape, that reason silently prayed.

Theodora, sister to Zoe, lost in grief for the deputy Patriarch Psellos, cut a sober and somewhat drab figure. But she was now with Alexius, previous differences buried. Their faith in their God absolute, both recognised there had to be a reason why the marriage would go ahead.

In the end, God's will would be done and his plans revealed. Until such time, they must remain quiet and compliant.

Fifty

Alone in the quiet of his stables, Maniakes brushed down the flanks of his prized warhorse. The messages sent, the orders given, soon he would ride to meet his men. The die cast. He looped his arm around the horse's neck and pressed his cheek against its warm flesh. Within a week, he would march on Constantinople and rid himself of his enemies forever. Then, to marry Zoe. Live out the life he always knew would be his.

The footfall made him turn, and he grinned.

"You killed her?"

He shrugged and drew her close. She purred, feeling the press of his arousal. "I had little choice. She'd been fucking Sclerus."

"So have I."

"Ah yes, but you did it because you had to …"

"He was good, my love."

"As good as me?"

She smiled. "What do you think?"

He laughed, swept her up into his arms and

carried her over to the piles of soft hay waiting in the far corner. He laid her down, ripped open his pants, and plunged into her.

"My lord was desperate," she said, sitting up after he had finished, and gathered her flimsy robe around her.

"I always am when I see you."

She smiled down at him. "What will you do with Sclerus?"

He shrugged. "What would you have me do, my sweet?"

"Kill him."

"Short, and to the point. Would you not have me make him suffer?"

"He betrayed you, betrayed his wife, and in time he would betray me." She shook her head. "You know he has sent messages to Monomachus? The fool laughed when he told me how he had tricked you into believing him. I almost told him that *he* was the fool."

Maniakes sat up. "He sent messages? When?"

She pulled a face. "Yesterday. Late at night."

He struck her, hard across the face, and she fell down, gasping, clutching at her split lip. "*Bitch,*" he screamed. "Why did you not tell me?" He stood up, tying together his pants.

"I thought you knew," she spluttered, pressing the back of her hand against the cut, which bled profusely. "You hurt me, you bastard!"

"Know this," he hissed. "I will hurt *anyone* who crosses me. Last night, you say?" She whimpered her reply. "Then I am already too late. Jesus." He went to his horse and threw on the saddle. "I shall ride to my men, gather them together with as much haste as I can and march on Constantinople. If I'm quick enough, I might be able to strike before Monomachus can make ready his defences." He bit his bottom lips. "Shit, if that bastard Hardrada stands in the field ..." He tugged hard on the straps. "Fucking Sclerus, I'll have his eyes for this." He swung round and his foot landed in a fresh pile of horse dung. He cursed, kicked it off on the fence post, which divided the stalls, then stopped and smiled. "Kill him, you say?"

She stood up, "I did. And I'm sorry, I thought you knew. If I had not—"

He held up his hand, "Enough of that. What's done is done. But you've given me an idea, or ..." He looked down at his boot and grinned, "Should I say *this* has given me an idea. Sclerus will play no more games of power and deceit with me."

"What will you do?"

"Something extremely entertaining." He turned to her, opened his arms, "My sweet. You have played your part well, and I am grateful."

"You are not angry with me?"

"My sweet," he beckoned her closer and she virtually ran into his arms and he bent down and kissed her. "You taste divine."

"I'm yours, my lord. Yours and no one else's."

"Yes. But you did say Sclerus was a good lover, did you not?"

She squirmed in his grip. "My lord, I told you ... he is nowhere near as good as you. I only did what you instructed me to do."

"Yes. You have, as I said, played your part well. You lived close, tending to your pathetic husband, and you won Sclerus with your ample charms. You did so very well." He kissed her nose. "And you were a good lover. One of the best."

A developing smile froze on her lips and then she gasped as Maniakes pushed the knife deep into her side, angling the blade upwards, eviscerating vital organs. She sagged in his arms and he let her drop to the ground, the blood leaking out over the hay. Before her breathing stopped, Maniakes strode out of the stables and made his way towards Sclerus's villa.

***

Kekaumenos readjusted his helmet and hauled himself up into the saddle. He nodded his head and grunted his satisfaction. The Imperial Guard, numbering some five thousand men, and a further three thousand Varangians, awaited his command. All he need do now was wait for Monomachus to grace them with his presence. No doubt the idle bastard was making merry with the Empress, so, patience never a strong point, Kekaumenos raised his hand before screaming out across the parade ground. "Men of Byzantium, we march to face the traitor George Maniakes. In the name of God, and the Emperor, victory is already ours!"

The soldiers roared out their agreement in

one mighty cheer, spears and axes held aloft.

***

Some way off, Monomachus tested his sword with a few strokes whilst Zoe looked on from the bed, her breasts exposed, licking her lips. "I had no idea you were so good, my love."

He laughed. "You mean my swordplay?"

"A quite beautiful sword, yes." She raised her arms above her head and stretched. "I thought you'd never let me sleep."

"If I didn't have to go to war, I would not have!" He slid the sword back into its scabbard and reached for his cloak. "I do not know how long I shall be. The messenger from Sclerus said Maniakes had yet to leave his villa. We might catch him before he can assemble all of his forces. If that is so, we should crush him with ease."

"*You* will crush him, my love."

"Aye. But we need more men. Mercenaries. I have some ideas, but they will take time. As soon as Maniakes is out of the way, I will set in motion new reforms, curtailing our spending but ensuring continued security."

"You are so clever." She smiled. "God, I wish we had met years ago."

He went over to her, ran his hand through her tussled hair. "And you, my sweet. You are so *giving*."

Her eyes closed. "Hurry back. I am already missing you."

"I will make the wait worthwhile."

"Yes." He stepped away and she eyed him from top to toe. "And as for that strumpet.

You will put her away, somewhere far away, my love."

Monomachus paused in the act of securing his cloak around his throat and narrowed his eyes. "That *strumpet* as you so heartlessly call her, is the love of my life. You had best remember that, my sweetness."

"I'll not share you with another woman."

"You'll share me with whoever I wish you to." He stepped over to her again. "Remember this – without me, this Empire will crumble. After I have defeated Maniakes, the whole of Byzantium will love me. And they will accept whatever I do, because I am the only one who can maintain the peace of this glorious Empire." His hand darted out like a viper striking its prey and he caught her hair in a powerful grip. She cried out as he twisted his fist. "You so much as lay one finger on her, my sweetness, and I'll cut out your tongue. You understand?"

She clawed at his hand, but it was useless, and after a moment she hissed, "*Yes, you bastard. Yes!*"

He released her and she fell back, clutching her head, breathing hard. "I can destroy you, my sweet. I can also deny you." He grabbed the bulge in his pants, thrusting his pelvis towards her. "You understand my meaning?"

"Merciless bastard!"

"*Do you understand my meaning?*"

"Yes! You fucking whore."

He laughed, "So speaks the biggest whore of them all." He swung away and swept up his helmet. "When I return, I'll show you how good it can be living with me, my sweet. But only if you do as you're told." He winked. "Sclerus will join our little family soon, my sweetness. We can all be happy together and, together, we will rule this magnificent Empire." And with that he left the room without another word.

***

But Sclerus would not be joining anybody.

Maniakes burst into his room at a rush as Sclerus was about to take a sliver of salted fish into his mouth. As he rose, Maniakes hit him hard across the side of the face, sending him crashing to the ground.

Wild now, flecks of spit spewing from his mouth, Maniakes hurled away a chair and kicked the half-risen Sclerus full in the face, pitching him backwards like a limp, wet rag. As the man writhed and groaned two of his servants took hold of him by the arms and lifted him to his feet.

"Welcome to the end of your days," said Maniakes, and landed a solid blow into the other's midriff. Sclerus's breath erupted out of his mouth, his face turning blue, and he sagged in the arms of his once loyal and diligent household workers. "How does it feel to know you are betrayed, eh?"

Sclerus lifted his head, sweat running down his strained features. A tiny frown and Maniakes laughed.

"I see you do not understand. Well, let me explain. You know that pathetic little whore you've been screwing? No, not my wife you poor fool. Your *neighbour's* wife? Sylvie? Well, she's been telling me everything, sending me reports about your many and varied little tricks." He grinned, casting his eyes over the servants. "Your household too. All in my service. All paid copious amounts so I can keep a close eye on everything you do." He leaned forward, the humour leaving his face, and gripped Sclerus's cheeks between finger and thumb. "You pathetic little shit. Did you really think you could outwit me, eh? I know everything. Your plans to ensconce your sister into the royal household, to make yourself chief administrator. But all the while you forgot about me and my ambitions and my absolute determination to see you rot in hell!" Maniakes snapped his fingers and a third servant, a young boy of perhaps a dozen years, entered, struggling with a large pail filled with steaming, stinking horse dung.

"You once told me you would ride my horse through the streets of Constantinople," laughed Maniakes, plunging a fist into the pile of excrement. "Well, my horse didn't take too fondly to that little remark and he asked me to give you a taste of just how angry he is." And with that he crammed the putrid mess into Sclerus's gaping mouth.

***

They stood in a small ring, peering up to the bodies suspended from coarse rope, swinging gently in the breeze. Their skin flayed, dried black blood ran like burnt tree branches down their naked thighs. Lifeless eyes bulged from bloated, pain-engrained faces with Sclerus himself the most hideous of the three, a grotesque manikin with mouth, ears and nose filled with excrement. Maniakes chuckled, touched his dead foe's feet with an index finger giving the corpse a little push to set up a more pronounced swing."Damn you to hell, Sclerus," he said and turned away.

No one else spoke, all mesmerised by the ghoulish sight before them.

Maniakes spurred his horse closer, "Once I am gone, torch his villa and his fields. I want nothing to remain when I return, is that clear?"

"Aye lord," said one of the others.

Maniakes looked to the sky, a few clouds drifting across the clear, endless blue. "I shall be back before the Moon is full once more. Destiny has called and I shall not be found wanting." He kicked his mount's flanks and rode off into the distance without another look back.

Fifty One

For the third time that day Andreas reined in his horse and scanned the nearby hillsides. Leoni came up beside him and sighed. "You think we are being followed?"

"Studied, I think."

She too ran her eyes over the skyline and shook her head. "I see nothing."

"No. Whoever it is they are good."

"How can you be sure someone is there?"

He smiled at her, "Because I am good too."

They moved on, following the winding trail through the mountains, setting an ambling gait, unconcerned by speed. Andreas made sure she was close. The girl had said little since the attack, but he knew she was close to breaking. Those huge, vivid eyes had lost their incandescence, her lips pale and thin, face gaunt. If he did not know otherwise, he might think her an old woman, dried up, weak and frail. If more Bulgars waited for the chance to strike they would not find her as the prize they wished for. Besides, Andreas thought, why did they not strike? He was one man and could do little against a determined attack. He had prevailed over the others due to his meticulous ambush. An assault by another group would be a very different matter.

One attacker, however, may result in a very different outcome.

And one man sat astride a horse right now, blocking their path.

Andreas pulled up, holding out his arm to bar Leonie's progress, and frowned towards the stranger.

He was a soldier, dressed in the uniform of the Royal Bodyguard, the elite force hand-picked from the Imperial Guard to defend the body of the Emperor, or Empress. He moved forward and Leoni gave a little cry.

Nikolias.

Andreas stiffened, reaching for his sword. But before he could react, Leoni kicked the flanks of her own mount to trot to the young Byzantine officer, reaching out as she drew near to fall into his arms, sobbing, out of control, her body melding into Nikolias's own.

He kissed the top of her head, then cupped her chin, pulling her even closer, and locked his mouth over hers. A sudden rush of desire enveloped him as the softness of her body yielded against him and they kissed for a long time.

When at last he pulled away, Nikolias locked his eyes upon Andreas, who stood, stony-faced, unmoved. Nikolias swung out of his saddle and then reached up to aid Leoni to do the same. He tied the horses loosely to a nearby fallen tree and smiled at Leoni when he told her to stay still. He then turned and took a step closer to his fellow Byzantine.

"I've been following you."

"Andreas nodded. "I knew it. For how long?"

"A day. I came across the men you killed. Bulgars?"

"Savages."

Nikolias gave a quick backwards glance to Leoni, trembling, her cloak gathered around her. "They hurt her?"

"I killed them before they could do that."

"Then for that I am grateful." He lowered his head for a moment. "And indebted."

"I am a warrior of Christ, Nikolias. I did what any other Byzantine would have done."

His words rang true and Nikolias smiled. "So, what happens now?"

"My orders are to find the girl, return her to the city."

"And mine are to travel to Kiev. To deliver dispatches to King Yaroslav." He slid his left foot forward slightly, tensing himself. "If you return her to Constantinople, they will kill her."

"Who will kill her?" Andreas dropped his eyes for an instant to the way Nikolias shifted position, and his hand hovered to his sword. "The General? The Empress? What possible good would that do?"

"Don't ask me to look into the hearts of those lost souls, Andreas. They killed my mother. They took Leoni away."

She rushed to him, grabbing hold of his arm. "A man, Niko. A terrible man, Heartless,

435

cruel. He broke into your home and snatched me away, said he wanted to lead me to Maniakes. Then the Bulgars came and ..." She sniffed, pressing the heel of her hand into her eye. "If Andreas had not saved me, they ..."

He turned and held her close again, allowing her to give full vent to her feelings. And as she remained trembling and crying in his arms, he fixed his stare on the other. "It was he who murdered my mother?" She sobbed, nodding her head into his chest. He let out his breath in a long, steady stream and narrowed his eyes towards his compatriot. "I'll not let you take her, Andreas, despite the service you have given us both."

Andreas snorted. "Very well. I have no wish to fight you, Nikolias. And as for the girl ..." He smiled. "I have an offer to make you."

"What sort of offer?"

"One that will serve us both well. I know Hardrada has plans to return to the north. He is betrothed to Yaroslav's daughter. Did you know that?"

"I have heard. But why would that be of any interest to me? My orders are simply to—"

"Deliver dispatches. I know, you said so." He took a step closer. "So here it is. Why not let me take the dispatches?"

Nikolias frowned, feeling Leoni tense in his arms. "*You*? But ... I don't understand."

"It's simple. I will take the dispatches to Kiev and you, my friend, you and Leoni can go to Maniakes's farm and get to the truth of it once and for all. Speak to his wife. Who knows, you might even get some answers."

And as Andreas grinned, Nikolias saw the sense in every single word.

***

They travelled with only the briefest of stops for refreshment, keeping clear of lonely households and hamlets. Once an aged market trader trundled by driving a haggard mule forward as it strained under the weight of piled-up bundles. An exchange of nods was all that passed between them. No one else broke into their thoughts.

On the second evening they made love under the stars, Nikolias groaning so loudly Leoni was forced to clamp her hand over his mouth. They lay naked and breathless staring at the night sky and she stroked his hair and told him she would teach him to be the finest lover in all of Christendom.

Later the following day they came upon Maniakes's villa, the stench of burning timbers thick in the air. On the horizon, a nearby farmhouse smouldered, its roof collapsed, walls broken. "What has befallen here?" asked Leoni. "You think it could be dangerous?"

Nikolias frowned, his hand falling to the hilt of his sword. He nodded towards the villa not so far away, "We shall soon find out."

They cantered down the slight incline. No one appeared to be about as Nikolias and Leoni took their horses into the yard, but then a thin man emerged from within, clutching a curved blade. He shivered with terror.

"There is no one here," he hissed, "except me and three others. We're armed and if you—"

Nikolias held up his hand. "Calm yourself, old man. We are not thieves. I am an officer of Byzantium, a captain in the Royal Bodyguard." The words eased the tension and the old man relaxed. "Where is the General?"

"Away to the east. He will not be back until the month is out." The scrawny man angled his head, his eyes lingering on Leoni. "I am sure the General would be more than willing to offer you the hospitality of his home. Although an unhappy place it is at the moment. Apart from a few remaining servants, everyone is dead, you see." His lip trembled and he broke down, the blade slipping from numbed fingers. He fell to his knees and within a blink others burst out from their hiding places, gathered around him, frightened faces looking out pleadingly towards the two visitors.

"What manner of devilment has occurred here?" demanded Nikolias.

"The worst kind," babbled one of the younger servants.

"Whose farm burns over yonder?"

The men exchanged wild, concerned looks.

Nikolias swung himself down from his horse then helped Leoni do the same. A young servant approached, bowed low, wringing his hands. "We are all still in shock, my lord. We are so afraid. But we have carried out the General's orders," he motioned towards the distant ruin of the neighbouring farmstead. "And we have buried the bodies. All with good, Christian grace, I swear it."

Nikolias placed his hand on the man's head, as if granting him pardon. "Clearly something dreadful has happened here, something far beyond my understanding. Perhaps when the General returns everything will be made clear."

The man nodded enthusiastically and turned to the house. "And until he does, my lord, we can offer you refreshment and rest."

Refreshment and rest. Nikolias smiled and drew Leoni close to his side, kissing her cheek. "We could do with plenty of that," he said, and together they followed the servant into the house whilst the others busied themselves with stabling the horses.

Fifty Two

George Maniakes scoured the desolate plain and knew it was not a good place. The scouts had brought in their reports and the news caused him to slump into his camp stool, bending forward to stare at the hard-packed earth, and mull over what he could do now.

Around him, soldiers prepared for battle, sharpening blades, adjusting panoplies, giving their horses a final check to ensure saddles fitted correctly. The buzz of anticipation filled the air; some men joked, many continued in grim silence. Over everything hung the knowledge that they were simply not enough.

The messages had gone out, sent two days previously. Nothing had come back. The General had waited, his patience stretched to breaking point. He needed more men, the regiments posted in the east, veterans, the same men who had accompanied Hardrada and him all that time ago in Sicily. The men around him right now were mainly mercenaries, Slavs and Asians. Would they hold, would they see it through?

Maniakes stood up and stretched his back. He snapped his fingers and a manservant handed over the goatskin gourd. He drank. Thessalonica. The air ran chill. Late autumn. Soon snows would fall and the campaigning season would draw to a close. He needed to hit the Walls of Theodosius before then. And to do so, he had to cut through the Byzantine force arrayed before him.

Adjusting the fit of his helmet, he stepped up onto the slight rise and joined his three generals. They all stood as still and silent as statues, staring down into the featureless bowl of dirt before them. Featureless except for one terrible thing.

The Byzantines.

***

The bishops wound their way through the steady formed-up ranks of soldiers, chanting prayers and sprinkling the men with holy water. Attendants streamed behind them, holding aloft gold inlaid crucifixes and icons of the Christ and the Holy mother. Many of the men crossed themselves, some fell to their knees shouting out their confessions. All received absolution. Way off in the distance, a small choir of black-robed monks sang in plainsong and Constantine Monomachus sat on his white warhorse and chewed at the inside of his cheek. Next to him, General Kekaumenos appeared unmoved, eyes closed, reciting what sounded to Monomachus as an old, family prayer.

"Penelope is your wife?"

Kekaumenos's eyes fluttered and he shook his head. "My daughter." He reached underneath his breastplate and fished out a small pendant. "I had this painted on her first birthday." He leaned forward and Monomachus studied the tiny portrait. A bright-eyed little girl, rosy-cheeked, plaited hair.

"When did you last see her?"

Kekaumenos shrugged and put the pendant back. He shifted position and nodded towards the distant rise. "Scouts have reported Maniakes has a force of some two thousand."

"We outnumber him almost three to one."

"The van is approaching his flank. Skirmishers are deployed, the blessings given."

Monomachus grunted. Kekaumenos gave so little away. Pious, stern and purposeful, he was not given to idle conversation. The troops respected him and he ensured absolution, properly conveyed. His faith seemed boundless. A sense of strong confidence oozed from every pore.

"I have made preparations to begin the minting of new coins," said Monomachus, hoping to tease out some response. "We need more men after this. I will disband Maniakes's forces on the eastern borders, employ mercenaries, paid in the new currency."

Kekaumenos remained silent. "Maniakes is a great general," he said, his voice flat. "I fought beside him on the island. But this day, he is weak and ill-prepared." He looked at Monomachus and his eyes burned with indignation. "It should never have come to this."

"You think me wrong to engage him in battle? The man is a traitor."

"Traitor? Or obstacle?"

"Don't bandy words with me, General. I am Emperor of New Rome. What I decree is what God decrees. You would do well to remember that."

"I am a soldier, nothing more. Politics is a game I do not wish to play."

"Maniakes thought differently." He turned in his saddle as the ranks of spearmen drew up in battle array, the *promakhos*or file leaders barking orders. "I have never fought in a battle before."

"Let us pray you will never have to again."

Monomachus snapped his head around and frowned. "You are certain we will win?"

Another shrug and Kekaumenos kicked his horse and cantered across to the men, arm raised, roaring, "Men, prepare to move forward at the command. God is with us this day." The many crucifixes rose higher, the chanting of the priests and bishops rang out. Kekaumenos made the sign of the cross, swung his horse around and screamed, "*Kinêson!*"

With the general's voice still ringing out across the field, echoed by the other officers, the army moved as one, their pace well-trained, hobnailed boots crunching over the earth in a great cacophony of sound. Under him, Monomachus's steed went into a small panic, and the new Emperor struggled to bring it under control as the ground rumbled. Over seven thousand spearmen, Varangians to the far left, archers to the fore, followed by a screen of javelinmen, lightly armed, already outpacing the ranks of armoured troops. Monomachus wondered how anyone could withstand such an onslaught. But as he soothed his mount and looked to the rise, his eyes settled on the distant figure of Maniakes and the knot tightened in his gut. If any man could withstand anything, it was George Maniakes, forged by war, fearless and indomitable. The greatest general Byzantium had ever known.

***

"Skirmishers to the right, my lord."

Maniakes swore, swung his horse about and spat into the dirt. "There are too many of them. Damn it, where are the reinforcements?"

The other generals exchanged looks. Maniakes saw the fear in their eyes.

"We should withdraw," said one of them, his voice barely a whimper.

Maniakes knew he spoke the truth. A strategic withdrawal, back to the east, meet with the others, and try again. A longer campaign, encroaching into winter. He had been too hasty, too hungry for power. For the first time in his life, impatience had mastered him.

"We draw in their skirmishers," he said, "then sweep around their rear with the light horse. As the main force comes over the lip of the hill, we will hit them in the flank and disrupt them as they fall the incline. We have more cavalry than they have. We use what we have, and then—"

His words caught in his throat as a rider came pounding over to the generals, eyes black-rimmed, blood on his lips. He reined in his horse, which snorted loudly, steam rising from its flanks, the stench of sweat and leather thick in the air. "Cavalry, lord."

Maniakes closed his eyes. "The scouts?"

"All dead, lord."

The weight pressed down upon his shoulders. Damn Kekaumenos. He'd taught the saintly upstart well. Whilst he was organising his own deployments, Kekaumenos had sucked him in, closed the trap.

"Orders, lord?"

Maniakes shook his head. "Deploy archers to the rear. How many have we got?"

"Perhaps three hundred."

He nodded, leaning across to grip the messenger's arm. "You hold them, you hear? You hold them until we have done with their infantry. Then we'll swing about."

But the man's eyes held nothing but terror. "They are as thick as locusts, lord. Three hundred archers cannot hold them."

Maniakes grinned, "You *will* hold them. By Christ, you will."

But Christ, if He ever did sit and gaze upon the horrors of battle, was not there that day.

In the blistered, battered landscape, the Byzantines came over the rise, their archers loosing flights of death before them. For each man who fell, medics took them to the rear where their wounds treated in the field hospital by expert doctors. Soon those men were back in the struggle.

Maniakes had no such organisation.

His was a hastily assembled force. Good judgment betrayed him that day.

He saw the Byzantines coming over the rise, their pikes levelled, cries of *'prothumos'* echoing across the barren field. However, their steady march proved useless on the steep incline. They slipped and fell and Maniakes, elated that the plan seemed to be working, sent in his cavalry and the fighting at once grew confused and ever more violent.

But the Byzantines were well trained and well led. They responded as if on the drilling grounds, pikes prepared, holding fast as Maniakes's cavalry struck hard, again and again, sweeping in to loose javelins and darts before swerving away, preparing for further attacks.

The mud mixed with the blood and the brains of the dead and dying, and in that slime of death and terror, a great groan of despair rose up.

And the loudest was from Maniakes.

***

The Byzantine cavalry broke through from the rear, a great incantation coming from their triumphant throats. They had smashed the archers, trampling like so many insects, and thundered forward whilst to the left, javelins whistled through the cold, steely air.

"The day is lost!"

Maniakes ignored his general's cry, turned away, reaching for his sword. He swung it above his head. Two hundred horsemen stood behind him. His hand-picked guard. One last throw. "We break through, lads, across the plain, and we cut down Monomachus. The day will be ours."

"George," screamed one of the generals, "You will never make it."

"If I do, I'll see you in Constantinople." He grinned. "If I don't, perhaps in heaven?" Laughter, his own, but strangely detached. Panic perhaps, causing him to lose grip of his sanity? He didn't know. He no longer cared. In Sicily, he remembered how Hardrada had argued with him over strategies, how his impudence and self-confidence had won the day.

He saw the Viking's face now, glaring at him, saying'We haven't the men, George. But if we strike where they least expect, we may still win through. Give me five hundred axemen, and I'll split the Normans in two. Once we have driven the wedge, you hit them in the side. With every man you have.'

Maniakes had studied the battle map, scratched at his stubble of beard. They had been in the field for months, hounded by Norman horsemen, drawing them closer into the mountains. A trap. Maniakes saw it, but as if hypnotised he had seen it too late. Only Hardrada with that insolence, his voice chipping away at him, bringing all of his uncertainty to the fore. Damn him. Damn his common sense.

'We strike before dawn. They will not know we are amongst them until they feel our axes cutting their throats. We strike hard, without falter. And you, you must time your charge to perfection. We will scatter them like seeds in the wind and you.'Hardrada's finger waggling in his face,'You will be the hero of Rome!'

And so he was.

But not this day. This day the numbers were too great, and he had been blind to the dangers. He needed Hardrada's counsel, not the squawking of inexperienced officers who knew nothing of death and battle. He laughed. "For our Holy mother church, and for the future of our Empire, we strike hard and we strike sure." He brought his sword blade down, pointing to the side of the hillside. "At the double, my beauties!"

They thundered off, making a wide arc around the hillside and away from the desperate struggle spread out all across the field; Maniakes at the lead, horses pounding across the earth, two hundred gallant, experienced guardsmen. One last throw of the dice. One last grasp for victory.

Fifty Three

They paraded the dead generals through the streets, secured by wooden boards to keep their bodies erect, strapped on the backs of donkeys, facing the rear.

People thronged the way to the Forum of Constantine, news of the great victory surging through the city like an irresistible tidal wave. Cheering, jeering, some threw rotten fruit, others handfuls of hard-packed earth. Everyone laughed, relieved at the victory, of prayers being answered.

In the Forum, Zoe stood on the raised balcony, resplendent in shimmering robes of ruby and emerald. Courtiers gathered around, their faces alive with expectation. Zoe alone appeared unmoved, her face a perfect mask. Behind her, away from the public glare, her sister had her hands clasped in prayer.

Alexius stood too, lost in thought. Exhausted, he'd spent the previous night sitting in his apartment, trying to read from the Gospels. The words blurred in the candlelight as his eyes, full of grit, tried vainly to focus. Memories took precedence. The past years. Of plans, hopes, wishes and prayers. Of how Michael betrayed his holy vows, of how Orphano and Maniakes manoeuvred, plotted and schemed. Of how death almost prevailed.

He had survived when so many had fallen.

Michael, Orphano. But never Maniakes. Until now.

His head turned as the great crowd roared like some beast of old. The once great General, his body stripped, the wounds gaping huge and black, looked out from dead, unseeing eyes.

They said he had fought to the last, hacking down his attackers, until a lance pierced his throat and he fell, overwhelmed by a frenzy of stabbing, slashing blades. Kekaumenos struggled to hold them back, and in the end had succeeded, declaring the General deserved better.

And how Monomachus himself had decreed Maniakesbe paraded so, body defiled, all glory thrown to the vultures of the mob.

Disgraced. His greatness nothing more than a whimsy. Soon, his name would be eradicated from the annals of history. So it had been decreed. Monomachus, the new Emperor, setting his seal.

Alexius walked away, nobody giving him more than a passing glance. Nobody cared, all of them too engrossed in the obscenity playing out below. He walked through the subterranean passageway, one of the many that crisscrossed beneath the city streets. By the time he reached the Royal Enclosure, he could no longer see where he was going the tears were so great.

He found an area of quiet, a small lime-grove not far from the great Church of Saint Sophia. And there he sat and muttered a final prayer, knowing paradise would not be his to see.

The hemlock tasted bitter.

He did not care.

No one cared.

When they found the Patriarch's body they put him in a hole in the ground and nobody thought to tell Zoe. When informed, Monomachus merely clicked his tongue, more out of annoyance than concern. How to tell the Empress?

He mulled it over, and decided some things were best left unsaid.

***

Some time later, Hardrada ordered the long ship to put in at the port of a small provincial town. The men had rowed for almost the entire day and they needed rest.

With the ropes secured, most of the men disembarked, a small skeleton crew left behind to guard the camouflaged treasure stored in the stern. Ulf stretched his limbs and scanned the sprawl of squat, white-washed buildings which spread along the small quay. "Where are we?"

"No idea." Hardrada cricked his neck, grunted and massaged his muscles. "Send some men into the town and get some idea where we are."

"We haven't made the Slavutayet."

"No. But with the help of God, we will."

Ulf scurried away and Hardrada found a nearby tree trunk and sat down, letting out a contented sigh. He tugged off the bandage on his arm and prodded the wound he'd received whilst capturing Sarah. He wondered how she would look back on their time together, their second meeting so unlike the first in every conceivable way. Would she hate him, or perhaps understand some of the reasons for why he did what he did?

A slight irritation played around inside him, causing him some discomfort. Why should he care? She was part of his past, to forgot and leave behind like everything else. Zoe, the City, the intrigues, the proximity of death. He smiled at the thought of how Maniakes would take the news of his departure. Rage, perhaps, at being outwitted? To be free of them all, he should be happy. But he wasn't. A curious blend of regret, even sadness.

"You shouldn't burden yourself so," said Haldor as he sat down next to his old friend. "Decisions made should be just that. Made. Not reconsidered."

"I'm not reconsidering anything," Hardrada quickly retied his bandage. "Just ...you know, reminiscing."

"Ah." Haldor nodded. "Well, you went through a lot. A lot to remember."

"Yes. More than most."

"A full life, and how old are you now?"

"Getting close to thirty."

"You've done more in those thirty years than most do in an entire lifetime. *Two* lifetimes."

"There is still much to do. Norway has been recued from the Danes. Time for a rightful king, I think."

"So that is why you left when you did? I thought there was something."

"I would have told you, but ..." He shrugged. "You gave me your news first. Stole my thunder, as was oft your way, you miserable bastard."

Haldor cackled. "Can't have you being the hero all the time, Harald. That would never do."

A long silence followed and Hardrada gave his bandage a final tug and rolled his sleeve down over it. He stood up and stared out towards the glittering Black Sea, its vastness stretching out into the far distance. Apart from his ship, no other vessel moved across the waters. He wondered about that. "Do you think this Empire will ever be as great as it was?"

"Something tells me no."

"So, it may not need the likes of us."

"I think this world will always need the likes of us, Harald. Whether it be now or a thousand years in the future, our skills will forever be required. Men who know how to die, and how to kill."

"A thousand years." He shook his head, allowed his shoulders to sag. "Dear Christ, do you think mankind will still be killing each other then?"

"Even more so."

Hardrada turned and looked down at his comrade. "Do you have to go?"

Haldor frowned, studying his old friend's face for a long time. "Like I said. Decisions."

"Aye. But some can be undone, surely?"

"Not the important ones."

With those words sounding so final, so

weighty, Hardrada knew, if he did not know before, that nothing, no amount of pleading or bargaining, would ever shift his friend's position. So he turned away anddragging his feet, shuffled over to the quayside and the waiting ship.

He did not know how long he stood there, his mind empty, body heavy, tired. When Ulf came up next to him, he barely flinched.

"It's some ten leagues south of Constantia," said Ulf. "The locals seem to think we could make the mouth of the Slavutain another day." He laughed. "Or we could ask them."

Hardrada followed his friend's extended finger to where a small merchantman appeared, like a smudge at first, but soon coming into clearer view. Its sails full, billowing, caught by the wind, it made straight for them.

"Should we be worried?"

"We should always be worried," said Hardrada, his hand falling to the hilt of his sword. "Rally the men, just in case."

As Ulf carried out the orders, Hardrada stood as if mesmerised. The small merchantman came up alongside, sweating, straining crew members hauling in ropes, adjusting the tack. The vessel bumped up alongside the quayside, men scurrying like rats this way and that, a large man in the rear barking out orders. His eyes met Hardrada's and for a moment panic caught hold of him. But then Hardrada raised his hand in welcome and all became calm again.

The man joined him on the quayside, nervous still, but no longer afraid. There could be no mistaking Hardrada, his sheer size making him instantly recognisable. Hardrada steered him away from earshot, spoke kindly, "You are from the city?"

The man paled, for what reason the Viking could not understand. He felt him quaking beneath the grip he had on the man's arm.

"The news is you are dead."

Hardrada pulled up short and for a moment a shudder of anger raced through him. He quelled it, found amusement in the news, and laughed out loud. "Dear Christ. *Dead*? Is that what they're saying?"

"The city is full of it." The man brought up both hands. "I ... I do not wish to insult you, my lord."

"I'm not your lord," said Hardrada. "And you tell me no insults. Simple untruths is all. As you can see," he hammered his chest with his fist, "I am still breathing."

"Aye. But many are not."

Hardrada frowned. "Tell me then, good friend. Tell me it all."

***

Later Haldor found Hardrada a little way off, sitting in a tiny glade, poking at the ground with a gnarled twig. He did not look up as his old friend approached.

"Is it true?"

Hardrada ceased scratching, peered at the worn end of the thin piece of wood, then tossed it into the undergrowth. "It seems that way."

"Maniakes? Alexius?"

"The old guard. All gone."

"Except you."

"Aye." Hardrada shook his head. "Although I don't feel it. I'm empty, Hal. As if part of me has also died."

"But you hated Maniakes. Why grieve for him now?"

"Hate? No, not hate. If I had hated him, I'd have killed him. We fought together, Hal, as brothers. We had *respect*."His voice grew quiet, "The way they treated him, to put him on a donkey, Hal. A man such as he." He slapped his knees with both hands, causing Hal to give a little jump, and the Viking stood. "Bastards the lot of them. At least Alexius was given the good grace of a funeral. Not sure if it was decent, but what they did to Maniakes ..." He shook his head, his distress too much.

"You're not thinking of going back there are you?" Hardrada looked at his old friend, arching a single eyebrow. "For revenge, Harald? Surely not?"

"Old friend." He smiled and put his hand on Haldor's shoulders. "Decisions. Remember?"

He turned Haldor around and together they walked back to the quay. The merchantman and long ship both bobbed in the water, crew members exchanging gossip, the day drawing into evening and already the air had turned chill.

"No. I won't be going back," said Hardrada, voice distant and thick with emotion. "Not yet, old friend." He grinned again and squeezed Haldor's arm. "Not *just yet*."

We hope you enjoyed *Varangian – King of the Norse* by Stuart G. Yates. Please turn the page for a preview of the next exciting book in the *Varangian* series, *Varangian — Origins*.

Varangian

ORIGINS

A preview of 'Hardrada', the third in the series of tales featuring Harald Hardrada, fabled Viking.

Stuart G. Yates

In a small glade by the side of the River Dneiper, the Varangians rested, many huddled around camp fires, warming their damp clothes, sending up great trails of steam. Watching the river flow past, Hardrada stood, lost in thoughts of home, of what he had left behind, of what might face him. Sarah, the playing piece in a game of twisted desires and forgotten hopes, had returned to Constantinople without a word. Not a hint of regret for the moment of passion they had shared. Eyes like bottomless pools, bereft of life. How could she have changed so completely? And the Empress too. Once, all of them, so giving, so willing, now ...

He breathed hard, looked beyond the gently bobbing longship to the distant shore opposite and wondered if life would always play out this way. In the far north, a princess awaited, and with her the promise of a new chapter in a life already full. To be King, his destiny fulfilled. Beside him a woman of grace, passion and beauty. A woman to bear him children. To ensure his line. King of the Norse. Father of greatness.

Something moved at his shoulder and he turned to see Ulf gnawing on a piece of coarse brown bread. "You should eat something," Hardrada's faithful companion said between mouthfuls.

"I don't feel much like eating."

"Why not? Everything is well. We have all the treasure. Byzantium is far behind us. What troubles you?"

Hardrada shrugged, turning again to the grey, cold river. "I'm feeling morose, that is all, wondering if I have made a mistake."

"How so?" Ulf finished his bread, wiped his hands on his jerkin, and sighed. "Listen, we did what we could for the Greeks. We've done well. *You've* done well. You have enough money now to buy up the Kievian Rus and ensure your journey to the throne of Norway. You can't regret any of it, Harald. Everything you've done has been for this moment. Seize it. Take what is yours. By right, not by force." He gripped Hardrada's arm. "No regrets, old friend. This isn't like you and it troubles me to see you this way. So, come on, share some wine and let's put Byzantium behind us – literally."

"You're right," said Hardrada, in a voice sounding heavy and resigned. "I thought ... I don't know, I thought that perhaps I could find happiness."

"*Happiness*? Dear Christ, what the hell is that? We're Vikings. We find happiness in the bottom of a wine jug and at the point of our swords. Nowhere else, old friend."

A footstep behind them, followed by a low voice, "Except home."

Both turned as Haldor approached. Regaining some his former strength, the eldest of the three companions still walked with a slight limp, hand forever clamped to his side. He stepped up alongside the others and breathed in the fresh salty air. "The smell of the north," he said. "I never dared believe we would turn our faces home. I wished it, of course, but I didn't want to tempt fate by saying so. You two," he grinned, without turning in their direction, "you seemed so hell-bent on adventure and money, but for me it was nothing more than an interval, a pause before I went back. And now that we are, I feel somewhat melancholy."

"You sound like a fucking philosopher," spat Ulf.

"Oh, and you don't? I heard what you said, all that about having no regrets. But we do, don't we? All three of us. And I am wondering if, when we return home, more regrets will follow."

"You truly think that?" asked Hardrada.

"Perhaps. We have been away for a long time. You were seventeen when you left Norway, Harald. Much has changed."

"I didn't leave. I fled. As well you know. Fled." He blew out a breath before closing his eyes, allowing the smell of the river to waft over him. Haldor's words spelled out the truth. The water promised dreams of the north, for at its end stood Kiev, and the next phase in the adventure. "You think the people will judge my actions as that of a coward?"

Ulf snorted, "Christ, Harald. A coward? You had no choice. Death or escape. Yarislav took you in, and he schooled you, and now you go back to help him. Debts paid. No one will judge you, you can depend on it."

"Regrets you said," Hardrada held Haldor's gaze. "You most of all, old friend. You have never held back from telling me the truth. So tell me now. Do I make a mistake in going back? Will the people accept me, or will they forever eye me with suspicion and fear?"

"The people will accept a king who treats them with fairness, who defends them against enemies, and fills their bellies with food. Nothing much else matters."

"So what I did? Running away?"

Ulf slammed down his fist. "Harald, you've got to stop thinking like this and—"

Hardrada cut off Ulf's words with a raised hand. "Haldor? Tell me, in truth. Will the people follow me?"

"You fled because the alternative was certain death. And many who lived then are now dead. They will see you as the returning star, to lead them forward. The great Viking age may have passed, but you Harald, you will restore it. Of that I have no doubt."

The silence stretched out, Haldor's words drifting out across the glade, to mingle with the encroaching trees and settle within the leaves, whilst all three men stood and allowed their own thoughts to cloud and become distilled.

When at last Hardrada's shoulders dropped and he turned to go, Ulf caught him by the arm. "Harald," he said, "I've followed you for many years, since we were both young. We have lived and fought as brothers and I will follow you to the ends of the earth if need be. Whatever you decide to do, I will be here."

"My good friend," said Hardada quietly, then nodded at Haldor. "Both of you. I would never have achieved any of it without you."

Haldor looked grim. "Harald. I too, as Ulf, have followed you, but ..." He shook his head. "I've thought long and hard since we spoke in the hospital in Constantinople. And you, you have tried so hard to dissuade me, but I am old, old and weary. I cannot go to Kiev."

"I thought you might have changed your mind," muttered Hardada, not daring to hold Haldor's eyes.

"No. Decisions. Like we said."

For a moment, it was as if the world had ground to a halt. Not a breath of wind, not a bird's song. Only the stillness of that place, and Haldor's words burning deep.

"You can't leave us, Hal," said Ulf at last. "You're one of us. You cannot turn away now, not when Harald needs you so much!"

"No, Ulf," said Hardrada. He smiled. "Hal, I always hoped, once your wounds healed, you might stand alongside me again, but ... I understand and accept your wishes."

"Do you?"

"Aye. I do. You wish to return home, as we too wish. But your home is not with us, and for that I give you everything I have, to send you with all speed."

"Everything you have?"

"Aye." Hardada nodded. "With Zoe returning the rest of my booty, I have more than enough to lay my claim to the throne of Norway. I will give you as much as you need to sail to Iceland and go home."

Haldor reeled backwards, his eyes filling with emotion, tears threatening to fall. "Harald, I cannot ask you to—"

"I know you would never ask, old friend. It is my gift to you. When we reach the far north, you take a ship and a crew, and make your way back to your island home."His smile grew broader."I knew this day would come. Your wounds have healed well enough, but your heart and soul, Hal, they are no longer bound with mine. I release you." He reached out his hand and took Haldor's, gripped it firmly. "Go with God, Haldor, and with all my blessings."

They embraced then and Ulf looked on, agog. Hardrada saw it in his friend's face, his incomprehension and when he stepped back, it was to Ulf that he now spoke. "But you, you will stay by my side and together we will make Norway the greatest kingdom in all the world. I have dreams, Ulf, dreams of greatness. We have such deeds to perform, such adventures. We will become legends, Ulf. Men will tell the stories of what we do for centuries to come. They will write poems and sing songs and for as long as the sun rises, the world will remember."

"They already sing songs," said Haldor.

"Your exploits, the legend that is Harald Hardrada, the whole world knows who you are and what you have done."

"I have done much, it is true. I would have been nothing if it were not for both of you."

"We are minor players," said Haldor. "Arriving as you did, in Constantinople, a young man, still stinging with the wounds you bore. It was you who recovered and made yourself into someone great."

"I do not know it all," said Ulf, "before we met, Harald, who you were, what brought you to Byzantium? It is a story of myth and legend, but neither of us knows the truth of it. Not the whole truth."

Hardrada nodded. "Well, whilst we wait here and the men dry themselves, and we eat and drink, I will tell you."

"All of it? How you came to be here?"

"Aye," said Hardrada. "It is a tale I have never spoken of, but now," he smiled at Haldor, "now perhaps is the best time to tell it, before you go your separate way, old friend."

With that, he put his arms around the shoulders of his two companions and guided them towards the camp fires of the Varangians and told them the story of who he was, what his roots were and how he became known as Harald Hardrada.

About the Author

Born on the Wirral, in the UK, Stuart Yates currently lives in Spain. A graduate of Liverpool Hope University, his passion is the teaching of history. He writes every day, and when he is not writing, he's *thinking* about writing.

Blessed with a fertile imagination which enables him to conjure stories in a wide range of genres, he has 16 books on the shelf, from paranormal YA, through contemporary adult thrillers, and historical fiction.

He writes whatever inspires him and loves every word.

Printed in Great Britain
by Amazon.co.uk, Ltd.,
Marston Gate.